The world has changed and so has Bond,
James Bond.

**Jeffery Deaver brings superspy 007 into the
twenty-first century with his #1 bestseller**

CARTE BLANCHE

"Brilliantly captures Fleming's style . . . with Deaver's
trademark twists flying."

—The Washington Post

"Ian Fleming was a master. . . . Deaver too is a genius and this
publishing marriage was truly made in heaven."

—The Sunday Express

"The pairing is as smooth as vodka and vermouth."

—Parade

"A new, streamlined incarnation for a new generation of global
fears."

—The Guardian

"[A] worthy homage. . . . Think of Jack Bauer let loose in
Whitehall."

—The London Times

"Thrilling and genuinely surprising."

—Heat

"Deaver combines the best of Fleming's crisp, eclectic style
without compromising his own ability to tell a cracking story."
—Literary Review

"Intricate and inventive, surprising and satisfying."
—Publishers Weekly

"Fantastic. . . . Jeffery Deaver truly *got it*."
—Ann Arbor News

Suspense fiction that "stokes our paranoia"
(*Entertainment Weekly*),
from the inimitable Jeffery Deaver!

EDGE

"Wildly twisted . . . a nail-biter."

—*Kirkus Reviews* (starred review)

"Ingenious."

—*The New York Times Book Review*

"Deaver unveils some nifty new tricks in this edge-of-your-seat thriller."

—*Publishers Weekly*

"Twist-filled. . . . The odds seem to change with each turn of the page."

—*The Wall Street Journal*

The "grand master of the ticking-clock thriller"
(Kathy Reichs) puts special agent Kathryn
Dance on a harrowing online manhunt

ROADSIDE CROSSES

Chosen as a Hot Summer Thriller on
TheDailyBeast.com!

"Clever and twisted. . . . Don't miss this one."

—*Library Journal*

"The techno-savvy Deaver . . . has one of those puzzle-loving minds you just can't trust."

—Marilyn Stasio, *The New York Times*

"Deaver's got the world of social networking and blogs down cold. . . . That dose of realism adds a fresh, contemporary edge."

—David Montgomery, TheDailyBeast.com

*Featuring Lincoln Rhyme and Amelia Sachs
**Featuring Kathryn Dance

JEFFERY DEAVER

SPEAKING IN TONGUES

Pocket Books

NEW YORK   LONDON   TORONTO   SYDNEY   NEW DELHI

Pocket Books
A Division of Simon & Schuster, Inc.
1230 Avenue of the Americas
New York, NY 10020

This book is a work of fiction. Names, characters, places, and incidents either are products of the author's imagination or are used fictitiously. Any resemblance to actual events or locales or persons, living or dead, is entirely coincidental.

This Pocket Books paperback edition September 2012

POCKET and colophon are registered trademarks of Simon & Schuster, Inc.

For information about special discounts for bulk purchases, please contact Simon & Schuster Special Sales at 1-866-506-1949 or business@simonandschuster.com.

The Simon & Schuster Speakers Bureau can bring authors to your live event. For more information or to book an event, contact the Simon & Schuster Speakers Bureau at 1-866-248-3049 or visit our website at www.simonspeakers.com.

Manufactured in the United States of America

10 9 8 7 6 5 4 3 2 1

ISBN 978-1-4516-7572-6
ISBN 978-0-7432-1167-3 (ebook)

In the beginning was the Word.
Man acts it out. He is the
act, not the actor.

—*Henry Miller*

I

THE
WHISPERING
BEARS

Chapter One

Crazy Megan parks the car.

Doesn't want to do this. No way.

Doesn't get out, listens to the rain . . .

The engine ticked to silence as she looked down at her clothes. It was her usual outfit: JNCO jeans. A sleeveless white tee under a dark denim work shirt. Combat boots. Wore this all the time. But she felt uneasy today. Embarrassed. Wished she'd worn a skirt at least. The pants were too baggy. The sleeves dangled to the tips of her black-polished fingernails and her socks were orange as tomato soup. Well, what did it matter? The hour'd be over soon.

Maybe the man would concentrate on her good qualities—her wailing blue eyes and blond hair. Oh, and her body too. He *was* a man.

Anyway, the clothes covered up the extra seven . . . well, all right, ten pounds that she carried on her tall frame.

Stalling. Crazy Megan doesn't want to be here one bit.

Rubbing her hand over her upper lip, she looked out the rain-spattered window at the lush trees and bushes of suburbia. This April in northern Virginia had been hot as July and ghosts of mist rose from the asphalt. Nobody on the sidewalks—it was deserted here. She'd never noticed how empty this neighborhood was.

Crazy Megan whispers, *Just. Say. No. And leave.*

But she couldn't do that. Mega-hassle.

She took off the wooden peace symbol dangling from her neck and flung it into the backseat. Megan brushed her blond hair with her fingers, pulled it away from her face. Her ruddy knuckles seemed big as golf balls. A glance at her face in the rearview mirror. She wiped off the black lipstick, pulled the blond strands into a ponytail, secured the hair with a green rubber band.

Okay, let's do it. Get it over with.

A jog through the rain. She hit the intercom and a moment later the door latch buzzed.

Megan McCall walked into the waiting room where she'd spent every Saturday morning for the past seven weeks. Ever since the Incident. She kept waiting for the place to become familiar. It never did.

She hated this. The sessions were bad enough but the waiting really killed her. Dr. Hanson *always* kept her waiting. Even if she was on time, even if there were no other patients ahead of her, he always started the session five minutes or so late. It pissed her off but she never said anything about it.

Today, though, she found the new doctor standing in the doorway, smiling at her, lifting an eyebrow in greeting. Right on time.

"You're Megan?" the man said, offering an easy smile. "I'm Bill Peters." He was about her father's age, handsome. Full head of hair. Hanson was bald and looked like a shrink. This guy . . . *Maybe a little George Clooney,* Crazy Megan decides. Her wariness fades slightly.

And he doesn't call himself "Doctor." Interesting.

"Hi."

"Come on in." He gestured. She stepped into the office.

"How's Dr. Hanson?" she asked, sitting in the chair across from his desk. "Somebody in his family's sick?"

"His mother. An accident. I hear she'll be all right. But he had to go to Leesburg for the week."

"So you're like a substitute teacher?"

He laughed. "Something like that."

"I didn't know shr—therapists took over other patients."

"Some don't."

Dr. Peters—*Bill* Peters—had called yesterday after school to tell her that Hanson had arranged for him to take over his appointments and, if she wanted, she could make her regular session after all. *No way,* Crazy Megan had whispered at first. But after Megan had talked with Peters for a while she decided she'd give it a try. There was something comforting about his voice. Besides, baldy Hanson wasn't doing diddly for her. The sessions amounted to her lame bitching about school and about being lonely and about Amy and Josh and Brittany, and Hanson nodding and saying she had to be friends with herself. Whatever the hell that meant.

"This'll be repeating some things," Peters now said, "but if you don't mind, could we go over some of the basics?"

"I guess."

He asked, "It's Megan *Collier?*"

"No, Collier's my father's name. I use my mother's. McCall." She rocked in the stiff-backed chair, crossing her legs. Her tomato socks showed. She uncrossed her legs and planted her feet squarely on the floor.

"You don't like therapy, do you?" he asked suddenly.

This was interesting too. Hanson had never asked that. Wouldn't ask anything so blunt. And unlike this guy, Hanson didn't look into her eyes when he spoke. Staring right back, she said, "No, I don't."

He seemed amused. "You know why you're here?"

Silent as always, Crazy Megan answers first. *Because I'm fucked up, I'm dysfunctional. I'm a nutcase. I'm psycho. I'm loony. And half the school knows and do you have a fucking* clue *how hard it is to walk through those halls with everybody looking at you and thinking, Shrink bait, shrink bait?* Crazy Megan also mentions what just plain Megan would never in a million years tell him—about the fake computerized picture of Megan in a straitjacket that made the rounds of Jefferson High two weeks ago.

But now Megan merely recited, "'Cause if I didn't come to see a therapist they'd send me to Juvenile Detention."

When she'd been found, drunk, strolling along the catwalk of the municipal water tower two months ago she'd been committing a crime. The county police got involved and she maybe pushed, maybe slugged a cop. But finally everybody agreed that if she saw a counselor the commonwealth's attorney wouldn't press charges.

"That's true. But it's not the answer."

She lifted an eyebrow.

"The answer is that you're here so that you can feel better."

Oh, please, Crazy Megan begins, rolling her crazy eyes.

And, okay, it was totally stupid, his words themselves. But . . . but . . . there was something about the *way* Dr. Peters said them that, just for a second, less than a second, Megan believed that he really meant them. This guy's in a different universe from Dr. Loser Elbow Patch Hanson.

He opened his briefcase and took out a yellow pad. A brochure fell out onto the desk. She glanced at it. A picture of San Francisco was on the cover.

"Oh, you're going there?" she asked.

"A conference," he said, flipping through the brochure. He handed it to her.

"Awesome."

"I love the city," he continued. "I'm a former hippie. Tie-dyed-in-the-wool Deadhead and Jefferson Airplane fan . . . Whole nine yards. Course, that was before your time."

"No way. I'm totally into Janis Joplin and Hendrix."

"Yeah? You ever been to the Bay Area?"

"Not yet. But I'm going someday. My mother doesn't know it. But I am."

He squinted. "Hey, you know, there *is* a resemblance—you and Joplin. If you didn't have your hair up it'd be the same as hers."

Megan now wished she hadn't done the pert 'n' perky ponytail.

The doctor added, "You're prettier, of course. And thinner. Can you belt out the blues?"

"Like, I wish . . ."

"But you don't remember hippies." He chuckled.

"Time out!" she said enthusiastically. "I've seen *Woodstock*, like, eight times."

She also wished she'd kept the peace symbol.

"So tell me, did you really try to kill yourself? Cross your heart."

"And hope to die?" she joked.

He smiled.

She said, "No."

"What happened?"

"Oh, I was just drinking a little Southern Comfort. All right, maybe more than a little."

"Joplin's drink," he said. "Too fucking sweet for me."

Whoa, the F-word. Cool. She was almost—almost—beginning to like him.

He glanced again at her hair—the fringes on her face. Then back to her eyes. It was like one of Josh's caresses. Somewhere within her she felt a tiny ping—of reassurance and pleasure.

Megan continued her story. "And somebody I was with said no way they'd climb up to the top and I said I would and I did. That's it. Like a dare is all."

"All right, so you got nabbed by the cops on some bullshit charge."

"That's about it."

"Not exactly the crime of the century."

"*I* didn't think so either. But they were so . . . you know."

"I know," he said. "Now tell me about yourself. Your secret history."

"Well, my parents are divorced. I live with Bett.

She has this business? It's really a decorating business but she says she's an interior designer 'cause it sounds better. Tate's got this farm in Prince William. He used to be this famous lawyer but now he just does people's wills and sells houses and stuff. He hires people to run the farm for him. Sharecroppers. Sound like slaves, or whatever, but they're just people he hires."

"And your relationship with the folks? Is the porridge too hot, too cold or just right?"

"Just right."

He nodded, made a small notation on his pad though he might've been just doodling. Maybe she bored him. Maybe he was writing a grocery list.

Things to buy after my appointment with Crazy Megan.

She told him about growing up, about the deaths of her mother's parents and her father's dad. The only other relative she'd been close to was her aunt Susan—her mother's twin sister. "She's a nice lady but she's had a rough time. She's been sick all her life. And she really, really wanted kids but couldn't have them."

"Ah," he said.

None of it felt important to her and she guessed it was even less important to him.

"What about friends?"

Count 'em on one hand, Crazy Megan says.

Shhhh.

"I hang with the goth crowd mostly," she told the doctor.

"As in 'gothic'?"

"Yeah. Only . . ." She decided she could tell him the truth. "What it is is I kinda stay by myself a lot. I meet people but I end up figuring, why bother? There're a lot of losers out there."

"Oh, yeah." He laughed. "That's why my business is so good."

She blinked in surprise. Then smiled too.

"What's the boyfriend situation?"

"This won't take much time," she said, laughing ruefully. "I was going with this guy? Joshua? And he was, like, all right. Only he was older. And he was black. I mean, he wasn't a gangsta or anything. His father's a soldier, like an officer in the Pentagon, and his mother's some big executive. I didn't have a problem with the race thing. But Dr. Hanson said I was probably involved with him just to make my parents nuts."

"Were you?"

"I don't know. I kinda liked him. No, I *did* like him."

"But you broke up?"

"Sure. Dr. Hanson said I ought to dump him."

"He *said* that?"

"Well, not exactly. But I got that impression."

Crazy Megan thinks that Mr. Handsome Shrink, Mr. *George Clooney* stud, ought to've figured it out: *How can a psycho nutcase like me go out with anybody? If I hadn't dumped Josh—which I cried about for two weeks—if I hadn't left, then everybody at his school would be on his case. "He's the one with the loony girl." And then his folks would find out— they're the nicest people in the universe and totally in love—and they'd be crushed . . . Well, of course I had to leave . . .*

"Nobody else on the horizon?" he asked.

"Nope." She shook her head.

"Okay, let's talk about the family some more. Your mother."

"Bett and I get along great." She hesitated. "Only it's funny about her—she's into her business but she also believes in all this New Age stuff crap. I'm, like, just chill, okay? That stuff is so bogus. But she doesn't hassle me about it. Doesn't hassle me about anything really. It's great between us. Really great. The only problem is she's engaged to a geek."

"Do you two talk, your mom and you? Chew the fat, as my grandmother used to say?"

"Sure . . . I mean, she's busy a lot. But who isn't, right? Yeah, we talk." She hoped he didn't ask her about what. She'd have to make up something.

"And how 'bout Dad?"

She shrugged. "He's nice. He takes me to concerts, shopping. We get along great."

"Great?"

C.M.—Crazy Megan—chides, *Is that the only word you know, bitch? Great, great, great . . . You sound like a parrot.*

"Yeah," Megan said. "Only . . ."

"Only what?"

"Well, it's like we don't have a lot to talk *about.* He wants me to go windsurfing with him but I went once and it's a totally superficial way to spend your time. I'd rather read a book or something."

"You like to read?"

"Yeah, I read a lot."

"Who're some of your favorite authors?"

"Oh, I don't know." Her mind went blank.

Crazy Megan isn't much help. *Yep, he's gonna think you're damaged.*

Quiet! Megan ordered her alter ego. She remembered the last book she'd read. "You know Márquez? I'm reading *Autumn of the Patriarch.*"

His eyebrow lifted. "Oh, I loved it."

"No kidding. I—"

Dr. Peters added, *"Love in the Time of Cholera.* Best love story ever written. I've read it three times."

Another ecstatic ping. The book was actually sitting on her bedside table. "Me too. Well, I only read it once."

"Tell me more," he continued, "about your father."

"Um, he's pretty handsome still—I mean for a guy in his forties. And he's in pretty good shape. He dates a lot but he can't seem to settle down with anybody. He says he wants a family."

"Does he?"

"Yeah. But if he does then why does he date girls named Bambi? . . . Just kidding. But they look like they're Bambis." They both laughed.

"Tell me about the divorce."

"I don't really remember them together. They split up when I was three."

"Why?"

"They got married too young. That's what Bett says. They kind of went different ways. Mom was, like, real flighty and into that New Age stuff I was telling you about. And Dad was just the opposite."

"Whose idea was the divorce?"

"I think my dad's."

He jotted another note then looked up. "So how mad are you at your parents?"

"I'm not."

"Really?" he asked, as if he were completely surprised. "You're sure the porridge isn't too hot?"

"I love 'em. They love me. We get along gre—fine. The porridge is just right. What the fuck is porridge anyway?"

"Don't have a clue," Peters said quickly. "Give me an early memory about your mother."

"What?"

"Quick! Now! *Do it!*" His eyes flashed.

Megan felt a wave of heat crinkle through her face. "I—"

"Don't hesitate," he whispered. "Say what's on your mind!"

She blurted, "Bett's getting ready for a date, putting on makeup, staring in a mirror and poking at a wrinkle, like she's hoping it'll go away. She always *does* that. Like her face is the most important thing in the world to her. Her looks, you know."

"And what do you think as you watch her?" His dark eyes were fervent. Her mind froze again. "No, you're hesitating. *Tell* me!"

"'Slut.'"

He nodded. "Now *that's* wonderful, Megan."

She felt swollen with pride. Didn't know why. But she did.

"Brilliant. Now give me a memory about your father. Fast!"

"Bears." She gasped and lifted a hand to her mouth. "No . . . Wait. Let me think."

But the doctor pounced. "Bears? At the zoo?"

"No, never mind."

"Tell me."

She was shaking her head, no.

"Tell me, Megan," he insisted. "Tell me about the bears."

"It's not important."

"Oh, it *is* important," he said, leaning forward. "Listen. You're with *me* now, Megan. Forget whatever Hanson's done. I don't operate his way, groping around in the dark. I go deep."

She looked into his eyes and froze—like a deer in headlights.

"Don't worry," he said softly. "Trust me. I'm going to change your life forever."

Chapter Two

"They weren't real bears."

"Toys?"

"Bears in a story."

"What's so hard about this?" Dr. Peters asked.

"I don't know."

Crazy Megan gives her a good burst of sarcasm. *Oh, good job, loser. You've blown it now. You had to tell him about the book.*

But the other side of her was thinking: Seven weeks of bullshit with Dr. Shiny Head Hanson and she hadn't felt a thing but bored. Ten minutes with Dr. Peters and she was hooked up to an electric current.

Crazy Megan says, *It's too hard. It hurts too much.*

But Bill couldn't hear C.M., of course.

"Go on," he encouraged.

And she went on.

"I was about six, okay? I was spending the weekend with Tate. He lives in this big house and nobody's around for miles. It's in the middle of his cornfields and it's all quiet and really, really spooky. I was feeling weird, all scared. I asked him to read me a story but he said he didn't have any children's books. I was really hurt. I started to cry and asked why didn't he have any.

He got all freaked and went out to the old barn—where he told me I wasn't ever supposed to go—and he came back with this book. It was called *The Whispering Bears*. Only it turned out it wasn't really a kid's story at all. I found out later it was a book of folk stories from Europe."

"Do you remember it?"

"Yeah."

"Tell me."

"It's stupid."

"No," Peters said, leaning forward again. "I'll bet it's anything *but* stupid. Tell me."

"There was a town by the edge of the woods. And everybody who lived there was happy, you know, like in all fairy stories before the bad shit happens. People walking down the street, singing, going to market, having dinner with their families. Then one day these two big bears walked out of the woods and stood at the edge of town with their heads down and it sounded like they were whispering to each other.

"At first nobody paid any attention then little by little the people stopped what they were doing and tried to hear what the bears were saying. But nobody could. That night the bears went back into the forest. And the townspeople stood around and one woman said she knew what they were whispering about—they were making fun of the people in the village. And then everybody started noticing how everybody else walked funny or talked funny or looked stupid and they all ended up laughing at each other, and everybody got mad and there were all kinds of fights in town.

"Okay, then the next day the bears came out of

the forest again and started whispering, blah, blah, blah, you get the picture. Then that night they went back into the woods. And this time some old man said *he* knew what they were talking about. They were gossiping about the people in town. And so everybody figured that everybody else knew all their secrets and so they went home and closed all their windows and doors and they were afraid to go out in public.

"Then—the third day—the bears came out again. And it was the same thing, only this time the duke or mayor or somebody said, '*I* know what they're saying! They're making plans to attack the village.' And they went to get torches to scare away the bears but they accidentally set a house on fire and the fire spread and the whole town burned down."

Megan felt a shiver. Her eyes slipped to the top of the desk and she couldn't look up at Dr. Peters. She continued, "Tate only read it to me once but I still remember the last line. It was, 'And do you know what the bears were really whispering about? Why, nothing at all. Don't you know? Bears can't talk.'"

This is so bogus, Crazy Megan scoffs. *What's he going to think about you now?*

But the doctor calmly asked, "And the story was upsetting?"

"Yeah."

"Why?"

"I don't know. Maybe 'cause everybody's lives got ruined for no reason."

"But there *was* a reason for it."

Megan shrugged.

He continued, "The town was destroyed because

people projected their own pettiness and jealousy and aggression on some innocent creatures. That's the moral of the story. How people destroy themselves."

"I guess. But I was just thinking it wasn't much of a kid's story. I guess I wanted *The Lion King* or *101 Dalmatians.*" She smiled. But Peters didn't. He looked at her closely.

"What happened after your father finished it?"

Why did he ask that? she wondered, her palms sweating. *Why?*

Megan looked away and shrugged again. "That's all. Bett came and picked me up and I went home."

"This is hard, isn't it, Megan?"

Get a clue.

Quiet! Megan snapped to C.M.

She looked at Dr. Peters. "Yeah, I guess."

"Would it be easier to write down your feelings? A lot of my patients do that. There's some paper."

She took the sheets that he nodded toward and rested them on a booklet he pushed forward for her to write on. Reluctantly Megan picked up a pen.

She stared at the paper. "I don't know what to say."

"Say what you feel."

"I don't know how I feel."

"Yes, you do." He leaned close. "I think you're just afraid to admit it."

"Well—"

"Say whatever comes into your mind. Anything. Say something to your mother first. Write a letter to her. Go!"

Another wave of that scalding heat.

Spotlight on Crazy Megan . . .

He whispered, "Go deep."

"I can't think!"

"Pick one thing. Why are you so angry with her?"

"I'm not!"

"Yes, you are!"

She clenched her fist. "Because . . ."

"*Why?*"

"I don't know. Because she's . . . She goes out with these young men. It's like she thinks she can cast spells on them."

"So what?" he challenged her. "She can date who she wants. She's single. What's *really* pissing you off?"

"I don't know!"

"Yes, you *do!*" he shot back.

"Well, she's just a businesswoman and she's engaged to this dweeb. She's not a fairy princess at all like she'd like to be. She's not a cover girl."

"But she wears an exotic image? Why does she do that?"

"I guess to make herself happy. She wants to be pretty and young forever. She thinks this asshole Brad's going to make her happy. But he isn't."

"She's *greedy?* Is that what you're saying?"

"Yes!" Megan cried. "That's it! She doesn't care about *me*. The night on the water tower? She was at Brad's and she was supposed to call me. But she didn't."

"Who? Her fiancé's?"

"Yeah. She went up there, to Baltimore, and she never called. They were *fucking*, I'll bet, and she forgot about me. It was just like when I was little. She'd leave me alone all the time."

"By yourself?"

"No, with sitters. My uncle mostly."

"Which uncle?"

"My aunt Susan's husband. My mom's twin sister. She's been real sick most of her life, I told you. Heart problems. And Bett spent all this time with her in the hospital when I was young. Uncle Harris'd baby-sit me. He was real nice, but—"

"But you missed your mother?"

"I wanted her to be with *me*. She said it was only for a little while because Aunt Susan was real sick. She said she and Susan were totally close. Nobody was closer to her than her sister."

He shook his head, seemed horrified. "She said that to *you*? Her own daughter?"

Megan nodded.

"*You* should have been the person closest to her in the world."

These words gripped her by the throat. She wiped more tears and struggled for breath. Finally she continued, "Aunt Susan'd do anything to have kids but she couldn't. Because of her heart. And here Mom got pregnant with me and Susan felt real bad about that. So Mom spent a lot of time with her."

"There's no excuse for neglecting children. None. Absolutely none."

Megan snagged a Kleenex and wiped her face.

"And you didn't let yourself be angry? Why not?"

"Because my mother was doing something good. My aunt's a nice lady. She always calls and asks about me and wants me to come visit her. Only I don't 'cause . . ."

"Because you're angry with her. She took your mother away from you."

A chill. "Yeah, I guess she did."

"Come on, Megan. What else? Why the guilt?"

"Because my aunt needed my mom more back then. When I was little. See—"

Crazy Megan interrupts. *Oh, you can't tell him that!*

Yes, I can. I can tell him anything.

"See, Uncle Harris killed himself."

"He did?"

"I felt so bad for my aunt."

"Forget it!" he snapped.

Megan blinked.

"You're Bett's *daughter*. You should have been the center of her universe. What she did was inexcusable. Say it. Say it!"

"I . . ."

"Say it!"

"It was inexcusable!"

"Good. Now write it to her. Every bit of the anger you feel. Get it out."

The pen rolled from Megan's lap onto the floor. She bent down and picked it up. It weighed a hundred pounds. The tears ran from her nose and eyes and dripped on the paper.

"Tell her," the doctor said. "Tell her that she's greedy. That she turned her back on her daughter and took care of her sister instead."

"But," Megan managed to say, "that's greedy of *me*."

"Of *course* it's greedy. You were a child, you're supposed to be greedy. Parents are there to fill *your* needs. That's the whole *point* of parents. *Tell* her what you feel."

Her head swam—from the electricity in the black eyes boring into hers, from her desire, her fear.

From her anger . . .

In ten seconds, it seemed, she'd filled the entire sheet. She dropped the paper on the floor. It floated like a pale leaf. The doctor ignored it.

"Now. Your father."

Megan froze, shaking her head. She looked desperately at the wall clock. "Next time. Please."

"No. Now. What are you mad about?"

Her stomach muscles were hard as a board. "Well, I'm mad 'cause why doesn't he want to *see* me? He didn't even fight the custody agreement. I see him every two or three months."

"Tell him."

"I—"

"Tell him!"

She wrote. She poured her fury onto the page. When the sheet was half full her pen braked to a halt.

"What else is it, Megan? What aren't you telling me?"

"Nothing."

"Oh, what do I hear?" he said. "The passion's slipping. Something's wrong. You're holding back." Dr. Peters frowned. "Whispering bears. Something about that story's important. What?"

"I don't know."

"Go into the place where it hurts the most. We go deep, remember. That's how I operate. I'm Super Shrink."

Crazy Megan can't take it anymore. She just wants to curl up into a little crazy ball and disappear.

The doctor moved closer, pulling his chair beside her. Their knees touched. "Come on. What is it?"

"No. I don't know what it is . . ."

"You want to tell me. You *need* to tell me." He dropped to his knees, gripped her by the shoulders. "Touch the most painful part. Touch it! Your father's read you the story. He comes to the last line. 'Bears can't talk.' He puts the book away. Then what happens?"

She sat forward, shivering, and stared at the floor. "I go upstairs to pack."

"Your mother's coming to pick you up?"

Eyes squinting closed painfully. "She's here. I hear the car in the driveway."

"Okay. Bett walks inside. You're upstairs and your parents are downstairs. They're talking?"

"Yeah. They're saying things I can't hear at first then I get closer. I sneak down to the landing."

"You can hear them?"

"Yes."

"What do they say?"

"I don't know. Stuff."

"What do they *say?*" The doctor's voice filled the room. "Tell me!"

"They were talking about a funeral."

"Funeral? Whose?"

"I don't know. But there was something bad about it. Something really bad."

"There's something else, isn't there, Megan? They say something else."

"No!" she said desperately. "Just the funeral."

"Megan, tell me."

"I . . ."

"Go on. Touch the place it hurts."

"Tate said . . ." Megan felt faint. She struggled to

control the tears. "He called me . . . They were talking about me. And my daddy said . . ." She took deep gulps of air, which turned to fire in her lungs and throat. The doctor blinked in surprise as she screamed, "My daddy shouted, 'It would all've been different without *her*, without that damn inconvenient child up there. She ruined everything!'"

Megan lowered her head to her knees and wept. The doctor put his arm around her shoulders. She felt his hand stroke her head.

"And how did you feel when you heard him say that?" He brushed away the stream of her tears.

"I don't know . . . I cried."

"Did you want to run away?"

"I guess I did."

"You wanted to show him, didn't you? If that's what he thinks of me I'll pay him back. I'll leave. That's what you thought, isn't it?"

Another nod.

"You wanted to go someplace where people weren't greedy, where people loved you, where people had children's books for you, where they read and talked to you."

She sobbed into a wad of Kleenex.

"Tell him, Megan. Write it down. Get it out so you can look at it."

She wrote until the tears grew so bad she couldn't see the page. Then she collapsed against the doctor's chest, sobbing.

"Good, Megan," he announced. "Very good."

She gripped him tighter than she'd ever gripped a lover, pressing her head against his neck. For a moment neither of them moved. She was frozen here, embracing him fiercely, desperately. He stiffened and for a moment she believed that he was feeling the same sorrow she was. Megan started to back away so that she could see his kind face and his black eyes but he continued to hold her tightly, so hard that a sudden pain swept through her arm.

A surge of alarming warmth spread through her body. It was almost arousing.

Then they separated. Her smile faded as she saw in his face an odd look.

Jesus, what's going on?

His eyes were cold, his smile was cruel. He was suddenly a different person.

"What?" she asked. "What's wrong?"

He said nothing.

She started to repeat herself but the words wouldn't come. Her tongue had grown heavy in her swollen mouth. It fell against her dry teeth. Her vision was crinkling. She tried once again to say something but couldn't.

She watched him stand and open a canvas bag that was resting on the floor behind his desk. He put away a hypodermic syringe. He was pulling on latex gloves.

"What're you? . . ." she began, then noticed on her arm, where the pain radiated, a small dot of blood.

"No!" She tried to ask him what he was doing but the words vanished in comic mumbling. She tried to scream.

A whisper.

He walked to her and crouched, cradling her head, which sagged toward the couch.

Crazy Megan is beyond crazy. She loves him, she's terrified of him, she wants to kill him.

"Go to sleep," he said in a voice kinder than her father's ever sounded. "Go to sleep."

Finally, from the drug, or from the fear, the room went black and she slumped into his arms.

Chapter Three

One hundred and thirty years ago the Dead Reb had wandered through this field.

Maybe shuffling along the very path this tall, lean man now walked in the hot April rain.

Tate Collier looked over his shoulder and imagined that he saw the legendary ghost staring at him from a cluster of brush fifty yards away. Then he laughed to himself and, crunching through rain-wet corn husks and stalks, the waste from last year's harvest, he continued through the field, inspecting hairline fractures in an irrigation pipe that promised far more water than it had been delivering lately. It'd have to be replaced within the next week, he concluded, and wondered how much the work would cost.

Loping along awkwardly, somewhat stooped, Tate was in a Brooks Brothers pinstripe beneath a yellow sou'wester and outrageous galoshes, having come here straight from his strip mall law office in Fairfax, Virginia, where he'd just spent an hour explaining to Mattie Howe that suing the *Prince William Advocate* for libel because the paper had accurately reported her drunk-driving arrest was a lawsuit doomed to failure.

He'd booted her out good-naturedly and sped back to his two-hundred-acre farm.

He brushed at his unruly black hair, plastered around his face by the rain, and glanced at his watch. A half hour until Bett and Megan arrived. Again, the uneasy twist of his stomach at the thought.

He glanced once more over his shoulder—toward where he'd seen the wisp of the ghostly soldier gazing at him from the cluster of vines and kudzu and loblolly pine. Tate returned to the damaged pipe, recalling what his grandfather—born Charles William Collier but known throughout northern Virginia as "the Judge"—had told him about the Dead Reb.

A young private in the bold experiment of the Confederacy took a musket ball between the eyes at the first battle of Bull Run. By all laws of mercy and physiology he should have fallen dead at the picket line. But he'd simply dropped his musket, stood up and wandered southeast until he came to the huge woods that bordered the dusty town of Manassas. There he lived for six months, growing dark as a slave, sucking eggs and robbing cradles (the human victuals were legend only, the Judge appended in a verbal footnote). The Dead Reb was personally responsible for the cessation of all foot traffic after dusk through the Centreville woods that fall—until he was found, stark naked and dead indeed, sitting upright in what was the middle of Jackson's Corner, now a prime part of Tate Collier's farm.

Well, no ghosts here now, Tate reflected, only a hundred feet of pipe to be replaced . . .

Straightening up now, he wiped his watch crystal.

Twenty minutes till they were due.

Look, he told himself, relax.

Through the misty rain Tate could see, a mile away, the house he'd built eighteen years ago. It was a miniature Tara, complete with Doric columns, and was white as a cloud. This was Tate's only real indulgence in life, paid for with some inheritance and the hope of money that a young prosecutor knows will be showered upon him for his brilliance and flair, despite the fact that a commonwealth's attorney's meager salary is a matter of public record. The six-bedroom house still groaned beneath a hearty mortgage.

When the Judge deeded over the fertile Piedmont land to Tate twenty years ago—skipping Tate's father for reasons never articulated though known to one and all of the Collier clan—the young man decided impulsively he wanted a family home (the Judge's residence wasn't on the farmland itself but was eight miles away in Fairfax). Tate kept a two-acre parcel fallow for one season and built on it the next. The house sat between the two barns—one new, one the original—in the middle of a rough, grassy field punctuated with patches of black-eyed Susans, hop clover and bluestem, a stand of bitternut hickory trees, a beautiful American beech and eastern white pines.

The eerily balmy wind grabbed his rain slicker and shook hard. He closed two buckles of the coat and happened to be gazing toward the house when he saw a downstairs light go out.

So Megan had arrived. It had to be the girl; Bett didn't have keys to the house. No hope of cancellation now. Well, if you live three miles from a Civil War battlefield, you have to appreciate the persistence of the past.

He glanced once more at the fractured pipe and started toward the house, heavy boots slogging through the untilled fields.

Like the Dead Reb. No, he reflected, nothing so dramatic. More like the introspective man of forty-four years that he'd become.

An enthymeme is an important rhetorical device used in formal debate.

It's a type of syllogism ("All cats see in the dark. Midnight is a cat. Therefore Midnight sees in the dark."), though the enthymeme is abbreviated. It leaves out one line of logic ("All cats see in the dark. Therefore Midnight sees in the dark."). Experienced debaters and trial lawyers like Tate Collier rely on this device frequently in their debates and courtroom arguments but it works only when there's a common understanding between the advocate and his audience. Everybody's got to understand that the animal in question is a cat; *they* have to supply the missing information in order for the logic to hold up.

Tate reflected now that he, his ex-wife and Megan had virtually none of this common understanding. The mind of Betty Susan McCall would be as alien to him as his was to her. Except for his ex-wife's startling reappearance seven weeks ago—with the news about Megan's drunken climb up the water tower—he hadn't seen her for nearly two years and their phone conversations were limited to practical issues about the girl and the few residual financial threads between people divorced fifteen years.

And as for Megan—how can anyone know a seventeen-year-old girl? Her mind was a moving target. Her only report on the therapy sessions was: "Dad, therapy's for, like, losers. Okay?" And her Walkman headset went back on. He didn't expect her to be any more informative—or articulate—today.

As he approached the house he now noticed that *all* of the inside lights had been shut off. But when he stepped out of the field he saw that neither Megan's nor Bett's car was in the drive.

He unlocked the door and walked into the house, which echoed with emptiness. He noticed Megan's house keys on the entryway table and dropped his own beside them, looking up the dim hallway. The only light in the cavernous space was from behind him—the bony light from outside, filtering through the entryway.

What's that noise?

A wet sound, sticky, came from somewhere on the first floor. Repetitive, accompanied by a faint, hungry gasping.

The chill of fear stirred at his neck.

"Megan?"

The noise stopped momentarily. Then, with a guttural snap of breath, it resumed again. There was a desperation about the sound. Tate's stomach began to churn and his skin prickled with sweat.

And that smell . . . Something pungent and ripe.

Blood! he believed. Like the smell of hot rust.

"Megan!" he called again. Alarmed now, he walked farther into the house.

The noise stopped though the smell was stronger, almost nauseating.

Tate thought of weapons. He had a pistol but it was locked away in the barn and there was no time to get it. He stepped forcefully into the den, seized a letter opener from the desk, flipped on the light.

And laughed out loud.

His two-year-old Dalmatian, her back to him, was flopped down on the floor, chewing intently. Tate set the opener on the bar and approached the dog. His smile faded. What *is* that? Tate squinted.

Suddenly, with a wild, raging snarl, the dog spun and lunged at him. He gasped in shock and leapt back, cracking his elbow on the corner of a table. Just as quickly the dog turned away from him, back to its trophy.

Tate circled the animal then stopped. Between the dog's bloody paws was a bone from which streamed bits of flesh. Tate stepped forward. The dog's head swiveled ominously. The animal's eyes gleamed with jealous hatred. A fierce growl rolled from her sleek throat and the black lips pulled back, revealing bloody teeth.

Jesus . . .

What *is* it? Tate wondered, queasy. Had the dog grabbed some animal that had gotten into the house? It was so badly mauled he couldn't tell what it had been.

"No," Tate commanded. But the dog continued to defend its prize; a raspy growl rose from her throat.

"Come!"

The dog dropped her head and continued to chew, keeping her malevolent eyes turned sideways toward Tate. The crack of bone was loud.

"Come!"

No response.

Tate lost his temper and stepped around the dog, reaching for its collar. The animal leapt up in a frenzy, snapping at him, baring sharp teeth. Tate pulled back just in time to save his fingers.

He could see the bloody object. It looked like a beef leg bone. The kennel owner from whom he'd bought the Dalmatian told him that bones were dangerous treats. Tate never bought them and he assumed Megan must have been shopping on her way here and picked one up. She sometimes brought chew sticks or rubber toys for the animal.

Tate made a strategic retreat, slipped into the hallway. He'd wait until the animal fell asleep tonight then throw the damn thing out.

He walked to the basement stairs, which led down to the recreation room Tate had built for the family parties and reunions he'd planned on hosting—people clustered around the pool table, lounging at the bar, drinking blender daiquiris and eating barbecued chicken. The parties and reunions never happened but Megan often disappeared down to the dark catacombs when she spent weekends here.

He descended the stairs and made a circuit of the small dim rooms. Nothing. He paused and cocked his head. From upstairs came the sound of the dog's growl once more. Urgent and ominous.

"Megan, is that you?" his baritone voice echoed powerfully.

He was angry. Megan and Bett were already twenty minutes late. Here he'd gone to the trouble of inviting them over, doing his fatherly duty, and this was what he got in return . . .

The growling stopped abruptly. Tate listened for footsteps on the ground floor but heard nothing. He climbed the stairs and stepped out into the drizzle once more.

He made his way to the old barn, stepped inside and called Megan's name. No response. He looked around the spooky place in frustration, straightened a stack of old copies of *Wallace's Farmer*, which had fallen over, and glanced at the wall—at a greasy framed plaque containing a saying from Seaman Knapp, the turn-of-the-century civil servant who'd organized the country's agricultural extension services program. Tate's grandfather had copied the epigram, for inspirational purposes, in the same elegant, meticulous lettering with which he filled in the farm's ledgers and wrote legal memos for his secretary to type.

> *What a man hears, he may doubt. What he sees, he may possibly doubt. But what he does, he cannot doubt.*

"Megan?" he called again as he stepped outside.

Then his eye fell on the old picnic bench and he thought of the funeral.

No, he told himself. Don't go thinking about *that*. The funeral was a thousand years ago. It's a memory deader than the Dead Reb and something you'll hate yourself for bringing up.

But think about it he did, of course. Pictured it, felt it, tasted the memory. The funeral. The picnic bench,

Japanese lanterns, Bett and three-year-old Megan . . . He pictured the cluster of week-old Halloween candy lying in grass, a hot November day long ago . . .

Until Bett had shown up at his door nearly two months ago with the news of Megan and the water tower he hadn't thought of that day for years.

What he does, he cannot doubt . . .

The rain began in earnest once again and he hurried back to the house, climbed to the second floor and looked in her bedroom. Then the others.

"Megan?"

She wasn't here either.

He walked downstairs again. Reached for the phone. But he didn't lift the receiver. Instead he sat on the living room couch and listened to the muted sound of the dog's teeth cracking the bone in the next room.

Dr. Peters—well, Dr. Aaron Matthews—sped away from Tate Collier's farm in Megan's Ford Tempo. His hands shook and his breath came fast.

A close call.

He didn't know why Collier had returned home this morning. He *always* kept Saturday hours at his office. Or had, every Saturday for the past three months. Ten to four. Clockwork. But not today. When Matthews had driven to Collier's farm—with Megan in the trunk, no less—he'd found, to his shock, that the lawyer had returned. Fortunately he was heading out into the fields. When he was out of sight Matthews had parked in a cul-de-sac of brush beside Collier's driveway, fifty feet from the house, had snuck into the large structure using Megan's keys. He'd tossed the Dalmatian a beef bone to keep it busy while he did what he'd come for.

He'd managed to escape to the Tempo just as Collier was returning.

Still, it unnerved him. It was bad luck. And although he was a Harvard-trained psychotherapist and did not, professionally, accept the existence of luck, sometimes it took little more than a shadow of superstition like this to drop him into the cauldron of a mood. Matthews was bipolar—the diagnosis that used to be called manic depression. In order for him to carry out the kidnapping he'd gone off his meds; he couldn't afford the dulling effects of the high doses of Prozac and Wellbutrin he'd been taking. Fortunately, once the medication had evaporated from his bloodstream he found himself in a manic phase and he'd easily been able to spend eighteen hours a day stalking Megan and working on his plan. But as the weeks had worn on he'd begun to worry that he was headed for a fall. And he knew from the past that it took very little to push him over the edge into a lethargic pit of depression.

But the near miss with Collier faded now and he remained as buoyant as a happy child. He sped to I-66 and headed east—to the Vienna, Virginia, Metro lot— the huge station for commuters fifteen miles west of D.C. It was Saturday morning but the lot was filled with the cars of people who'd taken the train downtown to visit the monuments and museums and galleries.

Matthews drove Megan's car to the spot where his gray Mercedes was parked then climbed out and looked around. He saw only one other occupied car—a white sedan, idling several rows away. He couldn't see the driver clearly but the man or woman didn't seem to be looking his way. Matthews quickly bundled Megan out of the Tempo's trunk and slipped her into the trunk of the Mercedes.

He looked down at the girl, curled fetally and unconscious, bound up with rope. She was very pale. He pressed a hand to her chest to make sure that she was still breathing regularly. He was concerned about her; Matthews was no longer a licensed M.D. in Virginia and couldn't write prescriptions so to knock the girl out he'd stockpiled phenobarb from a veterinarian, claiming that one of his rottweilers was having seizures. He'd mixed the drug with distilled water but couldn't be sure of the concentration. She was deeply asleep but it seemed that her respiration was fine and when he took her pulse her heart rate was acceptable.

Between the front seats of the Tempo he left the well-thumbed Amtrak timetable that Megan had used as a lap desk to write the letters to her parents and that now bore her fingerprints (and only hers—he'd worn gloves when handling it). He'd circled all the Saturday trains to New York.

He'd approached the abduction the way he once would have planned the treatment of a severely disturbed patient: every detail meticulously considered. He'd stolen the writing paper from Megan's room in Bett McCall's house. He'd spent hours in her room—when the mother was working and Megan was in school. It was there that he'd gotten important insights into her personality: observing the three Joplin posters, the black light, the Márquez book, notes she'd received from classmates laced with words like "fuck" and "shit." (Matthews had written a breakthrough paper for the APA *Journal* on how adolescents unconsciously raise and lower emotional barriers to their therapists according to the doctors' use of grammar and language; he'd observed, during the session that morning, how the expletives he'd used had opened her psyche like keys.)

He'd been careful to leave no evidence of his break-in at Bett McCall's. Or in Leesburg—where Dr. Hanson's mother lived. That had been the biggest problem of his plan: getting Hanson out of the way for the week—without doing something as obvious, though appealing, as running him over with a car. He'd done some research on the therapist and learned that his mother lived in the small town northwest of Washington, D.C., and that she was frail. On Wednesday night Matthews had loosened the top step leading from her back porch to the small yard behind her house. Then he'd called, pretending to be a neighbor, and asked her to check on an injured dog in the backyard. She'd been disoriented and reluctant to go outside after dark but after a few minutes he'd convinced her—nearly had her in tears over the poor animal, in fact. She'd fallen straight down the stairs onto the sidewalk. The tumble looked serious and for a moment Matthews was worried—if she died Hanson might schedule the funeral around his patients' sessions. But he waited until the paramedics arrived and noted that she'd merely broken bones. After Hanson had left a message canceling her regular session Matthews had called Megan and told her he was taking over Hanson's patients.

Now Matthews started the Mercedes and switched cars—parking Megan's in the space his had occupied—and then sped out of the parking lot.

He took his soul's pulse and found his mood intact. There was no paralysis, no anger, no sorrow dishing up the fishy delusions that had plagued him since he was young. The only hint of neurosis was understandable: Matthews found himself talking silently with Megan, repeating the various things he'd told her in the session and what she'd said to him. A bit obsessive but, as he'd occasionally said to patients, So what?

Finally, he turned the Mercedes onto the entrance ramp to I-66 and, doing exactly fifty-eight miles an hour, headed toward the distant mountains. Megan's new home.

Chapter Four

The woman walked inside the house of which she'd been mistress for three years and paused in the Gothic, arched hallway as if she'd never before seen the place.

"Bett," Tate said.

She continued inside slowly, offering her ex-husband a formal smile. She paused again at the den door. The Dalmatian looked up, snarling.

"Oh my, Tate . . ."

"Megan gave her a bone. She's a little protective about it. Let's go in here."

He closed the den door and they walked into the living room.

"Did you talk to her?" he asked.

"Megan? No. Where is she? I didn't see her car."

"She's been here. But she left. I don't know why."

"She leave a note?"

"No. But her house keys're here."

"Oh. Well." Bett fell silent.

Tate crossed his arms and rocked on the carpet for a moment. He walked to the window, looked at the barn through the rain. Returned.

"Coffee?" he asked.

"No, thank you."

Bett sat on the couch, crossed her thin legs, clad in tight black jeans. She wore a black silky blouse and a complicated silver necklace with purple and black stones. She sat in silence for a few moments then rose and examined the elaborate fireplace Tate'd had built several years ago. She caressed the mortar and with a pale pink fingernail picked at the stone. Her eyes squinted as she sighted down the mantelpiece. "Nice," she said. "Fieldstone's expensive."

She sat down again.

Tate examined her from across the room. With her long, Pre-Raphaelite face and tangle of witchy red hair, Betty Susan McCall was exotic. Something Virginia rarely offered—an enigmatic Celtic beauty. The South is full of temptresses and lusty cowgirls and it has matriarchs galore but few sorceresses. Bett was a businesswoman now but beneath that façade, Tate Collier believed, she remained the enigmatic young woman he'd first seen singing a folk song in a smoky apartment on the outskirts of Charlottesville twenty-three years ago. She'd performed a whaling song a cappella in a reedy, breathless voice.

It had, however, been many years since any woman had ensnared him that way and he now found himself feeling very wary. A dozen memories from the days when they were getting divorced surfaced, murky and unsettling.

He wondered how he could keep his distance from her throughout this untidy family business.

Bett's eyes had disposed of the fireplace and the furniture in the living room and were checking out the wallpaper and molding. His eyes dogged after hers and he concluded that she found the place unhomely and stark. It needed more upholstered things, more pillows, more flowers, new curtains, livelier paint. He felt embarrassed.

After several minutes Bett said, "Well, if her car's gone she probably just went out to get something."

"That's probably it."

Two hours later, no messages on either of their phones, Tate called the police.

The first thing Tate noticed was the way Konnie glanced at Bett.

With approval.

As if the lawyer had finally gotten his act together; no more young blondes for him. And it was damn well about time. This woman was in her early forties, very pretty. Smooth skin. She had quick eyes and seemed smart. Detective Dimitri Konstantinatis of the Fairfax County Police had commented once, "Tate, why're all the women you date half your age and, lemme guess, a third your intelligence? If that. Why's that, Counselor?"

Konnie strode into the living room and stuck his hand out toward her. He shook the startled woman's hand vigorously as Tate introduced them. "Bett, my ex-wife, this is Konnie. Konnie's an old friend from my prosecuting days."

"Howdy." Oh, the cop's disappointed face said, so she's the ex. Giving *her* up was one bad mistake, mister. The detective glanced at Tate. "So, Counselor, your daughter's up 'n' late for lunch, that right?"

"Been over two hours."

"You're fretting too much, Tate." He poked a finger at him and said to Bett, "This fella? Was the sissiest prosecutor in the commonwealth. We had to walk him to his car at night."

"At least I could *find* my car," Tate shot back. One of the reasons Konnie loved Tate was that the lawyer joked about Konnie's drinking; he was now in recovery—no alcohol in four years—and not a single soul in the world except Tate Collier would dare poke fun at him about it. But what every other soul in the world didn't know was that what the cop respected most was balls.

Bett smiled uneasily.

Tate and Konnie had worked together frequently when Tate was a commonwealth's attorney. The somber detective had been taciturn and distant for the first six months of their professional relationship, never sharing a single personal fact. Then at midnight of the day a serial rapist–murderer they'd jointly collared and convicted was sentenced to be "paroled horizontal," as the death row parlance went, Konnie had drunkenly embraced Tate and said that the case made them blood brothers. "We're bonded."

"Bonded? What kind of pinko touchy-feely crap is that?" an equally drunken Tate had roared.

They'd been tight friends ever since.

Another knock on the front door.

"Maybe that's her," Bett said eagerly. But when Tate opened the door a crew-cut man in a cheap, slope-shouldered gray suit walked inside. He stood very straight and looked Tate in the eye. "Mr. Collier. I'm Detective Ted Beauridge. Fairfax County Police. I'm with Juvenile."

Tate led him inside and introduced Beauridge to
Bett while Konnie clicked the TV's channel selector.
He seemed fascinated to find a TV that had no remote
control.

Beauridge was polite and efficient but clearly he
didn't want to be here. Konnie was the sole reason
Megan's disappearance was getting any attention at
all. When Tate had called, Konnie'd told him that it
was too early for a missing person's report; twenty-
four hours' disappearance was required unless the
individual was under fifteen, mentally handicapped
or endangered. Still, Konnie had somehow "accidentally forgotten" to get his supervisor's okay and
had run a tag check on Megan's car. And he'd put
in a request for Jane Doe admissions at all the area
hospitals.

Tate ushered them into the living room. Bett asked,
"Would you like some coffee or . . . ?" Her voice faded
and she laughed in embarrassment, looking at Tate,
undoubtedly remembering that this had not been her
house for a long, long time.

"Nothing, thanks, ma'am," Beauridge said for them
both.

In the time it had taken Konnie to arrive, Bett
had called some friends of Megan's. She'd spent the
night at Amy Walker's. Bett had called this girl first
but no one had answered. She left a message on the
Walkers' voice mail then called some of her other
friends. Brittany, Kelly and Donna hadn't seen Megan
or heard from her today. They didn't know if she had
plans except maybe showing up at the mall later. "To,
you know, like, hang out."

Konnie asked Tate and Bett about the girl's Saturday routine.

"She normally has a therapy session Saturday morning," Bett explained. "At nine. But the doctor had to cancel today. His mother was sick or something."

"Could she just've forgotten about coming here for lunch?"

"When we talked yesterday I reminded her about it."

"Was she good about keeping appointments?" Beauridge asked.

Tate didn't know. She'd always shown up on time when he took her shopping or to dinner at the Ritz in Tysons. He told them this. Bett said that she was "semigood about being prompt." But she didn't think the girl would miss this lunch. "The three of us being together and all," she added with a faint cryptic laugh.

"What about boyfriends?" Konnie asked.

"She didn't—" Tate began.

Then halted at Bett's glance. And he realized he didn't have a clue whether Megan had a boyfriend or not.

Bett continued, "She did but they broke up last month."

"*She* the one broke it off?"

"Yes."

"So is he trouble, you think? This kid?" Konnie tugged at a jowl.

"I don't think so. He seemed very nice. Easygoing."

So did Ted Bundy, Tate thought.

"What's his name?"

"Joshua LeFevre. He's a senior at George Mason."

"He's a senior in *college?*" Tate asked.

"Well, yes," she said.

"Bett, she's only seventeen. I mean—"

"Tate," Bett said again. "He was a nice boy. His mother's some executive at EDS, his father's stationed at the Pentagon. And Josh's a championship athlete. He's also head of the Black Students' Association."

"The *what?*"

"Tate!"

"Well, I'm just surprised. I mean, it doesn't *matter.*" Bett shrugged with some exasperation.

"It doesn't," Tate said defensively. "I'm just—"

"—surprised," Konnie repeated wryly. "Mr. ACLU speaks."

"You know his number?" Beauridge asked.

Bett didn't but she got it from directory assistance and called. She apparently got one of his roommates. Joshua was out. She left a message for him to call when he returned.

"So. She's been here and gone. No sign of a struggle?" Konnie looked around the front hall.

"None."

"What about the alarms?"

"I had them off."

"There a panic button she could hit if somebody was inside waiting for her?"

"Yep. And she knows about it."

Bett offered, "She left the house keys here. She has her car keys with her."

"Could somebody," Konnie speculated, "have stole her purse, got the keys and broken in?"

Tate considered this. "Maybe. But her driver's

license has Bett's address on it. How would a burglar know to come here? Maybe she had something with my address on it but I don't know what. Besides, nothing's missing that I could see."

"Don't see much worth stealing," Konnie said, looking at the paltry entertainment equipment. "You know, Counselor, they got TVs nowadays bigger'n cereal boxes."

Tate grunted.

"Okay," Konnie said, "how 'bout you show me her room?"

As Tate led him upstairs Beauridge's smooth drawl rolled, "Sure you got nothing to worry about, Mrs. Collier—"

"It's McCall."

Upstairs, Tate let Konnie into Megan's room then wandered into his own. He'd missed something earlier when he'd made the rounds up here: his dresser drawer was open. He looked inside, frowned, then glanced across the hall as the detective surveyed the girl's room. "Something funny," Tate called.

"Hold that thought," Konnie answered. With surprisingly lithe movements for such a big man he dropped to his knees and went through what must have been the standard teenage hiding places: under desk drawers, beneath dressers, wastebaskets, under beds, in curtains, pillows and comforters. "Ah, whatta we got here?" Konnie straightened up and examined two sheets of paper.

He pointed to Megan's open dresser drawers and the closet. "These're almost empty, these drawers. They normally got clothes in them?"

Tate hesitated, concern on his face. "Yes, they're usually full."

"Could you see if there's any luggage missing?"

"Luggage? No . . . Wait. Her old backpack's gone." Tate considered this for a moment. Why would she take that? he wondered. Looking at the papers, Tate asked the detective, "What'd you find?"

"Easy, Counselor," Konnie said, folding up the sheets. "Let's go downstairs."

Chapter Five

What would Sidney Poitier do?

Joshua LeFevre shifted his muscular, trapezoidal body in the skimpy seat of his Toyota and pressed down harder on the gas pedal. The tiny engine complained but slowly edged the car closer to the Mercedes.

Come on, Megan, what the hell're you up to?

He squinted again and leaned forward as if moving eight inches closer to the Merce were going to let him see more clearly through his confusion. He assumed the man, not Megan, was driving though he couldn't be sure. This gave him a sliver of comfort—for some reason the thought of this guy tossing Megan the keys to his big doctor's car and saying, "You drive, honey," riled the young man beyond words. Made him furious.

He nudged the car faster.

Sidney Poitier . . . What would you do?

LeFevre had seen *In the Heat of the Night* when he'd been ten. (On video, of course—when the film had originally come out, in the sixties, the man who would be his father was doing basic training push-ups in Fort Dix and his to-be mother was listening to Smokey Robinson and Diana Ross while she worked on her 4.0 average at National Cathedral School.)

The film had affected him deeply. The Poitier character, Detective Tibbs, ended up stuck in the small Southern town, butting horns with good-old-boy sheriff Rod Steiger. Moving slow, solving a local murder, step by step . . . Not getting flustered, not getting pissed off in the face of all the crap everybody in town was giving him.

Sure, the movie didn't have real guts, it was *Hollywood's* idea of race relations, more softball than gritty, but even at age ten Joshua LeFevre understood the film wasn't really about black or white—it was about being a man and being persistent and not taking no when you believed yes.

It choked him up, that flick—the way important movies always do, those films that give us our role models, whether it's the first time we see them or the hundredth.

Oh yes, Joshua Nathan LeFevre—an honors English major at George Mason University, a tall young man with his father's perfect physique and military bearing and with his mother's brains—had a sentimental side to him thick as a mountain. (The week that students in his nineteenth-century-lit seminar were picking apart a Henry James novel like crows, LeFevre had slunk back to his apartment with a very different book hidden in a brown paper bag. He'd locked his door and read the entire novel in one sitting, crying unashamedly when he came to the last page of *The Bridges of Madison County.*)

Sentimental, a romantic. And accordingly, Sidney Poitier—rather than Samuel L. Jackson or Wesley Snipes—appealed to him.

So, what would *Mr.* Tibbs do now?

Okay, he was saying to himself, let's analyze it. Step by step. Here's a girl's got a bad home life. None of that talk-show abuse, no, but it's clearly a case of Daddy don't care and Momma don't care. So she drinks more than she ought and hangs with a bad crowd—until she meets LeFevre. And seems to get her act together though she falls off the normal wagon every once in a while. And then one night she climbs up to the top of a water tower (and why didn't she call me, dammit, instead of guzzling a fifth of Comfort with Donna and Brittany, the Easy Sisters?). And once she's up there she does a little dance on the scaffolding and the cops and fire department come to get her down.

And she goes to see this shrink . . .

Who tells her she's got to break up with him.

And so she does.

"Why?" LeFevre had asked her a few weeks ago as they sat in his car, parked in front of her house, on what turned out to be their last date.

"Why?"

"It's not the differences . . ." Meaning the age, meaning the race. It was . . . what the hell was it? He replayed Megan's little speech.

"It's just that I'm not ready for the same kind of relationship you want."

And what kind is that? I don't remember proposing. I don't think we've even *talked* about our relationship. We just have fun together.

"Oh, Josh, honey, don't cry . . . I need to see things, do things. I feel, I don't know, all tied down or something . . . Living with Bett's like living with a roommate. You know, her date for Saturday's the biggest deal in the world. All she worries about is her skin getting old."

Old skin? I like your mom. She's pretty, smart, offbeat. I don't get it. What's her skin got to do with breaking up? LeFevre had been very confused as he sat in his tiny car beside the woman he loved.

"Oh, honey, I just need to get away. I want to travel, see things. You know."

Travel? Where was *this* coming from? I've got a trust fund, Mom and Dad're loaded. I've lived in Jeddah, Cyprus, London and Germany. I speak three languages. I can show you more of the world than the Cunard Line.

"Okay. What it is is this therapist. Dr. Hanson? See, he thinks it's not a good idea for me to be in a relationship with you right now."

Then we'll back off a bit. See each other once a week or so. How's that?

"No, you don't *understand*," Megan had said brutally, pulling away from him as he tried to take the Southern Comfort bottle out of her hand. And she'd climbed out of the passenger seat and run into her house.

Cruising down I-66 now, LeFevre leaned over and sniffed the headrest to see if he could smell her perfume. Heartbreakingly, he couldn't. He pushed the accelerator harder, edging up on the gray Mercedes.

"No, you don't understand."

No, he sure as hell hadn't.

Joshua LeFevre had waited a tormented three

weeks then—this morning—woke up on autopilot. He hadn't been able to take the girl's silence and the suffocating frustration anymore. He'd driven to Hanson's office around the time Megan's appointment would be over. He'd parked up the street, waiting for her to come out. Josh LeFevre could bench-press 220 pounds, he could bicycle 150 miles a day. But he wasn't going for intimidation. Oh no. He was going to Poitier the man, not Snipes him.

Why, he was going to ask the doctor, did you talk her into breaking up with me? Isn't that unethical? Let's sit down together. The three of us. Josh had a dozen arguments all prepared. He believed he could talk his way back into her heart.

"No, you don't understand."

But *now* he did.

God, I'm an idiot.

The doctor had her break up because he wanted to fuck her.

No psychobabble here. No inner child. Nope. The shrink wanted to play the two-backed beast with LeFevre's girlfriend. Simple as a shot in the head.

From where he'd been parked near the office he hadn't been able to see clearly but suddenly, before the appointment was supposed to be over, Megan's Tempo was pulling out of the lot—with the shrink himself driving, it seemed, and heading north.

He'd followed the car to Manassas—to Megan's dad's farm—where LeFevre'd waited for about twenty minutes. Then, just when he'd been about to pull into the long drive, the car had sped out again and they'd driven to the Vienna Metro parking lot. They'd switched cars—taking the German shrinkmobile—and headed west on I-66.

What was it all about? Had she picked up some clothes from her father's place? Was she going away for the weekend?

LeFevre was crazed. He had to do *something*.

But what would Sidney Poitier do? The script had changed.

Wait till they got to the doctor's house? The inn they were going to? Confront them there?

No, that didn't seem right.

Oh, hell, he should just go home . . . Forget this crap. Be a man.

His foot eased up on the gas . . . Good idea, get off at the next exit. Quit acting like a lovesick loser. It's embarrassing. Go home. Read your Melville. You've got a presentation due a week from Monday . . .

The Mercedes pulled ahead.

Then the thought burst within him: Bullshit. I'm going to deconstruct motifs in some fucking story about a big-ass whale while my girlfriend's in bed whispering into her therapist's ear?

He jammed his foot to the floor.

Would Poitier do this?

You bet.

And so LeFevre kept his sweating hands on the wheel of the car, straining forward, and sped after the woman whom he loved and, he believed somewhere in a portion of his sloppy heart, who loved him still.

"She's run away?" Bett whispered.

The four of them were in the living room, like

strangers at a cocktail party, knees pointed at one another, sitting upright and waiting to become comfortable. Konnie continued, "But y'all should consider that good news. The profile is most runaways come back on their own within a month."

Bett stared out the window at the misty darkness. "A month," she announced, as if answering a trivia question. "No, she wouldn't leave. Not without saying anything."

Konnie glanced at Beauridge. Tate caught the look.

"I'm afraid she did say something." Konnie handed Bett and Tate what he'd found upstairs. "Letters to both of you. Under her pillow."

"Why there?" Bett asked. "That doesn't make any sense."

"So you wouldn't find 'em right away," Konnie explained. "Give her a head start. I've seen it before."

Beauridge asked, "Is that her handwriting?"

Konnie added, "There's a buddy of mine, FBI document examiner, Parker Kincaid. Lives in Fairfax. We could give him a call."

But Bett said it was definitely Megan's writing.

"'Bett,'" she read aloud then looked up. "She called me Bett. Not Mom. Why would she do that?" She started again and read in a breathless, ghostly voice, "'Bett—I don't care if it hurts you to say this . . . I don't care how *much* it hurts . . .'"

She looked helplessly at her ex-husband then read to herself. She finished, sat back in the couch and seemed to shrink to the size of a child herself. She whispered, "She says she hates me. She hates all the time I spent with my sister. I . . ." Mystified, hurt, she shook her head and fell silent.

Tate looked down at his note. It was stained. With tears? With rain? He read:

> *Tate:*
>
> *The only way to say it—I hate you for what you've done to me! You don't listen to me. You talk, talk, talk and Bett calls you the silver-tongued devil and you are but you never listen to me. To what I want. To who I am. You bribe me, you pay me off and hope I'll go away. I should of run away when I was six like I wanted to. And never come back.*
>
> *I've wanted to do that all along. I still want to. Get away from you. It's what you want anyway, isn't it? To get rid of your inconvenient child?*

His mouth was open, his lips and tongue dry, stinging from the air that whipped in and out of his lungs. He found he was staring at Bett.

"Tate. You okay?" Konnie said.

"Could I see that again, Mrs. McCall?" Beauridge asked.

She handed the stiff sheet over.

"You're sure that's her writing paper?"

Bett nodded. "I gave it to her for Christmas."

In a low voice Bett answered questions no one had asked. "My sister was very sick. I left Megan in other people's care a lot. I didn't know she felt so abandoned . . . She never said anything."

Tate noted Megan's careless handwriting. In several

places the tip of the pen had ripped through the paper. In anger, he assumed.

Konnie asked Tate what he'd found in his own room.

He was so stunned it took him a minute to focus on the question. "She took four hundred dollars from my bedside drawer."

Bett blurted, "Nonsense. She wouldn't take . . ."

"It's gone," Tate said. "She's the only one who's been here."

"What about credit cards?" Konnie asked.

"She's on my Visa and MasterCard," Bett said. "She'd have them with her."

"That's good," Konnie offered. "It's an easy way to trace runaways. What it is we'll set up a real-time link with the credit card companies. We'll know within ten minutes where she's charged something."

Beauridge said, "We'll put her on the runaway wire. She's picked up anywhere for anything on the eastern seaboard, they'll let us know. Let me have a picture, will you?"

Tate realized that they were looking at him.

"Sure," he said quickly and began searching the room. He looked through the bookshelves, end-table drawers. He couldn't find any photos.

Beauridge watched Tate uncertainly; Tate guessed that the young officer's wallet and wall were peppered with snapshots of his own youngsters. Konnie himself, Tate remembered from some years ago, kept a picture of his ex-wife and kids in his wallet. The lawyer rummaged in the living room and disappeared into the den. He returned some moments later with a snapshot—a photo of Tate and Megan at Virginia Beach two years ago. She stared unsmilingly at the camera. It was the only picture he could find.

"Pretty girl," Beauridge said.

"Tate," Konnie said, "I'll stay on it. But there isn't a lot we can do."

"Whatever, Konnie. You know it'll be appreciated."

"Bye, Mrs. Coll—McCall."

But Bett was looking out the window and said nothing.

The white Toyota was staying right behind the Mercedes, Aaron Matthews noted. He wondered if it was the same auto he'd seen in the Vienna Metro lot when he was switching cars. He wished he'd paid more attention.

Matthews believed in coincidence even less than he believed in luck and superstition. There were no accidents, no flukes. We are completely responsible for our behavior and its consequences even if we can't figure out what's motivating us to act.

The car behind him now was not a coincidence.

There was a motive, there was a design.

Matthews couldn't understand it yet. He didn't know how concerned to be. But he *was* concerned.

Maybe he'd cut the driver off and the man was mad. Road rage.

Maybe it was someone who'd seen him heft a large bundle into the trunk of the Mercedes and was following out of curiosity.

Maybe it was the police.

He slowed to fifty.

The white car did too.

Sped up.

The car stayed with him.

Have to think about this. Have to do something.

Matthews slid into the right lane and continued through the mist toward the mountains in the west. He looked back as often as he looked forward.

As any good therapist will advise his patients to do.

Chapter Six

The rain had stopped but the atmosphere was thick as hot blood.

In her stylish shoes with the wide, high heels, Bett McCall came to Tate's shoulder. Neither speaking, they stood on the back porch, looking over the back sixty acres of the property.

The Collier spread was more conservative than most Piedmont farms: five fields rotating between soy one year and corn and rye the next. A classic northern Virginia spread.

"Listen to me, Tate," the Judge would say.

The boy always listened to his grandfather.

"What's a legume?"

"A pea."

"Only a pea?"

"Well, beans too, I think."

"Peas, beans, clover, alfalfa, vetches . . . they're all legumes. They help the soil. You plant year after year of cereals, what happens?"

"Don't know, sir."

"Your soil goes to hell in a handbasket."

"Why's that, Judge?"

The man had taught the boy never to be afraid to ask questions.

"Because legumes take nitrogen from the air. Cereals take it from the soil."

"Oh."

"We'll plant Mammoth Brown and Yellow for silage and Virginia soy too. Wilson and Haerlandts are good for seed and hay. How do you prepare the land?"

"Like you're planting corn," the boy had responded. "Sow them broadcast with a wheat drill."

Out of the blue the Judge might glance at his grandson and ask, "Do you cuss, Tate?"

"Nosir."

"Here. Read this." The man thrust into Tate's hand a withered old bulletin from the Virginia Department of Agriculture and Immigration. A dog-eared chapter bemoaned the rise of young farmers' profanity. *Even some of our girls have taken to this deplorable habit.*

"I'll keep that in mind, Judge," Tate had said, remembering without guilt how he'd sworn a blue streak at Junior Foote at school just last Thursday.

Gazing at his fields, the Judge had continued, "But if you *do* find it necessary to let loose just make sure there're no womenfolk around. Almost time for supper. Let's get on home."

Tate stayed at his grandparents' house in Fairfax as often as at his parents'. Tate's father was a kind, completely quiet man, best suited to a life as, say, a court reporter—a career he'd never dared pursue, of course, given the risk that he'd be assigned to transcribe one of his father's trials. The Judge had agonized over whether or not to leave the farm to his only son and had concluded the man just didn't have the mettle to handle a spread of this sort. So he deeded it over to

Tate while the other kin got money. (Ironically, as Tate learned during one of the few frank conversations he'd ever had with his father, the man had been dreading the day that the Judge would hand over the farm to him. His main concern seemed to be that running the farm would interfere with his passion of collecting Lionel electric trains.) Tate's timid, ever-tired mother suited her husband perfectly and Tate could remember not a single word of dissension, or passion, between the two. Little conversation either.

Which is why, given his druthers, adolescent Tate would hitch or beg a ride to his grandparents' house and spend as much time as he could with them.

As the Judge had presided at the head of the groaning board table on Sunday afternoons Tate's grandmother might offer in a whisper, "The only day to plant beans is Good Friday."

"That's a superstition, Grams," young Tate had said to her, a woman so benign that she took any conversation directed toward her, even in disagreement, as a compliment. "You can plant soy all the way through June."

"No, young man. Now listen to me." She'd looked toward the head of the table, to make sure her husband wasn't listening. "If you laugh loud while planting corn it's trouble. I mean, serious trouble. And it's good to plant potatoes and onions in the dark of the moon and you better plant beans and corn in the light."

"That doesn't make any sense, Grams."

"Does," she'd responded. "Root crops grow below ground so you plant them in the dark of the moon. Cereals are above ground so you plant in the light."

Tate admitted there was a certain logic there.

This was one of three or four simultaneous discussions going on around the dinner table—aunts and uncles and cousins, as well as the inevitable guest or two that the Judge would invite from the ranks of the bench and bar in Prince William and Fairfax Counties. One crisp, clear Sunday, young Tate shared an iced tea with one guest who'd arrived early while the Judge was en route from the farm. The slim, soft-spoken visitor showed a great interest in Tate's ant farm. The visitor was Supreme Court Justice William Brennan, taking a break from penning an opinion in a decision—maybe a landmark case—to come to Judge Collier's farm for roast beef, yams, collard greens and, of course, fresh corn.

"And," Grams would continue, scanning the table for the sin of empty serving bowls, "it's also bad luck to slaughter hogs in the dark of the moon."

"Sure is for the hogs," Tate had offered.

The dinner would continue until four or five in the afternoon, Tate sitting and listening to legal war stories and planning and zoning battles and local gossip thick as Grams's mashed potatoes.

Now, because his ex-wife stood beside him, Tate was keenly aware that those Norman Rockwell times, which he'd hoped to duplicate in his own life, had never materialized.

The vestige of a familial South for Tate hadn't survived long into his adulthood. He, Bett and Megan were no longer a family. Among the multitude of pretty and smart and well-rounded women he'd dated Tate Collier hadn't found a single chance for family.

And so, as concerned as he now was about Megan, the return of these two into his life was fraught with pain.

It brought practical problems too. He was preparing for the biggest case he'd had in years. A corporation was petitioning Prince William County for permission to construct a historical theme park near the Bull Run Battlefield. Liberty Park was going to take on King's Dominion and Six Flags. Tate was representing a group of residents who didn't want the entertainment complex in their backyard even though the county had granted tentative approval. Last week Tate had won a temporary injunction halting the development for ninety days, which the developer immediately challenged. Next week, on Thursday, the Supreme Court in Richmond would hear the argument and rule whether or not to let the injunction stand. If it did, the delay alone might be enough to put the kibosh on the whole deal.

Overnight Tate Collier had become the most popular—and unpopular—person in Prince William County, depending on whether you opposed or supported the project. The developer of the park and the lenders funding it wanted him to curl up and blow away, of course. But there were hundreds of local businessmen, craftsmen, suppliers and residents who also stood to gain by the park's approval and the ensuing migration of tourists. One editorial, lauding the project, called Tate "the devil's advocate." A phrase that certainly resonated in this fervent outpost of the Christian South.

Liberty Park's developer, Jack Sharpe, was one of

the richest men in northern Virginia. He came from
old money and could trace his Prince William ancestry
back to pre–Civil War days. When Tate had brought
the action for the injunction, Sharpe had hired a well-
known local firm to defend. Tate had chopped Sharpe's
lawyers into little pieces—hardly even sporting—and
the developer had fired them. For the argument in
Richmond he'd gone straight to Washington, D.C.,
to hire a law firm that included two former attorneys
general, one former vice president, and, possibly, a
future president.

Tate and Ruth, his secretary-assistant-paralegal,
had been working nonstop on the argument and
motion papers for a week, and would continue to do
so until, probably, midnight of the day before the
argument.

So Bett's reappearance in his life—and Megan's
disappearance from it—might have some serious
professional repercussions.

Queasy, he thought again of that day when he and
Bett had fought so bitterly—ten or eleven years ago.
He'd never known the girl had overheard his outburst.

Your inconvenient child . . .

Why had fate brought them back into his life?
Why now?

But however he wished otherwise, they *were* back.
And there was nothing he could do about it.

Finally Tate asked his ex-wife, "Think we should
call my mother?"

"No," Bett said. "Let's give it a few days. I don't
want to upset her unnecessarily."

"What about your sister?"

"Definitely not her."

"Why not?" Tate wondered aloud. He knew Susan cared very much for Megan. More than most aunts would for a niece. In fact, she'd always seemed almost jealous that Bett had a daughter and she didn't.

"Because we don't have any answers yet," Bett responded. Then, after a few moments, she sighed. "This isn't like her." She glanced at the letter in her hand. Then shoved it deep into her purse.

Tate studied his wife's face. Tate Collier had inherited several talents from the Judge. The main gift was, of course, a way with words, and the other, far rarer, was the ability to see the future in someone's face. Now he looked into his ex-wife's remarkable violet eyes, saw them narrow, alight on his and move on, and he knew exactly what was going through her mind. Debate is not just about words, debate is about intuition too. The advocate who can see exactly where his adversary is headed will always have an advantage, whatever rhetorical flourishes the opponent has in his repertoire.

He didn't like what he now saw.

Bett stepped determinedly off the porch and into the backyard, toward the west barn, where her car was parked. He followed and paused on the shaggy lawn, which was badly in need of a mowing. He stared intently at the white streak of the energetic Dalmatian, which had finally forsaken the bone and was zipping through the grass like a greyhound.

Tate glanced at the old barn, alien and yet very familiar. Then his eyes fell on the picnic bench that he and Bett had bought at one of the furniture stores along Route 28. They'd used it only once—for the gathering after the funeral fourteen years ago. He remembered the events with perfect clarity now. It seemed like last week.

He saw Bett looking at the bench too. Wondered what she was thinking.

That had been an unseasonably warm November— just as odd as this April's oppressive heat. He pictured Bett standing on the bench to unhook a Japanese lantern from the dogwood after the last of the family and well-wishers had left or gone to bed.

Today, Tate paused beside this same tree, which was in its expansive, pink bloom.

"Are you busy now?" she asked. "Your practice?"

"Lot of little things. Only one big case." He nodded at the house, where a paralyzing stack of documents for the Liberty Park argument rested. When they were married the house had been littered with red-backed legal briefs, forty or fifty pages long. *The Supreme Court of the Commonwealth of Virginia.* Many of them were for death penalty cases Tate was prosecuting. Although he'd been the Fairfax County commonwealth's attorney Tate had often argued down in Richmond on behalf of other counties. "Have voice, will travel," his staff had joked. His specialty had become special-circumstance murder cases—the official description of capital punishment cases.

These assignments and his eagerness to take such cases were a source of friction between husband and wife. Bett was opposed to the death penalty.

Death, Tate reflected, always seemed to lurk behind their relationship. Her sister Susan's continual battle with serious heart disease, and the suicide of Susan's husband, Harris. Then the death of Bett's parents and Tate's father and grandfather, all in the tragically short period of three years.

Tate kicked at piles of cornstalks.

"I have this *feeling*, Tate." Bett's hands lifted and dropped to her sides. "Do you understand what I mean?"

No. He didn't. Tate was dogged and smart, but feelings? No, sir. Didn't trust them for a minute. He saw how they got the people he'd prosecuted into deep, deep trouble. When they'd been married Bett lived on feelings. Intuition, sensations, impressions. And sometimes, it seemed, messages from the stars. Drove him crazy.

"Keep going," he said.

She shrugged. "I don't believe this." She tapped her purse. Meaning the letter, he supposed.

"Why do you think that?"

"I was remembering something."

"Hmm?" he offered noncommittally.

"I found a bag under Megan's bed at home. When I was cleaning last week. There was a soap dish in it."

He noticed the woman's tears. He wanted to step close, put his arm around her. Tate tried to remember the last time he'd held her. Not just bussed cheeks but actually put his arms around her, felt her narrow shoulder blades beneath his large hands. No memory came to mind.

"It was a joke between us. I never had a dish in my bathroom. The soap got all yucky, Megan said. So she bought this Victorian soap dish. It was for my birthday.

Next week. There was a card too. I mean, she wouldn't buy me a present and a card and then do this."

Wouldn't she? Tate wondered. Why not? When the pressure builds to a certain point the volcano blows—and it doesn't care about the time of year or who's picnicking on the slopes, drunken lovers or churchgoers. Any lawyer who's done domestic relations work will testify to that.

"You think someone *made* her do this? Or that it's a prank?" Tate asked.

"I don't know. She might've been drinking again. I checked the bottles at home and they didn't look emptier but . . . I don't know."

"That's not much to go on," her ex-husband said.

Suddenly she turned to him and spoke. "It's not a hundred percent thing we've got, Megan and me. There're problems. Of course there are. But our relationship deserves more than this damn letter. More than her running out . . ." She crossed her arms, gazed into the fields again. She repeated, "Something's wrong."

"But what? Exactly? What do you think?"

"I don't *know.*"

"Well, what should we do?"

"I want to go look for her," Bett said determinedly. "I want to find her."

Which is exactly what he'd seen in her purple eyes a few moments earlier. This is what he'd known was coming.

Yet now that he thought about it he was surprised. This didn't sound like Bett McCall at all. Bett the dreamer, Bett the tarot card consulter. Passive, she'd always floated where the breezes took her. Forrest Gump's feather . . . The least likely person imaginable to be a mother. Children needed guidance, direction, models. That wasn't Bett McCall. When he'd heard from Megan that Bett had become engaged last Christmas Tate was surprised only that it had taken her so long to accept what must have been her dozenth proposal since they'd divorced. When they'd been married she'd been charming and flighty and wholly ungrounded, relying on him to provide the foundation she needed. He'd assumed that once they'd split up she'd quickly find someone else to play that role.

He wondered if he was standing next to a Betty Susan McCall different from the one he'd been married to (and wondered too if *she* was thinking the same about him).

"Bett," he said to reassure her, "she's fine. She's a mature young woman. She vented some steam and's going off for a few days. I did it myself when I was about her age. Remember?" He doubted that she did but, surprising him, she said, "You made it all the way to Baltimore."

"And I called the Judge and he came to get me. A two-day runaway. Look, Megan's had a lot to deal with. I think the soap dish is the key."

"The dish?"

"You're right—nobody'd buy a present and a card and then not give them to you. She'll be back for your birthday. And know what else?"

"What?"

"There's a positive side to this. She's brought up

some things that we can talk about. That *ought* to be talked about." He nodded—toward the house, where *his* letter rested like a bloody knife.

Logic. Who could argue with it?

But Bett wasn't convinced.

"There's something else I have to tell you." She chewed on her narrow lower lip the way he remembered her doing whenever she'd been troubled. She gripped the porch banister and lowered her head.

Tate Collier, intercollegiate debate champion, national moot court winner, expert forensic orator, recognized the body language of an impending confession.

"Go ahead," he said.

"The night of the water tower thing—I was . . . out."

"Out?"

She sighed. "I mean, I didn't get home. I was at Brad's in Baltimore. I didn't plan on it; I just fell asleep. Megan was really upset I hadn't called."

"You apologized?"

"Of course."

"Well, it was one of those things. An accident. She'd know that."

Bett shook her head dismissingly. "I think maybe that's what started her drinking before she climbed up the tower. It didn't help that she doesn't like Brad much."

The girl had described Bett's fiancé as a nerd who parted his hair too carefully, thought sweaters with reindeer on them were stylish and spent too much time in front of the TV. Tate didn't share these observations with Bett now.

"It takes a little while to get used to stepparents. I see it all the time in my practice."

"I held off going over to his place for a while after that. But last night I went there again. I asked her if she minded and she said she didn't. I dropped her at Amy's on my way to Baltimore."

"So, there." Tate smiled and caught her eye as she glanced his way.

"What?"

He lifted his palms. "It's just a little payback. She's over at somebody's house, going to let you sweat a bit."

So, no need to worry.

You go your way and I'll go mine.

"That may be," Bett said, "but I'll never forgive myself if I just forget it and something happens to her."

Tate's phone buzzed. He answered it.

"Counselor," Konnie's gruff voice barked.

"Konnie, what's up?"

"Got good news."

"You found her?"

Bett's head swiveled.

The detective said, "She's on her way to New York."

"How do you know?" Tate asked.

"I put out a DMV notice and a patrol found her car at the Vienna Metro station. On the front seat was an Amtrak schedule. She'd circled Saturday trains to Penn Station. Manhattan." The Metro would take her from Vienna to Union Station in downtown D.C. in a half hour. From there it was three hours to New York City. Konnie continued. "You know anybody up there she'd go to visit?"

Tate told this to Bett, who took the news cautiously. He asked about where she might be going.

She shook her head. "I don't think she knows a soul up there."

Tate relayed the answer to Konnie.

"Well, at least you know where she's going. I'll call NYPD and have somebody meet the trains and ask around the station. I'll send 'em her picture."

"Okay. Thanks, Konnie." He hung up. Looked at his ex-wife. "Well," he said. "That's that."

But the violet eyes disagreed.

"What, Bett?" he asked.

"I'm sorry, Tate. I just don't buy it."

"What?"

"Her going off to New York."

"But *why?* You haven't told me anything specific."

Her palms slapped her hips. "Well, I don't *have* anything specific. You want evidence, you want proof. I don't have any." She sighed. "I'm not like you."

"Like me?"

"I can't *convince* you," she said angrily. "I don't have a way with words. So I'm not even going to try."

He started to say something more, to cinch his argument, to end this awkward reunion, to send her back out of his life. But he considered what she'd just said and recalled something—what the Judge had said after Tate had finished an argument before the Supreme Court in Richmond in a death penalty case, which Tate later won. His grandfather had been in the audience, proud as could be that his offspring was handling the case. Later, over whiskeys at the ornate Jefferson Hotel in Richmond, the somber old man had said, "Tate, that was wonderful, absolutely wonderful. They'll rule for you. I saw it in their faces."

I did too, he'd thought, wondering what else the Judge had in mind. The old man's eyes were dim.

"But I want you to understand something."

"Okay," the young man said.

"You've got it in you to be the most manipulative person on earth."

"How do you mean, sir?"

"If you were greedy you could be a Rockefeller. If you were evil you could be a Hitler. That's what I mean. You can talk your way into somebody's heart and get them to do whatever you want. Judge or jury, they won't have a chance. Words, Tate. Words. You can't see them but they're the most dangerous weapons on earth. Remember that. Be careful, son."

"Sure, sir," Tate had said, paying no attention to the old man's advice, wondering if the court's decision would be unanimous. It was.

What he does, he cannot doubt.

Bett gazed at him and in a soft voice—sympathetic, almost pitying—she said, "Tate, don't worry about it. It's not your problem. You go back to your practice. I can handle it."

She fished in her purse, pulled out her car keys.

He watched her walk away. Then he called, "Come on in here." She hesitated. "Come on," he said and wandered into the barn, the original one—built in the 1920s. Reluctantly she followed. It was a grimy place, the barn, filled with as much junk as farm tools. He'd played here as a boy, had a ream of memories: horses' tails twitching with muscular jerks on hot summer afternoons, sparks flying as the Judge edged an axe on the old grinding wheel. He'd tried his first cigarette here. And learned much about the world from the moldy stacks of *National Geographic*s. He also got his first glimpse of naked women—in the *Playboy*s the sharecroppers had stashed here.

He slipped off his suit jacket, hanging it up on a pink, padded coat hanger. What was that doing here? he wondered. A former girlfriend, he believed, had left it after they'd taken a trip to the Caribbean.

Bett stood near him, holding on to a beam that powder-post beetles had riddled. Tate rummaged through a box. Bett watched, remained silent.

He didn't find what he was looking for in one box and turned to another. He glanced up at her then continued to rummage. He finally found the old beat-up leather jacket. He pulled it on, took off his tie and unbuttoned the top button of his dress shirt.

Then he righted a battered old cobbler's bench, dropped down onto it and took off his oxford wing tips and socks. He massaged his feet.

His eyes fell again on the picnic bench, visible just outside the door. Thinking again of the night of the funeral. Megan in bed. Bett, unhooking the Japanese lantern, the November night still oddly balmy. She seemed to float like a ghost in the dim air above the bench. He'd come up next to her. Startled her by speaking to her in a heartrending whisper.

I have something to tell you.

Now he shoved that hard memory away and pulled on white work socks and his comfortable boots.

She looked at him in confusion, shook her head. "What're you doing?"

"You did it after all," he said with a faint laugh.

"What?"

"You convinced me." He laced the boots up tight. "I think you're right. Something happened to her. And we're going to find out what. You and me."

II

THE INCONVENIENT CHILD

Chapter Seven

The rain had started up again.

They were inside now, sitting at the old dining room table, dark oak and pitted with wormholes.

Tate poured wine, offered it to Bett.

She took the glass and cradled it between both hands the way he remembered her doing when they'd been married. In their first year of marriage, because he was a poor young prosecutor and Bett hadn't yet found her career, they couldn't afford to go out to dinner very often. But at least once a week they'd try to have lunch at a nice restaurant. They'd always ordered wine.

She sipped from the glass, set it on the table and watched the sheets of rain roll across the brown fields.

"What do we do, Tate?" she asked. "Where do we start?"

Prosecutors know as much about criminal investigations as cops do. But those gears in Tate's mind hadn't been used for a long time. He shrugged. "Let's start with her therapist. Maybe she said something about running away, about where she'd go. What's his name?" Tate felt he should have remembered.

"Hanson," Bett said. "He had to cancel the session today—an illness or something. I hope he's in town."

She looked up the number in her address book and dialed it. "It's his service," she whispered to Tate. "What's your cell number?"

She gave the doctor's answering service both of their mobile numbers and asked him to return the call. She said it was urgent.

"Try that friend again," Tate suggested. "Amy. Where she spent the night." He tried to picture Amy. He'd met her once. He'd counted nine earrings in the girl's left ear but only eight in her right. He'd wondered if the disparity had been intentional or if she'd merely miscounted.

Troubled, he thought again about her boyfriend. Well, she *was* seventeen. Why shouldn't she go out? But with a college *senior?* Tate's prosecutorial mind thought back to the Virginia provisions on statutory rape.

Bett shifted and cocked the phone closer to her ear. Apparently someone was now home.

"Amy? It's Megan's mother. Honey, we're trying to find her. She didn't show up for lunch. Do you know where she went this morning after she left you and your mom's?"

Bett nodded as she listened and then asked if Megan had been upset about anything. Her face was grim.

Tate was half listening but mostly he was studying Bett. The tangles of auburn hair, the striking face, the prominent neck bones, the complexion of a woman who looked ten years younger than her age. He tried to remember the last time he'd seen her. Maybe it was Megan's sweet sixteen party. An odd evening . . . For a fleeting moment, as he stood beside the girl and her mother, delivering what everyone declared to be a brilliant toast, he'd had a sense of them as a family. He and Bett had shared a momentary smile. But it had faded fast and the instant they'd stepped out of the spotlight they'd returned to their separate lives. When he'd seen her after that, Tate couldn't remember.

He thought: She's less pretty now but more beautiful. More confident, more assured, her sunset-sky eyes were narrowed and not flitting around—coy and ethereal—the way they'd habitually done fifteen years ago.

Maybe it's maturity, Tate reflected. And he wondered again what her impression of *him* might be.

Bett put her hand over the receiver and said, "Amy said Megan left about nine-thirty this morning and wouldn't tell her where she was going. She was secretive about it. She left her book bag there. I thought it might have something in it that'd give us a clue where she went. I said we'd be by to pick it up later."

"Good."

Bett listened to Amy again. She frowned in concern. "Tate . . . She said that Megan told her somebody'd been following her."

"Following? Who?"

"She doesn't know."

Okay, hard evidence. The latent prosecutor in Tate Collier awakened a bit more. "Let me talk to her."

Tate took the phone. "Amy? This is Megan's father."

A pause. The girl finally said, "Um, hi. Is Megan, like, okay?"

"We hope so. We just want to find out where she is. What's this about somebody following her?"

"She was, like, pretty freaked."

Not real helpful, he thought and asked, "Tell me exactly what happened."

"I mean, her and me, we were sitting around watching this movie, I don't know, on Wednesday, I guess, and it was about a stalker and she goes, 'I don't want to watch this.' And I'm like, 'Why not?' And she's like, 'There's this car with some older guy in it and I think he's been following me around.' And I go, 'No way.' But she's like, 'Yeah, really.'"

"Where?" Tate asked.

"Around school, I think," Amy said.

"Any description?"

"Of the guy?"

"Or the car."

"Naw. She didn't tell me. But I'm like, 'Right, somebody following you . . .' And she's like, 'I'm not bullsh—I'm not fooling.' And she goes, 'It was there yesterday. By the field.'"

"What field?"

"The sports field behind the school," Amy answered.

"That was this last Tuesday?"

"Um, yeah."

"Did you believe her?"

"I guess. She looked pretty freaked. And she says she told some people about it."

"Who?"

"I don't know. Some guys. She didn't tell me who. Oh, and she told Mr. Eckhard too. He's an English teacher at the middle school and he coaches volleyball after school and on the weekends. And he said if he saw it he'd go talk to the driver. And I'm like, 'Wow. This is totally fuck—totally weird.'"

"His name's Eckhard?"

"Something like that. I don't know how to spell it. But if you want to, like, talk to him there's usually volleyball practice on Saturday afternoon, only I don't know when. Volleyball's for losers, you know."

"Yeah, I know," Tate said. It had been the only sport he'd played in college.

"You think something, like, happened to her? That's way lame."

"We'd just feel a little better knowing where she is. Listen, Amy, we'll be around to pick up her book bag in the next couple of hours. If you hear from her give us a call."

"I will."

"Promise?" he asked firmly.

"Yeah, like, I promise."

As soon as Tate pushed the End button on Bett's phone it buzzed again. He glanced at her and she nodded for him to answer it. He pushed Receive.

"Hello?"

"Um, is this Megan's father?" a man's voice asked.

"That's right."

"Mr. McCall . . ."

"Actually it's Collier."

"That's right. Sure. Sorry. This is Dr. Hanson."

"Doctor, thanks for calling . . . I have to tell you, it looks like Megan's run away."

There was a pause. "Really?"

Tate tried to read the tone. He heard concern and surprise.

"We got some . . . well, some pretty angry letters from her. Her mother and I both did. And then she vanished. Is there any way we can see you?"

"I'm in Leesburg now. My mother's had an accident."

"I'm sorry to hear that. But if Bett and I drove up could you spare a half hour?"

"Well . . ."

"It's important, Doctor. We're really concerned about her."

"I suppose so. All right." He gave them directions to the hospital.

Tate looked at his watch. It was noon. "We'll be there in an hour or so."

"Actually," Hanson said slowly, "I think we *should* talk. There *were* some things she told me that you ought to know."

"What?" Tate asked.

"I want to think about them a little more. There are some confidentiality issues . . . But it's funny—I'd expect any number of things from Megan, but running away? No, that seems odd to me."

Tate thanked him. It was only after hanging up that he felt a disturbing twist in his belly. What were the "any number of things" Megan was capable of? And were they any worse than her running away?

His precious cargo was in the trunk. But while Aaron Matthews would have liked to meditate on Megan McCall and on what lay ahead for both of them he was instead growing increasingly anxious.

The fucking white car.

He was cruising down I-66. He'd planned to stop at the house he'd rented last year in Prince William County—only two or three miles from Tate Collier's farm—and pick up some things he wanted to take with him to the mountains.

But he couldn't risk leading anyone to that house, and this car was just not going away.

It was raining again, a gray drizzle. In the mist and rain he couldn't see the driver clearly though he was now certain he was young and black.

And because he followed Matthews so carelessly and obviously he sure wasn't a cop.

But who?

Then Matthews remembered: Megan had a black boyfriend. Josh or Joshua, wasn't it? The boy that Dr. Hanson had suggested she leave—if Megan had been telling the truth about that bit of advice, which he suspected she might not have been.

What was going through the young man's mind?

As a scientist, Matthews believed in logic. The only time people acted illogically—even psychotics—was when they were having seizures. We might not be able to *perceive* the logic they operated by and their actions might be illogical to rational observers but that was only because they were not being empathetic. *Once we climb into the minds of our patients,* he wrote in his well-received essay on delusional behavior in bipolars, *once we understand their fears and desires— their own internal system of logic—then we can begin to understand their motives, the reasons behind their actions, and we can help them change . . .*

So, what was this young man thinking?

Maybe Megan had planned to meet him at the office after the appointment. Maybe he'd just happened to see her car, being driven by a man he didn't recognize, and followed it.

Or maybe—this accorded with Matthews's perceptions on the frighteningly powerful dynamics of love—he'd been waiting at the office to confront the doctor about the breakup. Maybe even attack him.

Thanks for that, Dr. Hanson, he thought acerbically. Should have broken *your* hip, not Mom's . . . Rage shook him for a moment. Then he calmed.

Did the boy have a car phone? Had he called the police and reported the Mercedes's license number? It was a stolen plate but the number didn't belong to a gray Mercedes and that discrepancy would be reason enough for the cops to pull him over and look in the trunk.

But no, of course, he hadn't called the cops. They'd be after him by now if he had.

But what if he'd called her *parents?* What did Tate Collier know? Matthews brooded. What was the man thinking? What was he planning to *do?*

Matthews sped on until he came to a rest stop then he pulled suddenly into the long driveway, weaving slowly through the tractor trailers and four-by-fours filled with vacationers. He noticed that the white Toyota had made a panicked exit and was pulling into the rest stop after him. Fortunately the rain was heavy again. Which gave Matthews the excuse to hold an obscuring *Washington Post* over his head as he ran to the shelter.

Chapter Eight

They were trotting through the rain to Tate's black Lexus when his cell phone buzzed.

As they dropped into the front seats he answered. "Hello?"

"Tate Collier, please." A man's voice.

"Speaking."

"Mr. Collier, I'm Special Agent William McComb, with the FBI's Child Exploitation and Kidnapping Unit. We've just received an interagency notice about your daughter."

"I'm glad you called."

"I'm sorry about your girl," the agent said, speaking in the chunky monotone Tate knew so well from working with the feds. "Unfortunately, I have to say, sir, based on the facts we've got, there's not a lot we can do. But you made some friends here when you were a commonwealth's attorney and so we're going to open a file and put her name out on our network. That means there'll be a lot more eyes looking for her."

"Anything you can do will really be appreciated. My wife and I are pretty upset."

"I can imagine," the agent said, registering a

splinter of emotion. "Could you give me some basics about her and the disappearance?"

Tate ran through the physical details, Bett helping on the specifics. Blond, blue eyes, five six, 128 pounds, age seventeen. Then he told McComb about the letters. Tate asked, "You heard about her car?"

"Um, no sir."

"The Fairfax County Police found it at Vienna Metro. It looks like she went to Manhattan."

"Really? No, I didn't hear that. Well, we'll tell our office in New York about it . . . But do I hear something in your voice, sir? Are you thinking that maybe she *didn't* run away? Are you thinking there was some foul play?"

Tate had to smile. He'd never thought of himself— especially his speech—as transparent. "As a matter of fact, we've been having some doubts, my wife and I."

"Interesting," McComb said in a wooden monotone. "What specifically leads you to believe that?"

"A few things. Megan's mother and I are on our way to Leesburg right now to talk to her therapist. See what he can tell us."

"He's in Leesburg?"

"His mother's in St. Mary's Hospital. She had an accident."

"And you think he might be able to tell you something?"

"He said he wanted to talk to us. I don't know what he's got in mind."

"Any other thoughts?"

"Well, Megan told her girlfriend that there was a car following her over the past few weeks."

"Car, hm? They get any description?"

"Her girlfriend didn't. But we think a teacher at her school did. Eckhard's his name. He's supposed to be at the school later, coaching volleyball. But I'd guess that's only if the rain breaks up."

"And what's her friend's name?"

He gave the agent Amy Walker's name. "We're going to talk to her too. And pick up Megan's book bag from her. We're hoping it might have something in it that'll give us a clue where she's gone."

"I see. Does Megan have any siblings?"

"No."

"Is there anyone else who's had much contact with the girl?"

"Well, my wife's fiancé."

Silence for a moment. "Oh, you're divorced."

"That's right. Forgot to mention it."

"You have his name and number?" McComb asked.

Tate asked Bett, who gave him the information. Into the phone he said, "His name's Brad Markham. He lives in Baltimore." Tate gave him Brad's phone number as well.

"Do you think he was involved in any way?" the agent asked Tate.

"I've never met him but, no, I'm sure not."

"Okay. You working with anyone particular at the Fairfax County Police?"

"Konnie . . . That'd be Dimitri Konstantinatis."

"Out of which office?"

"Fair Oaks."

"Very good, sir . . . You know, nearly all runaways return on their own. And most of the ones that don't, get picked up and *sent* back home. A little counseling, some family therapy, and things generally work out just fine."

"Thanks for your thoughts. Appreciate it."

"Oh, one thing, Mr. Collier. I guess you know about the law. About how it could be, let's say, troublesome for you to take matters into your own hands here."

"I do."

"Bad for everybody."

"Understood."

"Okay. Then enough said."

"Appreciate *that* too. I'm just going to be asking a few questions."

"Good luck to both of you."

They hung up and he told Bett what the agent had said. Her face was troubled.

"What is it?" He felt an urge to append a "honey" but nipped that one fast.

"Just that it seems so much more serious with the FBI involved."

How foolish people are, how trusting, how their defenses crumble like sand when they believe they're talking to a friend. And oh how they want to believe that you *are* a friend . . .

Why, if wild animals were as trusting as human beings they'd have gone extinct ages ago.

Aaron Matthews, no longer portraying the stony-voiced FBI agent, protector of children, hung up the phone after speaking with Tate Collier. He almost felt guilty—it had been so easy to draw information out of the man.

And what information it was! Oh, Matthews was angry. His mood teetered precariously. All his preparation— such care, such finesse, everything constructed to paralyze Collier and his wife with sorrow and send them home to brood about their lost daughter . . . and what were they doing but playing amateur detectives?

Their talking to Hanson could be a real problem. Megan might have said something about loving her parents and never even considering running away. Or, even worse, they might become suspicious of Matthews's whole plan and have the police go through Hanson's office. He'd been careful there but hadn't worn gloves all the time. There were fingerprints—and the window latch in the bathroom where Matthews had snuck in was still broken. Then there was Amy Walker, Megan's friend. With a book bag that *probably* didn't have anything compromising but might—maybe a diary or those notes teenage girls are always passing around in school. And this Eckhard, the teacher and coach. What did he know?

Reports of a car following her . . .

Much of Matthews's reconnaissance had been conducted around the school. If the teacher *had* walked up to the car he might easily have gotten the license number of the Mercedes; Matthews hadn't changed the license plates to the stolen ones until yesterday. And even if Eckhard didn't *think* he'd seen much, there were probably some prickly little facts locked away in the teacher's subconscious; Matthews had done much hypnosis work and knew how many memories and observations were retained in the cobwebby recesses of the mind.

Why the hell was Collier doing this? Why hadn't the letters fooled him? He was a fucking lawyer! He was supposed to be *logical*, he was supposed to be *cold*. Why didn't he believe the bald facts in front of him?

A dark mood began to settle on Matthews but he struggled to throw it off.

No, I have no time for this now! Fight it, fight it, fight it . . .

(He thought of how many patients he'd wanted to grab by the lapels and shake as he shouted, Oh, quit your fucking complaining! You don't like her, leave. *She* left *you?* Find somebody else. You're a drunk, stop drinking.)

And closing his eyes fiercely, clenching his fists until a nail broke through the flesh of his palm, he struggled to remain emotionally buoyant. After a few minutes he forced the mood away. He returned to the phone and called three Walkers in Fairfax before he got the household that included a teenage Amy.

"Yes, Amy's my daughter," the woman's cautious voice said. "Who's this?"

"I'm William McComb, with the county. I've gotten a call from Child Protective Services."

"My God, what's wrong?"

"Nothing to be alarmed at, Mrs. Walker. This doesn't involve your daughter. We're investigating a case involving Megan McCall."

"Oh, no! Is Megan all right? She spent the night here!"

"That's what we understand. It seems she's missing and we've been looking into some allegations about her father."

There was a moment's pause.

"Tate Collier," Matthews prompted.

"Oh, right. I don't know him. You think *he's* involved? You think he did something?"

"We're just looking into a few things now. But I'd appreciate it if you'd tell your daughter she shouldn't have any contact with him."

"Why would she have any contact with him?" the edgy voice asked. How easily she'll cry, Matthews predicted.

"We don't *think* there'd be any reason for him to hurt or touch her . . ."

"Oh, God. You don't *think?*"

"We just want to make sure Amy stays safe until we get to the bottom of what happened to Megan."

"'Happened to Megan'? *Please* tell me what's going on."

"I can't really say any more at this time. Tell me, where's your daughter now?"

"Upstairs."

"Would you mind if I spoke to her?"

"No, of course not."

A moment later a girl's lazy voice: "Hello?"

"Hi, Amy. This is Mr. McComb. I'm with the county. How are you?"

"Okay, I guess. Like, is Megan okay?"

"I'm sure she's fine. Tell me, has Megan's father talked to you recently?"

"Um," the girl began.

"You answer," the mother said sternly from a second phone.

"Yeah, like, he said she's missing and asked me

about her. He was going to come by and get her book bag."

"So he's interested in what's in her bag? Did you get the impression he was concerned with what might be inside?"

"Like, maybe."

The mother: "You were going to let him in here? And not *tell* me?"

The girl snapped, "Mom, just, like, cut it out, okay? It's Megan's dad."

Matthews said sternly, "Amy, don't talk to him. And whatever you do, don't go anywhere with him."

"I—"

"If he suggests going away, getting into his car, going into his barn . . ."

"God, his *barn?*" her mother gasped. Yep, Matthews could hear soft weeping.

He continued, "Amy, if he offers you something to drink . . ."

Another gasp.

Oh my, this was fun. Matthews continued calmly, ". . . whatever he says tell him no. If he comes over don't answer the door. Make sure it's locked."

"Like, why?"

"You don't ask why, young lady. You do what the man says."

"Mom, like, come on . . . What about her book bag?"

"You just hold on to it until you hear from me or someone at Child Protective Services. Okay?"

"I guess."

"Should we call the police?" Mrs. Walker asked.

"No, it's not a criminal charge yet."

"Oh, God," said Amy's mother, the woman of the limited epithets. Then: "Amy, tell me. Did Megan's father ever touch you? Now, tell the truth."

"Who? Megan's father? Mom, you're such a loser. I never even met him."

"Mrs. Walker?"

"Yes. I'm here." Her voice cracked.

"I really don't want to alarm you unnecessarily."

"No, no. We appreciate your calling. What's your number, Mr. McComb?"

"I'm going to be in the field for a while. Let me call you later, when I'm back at the office."

"All right."

Matthews felt a cheerful little twinge as he heard her crying. Though Amy's silence on the other extension was louder.

He couldn't resist. "Mrs. Walker?"

"Yes?"

"Do you have a gun?"

A choked sob. "No, we don't. I don't. I've never . . . I wouldn't know how to use one. I guess I could go to Sports Authority. I mean—"

"That's all right," Matthews said soothingly. "I'm sure it's not going to come to anything like that."

"What if Megan's mother, like, calls?" the girl asked.

"Yes," Mrs. Walker echoed, "what if her mother calls?"

A concerned pause. "I'd be careful. We're investigating her too . . . It was a very troubled household, it seems."

"God," Mrs. Walker muttered.

Matthews hung up.

What a mess this could become. The kidnapping had been so simple in theory. But, in practice, it was growing so complicated. Just like the art of psychiatry itself, he reflected.

Well, there were other things to do to protect himself. But first things first. He had to get Megan to her new home—with his son, Peter—deep in the mountains.

Matthews returned to the Mercedes. He pulled back onto the highway, noting that the white car was still sticking with him like a lamprey to a fish.

Chapter Nine

Amy wasn't home.

Oh, brother. Tate sighed. Looked through a window, saw nothing. Walked back to the front door. Pressed the bell again. Standing on the concrete stoop of the split-level house in suburban Burke, Tate kept his hand on the doorbell for a full minute but neither the girl nor her mother came to the door.

Where'd she gone? Bett had said that they'd stop by soon. Why hadn't Amy stayed home? Or at least put the book bag out on the front stoop?

Didn't she care about Megan? Was this adolescent friendship nowadays?

"Maybe the bell's broken," Bett called from the car.

But Tate pounded on the door with his open palm. There was no response. "Amy!" he called. No answer.

"Go 'round back," Bett suggested.

Tate pushed through two scratchy holly bushes and rapped on the back door.

Still no answer. He decided to slip inside and find the bag; a missing teenager took precedence over a technical charge of trespass (thinking: I could make a good argument for an implied license to enter the premises). But as he reached for the doorknob he believed he heard a click. When he tried to open the latch he found the door was locked.

He peered through the window and thought he saw some motion. But he couldn't be sure.

Tate returned to the car.

"Not there." He sighed. "We'll call later."

"Leesburg?" Bett asked.

"Let's try that teacher first. Eckhard."

It was only a five-minute drive to the school. The rain had stopped and youngsters were gathering on the school yard—boys for baseball, girls for volleyball, both sexes for soccer. Hacky Sacks, Frisbees, skateboards abounded. After speaking with several parents and students they learned that Robert Eckhard, the volleyball coach, had put together a practice for three that afternoon. It was now a quarter to two.

Tate flopped down into the passenger seat of the Lexus. He stretched. "This police work . . . I don't see how Konnie does it."

Bett kicked her shoes off and massaged her feet. "Wish I'd worn comfy boots, like you." Then she glanced toward the school. "Look," she said.

When they'd been married Bett assumed that he knew exactly what she was thinking or talking about. She'd often communicate with a cryptic phrase, a gesture of her finger, an eyebrow raised like a witch casting a spell. And Tate would have no clue as to her meaning. Today, though, he turned his head toward where she was looking and saw the two blue-uniformed security guards, standing in one of the back doorways of the school.

"Good idea," he said. And they drove around to the door.

By the time they got there the guards had gone inside. Bett and Tate parked and walked inside the school. The halls had that smell of all high schools—sweat, lab gas, disinfectant, paste.

Tate laughed to himself at the instinctive uneasiness he felt being here. Classwork had come easily to him but he'd spent his hours and effort on Debate Club and the teachers were forever booting him into detention hall for skipped classes or missing homework. That he would pause at the door on the way out of class and resonantly quote Cicero or John Calhoun to his teacher didn't help his academic record any, of course.

The security offices in Megan's school were small cubicles of carpeted partitions near the gym.

One guard, a crew-cut boy with half-mast eyelids, wearing a perfectly pressed uniform, listened unemotionally to Tate's story. He adjusted his glistening black billy club.

"Don't know your daughter." He turned, called out, "Henry, you know a Megan McCall?"

"Nope," said his partner, who resembled him to an eerie degree. He stepped into the school proper and disappeared.

"What we're concerned about is this car. A man seemed to be following her."

"A car. Following her." The young man was skeptical.

Bett took over. "Around the school yard. This past week."

Tate: "We were wondering if anybody might've reported it."

The man's face eased into that put-upon look

security guards are very good at. Maybe they're resentful that they're not full-fledged cops and could carry guns. And use them.

"Are the police involved?" the man asked.

"Somewhat."

"Hm." Trying to figure that one out.

"What happens if somebody sees something unusual? Is there any procedure for that?"

"The Bust-er Book," the guard said.

Bett asked, "The . . . uh?"

"Bust-er. He's a dog. I mean, a cartoon dog. But it's like 'Bust' as in get busted. Arrested. Then a dash, then *e-r*. If the kids see something suspicious they come tell us and we write it down in the Bust-er Book and then there's a record of it for the police. If anything, you know, happens."

Tate recalled what Amy'd said. "It was on Tuesday. Out in the parking lot by the sports field. Could you take a look?"

"Oh, we can't let you see it," the guard said.

"I'm sorry?"

"Parents don't have, you know, access to it. Only the administration and police. That's the rule."

"That's it right there?"

The guard turned around and glanced at the blue binder with the words "Bust-er" on the spine and a cartoon effigy of a dog wearing a Sherlock Holmes deerstalker hat. "Yes sir."

"If you don't mind . . . See, our daughter's missing. As I was saying. Could *you* take a look?"

"Just have the police give us a call."

"Well, she's not officially a missing person."

"I don't have any leeway, sir. You understand." The guard's lean face crinkled. His still eyes looked Tate up and down and his muscular hand caressed his ebony billy club. He was everything Tate hated about northern Virginia. Snide and sullen, this young man would see nothing wrong with a tap on the wife's chin or a belt on his kids' butts to keep the family in line. He was master of the house; everyone did as he commanded. And never ask his opinion about the Mideastern and Asian immigrants settling in Fairfax because he'll tell you in no uncertain terms.

Tate looked at Bett. Her eyebrows were raised as if she were asking: Why was Tate hesitating? After all, he *was* the silver-tongued devil. He could talk anybody into anything. ("Resolved: The Watergate break-in was justifiable as a means to a valid end." Lifelong Democrat, grandson of a lifelong Democrat, Tate had leapt at the chance to take the pro side of the debate and argue that irreverent position—for the pure joy of going up against overwhelming odds. He'd won, to the Judge's shock and lasting amusement.)

"Officer," Tate began, thinking of the rhetorical tricks in his arsenal, the logic, the skills at persuasion. Ratiocination. He paused, then walked to the door and motioned the guard to follow.

The lean man walked slowly enough to let Tate know that nobody on earth was going to make him do a single thing he didn't want to do.

Tate, standing in the doorway, looked out over the school yard. "What do you see there?"

The guard hesitated uncertainly. He'd be thinking,

What kinda question's that? I see trees, I see cars, I see fences, I see clouds.

Tate waited just the right amount of time and said, "I see a lot of young people."

"Um." Well, what the hell else're you gonna see on a school yard?

"And those young people rely on us adults for everything. They rely on us for food, for shelter, for schooling, and you know what else?"

Video games, running shoes, Legos? What's this clown up to?

"They rely on us for their safety. That's what you're doing here, right? It's the reason they hired a big, strong guy like you. A man who's got balls, who's not afraid to mix it up with somebody."

"I dunno. I guess."

"Well, my daughter's relying on me for her safety. She needs me to find out where she is. Maybe she's in trouble, maybe she isn't. Hey, let's take an example: You see some tough big kids talking to a little kid. Maybe they're just buddies, fooling around. Or maybe they're trying to sell him some pot or steal his lunch money. You'd go and find out, right?"

"I would. Sure."

"That's all I'm doing with my daughter. Trying to find out if she's okay. And going through that book would sure be a big help."

The guard nodded.

"Well?" Tate asked expectantly.

"Rules is rules. Can't be done. Have a state trooper or a county officer stop by. I'll be happy to help."

Tate sighed. He glanced at Bett, who said icily,

"Let's go, Tate. Nothing more to be accomplished here."

As they walked toward the car, the guard called, "Sir?"

Tate turned.

"That was a good try, though. Kids and safety and everything. I almost bought it." He picked up a magazine on customized pickup trucks and sat down.

Tate and Bett continued to the car then climbed in and drove out of the lot.

Neither of them could contain the laughter for long. They both roared. Finally Bett gasped and said, "That was the biggest load of hogwash I ever heard. 'It's the reason they hired a big, strong guy like you.' You sounded like you were trying to pick him up."

Wiping tears from his eyes, Tate controlled his laughing. "That was some pretty good double-teaming."

Bett reached under her blouse and pulled out the twenty or thirty sheets of notebook paper she'd ripped from the Bust-er Book while Tate had distracted the guard with his absurd argument. "I figured I better leave the notebook itself." She muttered, "The Bust-er Book? The *Bust-er* Book? Do people really take that stuff seriously?"

Tate drove about three blocks and pulled over to the curb.

"Okay," she said, "Tuesday . . . Tuesday." Flipping through the pages. "If the storm trooper back there's the one who keeps the book he's got handwriting like a sissy. Okay, Tuesday . . ." She nodded then read: "'Two students reported a gray car, no school parking permit, parked on Sideburn Road. Single driver. Drove off without picking up student.'"

"A gray car. Not much to go on. Anything else?"

"Not then. But Amy said Megan'd been thinking she'd been followed for a while." Bett flipped back through the pages. Her perfect eyebrow rose in a delicate arc. "Listen. A week ago. 'M. McCall (Green Team)'—that's her class section at school—'reported gray car appeared to be following her. Security guard Gibson took report. Did not personally witness incident. Checked but no car seen. Subject did not know tag or make of vehicle.'" Bett looked at her ex-husband. "Why didn't she tell me about it, Tate? Why?"

Tate shrugged. He asked, "Any description of the driver?"

"None, no."

"What kind of car did her boyfriend drive?"

"White . . . I think a Toyota."

"He could've borrowed one to follow her," Tate mused.

"Could have, sure."

More questions than answers.

Tate stared at the turbulent clouds overhead. The sun tried to break through but a line of thick gray rolled over the sky heading eastward. "We'll come back and talk to Eckhard later," he said. "Let's go to Leesburg."

Chapter Ten

Joshua LeFevre glanced down at the odometer. He'd driven another twenty miles along I-66 in his battered old Toyota since the last time he'd checked. Which put him about seventy miles from Fairfax.

Mr. Tibbs, the unflappable police detective within him, had finally figured out where Megan and her therapist lover were going: to the doctor's mountain place. It was now chic for professionals to have vacation homes in the Blue Ridge or in West Virginia, where you could buy a whole mountaintop for a song.

The rain had stopped and he cranked the sunroof open, listening to the wind hissing through the Yakima bike rack on the roof.

It was early afternoon when he broke through the Shenandoahs and saw the hazy Blue Ridge in front of him. The rolling hills were not evocative gunmetal today, the literature major in him thought, but were tinted with the green frost of spring growth. Recalling that he and Megan had talked about a bike tour along Skyline Drive, which crested the ridge, later in the spring.

Without the rain LeFevre could see more clearly now and he realized that only the doctor was visible in the car. Where was Megan? Taking a nap? Wait . . . Was her head resting in his *lap?*

He was considering this appalling thought, distracted and angry, when the Mercedes got away from him.

Never would have happened to Sidney Poitier.

Damn . . .

The Merce had pulled out to pass a semi and he'd followed. But as soon as the big gray car had cleared the cab of the truck the doctor had steered hard to the right and pulled onto the exit ramp as the truck driver laid on his air horn and braked.

LeFevre's Toyota was caught in the left lane and he couldn't swerve back in time to make the exit.

His head swiveled and he saw the roof of the Mercedes sink below the level of the highway as it slowed on the ramp.

LeFevre slammed his fists on the wheel. Tantrums were definitely not Poitier's style but he couldn't help it. He thought about making an illegal U over the median, but he was a black kid with knobby dreads driving through the crucible of the Confederacy; the fewer laws he broke, the better.

The next exit was a mile down the highway and by the time he'd followed the Möbius strip of ramps and returned to the exit the Mercedes had taken, there was no sign of the big car—only an intersection of three different country roads, any one of which they might have taken.

And now that he thought about it, the doctor might just have stopped for gas and gotten back onto the interstate, continuing west.

He closed his eyes in frustration and pressed back hard into the headrest. Metal snapped.

What the hell'm I doing here?

The stuff love makes you do, he thought.

Hate it, hate it, hate it . . .

LeFevre pulled into the gas station, filled up at the self-service island then walked up to the skinny, sullen attendant with long hair sprouting from under a Valvoline giveaway cap, which was as greasy as his brown strands.

"How you doing?" Sidney Poitier asked very politely.

"Okay yourself?" the man muttered.

"Not bad. Not bad."

The man stared at LeFevre's hair, which was not exactly modeled on Mr. Poitier's, circa 1967, but was much closer to a rap star's.

"Helpya?"

It occurred to LeFevre that even Officer Tibbs, in suit, tie and polished oxfords, wouldn't get a lot of cooperation from a guy like this by asking which way a seventy-thousand-dollar automobile had just gone.

At least, not without some incentive.

LeFevre opened his wallet and extracted five twenties. Looked down at them.

So did the attendant. "That's cash."

"Yes, it is."

"You charged your gas. I seen you."

"I did."

"Well, whatsitfor?" The grimy hair swung as he nodded at the money.

"It's for you," LeFevre said in his most carefully crafted queen's English.

"Uh-huh. Uh-huh. Why's it for me?" The man seemed to sneer.

"I have a little problem."

The stubbly face asked, Who cares?

"I was driving down sixty-six and this Mercedes cut me off, ran me off the road. Nearly killed me." (This had happened to Sidney Poitier in *In the Heat of the Night*. More or less.) "Did it on purpose. The driver, I mean."

"Don't say." The man yawned.

"Front end's all screwed up now. And see what kind of bodywork I'll need?"

Thank goodness, LeFevre thought. He'd never fixed the damage after he'd scraped the side of the car on a barricade when he'd dropped his mother off at Neiman Marcus in Tysons Corner last month.

The attendant looked at the car without a splinter of interest.

"So you want me to lookit the front end?"

"No, I want the license number of that Mercedes. He came by here five, ten minutes ago. I was hoping he stopped here for gas."

This had seemed like a good way to break the ice—asking for the license number. It made things official—as if the police were going to get involved. LeFevre believed this trick was definitely something that Sidney Poitier would do.

"Why'd he run you off the road?" the man asked abruptly.

Which brought LeFevre up cold.

"Well, I don't know." LeFevre shrugged. Then he asked, "You know which car I mean?" He remained respectful but asked this firmly. He'd decided not to be too polite. Sidney Poitier had glared at Rod Steiger quite a bit.

"Maybe."

"So he stopped here for gas."

"Nope." The scrawny guy looked at the money. Then he shook his head; his slick grin gave LeFevre an unpleasant glimpse of bad teeth. "Fuck. Why're you bullshittin' me? You don't want that tag number."

"Um, I—"

"What you want is to find out where that sumvabitch lives. Am I right?"

"Well . . ."

"An' I'll tell you why you want that."

"Why?"

"'Cause he was drivin' his big old Mercedes and he thunk t'himself, Why, here's a black man—only he was thinking the N-word—driving a little shit Jap car and I can cut him off 'cause he don't mean shit to me and he don't got the balls to complain to nobody 'bout it." A faint laugh. "And you don't want no tag number for State Farm Insurance or the po-leece. Fuck. You wanna find him and you wanna beat the shiny crap outta him."

So, end of story. Well, it was a nice try. LeFevre was about to put the money away and return to his car—before the man called some real-life Rod Steigers—when the attendant shook his head and said, "God bless you."

"I'm sorry?"

"That frosts me, what he done. Truly does."

"I'm sorry?" LeFevre repeated.

"I mean, I got friends're black. Couple of 'em. And we have a good time together and one of 'em's wife cooks for me and my girlfriend nearly every week."

"Well, is that right?"

"Fuck, yeah, that's right." The twenties were suddenly in the man's stained fingers. "I say, more power to you. Find him and wail on him all you want. I know that sumvabitch."

"The man in the Mercedes?"

"Yeah."

"Dr. Hanson, right?"

"I don't know his name. But I seen him off and on for a spell. He comes and goes. Never stops here— probably thinks *my* gas ain't good enough—but I seen him. Pisses me off royal, people like him. Moving everybody down the mountain."

"What do you mean, 'moving down the mountain'?" Sidney Poitier asked politely, smiling now and giving the man plenty of thinking room.

"See, what happened was, when folk settled here they moved to the top of the Ridge. Naturally, where else? That's the best part. But they couldn't keep the land, most of 'em. Money troubles, you know. Taxes. So they kept selling to the government for the park or to rich folks wanted a weekend place, and families kept moving down the mountain. Now, most everybody's in the valley— most of the honest folk, I mean. Pretty soon there won't be no mountains left 'cept for the rich pricks and the government. 'S what my dad says. Makes sense to me."

"Where's his place?"

The skinny young man nodded toward one narrow road.

"That's the way he goes but I don't know where exactly his house is. Only place I know of up there's the hospital. Been for sale for years. He probably bought it and's gonna put a big fancy house on the land."

"What hospital?"

"Loony bin. Closed a while ago."

"How far is it?"

"Five miles, give'r take. At the end of Palmer Road yonder." He pointed. "Now, you ain't going to kill him, are you? I'd have some problems with that."

"No. I really do just want to talk."

"Uh-huh. Uh-huh." The man squinted then offered his bad-tooth grin again. "You know, you remind me of that actor."

"I do?"

"Yeah. He's a good one. Don't exactly *look* like him but you sorta hold yourself the same. What's his name? What's his name?"

LeFevre, grinning himself, answered his question.

The man blinked and shook his head. "Who the hell's Sidney Poitier?"

LeFevre said, "Maybe he was before your time."

"What's that guy's name? I can picture him . . . Kicked the shit out of some ninjas in this movie with Sean Connery. Wait! Snipes . . . Wesley Snipes. That's it. That man can *act*."

LeFevre walked to the edge of the tarmac. The smell of gasoline mixed with the scent of spring growth and clayish earth. Palmer Road vanished into a dark shaft of pine and hemlock, winding up into the mountains.

The young attendant stuffed a strand of slick hair

up under his hat. "You stay away from that hospital. I wouldn't go there for any money. Hear stories about it. People sometimes get attacked. By wild dogs or something."

Or something?

"Kids find bloody bones sometimes. Probably deer or boar but maybe not."

LeFevre's anger was turning to concern. Megan, what've you gotten yourself into? "I just follow that road?"

"Right. Five miles, I'd guess. Keeps to the high ground. Then circles back on itself like a snake."

"A snake," LeFevre said, absently staring into the murky forest. Thinking of the quote from Dante's *Divine Comedy:*

> *Halfway through life's journey I came to myself in a dark wood, where the straight way was lost.*

Recalling the story too: the author's guided tour of hell.

"Listen," the attendant said, startling him, "you stop on your way back, okay? Let me know what happens."

LeFevre nodded and shook the man's oily hand. He climbed into his car and sped along Palmer Road. In an instant, civilization vanished behind him and the world became black bark, shadows and the waving arms of tattered boughs.

The things we do for love, LeFevre thought. The things we do for love.

• • •

Aaron Matthews pulled the Mercedes into a grove of trees beside the asphalt and climbed out, looking back over Palmer Road.

No sign of the white car.

He was sure he'd tricked the boyfriend just fine when he'd sped off the highway beside the truck. The kid was probably in West Virginia by now and even if he managed to figure out which exit they'd taken and backtracked he'd have no way of knowing which way Matthews had gone into the maze of back roads here. Although Matthews had been coming to the deserted hospital for the past year, ever since he'd brought his son here, he'd made a point of never stopping for gas or food at the service station or grocery store near the exit ramp off I-66. He was sure the local hicks knew nothing about him.

He climbed back in the car and continued on to the Blue Ridge Mental Health Facility.

Just past the cleft where the road passed between two steep vine-covered hills, the ground opened into the shallow bowl of a valley. Through a picket line of scabby trees a sprawl of low, decrepit buildings was visible.

BRMHF had been the last destination for the hard-core crazies in the commonwealth of Virginia. Schizophrenics, uncontrollable bipolars, borderline personalities, delusionals, souls lost forever. Security was high—the patients (that is, inmates) were locked down at night in secure quarters (padded cells). The eight-foot chain-link fence enclosing the ten-acre grounds was "designed to provide comforting boundaries to patients and nearby residents alike" (it sported a live current of 500 volts).

The hospital had served its purpose well until two years ago, when it had been closed down by the state, and the patients were shipped to other facilities and halfway houses. BRMHF was soon overgrown with foliage and the place was forgotten.

Dr. Aaron Matthews was intimately familiar with the hospital; the patients here had found him a confidant, confessor, judge . . . a virtual father over the course of nearly four years. When he thought of home he thought first of this hospital and second of the Colonial house in Arlington, Virginia, he'd lived in with Margaret and their son, Peter.

Matthews now braked the Mercedes to a halt and examined the place carefully for signs of intruders though a break-in would have been very unlikely. The current to the fence had been shut off long ago but the chain link was intact and the grounds were patrolled by five knob-headed rottweilers, as raw and brutal as dogs could be, teeth sharp as obsidian; they hunted in packs and once or twice a week killed one of the deer that often strolled through the gate when it was open.

He listened carefully again—no sound of approaching cars—and unlocked the two tempered steel locks securing the gate. He drove inside and parked.

Then he lifted Megan from the trunk and carried her inside, pushing through a door with his shoulder. He'd reversed the locks on the doors—you could simply push in from the outside but couldn't get back out without a key.

He stepped into the lobby.

Asylums smell far more visceral than do regular hospitals because even though their province is the mind, the by-product of mental pathology is piss, shit, sweat, blood. This was still true of the Blue Ridge Facility years after its closing; the air stank of bodily functions and decay.

Through these murky halls Matthews carried his prize in his arms. Feeling every ounce of her weight— though it wasn't the weight of a burden; it was the weight of treasure: a golden or platinum artifact, solid and perfect.

Matthews carried Megan into the room he'd fixed up for her. He laid her on the bed and undressed her. First the blouse and the bra. Then jeans and panties and socks. His eyes coursed up and down her body. Yet he touched her only once—to make sure her pulse was regular.

Taking her clothes, he left the room, locked her door with a heavy padlock. He thought about stopping to see his son but the boy was in a different part of the hospital and Matthews had no time for a visit now. Tate Collier still troubled him. He left the building, got into his car and started through the gate. He'd driven only ten feet before he heard the thump-thump-thump of the flat tire.

Oh, not now! His mood suddenly darkened. And he fought once more to keep the blackness at bay. He thought of Megan. It buoyed him just enough to keep him functional. Matthews climbed out and walked to the rear of the car.

He took one look at the slash mark in the Michelin

and leapt toward the driver's door to get to the pistol in his glove compartment.

Too late.

"Don't move." The young man held the rusty machete, left over from the groundskeeping Matthews had done when he'd brought his son here. He gripped the long knife awkwardly but with enough manic determination to make Matthews freeze and raise his hands. The boy's muscles were huge.

He blurted, "I'll give you my wallet. And there's—"

"I want to know what's going on."

The young man's voice was astonishing. What a beautiful patois. Carolinian and Caribbean and some succulent English, which tempered the two. This man could fuck any woman he wanted simply by telling her she was beautiful.

"Don't hurt me," Matthews said desperately.

A flicker of uncertainty in the brown eyes.

"What've you done with Megan?"

Matthews frowned. "Who *are* you?"

Ah, young man, asked the silent therapist within Matthews, you're not a fighter at all, are you? You're out of your element, brandishing that knife like a squash racket . . . And why do you feel so guilty, why do you feel so unsure?

The pistol was in the glove compartment only feet away. But his assailant was riding on pure nerves. With his strength it wouldn't take much for the boy to injure Matthews seriously, without even trying. Besides, while he *believed* the young man wasn't dangerous Matthews had learned that premature diagnoses can be very risky.

He smiled and lowered his hands. He nodded knowingly. "Wait, wait. You're not . . . You must be Joshua."

The boy's face squirreled up into a frown. "You know me?"

"Sure, I know you," Matthews said smoothly. "I was *hoping* we'd get a chance to talk."

Chapter Eleven

"You startled me," said the soothing voice of Aaron Matthews. "I didn't mean to react the way I did." He glanced at the tire, laughed. "But, then again, you *did* attack my Mercedes with a machete."

With his voice trembling (love that voice, *love* it), the boy said, "I thought you'd just brought her here on a date. To show her some of your property or something. Then I saw you carry her inside. What the hell's going on? Tell me!"

"Wait. Carry who inside?" Matthews frowned.

Show her some of your property?

"Megan. I *saw* you two."

So he's thinking real estate development. Matthews shook his head, glanced toward the hospital. "You mean just a few minutes ago? Well, I carried in some bags of cleaning supplies. And a tarp. I bought this place and I'm turning it into condos."

A minuscule lessening of his suspicion. Not believing your own eyes, are you? How often we don't. Also, in his face was a suspicion that the young man himself had made a stupid error here. You don't do well with embarrassment, do you? A gift from the African-American executive mom, I'd say. The one

Speaking in Tongues / 119

with practiced elocution and the Chanel scarf over her shoulder and the defensive eyes?

Matthews noted, however, that the boy continued to hold the rusty blade firmly in his hand.

"Where is she? What were you doing with her car?"

"Joshua," Matthews said patiently, "I just dropped Megan off at my weekend place up the road." He pointed into the woods. "A couple miles from here. She wanted to get a head start on making lunch."

"Why'd you switch cars at the Metro?"

"Megan's got a friend. Amy." He paused.

Joshua said, "I know Amy."

"Amy's borrowing her car. We left it at the Metro for her and took the Mercedes."

The boy frowned. "I didn't think Amy had a license."

Matthews laughed. "Oh? She didn't share that with us. I wondered why she didn't want us to drop it off at her house."

Good, Matthews told himself, giving his performance high marks.

"But wait . . . I didn't see Megan in your car when I was behind you."

"You were following us?" Now a frown—at the boy's odd behavior.

"Yes, I was following you. How did you think I found you?"

"I assumed that Megan told you about me. And that we come up here sometimes."

Joshua blinked.

Matthews studied the young man for a moment

then tilted his head and said with sympathy, "Look, Joshua, don't do this to yourself."

"Do what?"

Oh, the desperation Matthews could see in the olive eyes was so sweet . . . He nearly shivered with pleasure. He whispered, "You should forget about her."

"But I love her!"

"Forget about her. For your own good."

Matthews realized he'd been right. The man had probably arrived at Hanson's office toward the end of the session, planning to confront Megan—and presumably the doctor too—about Hanson's advice on breaking up.

A little obsessive-compulsive, are we?

Or just too much testosterone in the blood?

If it weren't for romance we poor psychiatrists would have nothing to do. As Freud said, more or less, love's a bitch, ain't it?

"You talked her into breaking up with me so you could see her!" Joshua said.

"Megan said that?" he snapped. "Well, it's not true. That's completely unethical and I'd never do it."

Joshua blinked at the vehemence in Matthews's voice. The therapist had deduced that the boy would be a rules-and-regulations victim. Thanks to the other parent, of course—Dad the soldier.

The therapist continued, "She *decided* to break up with you on your own, Joshua. And *then* we started going out."

"That's not what she said. She said you told her to break up with me."

"No, Joshua. That's not the way it was at all."

"But she *told* me!"

"Well, we can't blame her for not being completely honest all the time, now, can we?"

"Blame her?"

"See, Megan has trouble taking responsibility for certain things. Not unusual, not a serious problem. We all suffer from it to varying degrees. It's hard for her to express her inner feelings. Given her parents . . . You know Tate and Bett?"

Hearing the names, the familiarity in Matthews's voice, the boy's defenses slipped a bit more. But he was still dangerous. Too confused, too much in love, riding on too much emotion. Matthews decided he couldn't win the boy's confidence; he'd have to go in a different direction.

"I've met her mother, not her father," Joshua said.

"Well, believe me, they're to thank for a lot of her problems. Her lying, for instance. And the way she'd lose her temper sometimes. It could be bad, couldn't it?"

"A couple of times. But who doesn't blow off steam?"

The question told Matthews that the boy was buying the argument. He laughed. "Joshua, put that thing down and go home. Forget about Megan. This is only going to mean heartache for you."

"I *love* her." He was nearly in tears.

By now Matthews had pegged the boy the way a geologist recognizes pyrite. An underachiever terrified of his parents. Military dad. Supermother cutting a swath through America Online or TRW. A couple who probably *were*—to use Megan's tired adjective—*great* people. And so Joshua wouldn't let himself be angry with them.

But the anger was there inside him. It had to be. But where?

Let's find out . . .

"Joshua, you don't understand. You—"

"Then tell me."

"It's not appropriate—"

Joshua persisted. "Tell me! What is going on?"

Matthews's eyes went wide, as if he were losing his temper. He said, "All right! You want to know the truth?"

"Yes!"

Matthews started to speak then shook his head as if he were struggling to control himself. "No, no, you don't."

"Yes I do!" The boy stepped forward, menacingly.

"All right. But don't blame me. The truth is, Megan didn't *like* you."

The young man's face froze into a glossy ebony mask. "That's not true!"

Matthews's mouth grew tight. "She told me that the first night we slept together."

Joshua gasped. "You're lying."

"You don't think we're lovers?" Matthews asked viciously, as befit a man no longer fearful but angry.

"No, I don't."

"Well, then how do I know about that birthmark just below her left nipple?"

Joshua couldn't hold Matthews's cold eyes and he looked down at the moss covering a fallen tree. His hands were shaking.

"What do we think of her pubic hair? A bit sparse?

And what does she like in bed? She likes men to go down on her all night long. And she loves to get fucked in the ass."

But not by you apparently, Matthews observed, noting the young man's shocked face.

"Stop it!"

"During our first session she asked me how she could get rid of you."

"No."

"Yes!" Matthews spat out. "You know what she called you? The white nigger."

The eyes glazed over in pain as the scalpel of these words incised the young man's soul.

"She'd *never* say that."

"You were the big minority experiment. She wanted a black man to fuck. But somebody who wasn't too black of course. She thought you'd be a good compromise. About as white as they come. But then she decided she'd got herself a clunker. She told me she had to drink a half bottle of Southern Comfort just so she could kiss you!"

"No!"

"She and Amy'd stay up all night making fun of you. Megan does a great impression of you. She's got you down cold."

"Go to hell!"

"Joshua, you asked for this!" Matthews shouted. "*You* pushed me, so you're going to hear the truth whether you want it or not. She wanted your pathetic face out of her life. White nigger. You were a toy. She told me again this morning. When we were fucking on the desk in my office."

The boy erupted. And while Matthews's words might have driven someone else to act ruthlessly and efficiently it drove Joshua manically forward toward Matthews, out of control. He dropped the machete and flailed away with his fists. *"She never said that!"* he cried. "She never said that never said that never said that—"

Matthews fell to the ground, covering his head with his left arm. And when he rose a moment later he was holding the machete.

The young man froze.

Matthews studied him for a moment—the boy suddenly realizing that something very bad was going on.

Joshua lowered his arms. "What are you going to do to me?" he asked in a soft, pathetic whisper.

Matthews tasted the extraordinary voice one last time and stepped forward, swinging the machete into Joshua's throat.

The boy gave a gurgling scream and stumbled forward. Matthews leapt back, away from the boy's swinging fist, and slashed his arm deeply. Then his leg. Joshua fell onto his back, cradling the gash in his throat.

Matthews plunged the rusty blade into the young man's abdomen. But with astonishing strength Joshua pushed Matthews off, twisted away, and rose to his knees, choking and coughing. The blood flowed between the fingers clutching his torn neck as Joshua crawled fast, like an animal, back through the gate toward the hospital. Matthews didn't bother to pursue him. Joshua got thirty feet into the field surrounding the hospital before collapsing in a stand of Queen Anne's lace, which turned a deep purple under the spray of his blood.

Matthews slowly walked toward him. Then stopped. He heard an animal snarling, growing closer. He backed quickly away from the quivering body.

The rottweilers appeared from behind the house. They paused, stood rigid for a moment then charged forward hungrily. Matthews stepped out of the gate and swung it closed as the dogs swarmed in a single muscular pack over the body, which had looked so strong and impervious moments ago and was now just ragged meat.

Matthews leaned against the bars of the gate, enraptured, watching the young man die. Joshua fought hard—he tried to rise and struggled to hit the dogs. But it was useless. The big male rottie closed his enormous jaws on the back of Joshua's neck and began to shake. After a moment the body went limp.

The animals dragged him into the ravine for the feast. His body vanished under the mass of snarling, bloody mouths.

Matthews quickly changed the Mercedes's tire and climbed into the car then sped down the rough road. He'd bury what remained of the boy's corpse later. He didn't have time now. Too many things to do. He was thinking that this was just like when he was a practicing therapist. Busy days, busy days. There were people to see, people to talk to.

I'm here to change your life forever.

Who is he? *Who?*

Megan McCall floated on a dark ocean, that one

question the only thing in her thoughts. She opened her eyes and gripped the thin, filthy mattress she lay on. The room swayed and bobbed.

She was dizzy and nauseated. Her mouth painfully dry, her eyes swollen half closed. She rolled onto her back and examined the small room. There were flaking cushions mounted on all the walls, bars on the windows.

A padded cell.

And the whole place stank so bad she thought she might puke.

She sat up briefly, trying to find a light. There was none. The overhead lamp had been removed and the room was dark. Maybe she—

Suddenly roaring filled her ears. Her vision dissolved into black grains and she collapsed back on the bed, passed out. Sometime later she opened her eyes again, managed to sit up then waited until the dizziness passed and she stumbled into the tiny bathroom. The drug he'd injected . . . it was still in her system. She'd have to take it slow.

Megan sat down on the toilet, spread her legs and finally worked up the courage to examine herself. No tenderness or pain. No come. He might have groped but he hadn't raped her. She sighed in relief then urinated and washed her hands and face in the basin. She drank a dozen handfuls of icy water. As she stood—careful, careful, take your time—she caught sight of herself in the metal mirror bolted to the wall. She gasped. Pale and haggard, blond hair knotted and filthy. Eyes red and puffy. And frightened. Megan stepped away from the mirror quickly.

She looked for her clothes. Nothing. She couldn't find anything to wrap herself in. No sheets or curtains. This started a crying fit. She huddled into a ball and sobbed.

Wondering how long she'd been unconscious. A week, a day? She wasn't hungry so she guessed it was still Saturday. Maybe Sunday at the latest.

Was anyone looking for her?

Did anyone know she was missing?

Her parents, of course. She'd missed the lunch. Which she'd been going to blow off anyway. Thank God she hadn't called her mother and told her she wasn't coming, the way she'd planned. If that had happened they *still* wouldn't miss her.

And Amy . . .

Should have told her where I was going.

But, no, Crazy Megan wouldn't hear of *that*. C.M. was embarrassed, didn't want anybody to know she's been seeing a shrink. Fuck. She should've gone to Juvie Detention after all. Ten days in jail and it'd be over with. But Mcgan had to pick the nut doctor.

Who *is* he? she screamed to herself. Was he the man in that car that'd been following her near school? She'd started to believe that was her imagination.

Guess not, honey, Crazy Megan offers with no sympathy whatsoever.

Standing by the bed, Megan looked out the barred window into a huge field of tall grass and brush. Some trees, many of them cut down and left to rot.

She gasped suddenly as a huge dog trotted past the window and stopped, staring up at her. A bit of bloody flesh dangled from its mouth, red, like a scrap of steak.

Its eyes were spooky—too human—and it seemed to recognize her. Then suddenly the dog tensed, wheeled and vanished.

She examined the window. The iron bars were thick and the space between them was far too small for her to get through.

Frustrated, she pounded her palms against the wall.

Who *is* he?

Megan strode to the door, gripped and pulled it hard. It was, of course, locked tight. The tears returned suddenly; they fell on her breasts, and her nipples contracted painfully from the sobbing and the dank cold of the dismal room.

Who *is* he?

Why did they make her go to see the doctor? If they hadn't this never would've happened.

What'd I do to deserve this? Nothing! I didn't do a thing!

If her mother was going to fuck nerds in Baltimore then for Christ's sake why didn't she call me? Just a three-minute phone call. *Sorry honey I'm going to be late call Domino's and use the charge card have Amy over and all right even Brittany too but no boys . . .*

If her father was going to waste his life chasing bimbettes why couldn't he at least spend more than one weekend a month with her?

This was *their* fault! Her parents!

I hate you so much! I fucking *hate* you. I—

A sound.

What was it?

A scuttling . . .

It came from the ceiling. Looking up, she saw a number of dark clusters where the wall met the ceiling. She moved closer. Spiders! Two huge black ones. And one had just given birth—a hundred hundred tiny dots of infants flowed down the wall like black water.

Megan shivered, overwhelmed with disgust, her skin crawling at the sight. She raced toward the door, slamming into it with all her weight, and collapsed onto the splintery floor. She crawled along it, pushing at the baseboards, trying to find a weak spot. Nothing.

She pulled a wad of toilet paper off the roll, hesitated then crushed the spiders with it. Megan flushed the messy shroud and curled up in a ball on the cold floor. Cried for five minutes.

What's that? Crazy Megan asks her alter ego.

This stopped the tears.

Squick, squick.

That sound again. In the ceiling and the walls.

Squirrels, she decided. Then stood and walked to the wall, which was made of cinder block. How could there be animals in the walls if they were made out of cement?

Then she glanced into the bathroom and squinted. *Those* walls were just plasterboard. And there was a rectangular plate about twelve by eighteen inches mounted on the wall beside the toilet. Where did it lead?

She walked inside, crouched down and ran her finger across the edge of the metal, which was covered with many layers of paint. In the corners she felt one screw head but three holes, from which the screws were missing. If she could break through the thick paint she might be able to pull the plate up and bend the metal till it snapped.

But the enamel was thick, like glue, and with her short nails she couldn't get a grip. She thought of her friend Brittany, with the killer fingernails, a regular at a local Vietnamese manicure parlor. That was what she needed—slut claws . . .

She searched the bedroom once more but couldn't find anything to use as a tool. Sighing, she returned to the bathroom, lay on the floor and slugged the metal plate. It resounded hollowly, tantalizing with the promise of an empty passageway on the other side. But it didn't move a millimeter. *Keep going,* Crazy Megan says.

Megan slammed her fist into it again and again, until her knuckles began to bruise and swell. She turned around and kicked with her heel. As the center pushed in slightly, a hairline crack formed around the edge and she kicked harder. Her foot felt as if it were going to shatter.

Go! C.M. encourages. *Go for it!*

Megan spun round and tried again to grab the side of the plate. But her nails just weren't long enough to get a purchase in the crack and she howled in frustration then lunged forward, bared her teeth and shoved her face against the wall, trying to dig her incisors into the crack.

Her gum tore open on the rough paint and plaster. Her jaw exploded with cramping pain and she tasted blood. Then suddenly, with a snap, her front teeth slipped into the crack and pulled the plate away from the wall a fraction of an inch. Megan pressed her hands to her face to ease the pain. Then she spit blood, grabbed the plate and yanked so furiously it gave way at once, ripping the remaining screw from the wall. She fell backward.

Jesus, Crazy Megan says respectfully. *Good job.*

With a gasp of joy she sat up, seeing faint light through the hole. She shoved her head into the opening, looking into another room. The plate had apparently covered an old heating vent. There was a thin grille on the other side about a foot away. On her back, she guided her leg into the wall and kicked. The grille fell clattering to the floor. She froze. Quiet! she reminded herself. He could be nearby.

Then she started crawling through the opening, headfirst. Her shoulders were broad but she managed to ease them through. She had to reach down, cramping her arm, and cradle her breasts to keep her nipples from scraping on the sharp bottom edge of the vent. One inch at a time she forced her way through the vent. As she eased through she examined the other room. There were bars on these windows too. But the door was open. She could see a dim corridor beyond the doorway.

Another ten or twelve inches. Then twelve more.

Until her hips. They stopped her cold.

Those fucking hips, Crazy Megan mutters. *Hate 'em, hate 'em, hate 'em. You just couldn't lose those ten pounds, could you?*

I don't need any of your crap now, okay? Megan thinks to her alter ego.

The vent on the other side of the wall was, it seemed, slightly smaller than the one in her room. Megan tried wriggling, tightening her muscles, licking her fingers and swabbing her sides with spit but she still remained stuck—halfway between each room, her butt dead center in the wall.

No way, she thought to herself. I'm not getting trapped here! A terrible burst of claustrophobia shook through her. She fought it down, wriggled slightly and moved forward an inch or two before she froze again.

Then she heard the noise. *Squick, squick.*

The scuttling of claws in the wall above. Accompanied by a high-pitched twitter.

Oh, my God, no. The squirrels.

Her heart began to pound.

Squick, squick.

Right above where she was stuck. Two of them, it sounded like. Then more, gathering where the wall met the ceiling.

Then she looked into the corner of the room—at an animal's nest. It rustled and a creature appeared, staring at her with tiny red eyes.

Oh, fuck, they're rats! Crazy Megan blurts.

Megan began to sob. The noise of their little feet started coming down the wall. She stifled a scream as something—a bit of insulation or wood—fell onto her skin.

Squick. Squick squick squick. Walking along the ceiling, several of them gathering above her, curious. Maybe hungry. Hundreds of terrible creatures moving toward her stuck body—cautiously but unstoppably.

More rats. *Squick.*

Twitters and scuttling, growing closer still. There seemed to be a dozen now, two dozen. She pictured needle-sharp yellow teeth. Tiny gray tongues.

Closer and closer. Curious. Attracted to her smell.

She'd just finished her period a day ago. They'd smell the blood. They'd head right for it. *Jesus* . . .

More scuttling.

Oh . . .

She closed her eyes and sobbed in terror. It seemed that the whole wall was alive with them. Dozens, hundreds of rats converging on her. Closer, closer. *Squick squick squick squicksquicksquick* . . .

Megan slapped her palms against the wall and pushed with all her strength, kicking her feet madly. Then, uttering a dentist's-drill squeal, one rat dropped squarely onto her. She gasped and felt her heart stutter in terror. She pounded the wall, wriggling furiously. The startled animal climbed off and she felt the snaky tail slip in between her legs as he moved back up the wall.

"Oh," she choked. "No . . ."

As she struggled to free herself and scrabbled her feet on the bathroom floor, another animal tentatively reached out with a claw and then stepped onto the small of her back. The paws gripped softly and began to move. A damp whiskered nose tapped on her skin as the creature sniffed along her body.

Her arms cramping, she shoved hard. Her foot caught the edge of the toilet in the bathroom behind her and she pushed herself forward two or three inches. It was just enough. She was able to wriggle her hips free. The rat leapt off her and Megan burst into the adjoining room. She crawled frantically into the far corner, as four rats escaped from the wall and vanished through the open door, joined by their friend in the nest.

She sobbed, gasping for breath, brushing her palms over her skin frantically to make sure none of them clung to her. After five minutes she'd calmed. Slowly she stepped back to the vent and listened. *Squick squick squick . . .* More scuttling, more twitters. She slammed the grille against the vent opening. The rest of the rats vanished up the wall. An angry hiss sounded from the hole.

God . . .

She found some stacks of newspapers, removed the grille, wadded up the papers and stuffed them inside the wall to keep the creatures trapped inside.

She collapsed back on the floor, trying to push away the horrible memory of the probing little paws, filthy and damp.

Looking into the dim corridor, cold and yellow, windows barred, filthy, she happened to glance up at a sign on the wall.

PATIENTS SHALL BE DELOUSED ONCE A WEEK.

That sign—a few simple words—brought the hopelessness home to her.

Don't worry about it, Crazy Megan tries to reassure.

But Megan wasn't listening. She shivered in fear and disgust and curled up, clutching her knees. Hating this place. Hating her life, her pointless life . . . Her stupid, superficial friends. Her sick obsession with Janis, the Grateful Dead and all the rest of the cheerful, lying, fake-ass past.

Hating the man who'd done this to her, whoever he was.

But most of all hating her parents.

Hating them beyond words.

Chapter Twelve

The forty-minute drive to Leesburg took Tate and Bett past a few mansions, some redneck bungalows, some new developments with names like Windstone and The Oaks. Cars on blocks, vegetable stands selling—at this time of year—jars of put-up preserves and relishes.

But mostly they passed farmland.

Looking out over just-planted land like this, some people see future homes or shopping malls or town houses and some see rows of money to be plucked from the ground at harvest time. And some perhaps simply drive past seeing nothing but where their particular journey is taking them.

But Tate Collier saw in these fields what he felt in his own farmland—a quiet salvation. Something he did, yet not of his doing, something that would let him survive, if not prosper, graciously: the silence of rooted growth. And if at times that process betrayed him— hail, drought, tumbling markets—Tate could still sleep content in the assurance that there was no malice in the earth's heart. And that, the former criminal prosecutor within him figured, was no small thing.

So even though Tate claimed, as any true advocate would, that it made no nevermind to him whether he was representing the plaintiffs or defendants in the Liberty Park case, say, his heart was in fact with the people who wanted to protect the farmland from the roller coasters and concession stands and traffic.

He felt this even more now, seeing these rolling hills. And he felt, too, guilt and a pang of impatience that he was distracted from his preparations for the Liberty Park hearing. But a look at Bett's troubled face put this discomfort aside. There'd be time to hone his argument. Right now there were other priorities.

They passed the Oatlands farm and as they did the sun came out. And he sped on toward Leesburg, into old Virginia. Confederate Virginia.

There weren't many towns like this in the northern part of the state; most people in Richmond and Charlottesville didn't really consider most of northern Virginia to be in the commonwealth at all. Tate and Bett drove through the city limits and slowed to the posted thirty miles per hour. Examining the trim yards, the white clapboard houses, the incongruous biker bar in the middle of downtown, the plentiful churches. They followed the directions Tate had been given to the hospital where Dr. Hanson was visiting his mother.

"Can he tell us much?" Bett wondered. "Legally, I mean."

She'd be thinking, he guessed, of the patient-doctor privilege, which allowed a doctor to keep secret the conversations between a patient and his physician. Years ago, when they'd been married, Tate had explained this and other nuances of the law to her. But she often grew offended at these arcane rules. "You mean if you don't read him his rights, the arrest is no good? Even if he *did* it?" she'd ask, perplexed. Or: "Excuse me, but why should a mother go to jail if she's shoplifting food for her hungry child? I don't get it."

He expected that same indignation now when he explained that Hanson didn't *have* to say anything to them. But Bett just nodded, accepting the rules. She smiled coyly and said, "Then I guess you'll have to be extra persuasive."

They turned the corner and the white-frame hospital loomed ahead of them.

"Well, busy day," Bett said, assessing the front of the hospital as she flipped up the car's mirror after refreshing her lipstick. There were three police cars parked in front of the main entrance. The red and white lights atop one of them flashed with urgent brilliance.

"Car wreck?" Bett suggested. Route 15, which led into town, was posted fifty-five but everybody drove it at seventy or eighty.

They parked and walked inside.

Something was wrong, Tate noted. Something serious had happened. Several nurses and orderlies stood in the lobby, looking down a corridor. Their faces were troubled. A receptionist leaned over the main desk, gazing down the same corridor.

"What is it?" Bett whispered.

"Not a clue," Tate answered.

"Look, there he is," somebody said.

"God," someone else muttered.

Two policemen were leading a tall, balding man

down the corridor toward the main entrance. His hands were cuffed behind him. His face was red. He'd been crying. As he passed, Tate heard him say, "I didn't do it. I *wouldn't* do it! I wasn't even *there!*"

Several of the nurses shook their heads, eyeing him with cold expressions on their faces.

"I didn't do it!" he shouted.

A moment later he was in a squad car. It made a U-turn in the driveway and sped off.

Tate asked the receptionist, "What's that all about?"

The white-haired woman shook her head, eyes wide, cheeks pale. "We nearly had an assisted suicide." She was very shaken. "I don't believe it."

"What happened?"

"We have a patient—an elderly woman with a broken hip. And it looks like he"—she nodded toward where the police car had been—"comes in and talks to her for a while and next thing we know she's got a syringe in her hands and's trying to kill herself. Can you imagine? Can you just *imagine?*"

"But they saved her?" Tate asked.

"The Lord was watching over her."

Bett blinked. "I'm sorry?"

The receptionist continued, "A nurse just happened by. My goodness. Can you imagine?"

Bett shook her head, very troubled. Tate recalled that she felt the same about euthanasia as she did about the death penalty. He thought briefly of her sister's husband's death. Harris. He'd used a shotgun to kill himself. Like Hemingway. Harris had been an artist—a bad one, in Tate's estimation—and he'd shot himself in his studio, his dark blood covering a canvas that he'd been working on for months.

Absently he asked the receptionist, "That man. Who is he? Somebody like Kevorkian?"

"Who *is* he?" the woman blurted. "Why, he was the poor woman's *son!*"

Tate and Bett looked at each other in shock. She said in a whisper, "Oh, no. It couldn't be."

Tate asked the woman, "The patient? Was her name Hanson?"

"Yes, that's the name." Shaking her head. "Her own son tried to talk her into killing herself! And I heard he was a therapist too. A doctor! Can you *imagine?*"

Tate and Bett sat in the hospital cafeteria, brooding silence between them. They'd ordered coffee that neither wanted. They were waiting for a call from Konnie Konstantinatis, whom Tate had called ten minutes ago—though the wait seemed like hours.

Tate's phone buzzed. He answered it before it could chirp again.

"'Lo."

"Okay, Counselor, made some calls. But this is all unofficial. There's still no case. *Got* it? Are you *comfortable* with that?"

"Got it, Konnie. Go ahead."

The detective explained that he had called the Leesburg police and spoken to a detective there. "Here's what happened. This old lady, Greta Hanson, fell and broke her hip last week. Fell down her back stairs. Serious but not too serious. She's eighty. You know how it is."

"Right."

"Okay, today she's tanked up on painkillers, really out of it, and she hears her son—*your* Dr. Hanson—hears him telling her that it looks like the end of the road, they found cancer, she only has a few months left. Yadda, yadda, yadda. The pain's gonna be terrible. Tells her it's best to just finish herself off, it's what everybody wants. He's pretty persuasive, sounds like. Leaves her a syringe of Nembutal. She says she'll do it. She sticks herself but a nurse finds her in time. Anyway, she's pretty doped up but tells 'em what happened and the administrator calls the cops. They find the son in the gift shop buying a box of candy. Supposedly for her. They collar him. He denies it all, of course. What else is he going to say? So. End of story."

"And this all happens fifteen minutes before Bett and I are going to talk to him about Megan? It's no coincidence, Konnie. Come on."

Silence from Fairfax.

"Konnie. You hear me?"

"I'm telling you the facts, Counselor. I don't comment otherwise."

"She's sure it was her son who talked to her?"

"She said."

"But she was drugged up. So maybe it was somebody *else* talking to her."

"Maybe. But—"

"We can talk to Hanson?"

"Nope. Not till the arraignment on Monday. And he's probably not gonna be in any mood even then."

"All right. Answer me one question. Can you look up what kind of car he drives?"

"Who? Hanson? Yeah, hold on."

Tate heard typing as he filled Bett in on what Konnie'd said.

"Oh, my," she said, hand rising to her mouth.

A moment later the detective came back on the line. "Two cars. A Mazda nine two-nine and a Ford Explorer. Both this year's models."

"What colors?"

"Mazda's green. The Explorer's black."

"It was somebody else, Konnie. Somebody was following Megan."

"Tate, she took the train to New York. She's going to see the Statue of Liberty and hang out in Greenwich Village and do whatever kids do in New York and—"

"You know the Bust-er Book?"

"What the hell is a buster book?" the detective grumbled.

"Kids at Jefferson High are supposed to write down anybody who comes up and offers them drugs or candy or flashes them."

"Oh, that shit. Right."

"A friend of Megan's said there'd been a car following her. In the Bust-er Book, some kids reported a gray car parked near the school in the afternoon. And Megan herself reported it last week."

"Gray car?"

"Right."

A sigh. "Tate, lemme ask you. Just how many kids go to that school of hers?"

"I'm not saying it's a *good* lead, Konnie—"

"And just how many parents in gray cars pick 'em up?"

"—but it *is* a lead."

"Tag number? Make, model, year?"

Tate sighed. "Nothing."

"Look, Counselor, get me at least one of the above and we'll talk . . . So, what're you thinking, somebody snatched her? The Amtrak schedule is bogus?"

"I don't know. It's just fishy."

"It's not a case, Tate. That's the watchword for today. Look, I gotta go."

"One last question, Konnie. *Does* she have cancer? Hanson's mother?"

The detective hesitated. "No. At least it's not what they're treating her for."

"So somebody talked her into believing she's dying. Talked her into trying to kill herself."

"Yeah. And that somebody was her son. He could have a hundred motives. Gotta go, Counselor."

Click.

He relayed to Bett the rest of his conversation with Konnie.

"Megan was seeing a therapist who tried to kill his mother? God."

"I don't know, Bett," he said. "You saw his face. Did he look guilty?"

"He looked caught," she said.

Tate glanced at his watch. It was two-thirty. "Let's get back to Fairfax and find that teacher. Eckhard."

Crazy Megan finally gets a chance to talk.

Listen up, girl. Listen here, kiddo. Biz-nitch, you listening? Good. You need me. This is serious . . . You're not sneaking cigarettes in the Fair Oaks mall parking lot. You're not flirting with a George Mason junior to get him to buy you a pint of Comfort or Turkey. You're not sitting in Amy's room, snarfing wine, hating it and saying it's great, while you're like, "Sure, I come every time Josh and I fuck . . ."

Leave me alone, Megan thought.

But C.M. won't have any of her *attitude*. She snaps, *You hate the world. Okay. What you want—*

A family is what I want, Megan responded. That's all I wanted.

Oh. Well, that's precious, her crazy side offers, nice and sarcastic. *Who the fuck doesn't? You want Mommy and Daddy to wave their magic wand and get you out of here? Uh-huh. Uh-huh. Well, ain't going to happen, girl. So get off your fat ass and get out.*

I can't move, Megan thought. I'm scared, I'm tired.

Up, girl. Up. Look, he—

And who *is* he?

Crazy Megan is in good form today. *What difference does it make? He's the bogeyman, he's Jason, he's Leatherface, he's Freddy Krueger, he's your father—*

All right, stop it. You're like so . . . tedious.

But C.M.'s wound up now. *He's everything bad, he's your mother giving Brad a blow job, he's the barn at your father's farm, he's an inconvenient child, he's a whispering bear—*

"Stop it, stop it, stop it!" Megan screamed out loud.

But nothing stops Crazy Megan when she gets going. *It doesn't matter who he is. Don't you get it? He thinks you're locked up tight in your little padded cell. But you're not. You're out. And you may not have much time. So get your shit together and get the hell out of here.*

I don't have any clothes, Megan pointed out.

That's the girl I love. Oooo. The sarcasm is thick as Noxema. *Sit back and find excuses. Let's see: You're pissed 'cause Mom's off to Baltimore to fuck Mr. Rogers and do you say anything about it? No. It rags you that Dad fits you in around his dates with girls who've got inflatable boobs but do you bitch about it? Do you call him on it? No. You go off and get drunk. You have another cigarette. What other distractions can we come up with? Nail polish, CDs, Victoria's Secret Taco Bell the mall the multiplex a boy's fat dick gossip . . .*

I hate you, Megan thought. I really, really hate you. Go away, go back where you came from.

I am where I came from, Crazy Megan responds. *You may have some time to fuck around like this, whining, and you may not. Now, you're buck naked and you don't like it. Well, if that's an issue, go find some clothes. And, no, there's no Contempo Casual around here. Of course, I personally would say, Fuck the clothes, find a door and run like hell. But that's up to you.*

Megan rolled to her feet.

She stepped into the corridor.

Cold, painful. Her feet stung from kicking the wall. She started walking. Looking around, she saw it was a rambling place, one story, and built of concrete blocks. All the windows had thick bars on them. With the padded cell, she figured it was a mental hospital but she couldn't imagine treating patients here. It was totally depressing. No one could have gotten better here.

She found a door leading outside and pushed it. It was locked tight. The same with two others. She looked outside for a car, didn't see one in the lot. At least she was alone. Dr. Peters must have left.

Keep going, Crazy Megan insists.

But—

Keep. Going.

She did.

The place was huge, wing after wing, dozens of corridors, gloomy wards, private rooms, two-bed rooms. But all the doors leading outside were sealed tight and all the windows were barred. Every damn one of them. Two large interior doorways had been bricked off sloppily with cinder blocks and Sakrete—maybe because they led to less restricted wings. Dozens of the large concrete blocks that hadn't been needed lay scattered on the floor. She picked up one and slammed it into a barred window. It didn't even bend the metal rods.

For several hours she made a circuit of the hospital, moving quietly. She was careful; in the dim light she could make out footprints, hundreds of them. She couldn't tell if they'd been left by Dr. Peters alone or by him and someone else but she was all too aware that she might not be alone.

By the time she'd made it back to her cell she hadn't found a single door or window that looked promising. Shit. No way out.

Okay, Crazy Megan offers, chipper as ever. *At least find something you can use to nail his ass with.*

What do you mean?

A weapon, bitch. What do you think?

Megan remembered seeing a kitchen and returned there.

She started going through drawers and cupboards. But there wasn't anything she could use. There were no metal knives or forks, not even dinner knives, only hundreds of packages of plastic utensils. No glasses or ceramic cups. Everything was paper or Styrofoam.

She pulled open a door. It was a pantry full of food. She started to close the door but stopped, looked inside again.

There was enough food for a family to live on for a year. Cheerios, condensed milk, Diet Pepsi, Doritos, Lay's potato chips, tuna, Hostess cupcakes, Cup-A-Soup, Chef Boyardee . . .

What's funny here?

Jesus. Crazy Megan catches on first.

Megan's hand rose to her mouth as she too understood and she started to cry.

Jesus, Crazy Megan repeats.

These were exactly the same brands that Megan liked. This was what her mother's cupboards were stocked with. Here too were her shampoo, conditioner and soap.

Even the type of tampon that Megan used.

He'd been in her house, he knew what she liked.

He'd bought this all for her!

Don't lose it, babes, don't . . .

But Megan ignored her crazy side and gave in to the crying.

Thinking: If a family of four could live on this for a year, just think how long it would last her by herself.

• • •

Twenty minutes later Megan rose from the floor, wiped her face and continued her search. It didn't take her long to find the source of the footprints.

In a far wing of the hospital were two rooms that had been "homified," as Bett would say when she'd dress up a cold-looking house to make it warmer and more comfortable. One room was an office, filled with thousands of books and files and papers. An armchair and lamp and desk. The other room was a bedroom. It smelled stale, turned her stomach. She looked inside. The bed was unmade and the sheets were stained. Off-white splotches.

Guys're so disgusting, Crazy Megan offers.

Megan agreed; who could argue with that?

This meant that someone else probably lived here—someone young (she supposed older guys jerked off too but tried to imagine, say, her father doing it and couldn't).

Way gross thought. From C.M.

Then she saw the closet.

Oh, please! She mentally crossed her fingers as she pulled the door open.

Yes! It was filled with clothes. She pulled on some jeans, which were tight around her hips and too long. She rolled the cuffs up. She found a work shirt—which was tight, too, but that didn't matter. She felt a hundred percent better. There were no shoes but she found a pair of thick black socks. For some reason, covering her feet gave her more confidence than covering the rest of her body.

She looked through the closet for a knife or gun but found nothing. She returned to the other room. Rummaged through the desk. Nothing to use as a weapon, except a Bic pen. She took it anyway. Then she looked through the rest of the room, focusing at first on the bookshelves.

Some books were about psychiatry but most were fantasy novels and science fiction. Some were pretty weird. Stacks of comic books too—Japanese, a lot of them. Megan flipped through several. Totally icky— girls being raped by monsters and gargoyles and aliens. X-rated. She shivered in disgust.

The name inside the books and on the front of the comic books was *Pete Matthews.* Sometimes he'd written *Peter M.* It was written very carefully but in big block letters. As if he was a young kid.

Megan looked through the files, most of them filled with psychological mumbo jumbo she couldn't understand. There were also stacks of the American Psychiatric Association *Journal.* Articles were marked with yellow Post-its. She noticed they'd been written by a doctor named Aaron Matthews. The boy's father? she wondered. His bio gave long lists of credentials. Dozens of awards and honorary degrees. One newspaper clipping called him "the Einstein of therapists" and reported, "He can detect and categorize a psychosis from listening to a patient's words for three or four minutes. A master diagnostician."

In between two file folders was another clipping. Megan lifted it to the light. It showed Dr. Peters and a young man in his late teens. But wait . . . The doctor's last name wasn't Peters. The caption read: "Dr. Aaron Matthews leaves the funeral home after the memorial service for his wife. He is accompanied by his son, Peter." Matthews . . . the one who wrote those articles.

So he must have been a doctor here. That's how he knew about the hospital—and that it would make a perfect prison.

Megan studied the picture again, feeling crawly and scared. The doctor's son was . . . well, just plain weird. He was a tall boy, lanky, with long arms and huge hands. He had thick floppy hair that looked dirty and his forehead jutted over his dark eye sockets. He had a sick smile on his face.

Leaving his mother's funeral and he's *smiling?*

So this was his room—the son's. Maybe Peters— well, Matthews—kept the boy locked up here, a prisoner too.

Her eyes fell to an official-looking report. She read the top page.

EMERGENCY INTAKE EVALUATION

Patient Peter T. Matthews presents with symptoms typical of an antisocial and paranoid personality. He is not schizophrenic, under DSM-III criteria, but he has, or claims to have, delusions. More likely these are merely fantasies, which in his case are so overpowering that he chooses not to recognize the borderline between his role-playing and reality. These fantasies are generally of a sadoerotic nature, with him playing a nonhuman entity—stalking and raping females. During our sessions Peter would sometimes portray these entities—right down to odd mannerisms and garbled language. He was often "in character," and quite consistent in his role-playing. However, there was no evidence of fugue states or multiple personalities. He changed personas at his convenience, to achieve the greatest stimulation from his fantasies.

Peter is extremely dangerous. He must be hospitalized in a secure facility until the determination is made for a course of treatment. Recommend immediate psychopharmacological intervention.

Stalking . . . rape.

Megan put the report back on the desk. She found a notebook. Peter's name was written on this too. She read through it. In elaborate passages Peter described himself as a spaceman or an alien stalking women, tying them up, raping them. She dropped the book.

Tears again.

Then another thought: Her cell! This Dr. Matthews, her kidnapper, had locked her up not only to keep her from getting out but to keep his son from getting *in*. He was—

A creak, a faint squeal. A door closed softly in a far part of the hospital.

Megan shivered in terror.

Move it, girl! Crazy Megan cries, in a silent voice as panicked as uncrazy Megan's. *It's him, it's the son.*

She grabbed a pile of things to take with her— several of the magazines, file folders about the hospital, letters. Anything that might help her figure out who this Dr. Matthews was. Why he'd taken her. How she might get out.

Footsteps . . .

He's coming. He's coming here . . . Move it. Now!

Holding the files and clippings under her arm, Megan fled out the door. She ran down the corridors, getting lost once, pausing often to listen for footsteps. He seemed to be circling her.

Finally she found her way and raced into the room that adjoined hers, the "rat room." She rubbed the grate along the edges of the hole in the wall to widen it. She started through and, whimpering, clawed her way forward. Five inches, six, a foot, two feet. Finally she grabbed the toilet in her room and wrenched herself through the hole. She replaced the grate on the far side of the wall and then slammed the metal plate into place in her bathroom.

She ran to the door and pressed her ear against it. The footsteps grew closer and closer. But Peter didn't stop at her door. He kept moving. Maybe he didn't know she was here.

Megan sat on the icy floor with her hands pressing furiously against the plate until they cramped.

Listen, C.M. starts to say. *Maybe you can—*

Shut up, Megan thought furiously.

And for once Crazy Megan does what she's told.

Chapter Thirteen

The eyes.

The eyes tell it all.

When Aaron Matthews was practicing psychotherapy he learned to read the eyes. They told him so much more than words. Words are tools and weapons and camouflage and shields.

But the eyes tell you the truth.

An hour ago, in Leesburg, he'd looked into the glassy, groggy eyes of a drugged Greta Hanson and knew she was a woman with no reserves of strength. And so he'd leaned close, become her son and spun a tale guaranteed to send her to the very angels that she was babbling on and on about. It's quite a challenge to talk someone into killing herself and he'd thoroughly enjoyed playing the game.

He doubted she'd die from the dosage of Nembutal he'd given her and he doubted that she could find a vein anyway. Besides, it was important for her to remain alive—to blame her son for the Kevorkian number. Poor Doc Hanson now either in jail or on the run. In any case, he'd be no help as a witness to Tate Collier.

Now, as he strolled along the sidewalk near

Jefferson High School, Aaron Matthews was looking at another set of eyes.

Robert Eckhard's—the teacher who'd seen his car as he stalked Megan.

Studying the man's eyes, Matthews was concluding that Eckhard might or might not have been a good English teacher but he didn't doubt that he was one hell of a girls' volleyball coach. The diminutive, tweedy man sat with a sports roster on his lap outside the sports field between the grade and high schools.

Wearing a baseball cap and thick-framed reading glasses he'd bought at Safeway—he remembered that Eckhard might have seen him near the school in the Mercedes—Matthews walked slowly past. He studied his subject carefully. The teacher was a middle-aged man, in Dockers and a loose tan shirt. Matthews took in all these observations and filed them away but it was the eyes that were most helpful; they told him everything he needed to know about Mr. Eckhard.

Continuing down the sidewalk, Matthews walked into a drugstore and made several purchases. He slipped into the rest room of the store and five minutes later returned to the school yard. He sat down on the bench next to Eckhard's and rested the *Washington Post* in his lap. He gazed out at the young girls playing informal games of soccer or jump rope in the school yard.

Once, then twice, Eckhard glanced at him. The second time, Matthews happened to turn his way and saw the teacher looking at him with a hint of curiosity in his tell-all eyes.

Matthews's face went still with uneasy alarm. He waited a judicious moment then stood quickly and walked past Eckhard. But as he did, the disposable camera fell from the folds of his newspaper. Matthews blinked then stepped forward suddenly to pick it up but his foot struck the yellow-and-black box. It went skidding along the sidewalk and stopped in front of Eckhard.

Matthews froze. The teacher, his eyes on Matthews's, smiled again. He reached down and picked up the camera, looked at it. Turned it over.

"I—" Matthews began, horrified.

"It's okay," Eckhard said.

"Okay?" Matthews's voice faltered. He looked up and down the sidewalk, uneasy.

"I mean, the camera's okay," Eckhard said, rattling it. "It doesn't seem to be broken."

Matthews began speaking breathlessly, over-explaining—as his script required. "See, what it was, I was going to D.C. later today. I was going to the zoo. Take some pictures of the animals."

"The zoo." Eckhard examined the camera.

Matthews again looked up and down the sidewalk.

"You like photography?" the teacher asked.

After a moment, Matthews said, "Yes, I do. A hobby." Smiled awkwardly, summoning a blush. "Everybody should have a hobby. That's what my father said." He fell silent.

"It's my hobby too."

"Really?"

"Been doing it for about fifteen years," Eckhard said.

"Me too. Little less, I guess."

"You live around here?" the teacher asked.

"Fairfax."

"Long time?"

"A couple of years."

Silence grew between them. Eckhard still held the camera. Matthews crossed his arms, rocked on his feet. Looking out over the school yard. Finally he asked, "You do your own developing and printing?"

"Of course," Eckhard said.

Of course. The expected answer. Matthews's eyes narrowed and he appeared to relax. "Harder with color," he offered. "But they don't make the throwaways in black and white."

"I'm getting a digital camera," Eckhard said. "I can just feed the pictures into my computer at home."

"I've heard about those. They're expensive, aren't they?"

"They are . . . But you know hobbies. If they're important to you you're willing to spend the money."

"That's my philosophy," Matthews admitted. He sat down next to Eckhard. They looked out on the playing field, at a cluster of girls, who were around ten or eleven years old. Eckhard looked through the eyepiece of the camera. "Lens isn't telephoto."

"No," Matthews said. Then after a moment: "She's cute. That brunette there."

"Angela."

"You know her?"

"I'm a teacher at the high school. I'm also a grade school counselor."

Matthews's eyes flashed enviously. "Teacher? I work

for an insurance company. Actuarial work. Boring. But summers I volunteer at Camp Henry. Maryland. Ages eight through fourteen. You know it?"

Eckhard shook his head. "I also coach girls' sports."

"That's a good job too." Matthews clicked his tongue.

"Sure is." Eckhard looked out over the field. "I know most of these girls."

"You do portraits?"

"Some."

"You ever photograph her? That girl by the goal-post?"

But Eckhard wouldn't answer. "So, you take pictures just around the area here?"

Matthews said, "Here, California. Europe some. I was in Amsterdam a little while ago."

"Amsterdam. I was there a few years ago. Not as interesting as it used to be."

"That's what I found."

"Bangkok's nice, though," Eckhard volunteered.

"I'm planning on going next year," Matthews said in a whisper.

"Oh, you have to," Eckhard encouraged, kneading the yellow box of the camera in his hands. "It's quite a place."

Matthews could practically see the synapses firing in Eckhard's mind, wondering furiously if Matthews was a cop with the Child Welfare Unit of the Fairfax County Police or an FBI agent. Matthews had treated several pedophiles during his days as a practicing therapist. He recognized the classic characteristics in Eckhard. He was intelligent—an organized offender—and he'd know all about the laws of child molestation and pornography. He could probably just keep the testosterone under control to avoid actually molesting a child but photographing young girls was a compulsion that ruled his life.

Matthews offered another conspiratorial smile then glanced at a girl bending down to pick up a ball. Gave a faint sigh. Eckhard followed his gaze and nodded.

The girl stood up. Eckhard said, "Nancy. She's nine. Fifth grade."

"Pretty. You wouldn't happen to have any pictures of her, would you?"

"I do." Eckhard paused. "In a nice skirt and blouse, I seem to recall."

Matthews wrinkled his nose. Shrugged.

He wondered if the man would take the bait.

Snap.

Eckhard whispered, "Well, not the blouse in all of them."

Matthews exhaled hard. "You wouldn't happen to have any with you?"

"No. You have any of yours?"

Matthews said, "I keep all of mine on my computer."

One of Matthews's patients had seven thousand images of child pornography on a computer. He'd traded them with other pedophiles while he'd been serving time for a molestation charge; the computer they resided on was the warden's at Hammond Falls State Penitentiary in Maryland. The prisoner had written an encryption program to keep the files secret.

The FBI cracked it anyway and, despite his willingness to go through therapy, the offense earned him another ten years in prison.

Matthews said, "I don't have too many in my collection. Only about four thousand."

Eckhard's eyes turned to Matthews and they were vacuums. He whispered a long, envious "Well . . ."

Matthews added, "I've got some videos too. But only about a hundred of them."

"A *hundred?*"

Eckhard shifted on the bench. Matthews knew the teacher was lost. Completely. He'd be thinking: At worst, it's entrapment and I can beat it in court. At worst, I can talk my way out of it. At worst, I'll flee the country and move to Thailand . . . As a therapist Matthews was continually astonished at how easily people won completely unwinnable arguments with themselves.

Still, you land a fish with as much care as you hook it.

"You seem worried . . ." Matthews started. "And I have to say, I don't know you, and I'm a little nervous myself. But I've just got a feeling about you. Maybe we could help each other out . . . Let me show you a couple of samples of what I've got."

The teacher's eyes flickered with lust.

Always the eyes.

"That'd be fine. That'd be good. Please." Eckhard cleared his excited throat.

Oh, you pathetic thing . . .

"I could give you a computer disk," Matthews suggested.

"Sure. That'd be great."

"I only live about three blocks from here. Let me run up to my house and get some samples."

"Good."

"Oh," Matthews said, pausing. A frown. "I only have girls."

"Yes, yes. That's fine," Eckhard said breathlessly. A bead of spit rested in the corner of the mouth. Desperately he asked, "Can you go now?"

"Sure. Be right back." Matthews started up the street.

He turned and saw the teacher, a stupid smile on his face, grinning from ear to ear, looking out over the field of his sad desire, rubbing his thumb over the disposable camera.

In the drugstore once again, Matthews walked up to the pay phone and called 911.

When dispatch answered he said urgently, "Oh, you need somebody down to Markus Avenue right away! The sports field behind Jefferson School." He described Eckhard and said, "He took a little girl into the alley and pulled his, you know, penis out. Then took some pictures. And I heard him ask her to his house. He said he's got lots of pictures of little girls like her on his computer. Pictures of little girls, you know . . . doing it. Oh, it's disgusting. Hurry up! I'm going back and watch him to make sure he doesn't get away."

He hung up before the dispatcher could ask for his identity.

Matthews didn't know if snapshots of a fully dressed little girl in a school yard next to frames of a man's erect dick (Matthews's own penis, taken in the drugstore rest room twenty minutes ago) were an offense, but once the cops got a search warrant for the man's house Eckhard would be out of commission—and a completely unreliable witness about a gray Mercedes or anything else—for a long, long time.

By the time he was back on the street, walking toward his car, Matthews heard the sirens.

Fairfax County apparently took children's well-being very seriously.

Tate and Bett arrived at the school yard, taking care to avoid the main building, just in case the clean-cut young fascist of a security guard had happened to glance inside the Bust-er Book after Tate and Bett had left and found twenty pages missing.

But volleyball practice had been canceled for today, it seemed. Nobody quite knew why.

In fact the yard was almost deserted, despite the clear skies.

They found two students and asked if they'd seen Eckhard. They said they hadn't. One teenage girl said, "We were coming here for the practice."

"Volleyball?"

"Right. And what it was was somebody said it's been canceled and we should all go home. And stay away from here. Totally weird."

"And you haven't seen Mr. Eckhard?"

"Somebody said he had to go someplace. But they didn't tell us where. I don't know. He was here earlier. I don't get it. He's *always* here. I mean, always."

"Do you know where he lives?"

"Fairfax someplace. I think."

"What's his first name?"

"Robert."

Tate called directory assistance and got his number then called. There was no answer. He left a message. He looked out over the school yard for a moment and had a thought. Tate asked his ex-wife, "Where did she hang out?"

"Hang out?" Bett asked absently. He saw her looking into her purse, eyes on the letter containing her daughter's searing words.

"Yeah, with her friends. After school."

She looked up. "Just around. You know."

"But where? We'll go there, ask if anybody's seen her."

There was a long hesitation. Finally she said, "I'm not sure."

"You're not?" Tate asked, surprised. "You don't know where she goes?"

"No," Bett answered testily. "Not all the time. She's a seventeen-year-old girl with a driver's license."

"Oh. So you don't know where she'd spend her afternoons."

"Not always, no." She glanced at him angrily. "It is not like she hangs out in southeast D.C., Tate."

"I just—"

"Megan's a responsible girl. She knows where to go and where not to go. I trust her."

They walked in silence back to the car. Bett grabbed her phone again and her address book. She began making calls—to Megan's friends, he gathered. At least she had *their* numbers, if not Megan's boyfriend's. Still, it irked him that she didn't seem to know much basic information—important information—about the girl.

When they arrived at the car she folded up the phone. "Her favorite place was called the Coffee Shop. Up near Route fifty." Bett sounded victorious. "Like Starbucks. All right? Happy?"

She dropped into the seat and crossed her arms. They drove in silence north along the parkway.

Chapter Fourteen

Braking to five miles an hour, Tate surveyed the crowded parking lot.

He found a space between a chopped Harley-Davidson and a pickup bumper-stickered with the Reb stars 'n' bars. He navigated the glistening Lexus into this narrow spot.

He and Bett surveyed the cycles, the tough young men and women, all in denim, defiantly holding open bottles, the tattoos, the boots. At the other end of the parking lot was a very different crowd, younger—boys with long hair, girls with crew cuts, layers of baggy clothes, plenty of body piercing. Bleary eyes.

Welcome to the Coffee Shop.

"Here?" Bett asked. "She came *here?*"

Starbucks? Tate thought. I don't think so.

She glanced at the notes she'd jotted. "Off fifty near Walney. This's it. Oh my."

Tate glanced at his ex-wife. Her horrified expression didn't diminish his anger. How could she have let Megan come to a place like this? Didn't she check up on her?

Her own daughter, for Christ's sake . . .

Tate pushed the door open and started to get out.

Bett popped her seat belt but he said abruptly, "Wait here."

He walked up to the closest cluster—the bikers; they seemed less comatose than the slacker gang at the other end of the lot.

But no one he queried had heard of Megan. He was vastly relieved. Maybe it was a misunderstanding. Maybe her friend meant a generic coffee shop someplace.

At the far end of the lot he waded into a grungy sea of plaid shirts, Doc Marten boots, JNCO jeans and bell-bottom Levi's. The girls wore tight tank tops over bras in contrasting colors. Their hair was long, parted in the middle, like Megan's. Peace symbols bounced on breasts and there was a lot of tie-dyed couture. The images reminded Tate of his own coming-of-age era, the early seventies.

"Megan? Sure, like I know her," said a slim girl, smoking a cigarette she was too young to buy.

"Have you seen her lately?"

"She's here a lotta nights. But not in the last week, you know. Like, who're you?"

"I'm her father. She's missing."

"Wow. That sucks."

"How'd she get in? She was seventeen."

"Uhm. I don't know."

Meaning: a fake ID.

He asked, "Do you know if anybody's been asking about her? Or been following her?"

"I dunno. But her and me, we weren't, like, real close. Hey, ask him. Sammy! Hey, Sammy." To Tate she added, "They'd hang out some."

A large boy glanced their way, eyed Tate uneasily. He set a paper cup behind a garbage can and walked up to him. He was about the lawyer's height, with a pimply face, and wore a baseball cap backward. He wore a pager and a cell phone.

"I'm looking for Megan McCall. You know her?"

"Sure."

"Have you seen her lately?"

"She was here this week."

"She comes here a lot?" Tate asked.

"Yeah, she, like, hangs here. Her and Donna and Amy. You know."

"How about her boyfriend?"

"That black dude from Mason?" Sammy asked. "The one she broke up with? Naw, this wasn't his scene. I only saw 'em together once, I think."

"Was somebody—some man in a gray car—asking about her, following her around?"

Sammy gave a faint laugh. "Yeah, there was. Last week, Megan and me, we were here and she was like, 'What's he want? Him again.' And I'm like, 'You want me to go fuck him up?' And she goes, 'Sure.' I go up to the car but the asshole takes off."

"Did you get a look at him?"

"Not too close. White guy. Your age, maybe a little older."

"You get the plate number?"

"No. Didn't even see what state. But it was a Mercedes. I don't know what model. All those fucking numbers. American cars have names. But German cars, just fucking numbers."

"And you don't have any idea who he was?"

"Well, yeah, I mean, I *knew* who he was. But Megan doesn't like to talk about it. So I let it go."

Tate shook his head. "Talk about what?"

"You know."

"No, I *don't* know," Tate said. "What?"

"Well, just . . ." Sammy lifted his hands. "What she used to do. I figured he was looking for some more action and had tracked her down here."

"Action? I don't understand. What are you saying?"

"I figured him and Megan had . . . get it? And he wanted some more."

"What are you talking about?" Tate persisted.

"What d'you think I'm talking about?" The kid was confused. "He fucked Megan and liked what he got."

"Are you saying she had a boyfriend in his forties?"

"Boyfriend?" Sammy laughed. "No, man. I'm saying she had a *customer.*"

"*What?*"

"Sure, she—"

The boy probably had twenty or thirty pounds on Tate but farmwork keeps you strong and in two seconds Sammy was flat on his back, the wind knocked out of him. Both hands were raised, protecting his face from Tate's lifted fist.

"What the fuck're you saying?" the lawyer raged.

Sammy shouting back, "No, man, no! I didn't do anything. Hey . . ."

"Are you saying she had sex for money?"

"No, I'm not saying nothing! I'm not saying a fucking thing!"

The girl's voice was close to his ear, the blonde he'd

first spoken to. "It's, like, not a big deal. It was a couple years ago."

"Couple years ago? She's only seventeen *now*, for Christ's sake." Tate lowered his hand. He stood up, brushed the dust off. He looked at the people in front of the bar, staring at him. The huge, bearded bouncer was amused. Bett was half out of the car, looking at her ex-husband with alarm. He motioned her to stay where she was.

Sammy said, "Fuck, man, what'd you do that for? I didn't fuck her. She gave it up a while ago. You asked me what I thought and I told you. I figured the guy liked what he had and wanted more. Jesus."

The girl said, "Sorry, mister. She had a thing for older men. They were willing to pay. But it was okay, you know."

"Okay?" Tate asked, numb.

"Sure. She always used rubbers."

Tate stared at her for a moment then walked back to the car.

Sammy stood up, picked up his beeper, which had fallen off his belt in the struggle. "Fuck you, man. *Fuck* you! Who're you anyway?"

Turning back, Tate snapped, "I'm her father."

"Father?" the boy asked, frowning.

"Yeah. Her father."

Sammy looked at the girl, who shrugged. The boy said, "Megan said she didn't have a father."

Tate frowned and Sammy continued, "She said he was a lawyer or something but he ran off and left her when she was six. She hasn't heard from him since."

• • •

In the car Tate asked angrily, "You didn't know she went there?"

"I told you I didn't. You think I'd *let* her go to a place like that?"

"I just think you might want to know where she was hanging out. From time to time."

"You 'just think.' You know when people say that?"

"What are you—?" he began.

"They say that when they mean, you damn well *ought* to know where she was."

"I didn't mean that at all," Tate snapped.

Though, of course, he had.

He sped out onto the highway, tires squealing, gravel flying from beneath the tires. Putting the Coffee Shop far behind them.

She finally asked, "What was that all about?"

He didn't answer.

"Tate? What were you fighting with that boy about?"

"You don't want to know," he said darkly.

"Tell me!"

He hesitated but then he had to say it. "He said he thought the guy in the gray car might've been a customer."

"Customer?"

"Of Megan's."

"What? . . . Oh, God. You don't mean . . . ?"

"That's exactly what I mean. That's what the boy said. And that girl too."

"Vile. You're disgusting . . ."

"Me? *I'm* just telling you what he said."

Tears coming down her face. "She wouldn't! There's no way. It's impossible."

"*They* didn't seem to think it was impossible. They seemed to think she did it pretty often."

"Tate! How can you say that?"

"And he said it was a couple years ago. When she was *fifteen*."

"She didn't. I'm certain."

A wave of fury consumed him. His hands cramped on the steering wheel. "How could you not know? What were you so busy doing that you didn't notice any condoms in your daughter's purse? Didn't you check who called her? Didn't you notice what time she got home? Maybe at midnight? At one? Two?"

"Stop it!" Bett cried. "Don't attack me. It's not true! It's a misunderstanding. We'll find her and she'll explain it."

"They seemed to think—"

She screamed, "It's a lie! It's just gossip. That's all it is! Gossip. Or they're talking about somebody else. Not Megan."

"Yes, Megan. And you should have—"

"Oh, you're blaming me? It isn't my fault! You know, you *might* have been more involved with her life."

"Me?" he snapped.

"Okay—sure, your happy family didn't turn out the way you wanted. Well, I'm sorry about that, Tate. But you could have checked on her once in a while."

"I did. I paid support every month—"

"Oh, for Christ's sake, I don't mean money. You know how often she'd ask me, Why doesn't Daddy like me? And I'd say, He does, he's just busy with all his cases. And I'd say, It's hard to be a real daddy when he and Mommy are divorced. And I'd say—"

"I spent Easters with her. And the Fourth of July."

"Yeah, and you should've heard the debriefings on *those* joyous holidays." Bett laughed coldly.

"What do you mean? She never complained."

"You have to *know* somebody before you complain to them."

"I took her shopping," he said. "I always asked her about school. I—"

"You could've done more. We might've made some accommodation. Might've been a little more of a family."

"Like hell," he spat out.

"People've done it. In worse situations."

"What was I supposed to do? Take up your slack?"

"This isn't about me," she snapped.

"Well, apparently it is. You're her mother. You want somebody else to fix what you've done? Or haven't done?"

"I've done the best I could!" Bett sobbed. "By myself."

"But it wasn't you yourself. It was you and the boyfriends."

"Oh, I was supposed to be celibate?"

"No, but you were supposed to be a mother first. You should've noticed that she had problems."

Tate couldn't help but think of Bett's sister, Susan. The woman had desperately wanted children, while Bett had always been indifferent to the idea. After her husband, Harris's, death Susan had moved in with a man very briefly—he was abusive and, from what Tate heard, half crazy. But he was a single man—divorced or widowed—with a child. And Susan put up with a lot of crap from him just to have the young boy around; she desperately wanted someone to mother. After they'd broken up, the lover had turned dangerous and stalked her but even at the worst moments Susan still seemed to regret the loss of that child in her life. Tate now wished Bett had shown some of that desire for Megan.

"I saw she was unhappy," Bett said. "But who the hell isn't? What was I supposed to do? Wave a magic wand?"

His anger wouldn't release the death grip it had on his heart. "Hell, that's probably exactly your idea of mothering. Sure. Or cast a spell, look up something in the *I Ching*. Read her tarot."

"Oh, stop it! I gave up all that shit years ago . . . I tried to be a good mother. I tried."

"Did you?" he was astonished to find himself saying. "You sure you weren't out looking for your King Arthur? Easier than changing diapers or helping her with homework or making sure when she was home after school. Making sure she wasn't fucking—"

"I tried . . . I tried . . ." Bett was sobbing, shaking.

Tate realized the car was nudging eighty. He slowed. A deep breath. Another.

Long, long silence. His eyes, too, welled up with tears. "Listen, I'm sorry."

"I tried. I wanted . . . I wanted . . ."

"Bett, please. I'm sorry."

"I wanted a family too, you know," she whispered, wiping her face on the sleeve of her blouse. "I saw the Judge and his wife and you and the rest of the Colliers.

I didn't talk about it the way you did but I wanted a family too. But then things happened . . . You know."

"I lost my temper. I don't . . . You're right. Those kids back there . . . it was probably just gossip."

But his words were flaccid. And, of course, they came far too late. The damage had been done. He wondered if they'd separate now and never speak to each other again. He supposed that would happen. He supposed that it would *have* to.

And oddly, he realized how much the idea upset him. No, it *terrified* him; he had no idea why.

A long moment passed.

Bett spoke first. He was surprised to hear her say, in a calm, reasoned voice, "Maybe it's true, Tate—what you heard about her. Maybe it is. And maybe part of it's my fault. But you know, people change. They can. They really can."

They continued on in silence. Bett closed her eyes and leaned her head back on the headrest.

What a man hears, he may doubt.

What he sees, he may possibly doubt.

"Bett? I am sorry."

What he does . . .

"Bett?"

But she didn't answer.

Chapter Fifteen

She decided she was safest here, in her cell.

If the father—Aaron Matthews—had wanted to kill her he could have done so easily. He didn't have to stash her away here, he didn't have to buy all the food. No, no, she had this funny sense that though he kidnapped her he didn't want to hurt her.

But the son . . . *He* was the threat. She needed protection from him. She'd stay here locked in Crazy Megan's padded cell until she figured out how to escape.

She opened one of the files she'd taken from Peter's room. In the dim light she scanned the pages, trying to find something that might help her. Maybe the hospital was near a town. Were there photos or brochures of the hospital and grounds? Maybe she could find a map. If she started a fire, people might see the smoke. Or maybe she'd find ventilation shafts or emergency exits.

She remembered a padlocked door marked *Basement* down one of the corridors nearby. If she could break the lock on the door, were there exits down there she might get through? She flipped through the documents, looking for a picture or photo of the hospital—trying to find basement windows or doors she might climb out of.

Damn, that's smart, says an impressed Crazy Megan.

Shhhh . . .

Megan happened to glance at the papers on the top of the pile.

. . . patient Victoria Skelling, 37, paranoid schizophrenic, was found dead in her room at 0620 hours, April 23. COD was asphyxia, from inhalation of mattress fibers. County police (see annexed report) investigated and declared the death suicide. It appeared patient Skelling gnawed through the canvas ducking of her mattress and pulled out wads of stuffing. She inhaled approximately ten ounces of this material, which lodged in her throat. The patient had been on Thorazine and Haldol, delusions were minimal. Orderlies described her in "good spirits" for much of the morning of her death but after spending the day on the grounds with a group of other patients she grew increasingly depressed and agitated. She complained that rats were coming to get her. They were going to chew her breasts off (earlier delusions and certain dreams centered around poisoned breast milk and suckling). She calmed again at dinnertime and spent the evening in the TV room. She was extremely upset when she went to bed and orderlies considered using restraints. She was given an extra dose of Haldol and locked into her room at 2200 hours. She said. "It's time to take care of the rats. They win, they win." She was found the next morning dead . . .

Gross, both Megan and C.M. think simultaneously. She flipped through more pages.

. . . Patient Matthews (No. 97–4335) was the last person to see her alive and he reported that she seemed "all spooky."

So Aaron Matthews's son, Peter, had been hospitalized here. And after the hospital was closed his father brought him back. Why, she couldn't guess. Maybe he felt at home here. Maybe his father broke him out of the hospital for the criminally insane to have him nearby.

She flipped through another report and learned that someone else had committed suicide.

. . . The body of Patient Garber (No. 78–7547) was found behind the main building. The police and coroner had determined that he had swallowed a garden hose and turned the water on full force. The pressure from the water ruptured his stomach and several feet of intestine. He died from internal hemorrhaging and shock. Although several patients were nearby when this happened (Matthews, No. 97–4335, and Ketter, No. 91–3212), they could offer no further information. The death was ruled suicide by the medical examiner.

Megan read through several other files. They were all similar—reports of patients killing themselves. One victim was found in the library. He'd apparently spent hours tearing apart books and magazines, looking for a sheet of paper sturdy enough to slice through the artery in his neck. He finally succeeded.

She shivered at the thought.

Someone else had leapt out of a tree and broken his neck. He didn't die but was paralyzed for life. When asked about why he'd done it he said, *"He'd been talking to 'some patients' and he realized how pointless life was, how he was never going to get better. Death would bring some peace."*

Yet another report stated, *"Patient Matthews was the last person to see victim alive."* The administrator wondered if he'd been involved and the boy had been interviewed and evaluated but no charges were brought.

Reading more, she found that not long after the last suicide a reporter from the *Washington Times* heard of the deaths and filed an investigative report. The state board of examiners looked into the matter and closed the hospital.

But Megan understood that the deaths weren't suicides at all. How could they have missed it? Peter Matthews had killed the other patients and somehow covered up the evidence to make the deaths look like suicide.

She flipped through the rest of the files and clippings.

Nothing she found told her anything helpful. She shoved them under the bed. What can I do? There has to—

Then she heard the footsteps.

Faint at first.

Oh, no . . . Peter was coming back up the hall.

Well, he'd missed her before.

Closer, closer. Very soft now, as if he was trying not to make any noise. But she heard his breathing and remembered the picture of the eerie-looking boy—his twisted mouth, the tip of his pale tongue in the corner of his lips. She remembered the stained sheets and wondered if he was walking around, looking for her, masturbating . . .

Megan shivered violently. Started to cry. She eased up to the door, put her head against it, listened.

No sounds from the other side.

Had he—?

A fierce pounding on the door. The recoil knocked her to her knees.

Another crash.

A whispered voice. "Megan . . ." And in that faint word she heard lust and desperation and hunger. "Megan . . ."

He knows I'm here . . . He knows who I am!

Peter was rattling the lock. A few loud slams of a brick or baseball bat on the padlock.

No, please . . . Why'd Matthews leave her alone with him? As much as she hated the doctor, Megan prayed he'd return.

"Megannnnnnn?" It now sounded as if the boy was laughing.

A sudden crash, into the door itself. Then another. And another. Suddenly a rusty metal rod— like the spears in his horrible comic books—cracked the wood and poked through a few inches. Just as Peter pulled the metal back out Megan leapt into the bathroom, plastered herself against the wall. She heard his breath on the door and she knew he was looking through the hole he'd made. Looking for her.

"Megan . . ."

But from that angle he couldn't see that there was a bathroom; the door was to the side.

For an eternity she listened to his lecherous breathing. Finally he walked off.

She started back into the room. But stopped.

Had he really gone? she wondered.

She decided she'd wait until dark. Peter might be outside and he'd see her. And if she plugged up the hole he'd know for certain she was there.

She sat on the toilet, lowered her head to her hands and cried.

Come on, girl. Get up.

I can't. No, I can't. I'm scared.

Of course you're scared, Crazy Megan chides. *But what's that got to do with anything? Lookit that. Lookit the bathroom window.*

Megan looked at the bathroom window.

No, it's nuts to think about it.

You know what you've got to do.

I can't do it, Megan thought. I just can't.

Yeah? What choice've you got?

Megan stood and walked to the window, reached through the bars and touched the filthy glass.

I can't.

Yes, you can!

Megan crawled back into the room, praying that Peter wasn't outside the door and looking through the peephole he'd made. She reached under the bed, sure she'd come up with a handful of rat. But no, she found only the manila file folder she'd been looking for. She returned to the bathroom and eased up to the window, pressed the folder against the glass. She drew back her fist and slugged the pane. The punch was hard but the glass held. She hit it again and this time a long crack spread from the top to the bottom of the window. Finally, another slug and the glass shattered. She pulled her fist back just as the sharp shards fell to the windowsill.

She picked a triangular piece of glass about eight inches long, narrow as a knife. Taking her cue from patient Victoria Skelling's sad end, Megan, using her teeth, ripped a strip off one of the mattress pads on the wall. She wound this around the base of the splinter to make a handle.

Good, C.M. says with approval. Proud of her other self.

No, better than good Megan reflected: *great.* Fuck you, Dr. Matthews. I feel *great!* It reminded her of how she'd felt when she'd written those letters to her parents in Dr. Hanson's office. It was scary, it hurt, but it was completely honest.

Great.

Crazy Megan wonders, *So what's next?*

"Fuck the kid up with the knife," Megan responded out loud. "Then get his keys and book on out of here."

Atta girl, C.M. offers. *But what about the dogs?*

They've got claws, *I've* got claws. Megan dramatically held up the glass.

Crazy Megan is impressed as hell.

"There's a van."

"A van?" Bett asked.

"Following us," Tate continued, as they drove past the Ski Chalet in Chantilly.

Bett started to turn.

"No, don't," he said.

She turned back. Looked at her hands, fingers tipped in faint purple polish. "Are you sure?"

"Pretty sure. A white van."

Tate made a slow circle through the shopping center then exited on Route 50 and sped east. He pulled into the Greenbriar strip mall, stopped at the Starbucks and climbed out. He bought two teas topped with foamed milk and returned to the car.

They sipped them for a moment and when a red Ford Explorer cut between his Lexus and the van he hit the gas and took off past a bookstore, streaking onto Majestic Lane and just catching the tail end of the light that put him back on Route 50, heading west this time.

When he settled into the right lane he noticed the white van was still with him.

"How'd he do that?" Tate wondered aloud.

"He's still there?"

"Yep. Hell, he's good."

They continued west, passing under Route 28, which was the dividing line between civilization here and the farmland that led eventually to the mountains.

"What're we going to do?"

But Tate didn't answer, hardly even heard the question. He was looking at a large sign that said, FUTURE HOME OF LIBERTY PARK . . .

He laughed out loud.

This was one of those odd things, noticing the sign at the same time the van was following them. A high-grade coincidence, he would have said. Bett—well, the old Bett—would of course have attributed it to the stars or the spirits or past lives or something. Didn't matter. He'd made the connection and at last he had a solid lead.

"What?" she cried, alarmed, responding both to his outrageous U-turn, skidding 180 degrees over the grassy median and the harsh laugh coming from his throat.

"I just figured something out. We're going to my place for a minute. I have to get something."

"Oh. What?"

"A gun."

Bett's head turned toward him then away. "You're serious, aren't you?"

"Oh, yep. Very serious."

Some years ago, when Tate had been prosecuting the improbable case of the murder of a Jamaican drug dealer at a Wendy's restaurant in suburban Burke, Konnie Konstantinatis had poked his head into Tate's office.

"Time you got yourself a piece."

"Of what?"

"Ha. You'll want a revolver 'cause all you do is point 'n' shoot. You're not a boy to mess with clips and safeties and stuff like that."

"What's a clip?"

Tate had been joking, of course—every commonwealth's attorney in Virginia was well versed in the lore of firearms—but the fact was he really didn't know guns well. The Judge didn't hold with weapons, didn't see any need for them and believed the countryside would be much more highly populated without weaponry.

But Konnie wouldn't take no for an answer and within a week Tate found himself the owner of a very unglamorous Smith & Wesson .38 Special, sporting six chambers, only five loaded, the one under the hammer being forever empty, as Konnie always preached.

This gun was locked away where it'd been for the past three or four years—in a trunk in Tate's barn. He now sped up his driveway and leapt out, observing that with his manic driving he'd lost the white van without intending to. He ran into the barn, found the key on his chain and after much jiggling managed to open the trunk. The gun, still coated with oil as he'd left it, was in a Ziploc bag. He took it out, wiped it clean and slipped it into his pocket.

In the car Bett asked him timidly, "You have it?" the way a college girl might ask her boyfriend if he'd brought a condom on a date.

He nodded.

"Is it loaded?"

"Oh." He'd forgotten to look. He took it out and fiddled with the gun until he remembered how to open it. Five silver eyes of bullets stared back from the cylinder.

"Yep."

He clicked it shut and put the heavy gun in his pocket.

"It's not going to just go off, is it? I mean, by itself."

"No." He noticed Bett staring at him. "What?" he asked, starting the engine of the Lexus.

"You're . . . you look scary."

He laughed coldly. "I *feel* scary. Let's go."

Manassas, Virginia, is this:

Big-wheeled trucks, sullen pick-a-fight teenagers (the description fitting both the boys and the girls), cars on the street and cars on blocks, Confederate stars 'n' bars, strip malls, PCP labs tucked away in the woods, concrete postwar bungalows, quiet mothers and skinny fathers struggling, struggling, struggling. It's domestic fights. It's women sobbing at Garth's concerts and teens puking at Aerosmith's.

And a little of it, very little, is Grant Avenue.

This is Doctors' and Lawyers' Row. Little Taras, Civil War mansions complete with columns and detached barns for garages, surrounded by expansive landscaped yards. It was to the biggest of these houses—a rambling white Colonial on four acres—that Tate Collier now drove.

"Who lives here?" Bett asked, cautiously eyeing the house.

"The man who knows where Megan is."

"Call Konnie," she said.

"No time," he muttered and he rolled up the drive, past the two Mercedeses—neither of them gray, he noticed—and skidded to a stop about five feet from the front door, nearly knocking a limestone lion off its perch beside the walk.

"Tate!"

But he ignored her and leapt from the car.

"Wait here."

The anger swelled inside him even more powerfully, boiling, and he found himself pounding fiercely on the door with his left hand, his right gripped around the handle of the pistol.

A large man opened the door. He was in his thirties, muscular, wearing chinos and an Izod shirt.

"I want to see him," Tate growled.

"Who are you?"

"I want to see Sharpe and I want to see him now."

Pull the gun now? Or wait for a more dramatic moment?

"Mr. Sharpe's busy right at the—"

Tate lifted the gun out of his pocket. He displayed it, more than brandished it, to the assistant or bodyguard or whatever he was. The man lifted his hands and backed up, alarm on his face. "Jesus Christ!"

"Where is he?"

"Hold on there, mister, I don't know who you are or what you're doing here but—"

"Jimmy, what's going on?" a voice called from the top of the stairs.

"Got a problem here, Mr. Sharpe."

"Tate Collier come a-calling," Jack Sharpe sang out. He glanced at the gun as if Tate were holding a butterfly net. "Collier, whatcha got yourself there?" He laughed. Cautious, sure. But it was still a laugh.

"Was he driving the white van?" Tate pointed the

gun at the man in the chinos, who lifted his hands. "Careful, sir, please!" he implored.

"It's okay, Jimmy," Sharpe called. "Just let him be. He'll calm down. What van, Collier?"

"You know what van," Tate said, turning back to Sharpe. "Was he the asshole driving?"

"Why'n't you put that thing away so's nobody gets hurt. And we'll talk . . . No, Jimmy, it's okay, really."

"I can shoot him if you want, Mr. Sharpe."

Tate glanced back and found himself looking into the muzzle of a very large pistol, chrome plated, held steadily in Jimmy's hand. It was an automatic, he noticed—with clips and safeties and all the rest of that *stuff*.

"No, don't do that," Sharpe said. "He's not going to hurt anybody. Collier, put it away. Be better for everybody."

Jimmy kept the gun pointed steadily at Tate's head.

Tate put his own pistol back into his pocket with a shaking hand.

"Come on upstairs."

"Should I come too, Mr. Sharpe?"

"No, I don't think we'll needya, Jimmy. Will we, Collier?"

"I don't think so," Tate said. "No."

"Come on up."

Tate, breathless after the adrenaline rush, climbed the stairs. He followed Jack Sharpe into a sunlit den. He glanced back and saw that Jimmy was still holding the shiny pistol pointed vaguely in Tate's direction.

Sharpe—wearing navy-blue polyester slacks and a

red golfing shirt—was now all business. No longer jokey.

"What the fuck's this all about, Collier?"

"Where's my daughter?"

"Your daughter? How should I know?"

"Who's driving the white van?"

"I assume you're saying that somebody's been following you."

"Yeah, somebody's been following me."

When Tate had seen the Liberty Park sign he'd remembered that his clients in that case had complained to him last week that private eyes had been following them. Tate'd told them not to worry—it was standard practice in big cases (though he added that they shouldn't do anything they wouldn't want committed to videotape). "Same as somebody's been following my clients. And probably my wife—"

"Thought you were divorced," Sharpe noted.

"How'd you know that?"

"Seem to remember something."

"So if you were following us—"

"*Me?*" Sharpe tried for innocence. It didn't take.

"—you've been following my daughter too. Who just happened to disappear today."

Sharpe slowly lifted a putter from a bag of golf clubs sitting in the corner of his study, addressed one of the dozen balls lying on the floor and sent it across the room. It missed the cup.

"I hire lawyers to fight my battles for me. As *you* well know, having decorated the walls of the courtroom with their hides recently. That's *all* I hire."

Tate asked, "No security consultants?"

"Ha, security consultants. That's good. Yeah, that's good. Well, no, Collier. There ain't no private eyes and no see-curity consultants on my payroll. Now, what's this about your daughter?"

"She's missing and I think you're behind it."

Another putt. He missed the cup again.

"Me? Why? Oh, I get it. To take you outta the running at the oral argument next Thursday down in Richmond, right?"

"Makes sense to me."

"Well, it *don't* make sense to me. I don't need to do that to beat you. You know, I fired those half-assed shysters you reamed at the trial. I got the big boys involved now. Lambert, Stone and Burns. They're gonna run right over you. Don't flatter yourself. They'll burn you up like Atlanta."

"Liberty Park, Sharpe. Tell me. How much'll you lose if it doesn't get built?"

"The park? It don't go through? I don't lose a penny." Then he smiled. "But the amount I won't *make* is to the tune of eighteen million. Say, ain't it unethical for you to be here without my lawyer being present?"

Tate said, "Where is she? Tell me."

"I don't know what you're talking about."

"Come on, Jack. You think I don't know about defendants harassing clients and lawyers so they'll drop cases?"

Sharpe ran his hand through his white hair. He sat down beneath a picture of himself on the eighteenth tee of the Bull Run Country Club, a place that proudly had not a single member who wasn't white and Protestant. Male too—though that went without saying.

"Collier, I don't kidnap people."

"But how about some of those little roosters that work for you? I wouldn't put it past a couple or three of them. That project manager of yours. Wilkins? He was in Lorton for eighteen months."

"For passing bad paper, Collier, not kidnapping girls."

"Who knows who they might've hired? Some psycho who *does* kidnap girls. And maybe likes it."

"Nobody hired nobody," Sharpe said, though Tate could see in his eyes that he was considering the possibility that one of his thugs had snatched Megan. But five seconds on the defensive was too much for Jack Sharpe. "Running outta patience here, Collier. And whatta I know—I'm just a country boy—but if I'm not mistaken isn't that slander or libel or some such you're spouting?"

"So file suit, Jack. But tell me where she is."

"You're barking up the wrong tree, Collier. You're gonna have to look elsewhere. You're not thinking clear. You know Prince William as good as your grandfather did before you. If you do a deal like Liberty Park you play hardball. That's the way business works in these parts. But for Christ's sake, this ain't southeast D.C. I'm not gonna hurt a seventeen-year-old girl. Now it's time for you to leave. I got work to do."

He sank the next putt into the small cup, which spit the ball back to him.

Tate, chin quivering with rage, stared back at the much calmer face of his opponent.

From the doorway, Jimmy asked calmly, "You want me to help him outside?"

Sharpe said, "Naw. Just show him to the door. Hey, so long, Counselor. See you in Richmond next Thursday. Hope you're rested and comfy. They're going to rub every inch of your skin off. It's gonna be pretty to watch."

Chapter Sixteen

Rhetoric, Plato wrote, is the universal art of winning the mind by argument.

Tate Collier, at eleven years of age, listened to the Judge recite that definition as the old man rasped a match to light his fragrant pipe and decided that one day he would "do rhetoric."

Whatever that meant.

He had to wait three years for the chance but finally, as a high school freshman, he argued (what else?) his way into Debate Club, even though it was open only to upperclassmen.

Tournament debating started in colonial America with the Spy Club at Harvard in the early 1700s and opened up to women a hundred years later with the Young Ladies Association at Oberlin, though hundreds of less formal societies, lyceums and bees had always been popular throughout the colonies. By the time Tate was in school, intercollegiate debate had become a practiced institution.

He argued in hundreds of National Debate Tournament bouts as well as the alternative-format—Cross Examination Debate Association—tournaments. He was a member of the forensic honorary fraternities—Delta Sigma Rho, Phi Rho Pi and Pi Kappa Delta—and was now as active in the American Forensics Association as he was in the American Bar Association.

In college—when it was fashionable to be antimilitary, antifrat, anti-ROTC—Tate shunned bell-bottoms and tie-dye for suits with narrow ties and white shirts. There he honed his technique, his logic, his reasoning. If . . . then . . . Major premise, minor premise, conclusion. Knocking down straw men, circular logic and *ad hominem* tactics by his opponents. He fought debaters from Georgetown and George Washington, from Duke and North Carolina and Penn and Johns Hopkins, and he beat them all.

With this talent (and, of course, with the Judge for a grandfather) law school was inevitable. At UVA he'd been the state moot court champion his senior year at the Federal Bar Moot Court Open in the District. Now he frequently taught well-attended appellate advocate continuing-ed courses, and his American Trial Lawyers' Association tape was a best-seller in the ABA catalogue.

When he'd been a senior at UVA and the champion debater on campus the Judge had traveled down to Charlottesville to see him. As predicted, he'd won the debate (it was the infamous pro-Watergate contest). The Judge told him that he'd heard someone in the audience say, "How's that Collier boy do it? He looks like a farm boy but when he starts to talk he's somebody else. It's like he's speaking in tongues."

No, there was no one Tate Collier would not match words with. Yet the incident with Sharpe had left him unnerved. He'd let emotions dictate what he'd said. What was happening to him? He was losing his orator's touch.

"I blew it," he muttered. And told Bett what had happened.

"Did he have anything to do with it?"

"I think he did, yeah. He was slick, too slick. He was expecting me. But he was also surprised about something."

"What?"

"I think something happened he hadn't planned on. It's true. I don't think his boys would kidnap Megan themselves. But I think they hired somebody to do it. Oh, and he knew we were divorced and that Megan was seventeen. Why would he know that if he hadn't looked into our lives?"

"Are you going to tell Konnie?"

"Oh, sure I am. But people like Sharpe are good. They don't leave loose ends. You follow the trails and they vanish."

She picked up the pistol, which he'd set on the dashboard. She slipped it in the glove compartment distastefully. "Aren't we a pair, Tate? Guns, private eyes."

He said, "Bett, I'm sorry. About before."

She shook her head. "No," she said firmly. "There was truth in what you said."

They drove in silence for several moments.

She sighed then asked reflectively, "Do you like your life?"

He glanced at her. Responded: "Sure."

"Just sure?"

"How much more can you be than sure?"

"You can be convincing," she said.

"What's life," he asked, "but ups and downs?"

"You ever get lonely?"

Ah, there's a question for you. . . . Sometimes the women would stay the night, sometimes they'd leave. Sometimes they decided to return to their husbands or lovers or leave him for other men, sometimes they'd talk about getting divorced and sometimes they were single, unattached and waiting for a ring. Sometimes they'd introduce Tate to their parents or their cautious-eyed children or, if they had none, talk about how much they wanted youngsters. A boy first, they'd invariably say, and then a girl.

They all faded from his life and, yes, most nights he *was* lonely.

"I keep pretty busy," he said. "You?"

She said quickly, "I'm busy too. Everybody needs interior design."

"Sure," he agreed. "Things working out well with Brad?"

"Oh, Brad's a dear. He's a real gentleman. You don't see many of them. You were one. I mean, you still are." She laughed. "You know, I keep expecting to see you on Court TV," she said. "Prosecuting serial killers or terrorists or something. Channel Nine loved you. You gave great interviews."

"Those were the days."

"Why'd you quit practice?"

He kept his hands at ten to two on the wheel and his eyes straight ahead.

"Tate?" she repeated.

"Prosecuting's a young man's game," he said. Thinking he was the epitome of credibility.

But Bett said, "That's *an* answer. But not *the* answer."

"I didn't quit practice."

"You know what I mean. You were the best in the state. Remember those rumors that you'd get that job you wanted?"

Solicitor general—the lawyer who represented the government in cases before the Supreme Court—the most important forensic orator in the country. Tate's grandfather had always hoped his grandson might get that job. And Tate himself had for years had his sights on that job.

"I wanted to spend more time on the farm."

"Bullshit." Well, this was *definitely* a new Bett McCall. The ethereal angel had come to earth with muddy cheeks. "Why won't you tell me?"

"Okay. I lost my taste for blood," he explained. "I prosecuted a capital case. I won. And I wished I hadn't."

Bett had been deeply ashamed that while they were married Tate had sent six men to death row in Jarratt, Virginia. Her horror at this achievement had always seemed ironic to him for she believed in the immortality of souls and Tate did not.

"He was innocent?" she asked.

"No, no. It was more complicated than that. He killed the victim. There was no question about that. But he was probably only guilty of manslaughter at best. Criminally negligent homicide, most likely. The defense offered a plea—probation and counseling.

I rejected it and went for lethal injection. The jury gave him life imprisonment. The first week he was in prison, he was killed by other inmates. Actually"—his voice caught—"he was tortured and then he died."

"God, Tate."

What a man hears, he may doubt . . .

"I talked him to death, Bett. I conjured the jurors. I had the *gift* on my side, not the law. And he's dead when he shouldn't be. If he'd been out of prison, had some help, he'd be alive now and probably a fine person."

But what he does, he cannot doubt.

He waited for her disgust or anger.

But she said only, "I'm sorry." He looked at her and saw not pity or remorse but simple regret at his pain. "They fired you? The commonwealth's attorney's office?"

"Oh, no. No. I just quit."

"I never heard about it."

"Small case. Not really newsworthy. The story died on the Metro page."

Staring at the road, Tate confessed, "You know something?"

He felt Bett's head turn toward him.

He continued, "I wanted to tell you about what happened. When I heard that he'd died I reached for the phone to call you—before anybody else. Even before Konnie. I hadn't seen you in over a year. Two years maybe. But you were the one I wanted to tell."

"I wish you had."

He chuckled. "But you hated me taking capital cases."

There was a long pause. She said, "Seems to me you've served enough time over that one. 'Most everybody gets a parole hearing, don't they?" As Tate signaled to make the turn for Bett's exit she said, "Could we just drive a bit? I don't feel like going home."

His hand wavered over the signal stem. He clicked it off.

Chapter Seventeen

Tate piloted his Lexus back through Centreville, which some of the redder of the rednecks around these parts disparagingly called New Calcutta and New Seoul—because of the immigrants settling here. He made a long loop around Route 29 and turned down a deserted country road.

The sun was low now but the heat seemed worse. The sour, sickly aroma of rotting leaves from last year's autumn was in the air.

"Tate," Bett asked slowly, "what if nothing happened?"

"Nothing happened?"

"What if nobody kidnapped her? What if she really did run off? Because she hates us."

He glanced at her.

She continued, "If we find her—"

"*When* we find her," he corrected.

"What if she's so mad at us that she won't come home?"

"We'll convince her to," he told her.

"Could you do it, do you think? Talk her into coming back home?"

Can I? he wondered.

There's a transcendent moment in debate when your opponent has the overwhelming weight of logic and facts on his side and yet still you can win. By leading him in a certain direction you get him to build his entire argument on what appears to be an irrefutable foundation, the logic of which is flawless. But which you nonetheless destroy at the same time as you accept the perfection of his argument.

It's a moment, Tate tells his classes, just like in fencing, when the red target of a heart is touched lightly with the button of the foil while the fencer's attention is elsewhere. No flailing away, no chops or heavy strokes, but a simple, deadly tap the opponent never sees coming.

All cats see in the dark.

Midnight is a cat.

Therefore Midnight can see in the dark.

Irrefutable. The purest of logic.

Unless . . . Midnight is blind.

But what kind of argument could he make to convince Megan to return home?

He thought about the two letters she'd written and he didn't have any thoughts at all; he saw only her perfect anger.

"We'll get her back," he told Bett. "I'll do that. Don't worry."

Bett pulled down the makeup mirror in the sun visor to apply lipstick. Tate was suddenly taken back to the night they met—at that party in Charlottesville. He'd driven her home afterward and had spent a passionate half hour in the front seat of the car removing every trace of her pink Revlon.

Five weeks later he'd suggested they move in together.

A two-year romance on campus. He'd graduated from law school the year Bett got her undergraduate degree. They left idyllic Charlottesville for the District of Columbia and his clerkship at federal District Court; Bett got a job managing a New Age bookstore. They lived the bland, easy life that Washington offered a young couple just starting out. Tate's consolation was his job and Bett's that she finally was close to her twin sister, who lived in Baltimore and had been too ill to travel to Charlottesville.

Married in May.

His antebellum plantation built the next spring.

Megan born two years later.

And three years after that, he and Bett were divorced.

When he looked back on their relationship his perfect memory was no longer so perfect. What he recalled seemed to be merely sharp peaks of an island that was the tip of a huge undersea mountain range. The wispy, ethereal woman he'd seen at the party, singing a sailor's mournful song of farewell. Walks in the country. Driving through the Blue Ridge toward Massanutten Mountain. Making love in a forest near the Luray Caverns. Tate had always enjoyed being out of doors—the cornfields, the beach, backyard barbecues. But Bett's interest in the outside arose only at dusk. "When the line between the worlds is at its thinnest," she'd told him once, sitting on the porch of an inn deep in the Appalachians.

"What worlds?" he asked.

"Shhh, listen," she'd said, enchanting him even while

he knew it was an illusion. Which was, he supposed, irrefutable proof of her ability to cast a spell. Betty Sue McCall, devoted to her twin sister, with whom she had some mystical link that unnerved even rationalist Tate, reedy folk singer, collector of the unexplained, the arcane, the invisible . . . Tate had never figured out if her sublime mystique magnified their love falsely, or obscured it, or indeed if it was the essence of their love.

Magic . . .

In the end, of course, it didn't matter, for they separated completely, moved far away from each other emotionally. She became for him what she'd been when he was first captivated by her: the dark woman of his imagination.

Today she prodded her face in the mirror, rubbed at some invisible blemish as he remembered her doing many times. She'd always been terribly vain.

She flipped the mirror back.

"Pull over, Tate."

He glanced at her. No, it was not an imperfection she'd been examining; she'd been crying again.

"What is it?"

"Just pull over."

He did, into the Park Service entrance to the Bull Run Battlefield.

Bett climbed from the car and walked up the gentle slope. Tate followed and when they were on level ground they stopped and simultaneously lifted their eyes toward the tumultuous clouds overhead.

"What is it, Bett?" He watched her stare at the night sky. "Looking for an angel to help you decide something?"

Suddenly he was worried that she'd take offense at this—an implicit reference to her flighty side—though he hadn't meant it sardonically.

But she only smiled and lowered her eyes from the sky. "I was never into that angel stuff. Too Hallmark card, you know. But I wouldn't mind a spirit or two."

"Well," he said, "this'd be the place. General Jackson came charging out of those trees right over there and stopped the Union boys cold in their tracks. Right here's where he earned himself the name Stonewall." The low sun glistened off the Union cannons' black barrels in the distance.

Bett turned, took his hands and pulled him to her. "Hold me, Tate. Please."

He put his arms around her—for the first time in years. They stood this way for a long moment. Then found a bench and sat. He kept his arm around her. She took his other hand. And Tate wished suddenly, painfully, that Megan were here with them. The three of them together and all the hard events of the past dead and buried, like the poor bodies of the troops who'd died bloody and broken on this very spot.

Wind in the trees, billowing clouds overhead.

Suddenly a streak of yellow flashed past them.

"Oh, what's that?" Bett said. "Look."

He glanced at the bird that alighted near them.

"That'd be, let me see, a common yellowthroat. Nests on the ground and feeds in the tree canopy."

Her laugh scared it away. "You know all these *facts*. Where do you learn them?"

A girlfriend, age twenty-three, had been a bird-watcher.

"I read a lot," he said.

More silence.

"What are you thinking?" she wondered after a moment.

A question women often ask when they find themselves in close contact with a man and silence descends.

"Unfinished business?" he suggested. "You and me?"

She considered this. "I used to think things were finished between us. But then I started to look at it like doing your will before you get on a plane."

"How's that?"

"If you crash, well, maybe all the loose ends're tied up but wouldn't you still rather hang around for a little while longer?"

"There's a metaphor for you." He laughed.

She spent a moment examining the sky again. "When you argued before the Supreme Court five or six years ago. That big civil rights case. And the *Post* did that write-up on you. I told everybody you were my ex-husband. I was proud of you."

"Really?" He was surprised.

"You know what occurred to me then, reading about you? It seemed that when we were married you were my voice. I didn't have one of my own."

"You were quiet, that's true," he said.

"That's what happened to us, I think. Part of it anyway. I had to find mine."

"And when you went looking . . . so long. No half measures for you. No compromises. No bargaining."

The old Bett would have grown angry or dipped into her enigmatic silence at these critical words. But she merely nodded in agreement. "That was me, all right. I was so rigid. I had all the right answers. If something wasn't just perfect I was gone. Jobs, classes . . . husband. Oh, Tate, I'm not proud of it. But I felt so young. When you have a child, things do change. You become more . . ."

"Enduring?"

"That's it. Yes. You always know the right word."

He said, "I never had any idea what you were thinking about back then."

Bett's thoughts might have been on what to make for dinner. Or King Arthur. Or a footnote in a term paper. She might have been thinking of a recent tarot card reading.

She might even have been thinking about him.

"I was always afraid to say anything around you, Tate. I always felt tongue-tied. Like I had nothing to say that interested you."

"I don't love you for your oratorical abilities." He paused, noting the tense of the verb. "I mean, that's not what attracted me to you."

Then reflected: Oh, she's so right—what she'd said earlier . . . We humans have this terrible curse; we alone among the animals believe in the possibility of change—in ourselves and those we love. It can kill us and maybe, just maybe, it can save our doomed hearts. The problem is we never know, until it's too late, which.

"You know when I missed you the most?" she said finally. "Not on holidays or picnics. But when I was in Belize—"

"What?" Tate asked suddenly.

She waved lethargically at a yellow jacket. "You know, you and I always talked about going there."

They'd read a book about the Mayan language and the linguists who trooped through the jungles in Belize on the Yucatán to examine the ruins and decipher the Indian code. The area had fascinated them both and they planned a trip. But they'd never made the journey. At first they couldn't afford it. Tate had just graduated from law school and started working as a judge's clerk for less money than a good legal secretary could make. Then came the long, long hours in the commonwealth's attorney's office. After that, when they had the money saved up, Bett's sister had a serious relapse and nearly died; Bett couldn't leave home. Then Megan came along. And three years after that they were divorced.

"When did you go?" he asked.

"Three years ago January. Didn't Megan tell you?"

"No."

"I went with Bill. The lobbyist?"

Tate shook his head, not remembering who he was. He asked, "Have a good time?"

"Oh, yeah," she said haltingly. "Very nice. It was hotter than Hades. Really hot."

"But you like the heat," he remembered. "Did you see the ruins?"

"Well, Bill wasn't into ruins so much. We did see one. We took a day trip. I . . . Well, I was going to say—I wished you'd been with me."

"Two years ago February," Tate said.

"What?"

"I was there too."

"No! Are you serious?" She laughed hard. "Who'd *you* go with?"

Her face grew wry when it took him a moment to remember the name of his companion.

"Cathy."

He *believed* it was Cathy.

"Did *you* get to the ruins?"

"Well, we didn't exactly. It was more of a sailboarding trip. I don't believe it . . . Damn, how 'bout that. We finally got down there. We talked about that vacation for years."

"Our pilgrimage."

"Great place," he said, wondering how dubious his voice sounded. "Our hotel had a really good restaurant."

"It was fun," she said enthusiastically. "And pretty."

"Very pretty," he confirmed. The trip had been agonizingly dull.

Her face was turned toward a distant line of trees. She was thinking probably of Megan now, and the Yucatán had slipped far from her thoughts.

"Let me take you home," he said. "There's nothing more we can do tonight. We should get some rest. I'll call Konnie, tell him about Sharpe."

She nodded.

They drove to Fairfax and he pulled up in front of her house. She sat in the front seat in silence for a while.

"You want to come in?" she asked suddenly.

His answer was balanced on the head of a pin and for a long moment he didn't have a clue which way it was going to tilt.

Tate pulled her to him, hugged her, smelled the scent of Opium perfume in her hair. He said, "Better not."

Chapter Eighteen

Crazy Megan reveals her true self.

She isn't crazy at all and never has been. What C.M. is is furious.

He's going down, she mutters. *This asshole Peter is going down hard.*

Megan McCall was angry too but she was much less optimistic than her counterpart as she moved cautiously through the corridors of the hospital, clutching three boxes of plastic dining utensils under her arm and her glass knife in the other.

Though she was feeling better physically, having eaten half a box of her favorite cereal—Raisin Bran—and drunk two Pepsis.

Listening.

There!

She heard a shuffle, a few steps of Peter's feet. Maybe a whisper of breath.

Another shuffle. A voice.

Was he muttering her name?

Yes, no?

She couldn't tell.

This could be it! Got a good grip on the knife?

Be quiet! Megan thought. She shivered and felt a

burst of nausea from the fear. Wished she hadn't eaten so fast. *If I puke he'll hear and that'll be it . . .*

She inhaled slowly.

A clunk nearby. More footsteps. These were close.

Megan gasped and closed her eyes, remaining completely still, huddling behind an orange fiberglass chair.

She pressed into the wall and began mentally working her way through Janis Joplin's *Greatest Hits* album line by line. She cried noiselessly throughout "Me and Bobby McGee," then grew defiant once more when she mind-sang "Down on Me."

Peter Matthews wandered away, back toward his room, and she continued on. Ten endless minutes later she made it to the end of the corridor she'd decided to use.

It was here that she was going to lay the trap.

She needed a dead end—she had to be sure of which direction he'd come from. Crazy Megan points out, though, that it also means she'll have no escape route if the trap doesn't work.

Who's the pussy now? Megan asked.

Like, excuse me, C.M. snaps in response. *Just letting you know.*

She rubbed her hand over the wall.

Sheetrock.

Megan had recalled one time she'd been at her father's house. A few years ago. He'd been dating a woman with three children. As usual he'd been thinking about marrying her—he *always* did that, it was *so* weird—and had gone so far as to actually hire a contractor to divide the downstairs bedroom into two smaller ones for her young twins. Halfway through the project they'd broken up; the construction went unfinished but Megan recalled watching the contractors easily slice through the Sheetrock with small saws. The material had seemed as insubstantial as cardboard.

She took a plastic dinner knife from the box. It was like a toy tool. And for a moment the hopelessness of her plan overwhelmed her. But then she started to cut. Yes! In five minutes she'd sliced a good-sized slit into the wall. The blades were sharper than she'd expected.

For about fifteen minutes the cutting went well. Then, almost all at once, the serrated edge of the knife wore smooth and dull. She tossed it aside and took a new one. Started cutting again.

She lowered her head to the plasterboard and inhaled its stony moist smell. It brought back a memory of Joshua. She'd helped him move into his cheap apartment near George Mason University. The workmen were fixing holes in the walls with plasterboard and this smell reminded her of his studio. Tears flooded into her eyes.

What're you doing? an impatient Crazy Megan asks.

I miss him, Megan answered silently.

Shut up and saw. Time for that later.

Cutting, cutting . . . Blisters formed on the palm of her right hand. She ignored them and kept up the hypnotic motion. Resting her forehead against the Sheetrock, smelling mold and wet plaster. Hand moving back and forth by itself. Thoughts tumbling . . .

Thinking about her parents.

Thinking about bears . . .

No, bears can't talk. But that didn't mean you couldn't learn something from them.

She thought of the *Whispering Bears* story, the illustration in the book of the two big animals watching the town burn to the ground. Megan thought about the point of the story. She liked her version better than Dr. Matthews's; the moral to her was: people fuck up.

But it didn't have to be that way. Somebody in the village could have said right up front, "Bears can't talk. Forget about 'em." Then the story would have ended: "And they lived happily ever after."

Working with her left hand now, which was growing a crop of its own blisters. Her knees were on fire and her forehead too, which she'd pressed into the wall for leverage. Her back also was in agony. But Megan McCall felt curiously buoyant. From the food and caffeine inside her, from the simple satisfaction of cutting through the wall, from the fact that she was doing *something* to get out of this shithole.

Megan was thinking too about what she'd do *when* she got out.

Dr. Matthews had tricked her—to get her to write those letters. But the awesome thing was that what she'd written had been true. Oh, she *was* pissed at her parents. And those bad feelings had been bottled up in her forever, it seemed. But now they were out. They weren't gone, no, but they were buzzing around her head, getting smaller, like a blown-up balloon you let go of. And she had a thought: The anger goes away; the love doesn't. Not if it's real. And she thought maybe, just maybe—with Tate and Bett—the love might be real. Or at least she might unearth a patch of real love. And once she understood that she could recall other memories.

Thinking of the time she and her father went to Pentagon City on a spur-of-the-moment shopping spree and he'd let her drive the Lexus back home, saying only, "The speedometer stops at one forty and you pay any tickets yourself." They'd opened the sunroof and laughed all the way home.

Or the time she and her mother went to some boring New Age lecture. After fifteen minutes Bett had whispered, "Let's blow this joint." They'd snuck out the back door of the school, found a snow saucer in the playground and huddled together on it, whooping and screaming all the way to the bottom of the hill. Then they'd raced each other to Starbucks for hot chocolate and brownies.

And she even thought of her sweet sixteen party, the only time in—how long?—five, six years she'd seen her parents together. For a moment they'd stood close to each other, near the buffet table, while her father gave this awesome speech about her. She'd cried like crazy, hearing his words. For a few minutes they seemed like a perfectly normal family.

If I get home, she now thought . . . No, *when* I get home, I'll talk to them. I'll sit down with them. Oh, I'll give 'em fucking hell but then I'll *talk*. I'll do what I should've done a long time ago.

The anger goes away; the love doesn't . . .

A blister burst. Oh, that hurt. Oh, Jesus. She closed her eyes and slipped her hand under her arm and pressed hard. The sting subsided and she continued to cut.

After a half hour Megan had cut a six-by-three-foot hole in the Sheetrock. She worked the piece out and rested it against the floor then leaned against the wall for a few minutes, catching her breath. She was sweating furiously.

The hole was ragged and there was plaster dust all over the floor. She was worried that Peter would see it and guess she'd set a trap for him. But the window at this end of the corridor was small and covered with grease and dirt; very little light made it through. She doubted that the boy would ever see the trap until it was too late.

She snuck back to where his father—or someone— had bricked up the entrance to the administration area of the hospital and, quietly, started carting cinder blocks back to the trap, struggling under their weight. When she'd lugged eight bricks back to the corridor she began stacking them in the hole she'd cut, balancing them on top of one another, slightly off center.

Megan then used her glass knife and sliced strips off the tail of her shirt. She knotted them into a ten-foot length of rope and tied one end to one of the blocks in the stack. Finally she placed the piece of Sheetrock back in the opening and examined her work. She'd lead Peter back here and when he walked past the trap she'd pull the rope. A hundred pounds of concrete would crash down on top of him. She'd leap on him with the knife and stab him—she decided she couldn't kill him but would slash his hands and feet— to make sure he couldn't attack or chase her. Then she'd demand the keys and run like hell.

Megan walked softly down to the main corridor

and looked back. Couldn't see anything except the tail of rope.

Now, she just needed some bait.

"Guess that's gonna be us, right?" she asked, speaking out loud, though in a whisper.

Who else? Crazy Megan answers.

Bett McCall poured herself a glass of chardonnay and kicked her shoes off.

She was so accustomed to the dull thud of the bass and drums leaching through the floor from Megan's room upstairs that the absence of the sound of Stone Temple Pilots or Santana brought her to tears.

It's so *frustrating,* she thought. People can deal with almost anything if they can *talk* about it. You argue. You make up and live more or less comfortably for the rest of your lives. Or you discover irreconcilable differences and you slowly separate into different worlds. Or you find that you're soul mates. But if the person you love is physically gone—if you *can't* talk— then you have less than nothing. It's the worst kind of pain.

The house hummed and tapped silently. A motor somewhere clicked, the computer in the next room emitted a pitch slightly higher than the refrigerator's.

The sounds of alone.

Maybe she'd take a bath, Bett thought. No, that would remind her of the soap dish Megan was going to give her. Maybe—

The phone rang. Heart racing, she leapt for it. Praying that it was Megan. Please . . . Please . . . Let it be her. I want to hear her voice so badly.

Or at least Tate.

But it was neither. Disappointed at first, she listened to the caller, nodding, growing more and more interested in what she heard. "All right," she said. "Sure . . . No, a half hour would be fine . . . Thank you. Really, thank you."

After she hung up she dropped heavily into the couch and sipped her wine.

Wonderful, she thought, feeling greatly relieved after talking to him for only three minutes. The caller was Megan's other therapist—a colleague of Dr. Hanson's, a doctor named Bill Peters, and he was coming over to speak to her about the girl. He didn't have any specific news. But he wanted to talk to her about her daughter's disappearance. He'd sounded so reassuring, so comforting.

She was curious only about one thing that the doctor had said during his call. Why did he want to see her alone? Without Tate there?

III

THE DEVIL'S ADVOCATE

Chapter Nineteen

"When you called," Bett McCall confessed, "I was a little uneasy."

"Of course," the man said, walking into the room. Dr. Bill Peters seemed confident, comfortable with himself. He had a handsome face. His eyes latched onto Bett's and radiated sympathy. "What a terrible, terrible time for you."

"It's a nightmare."

"I'm so sorry." He was a tall man but walked slightly stooped. His arms hung at his side. A benign smile on his face. Bett McCall, short and slight, was continually aware of the power of body stature and posture. Though she was a foot shorter and much lighter, she felt—from his withdrawing stance alone—that he was one of the least threatening men she'd ever met.

He looked approvingly at the house. "Megan said you were a talented interior designer. I didn't know quite *how* talented, though."

Bett felt a double burst of pleasure. That he liked her painstaking efforts to make her house nice. But, much more significant to her, that Megan had actually complimented her to a stranger.

Then the memory of the letter came back and her

mood darkened. She asked, "Have you heard about Dr. Hanson? That terrible thing with his mother?"

Dr. Peters's face clouded. "It's got to be a mix-up. I've known him for years." He glanced at a crystal ball on her bookshelf. "He's been an advocate for assisted suicide and I think he *did* talk about it with his mother."

"You do?"

"But I think she misinterpreted what he said. You know that a nurse said his mother lifted the hypodermic off a medicine cart."

Bett considered this. Maybe Tate had been wrong about somebody framing Dr. Hanson to get him into jail and unavailable to speak to them.

"Doctor . . ."

"Oh, call me Bill. Please."

"Is he a good therapist? Dr. Hanson?"

The therapist examined a framed tapestry from France, mounted above the couch.

Why was he hesitating to answer?

"He's very good, yes," Dr. Peters said after a moment. "In certain areas. What was *your* impression of him?"

"Well," she said, "we've never met."

"You haven't?" He seemed surprised. "He hasn't talked to you about Megan?"

"No. Should he have?"

"Well, maybe with his mother's accident . . . he's had a lot on his mind."

"But that just happened this week," Bett pointed out. "Megan's been seeing him for nearly two months."

In his face she could see that he couldn't really defend his friend.

"Well, frankly, I think he *should* have talked to you. I would have. But he and I have very different styles. Mrs. McCall—"

"Bett, please."

"Betty?"

"Betty Sue." She smiled, and then blushed. Hoped he couldn't see it, thankful for the dimmed lighting. "All right . . . Deep, dark secret? The name's *Beatrice* Susan McCall. My sister—"

"Your twin. Megan told me."

"That's right. She's Susan Beatrice. We were named dyslexically. I can't tell you how many years we plotted revenge against Mom and Dad for *that* little trick."

He laughed. "Say, could I trouble you for a glass of water?"

"Of course."

She noticed that he examined her briefly—the tight black jeans and black blouse. Wild earrings dangled; crescent moons and shooting stars. She started toward the kitchen. "Come on in here. Would you rather have a soda? Or wine?"

"No, thanks . . . Oh, look." He picked up a bottle of Mietz merlot, which Brad had bought for them last week and they hadn't gotten around to drinking yet. He glanced at the eighteen-dollar price tag. "Funny, I just bought a case of this. It's a wonderful wine. Eighteen's a great price. I paid twenty-one a bottle— and that was supposed to be a discount."

"You know the vineyard? Brad said it's real hard to find."

"It is."

She said, "Let's open it."

"You're sure?"

"Yep." Bett was happy to impress him. She opened and poured the wine. They touched glasses.

"Do you live in the area?" she asked.

"In Fairfax. Near the courthouse. It's a nice place. Only . . . there're a lot of law offices around there and I get these lawyers coming and going at all hours. Drives me crazy sometimes."

She gave a brief laugh. He lifted an eyebrow. She'd been thinking of all the nights Tate had spent in that very neighborhood, interviewing prisoners and police and getting home at ten or eleven. "Tate—"

"Your ex."

"Right. I'm afraid he's one of them. Working late, I mean."

"Oh, that's right. Megan told me he was an attorney. But he doesn't live in Fairfax, does he? Didn't she tell me he's got a farm somewhere?"

"Prince William. But his office is here."

Dr. Peters smiled and examined the collection of refrigerator magnets that she and Megan had collected. It pinched her heart to see them. And she had to look away before the tears started.

He asked her some questions about the interior design business in Virginia. It turned out his mother had been a decorator.

"Where?" she asked.

"Boston."

"No kidding! That's where the McCalls are from." She pointed to some pictures of her family in front of *Old Ironsides* and in their front yard, the Prudential building towering over the skyline in the background.

"Sure," he said. "I thought I detected a bit of accent. I'm driving the cah to the pahty . . ."

She laughed.

"You miss it?" he asked.

"No. We moved here when I was ten. The South definitely appeals to me more than New England."

"To the extent this is the South," he offered.

"That's true."

He took her glass and refilled it. He handed it back and leaned against the island, glanced at the expensive stainless-steel utensils. "I love to cook," he said. "It's a hobby of mine."

"Me too. It's relaxing to open some wine, come out to the kitchen and start slicing and dicing."

He lifted the heavy Sabatier butcher knife and tested the edge carefully with his thumb. Nodded. "Sharp knives are—"

"—safer than dull ones," she said. "My mother taught me that."

"Mine too," he said, weighing the knife in his hand for a moment, studying the blade carefully. Then he set it on the table. "Should we go back in the other room?"

"Sure."

He nodded toward the door. She preceded him into the living room. Bett sat on the couch and he walked over to the bookshelves, looked at her collection of crystals and several boxes of tarot cards.

He chided, "Didn't you know you're supposed to keep your tarot cards wrapped in silk?"

"You *know* about that?" She laughed.

"Sure do."

"I was really into the occult a long time ago." She smiled and realized that she was relaxing for the first time all day. "I was kind of crazy when I was young."

"You look embarrassed. You shouldn't be. I think our spiritual side's as important as our physical and our psychic sides. I use a holistic approach in my treatment. A lot of times I'll prescribe herbs—they have both organic and psychosomatic effects."

"I try to use them whenever I can," Bett said.

"If my patients need *something* I'd rather it was Saint-John's-wort instead of Prozac."

He was a *doctor* who felt this way? How often had she explained these things to doctors, or to friends, or to *Tate,* only to be met with a politely wary gaze—at best.

Dr. Peters continued. "It makes a lot of sense to me. Take tarot cards . . . do they predict the future? Well, in a way they do. They make us look at who we are, where we fit in with the godhead or the Oversoul—"

"Oh, you know Emerson?" she asked, pointing to a book of his writings.

Dr. Peters walked to it and pulled the volume off the shelf. He flipped through it, held up the book and showed her the title of an essay, "The Oversoul." "I've been reading him since college . . . I think fortune-telling makes us look at where we fit in with the life force, what our relationships are like, makes us question where we're going. That *has* to affect our future."

"That's true," she said, feeling warm and comfortable. She sipped more wine. "That's what I've always felt. Most people don't get it. They just make fun of the Madame Zostra's fortune-telling stuff. It's not fair. My ex . . ."

But she decided to let the thought die. And Dr. Peters didn't push her to finish.

The doctor was looking at her bookshelf, head cocked sideways. Pointing out volumes. "Ah, Joseph Campbell. That's very good. Sure, sure . . . You know Jung?"

"Sort of, not really."

"About the archetypes? There are certain persistent myths we see surfacing in people's lives. The Arthurian legend—you know it?"

Know it? she thought, laughing to herself. I lived it.

"T. H. White, Camelot, the whole thing." She pointed out an old copy of *The Once and Future King*.

"What a book that is," he said. "Oh, and *The Mists of Avalon,*" nodding at the book.

"The best," she said enthusiastically. Remembering how Tate didn't have time for any of this. She found the old angers and resentments churning up again and recalled how much comfort she'd found in the New Age world. Here was a man who truly understood her. It was so refreshing . . .

Dr. Peters tapped his glass to hers and they sipped. Her glass was nearly empty. Yet she didn't feel drunk, she felt elated. He sat down close to her. "Um, Bett . . . I don't know how much Megan told you about me."

"Nothing, really. But she didn't want to talk about her therapy sessions. That's what we were going to do today, Tate and I. Meet her for lunch and find out how it was going."

He nodded. He was really quite a handsome man,

well built. Interior designer Bett McCall thought: Proportions are everything.

"Dr. Hanson saw her more frequently than I did. But I wanted to come over tonight and just talk to you about her a little. Try to reassure you."

Oh, I'll take that. Anything you want to give me in the reassurance department, I'll take.

"Have you heard anything from her?" he asked.

"Not a word. But there are some funny things going on."

"What sort of things?"

"We think maybe somebody was following her. My husband . . . my ex-husband thinks it might have to do with a case he's working on. He thinks the man he's suing is trying to distract him or something. I don't know."

"Any . . . what would they say on *NYPD Blue*? Any concrete leads?"

"Not really. But Tate's been in touch with a friend of his at the police."

"Oh, is that the detective who called me? He asked me a few questions about Megan. Um, what's his name again?"

"Konstantinatis."

"Right. Well," he continued, pouring more wine, "I think you should know what I told him."

"What's that?"

"That I don't think she's in any danger."

"Oh, did she say something to you about running away?" Bett asked quickly. "You'd tell me if she did."

"Ordinarily that'd be confidential. But . . . yes, I would tell you. And she didn't say anything specific about it though she was always talking about going to a big city like San Francisco or New York."

"They found an Amtrak timetable in her car. She'd marked trains to New York."

He nodded, as if a mystery had been explained. "I'd guess that's what happened. No, I'd say I'm *positive* that's what happened. I really doubt there are stalkers or bogeymen out to get her."

"Why're you so sure?"

He didn't answer her. Instead he said, "I think we need more wine. I'll get it. Okay?"

"Sure."

Dr. Peters vanished into the kitchen. He returned a moment later, sat down and poured. After a moment he asked, "How does your husband feel about his daughter?"

"Tate's . . ." She groped for words.

He supplied one. "Indifferent?"

"Yes. He's never been very involved with Megan."

"I understand that. But why?"

She now looked at the crystal ball. In it was captured the orange glow from a wall lamp. She stared at the distorted trapezoid of light and said, "Tate wanted to be his grandfather. He was a famous lawyer and judge in the area. He had a big family, a traditional lifestyle. Well, Tate wanted that—and a good, dependable farmwife." She lifted her hands and slapped her thighs. "He got me instead. Big disappointment."

"No, that's not you." The doctor smiled wryly. "I can see that. That was very unfair to you for him to expect that."

"To me?" she asked. "Unfair?"

"Of course," he offered as if it were obvious. "Your husband had a distorted level of expectations—based on a child's view of the past—and he tried to project that onto you. I'll bet he worked a lot, spent time away from home."

"He did, yes. But I was busy too. My sister was sick—"

"Her heart condition."

Oh, she could talk to this man for hours! She'd met him only thirty minutes ago and yet he *knew* her. Knew her better than Tate did—even after all those years of marriage.

"That's right."

"But why are you taking the blame? You're attractive, intelligent, have a mind of your own. If you wanted an independent life, why should you feel bad about that? It seems to me that *he's* the one to blame for all this. He went into the marriage knowing who you were and tried to change you. And probably in some less-than-honest ways."

"Less than honest?"

"He *appeared* supportive, I'll bet. He probably said, 'Honey, do whatever you want to do. I'll be behind it.'"

She was stunned. It was as if Dr. Peters were looking directly into her memories. "Yes, that's exactly what he'd say."

"But in fact, what he was doing was the opposite. Little comments, even body language, that'd whittle away at your spirit. He wanted you barefoot and pregnant and wanted you to give up your life, have dinner on the table for him, give him a brood of kids, ignore your ill sister. And he was going to make a name for himself as a prosecutor and to hell with everybody else." His eyes flickered with pain—*her* pain. "It was horrible what he did to you. Inexcusable. But I suppose it's understandable. His character, you know."

"Character."

"You know the old expression? 'A man's character is his fate.' That's your ex-husband. He's reaping now what he sowed. With Megan running away."

I wish I could believe that, Bett thought. Please . . . Tears now. From the wine, from the astonishing comfort she felt, years and years of pain and confusion and loneliness being stripped away. "I . . ." She caught her breath. "He'd sit down and talk to me and say that he loved me and what could he do for me—"

"Tricks," Dr. Peters said quickly. "All tricks."

"I couldn't argue with him. He had an answer for everything."

"He's smooth, isn't he? A slick talker. Megan told me that."

"Oh, you better believe it. I couldn't win against him. Not at words. Never. I always came away feeling, I don't know, violated, I guess."

"Bett, most women would've put up with that. They would've stayed and stayed and destroyed themselves. And their children. But you had the courage to do something about it. To strike out on your own."

"But Megan . . . she's suffered . . ."

"Suffered?" He laughed. "Because of *him,* yes. Not because of you. You've done a *miraculous* job with her. Here's to you." He tapped her glass and they drank. The room was swimming. She realized he'd moved very close to her and she enjoyed the proximity.

"A miraculous job?" Bett shook her head, felt her eyes swimming with tears. "Oh, I don't think so."

Dr. Peters said firmly, "Why, if every mother cared for her children the way you care for Megan I'd be out of business."

"Do you really think that?" she asked in a choked voice. The tears were coming fast now. But she wasn't the least embarrassed. Not in front of this man. She could tell him anything, she could do anything. He'd understand, he'd forgive, he'd comfort. She said wistfully, "Too bad Megan doesn't think so."

"Oh, but she does." He frowned in confusion.

"No, no . . . there's a letter . . ." She glanced toward her purse, where the girl's horrible note sat like a puddle of cold blood.

"The detective told me about it. That's the main reason why I wanted to see you. Alone, without your husband here." He took the wineglass from her and set it on the table. Then he sat forward, took her hands in his. Looked at her until she was gazing into his dark eyes, nearly hypnotized. "Listen to me. Listen carefully. She didn't mean what she wrote you."

"She—"

"She. Didn't. Mean. It. Do you hear what I'm saying?"

Bett was shaking with sobs. "But what she wrote, it was so terrible . . ."

"No," he said in a firm whisper. "No." He was completely focused on her. She thought of the other men in her life with whom she'd had serious talks. Tate was often elsewhere—thinking of cases or trying to dissect what she was saying. Brad would smother

her with an adoring gaze. But Dr. Peters was looking at *her* as a person.

"Here's what you have to understand. Your letter doesn't mean anything."

Oh, please, she thought, please explain how this happened. Please explain to me why I'm not a witch, please explain how my daughter still loves me. She thought of an expression she'd heard once and believed was true: You'd kill for your mate; but you'd die for your child. Well, I would, she thought. If only Megan knew that she felt that way.

He squeezed her hands. "Your daughter hates your husband. I don't know what the genesis of that is but it's a very deeply ingrained feeling."

Bett felt the impossibility of compressing seventeen years into a few minutes. Her eye went to a board game, Monopoly, sitting dusty on the shelf. "There were so many things she wanted from Tate . . . Megan wanted us to play games together, Tate, her and me. But he never would. And then—"

"It doesn't matter," the doctor interrupted. "The fact is that she was the child and he was the parent and he failed her. Megan knows it and she hates him. The anger inside her is astonishing. But it's only directed at *him*—I guarantee you that. She loves you so much."

Shaking with tears. "But the letter . . ."

"You know the Oedipus and Electra principles? The attractions of sons and mothers and daughters and fathers?"

"A little, I guess."

"In Megan's subconscious her anger at your ex-husband makes her feel terribly guilty. And directing it *only* at him is intolerable. With the natural attraction between fathers and daughters she either had to write no letter at all or write you both. She was psychically unable to point her anger only at its true source."

"Oh, if I could believe that . . ."

"During our sessions she was always telling me how proud she was of you. How she wants to be like you. How hard a life you've had. I promise you, without a doubt, she regrets writing that letter to you. She doesn't mean it. She'd give anything to take it back."

Bett lowered her head and put her face in her hands. Why was the room swimming so badly? His arm went around her shoulders.

"You okay?"

She nodded.

"Will she be coming back?" Bett asked.

"I don't doubt it for a minute. It might be awhile— your husband's caused some serious damage. But nothing that's irreparable. Megan knows that she couldn't ask for a better mother in the world. You've done everything right. She loves you and misses you."

Bett sagged against his chest, felt the muscles in his arms tighten as he held her. Oh, when was the last time she'd felt this good, this easy, this comforted? Years. She felt his hot breath on the top of her head. She smelled a faint aftershave.

"I feel so light-headed."

Did she say that? Or think it?

She wept and she laughed.

The doctor's hand went to her forehead. "You're so hot . . ."

He hugged her harder and his hand slid downward,

fingers encircling her neck. An electric chill went through her and then her arms were snaking around him, pulling him to her. Her head was up and she pressed her cheek against his.

No, no, she thought. I can't be doing this . . .

But she was thinking these words from a very different place, very remote. And it was impossible for her to release her grip on the man who'd repaired her bleeding soul. He thinks I'm a good mother, he thinks I'm a good mother, he thinks . . .

He leaned down and kissed her tears.

The light touch of his lips felt so good . . .

She was so giddy, so happy . . .

Stretching out, getting comfortable . . . The room was hot, the room was wonderful . . .

And what was this? she thought like an excited high school girl.

He was kissing her on the mouth. Or am I kissing him? Bett didn't know. All she knew was that she wanted to be close to him. To the man who'd found her single worst fear and killed it dead.

"No," he protested. But his voice was a whisper.

But she was not letting him go. She knew she should stop but she couldn't. She pulled him down next to her on the couch, refusing to let go, arms fixed forever around his neck. The room filling with heat, spinning, orange lights, yellow lights . . .

Kissing harder now.

Hands on her belly, then her chest. She glanced down and wasn't surprised to see her blouse was undone. Her bra up, his fingers cupping her breast. This seemed completely natural. A pop, the snap of her jeans opened. Had he done that, or had she? It didn't matter. Getting close to him was all that mattered, hearing him whisper whatever he would whisper in her ear as he lay on top of her. *That* was what she wanted, hearing him speak to her. The sex wasn't important but she'd gladly give him that if only he'd keep reassuring her, keep speaking to her . . .

She opened her mouth and kissed him hard.

And then the world ended.

The front door was swinging open. And a familiar voice was crying, "Bett . . . why, Bett!"

Gasping, she sat up.

Dr. Peters backing away, a shocked look on his face.

Brad Markham stood in the doorway, his face a horrified mask. His key to her house dropped to the floor with a loud ring. "What . . ." He was breathless. "What . . ."

"Brad, I thought . . ."

"I was in Baltimore?" he spat out. He shook his head. "I was. A policeman called and told me about Megan. I drove down to be with you . . . Your daughter's missing and you're fucking somebody. You're *cheating* on me?"

"No," she said, feeling faint and nauseous from the wine and shock. Tears coming again. Tears of horror. "You don't understand. I didn't mean it. I didn't know what I was doing."

"I'm sorry." Dr. Peters looked horrified. "I didn't know you had a boyfriend. You never said anything."

"Boyfriend?" Brad spat out. "We're engaged."

"You're *what?*" The doctor stared at Brad. "I'm so sorry. She never said anything."

"How could you?" Brad spat out, raging at her. "After everything I've done for you? And Megan? How could you?"

"I don't know what happened . . ."

Brad stalked outside leaving the door open.

"No!" Bett cried, sobbing, pulling her bra down and buttoning her blouse as she stumbled toward the door. "Wait."

Through her tears she saw Brad's car squeal off down the street.

Leaning against the doorjamb, sobbing, sinking to the floor. Close to fainting, wishing to die . . .

"No, no, no . . ."

Then the doctor was standing next to her, crouching down. His mouth close to her ear. When he spoke the voice was so different from the soothing drone of ten minutes ago. It was flint, it was ice water. "What I told you Megan said about you? That wasn't true. I only said it to make you feel better . . . All she told me was that you were a selfish whore. I didn't believe her. But I guess she was right." He took a final sip of wine. "What a pitiful excuse for a mother you are."

The doctor rose, set the glass on the table and stepped over her, out the door. It seemed he was smiling, though Bett was blinded by the tears and couldn't say for certain.

Tate Collier hung up the phone. Sighed.

No, man, Josh still isn't home. I don't know where he is. You called, like, three times already. Maybe we'll give it a rest now? Okay?

Well, where the hell was Megan's boyfriend?

Konnie too was still out of the office. And it irked Tate that the detective hadn't returned his page.

He fed the Dalmatian and paced up and down his front porch, looking at the clear early evening skies and the dusting of April growth over his fields.

No more Dead Rebs that he could see.

Again his eye settled on the dilapidated picnic bench in the backyard. Remembering Bett unhooking the Japanese lanterns, feeling the odd heat of that fall so many years ago, feeling the residual exhaustion from the funeral. Sweating in November, the hot wind pushing crisp, curled leaves over the shaggy grass.

He remembered:

Bett looking down at him. Asking, "What is it?"

Alarmed, as she gazed at the expression on his face.

What is it, what is it, what is it? . . . A simple question. Yet simple words can't convey the answer— that two people who were once in love no longer are.

He'd closed his eyes. "I don't want to be married to you anymore," he'd said.

Good-bye . . .

Tate now looked away from the bench and glanced impatiently at the cordless phone, sitting on the porch swing. Why wasn't—

It rang. He blinked and snagged it from the cradle. "Hello?"

Silence for a moment. Then: "Tate?"

"I'm here, Bett. What's wrong?" His heart went cold at the sound in her voice.

"I'm on my way to Baltimore."

"You are? Why?"

More silence. "Brad left me."

"What? At a time like this?"

"It's not his fault. I did something stupid. I don't know . . . I don't want to go into it. It's . . . Oh, Jesus, it's a mess."

"Bett, you sound terrible. Are you crying?"

"I can't talk about it. Not now."

"When'll you be back? What about Megan?"

"I don't care."

He heard utter defeat in her voice. "What do you mean?"

"Oh, Tate. We've blown it. There's nothing we can do. We've ruined her life, she's ruined ours. Maybe she'll come back, maybe she won't. Let's just let her go and hope for the best. I don't care anymore."

"This doesn't sound like you."

"Well, it *is* me, all right? It was stupid looking for her, it was stupid getting together like this, you and me. We should have kept our lives on different sides of the universe, Tate. What've we got to show for it? Just pain."

"We're going to find her."

"She doesn't *want* to be found. Don't you get that? Let her go and don't worry about it. She's part of the past, Tate. Let her go. The phone's breaking up. I'm coming to a tunnel. Good-bye, Tate . . . Good-bye . . ."

Chapter Twenty

Bait.

That's me, yes sir. That's me.

He's on to you, Crazy Megan says. *Move, move, move.*

She went to the right and Peter Matthews went to the right.

Left and left, straight and straight.

Getting closer all the time.

Whispering, "Megan, Megan, Megan."

Other words too. She wasn't sure but she thought he was muttering, "I want to fuck you, I want to fuck you." Or maybe "cut you."

Megan was part of his fantasy now. She was a victim from those disgusting comic books. The tentacles, the monsters, the purple dicks, the claws and pincers . . .

And was nothing more than a game to the boy—if you can call a six-foot, two-hundred-pound *thing* a boy.

As she moved up and down the corridors, gripping the handle of her glass knife in her right hand, which stung fiercely from the blisters, she had all sorts of terrible thoughts: why the father had brought her here, for instance. As a bride for his son. Jesus . . . Maybe Aaron Matthews had wanted grandchildren. Maybe

Peter'd been at Jefferson High—they had a special ed department—and he'd gotten obsessed with her. That might be it. And his father had kidnapped her to be a present for his son.

Down the corridor toward the kitchen.

Scuffling, muttering, but no sight of him.

Down the corridor that led past the door to the basement. The lock looked flimsy but not *that* flimsy. Breaking it open would make a hell of a noise. And what was down there anyway?

No, Crazy Megan tells her. *Stick to your plan. He's gotta go down.*

Well, *one* of us does, thought the less confident half of the duo.

Keep going, keep looking for him. Up and down the dim halls.

It didn't seem that late but the hospital was in a valley and the sun was behind a mountain to the west. The whole place was bathed in cold blue light and she was having trouble seeing.

She stopped. The boy's footsteps were getting closer.

This is it, Crazy Megan says. *Just stab the fucker in the back and get it over with.*

But Megan reminded her that she couldn't do that. As much as she hated him, she couldn't kill.

He wants to fuck you. He wants to pretend he's one of those insect monsters and fuck you till you bleed. You have to—

Be quiet! I'm doing the best I can.

Closer. The steps got closer. The sound coming from around the corner. She didn't have time to get into the main corridor—he was too close.

She stepped into a little nook. Trapped.

He moved closer, paused. Maybe hearing her.

Maybe *smelling* her. He'd stopped whispering her name. Which scared her more because he knew he was close to his prey and didn't want to be heard. He was sneaking up on her. He was playing the invisible monster; she'd seen that story in one of the comic books. Some creature you couldn't see snuck into girls' locker rooms and raped stragglers after gym class. The comic had been limp, as if Peter'd read that one a thousand times.

He moved forward another few cautious steps.

Her hand started to shake.

Should she jump out into the corridor and just run like hell?

But he couldn't be more than ten feet away. And he'd looked so big in the photographs! He could lunge like a snake and grab her by the throat in two steps.

Suddenly a flash of pain went through her hand—from one of the blisters—and she dropped the knife. Gasped involuntarily.

Megan froze, watching the knife tumble to the floor. It can't break! No . . .

Just before the icy glass hit the floor she shoved her foot under it, waiting for the pain as the tip of the blade sliced into the top of her foot.

Thunk. The knife hit her right foot flat and rolled, unbroken, to the floor.

Thank you, thank you . . .

She bent down and picked it up.

Another two footsteps, closer, closer.

No choice. She had to run. He was only three or four feet away.

Megan took a deep breath, another. Jump out, slash with the knife and run like hell toward the trap.

Now!

She leapt out, turned to the right.

Froze. Gasping. Her ears had played tricks on her. No one was there. Then she looked down. The rat—a large one, big as a cat—standing on his haunches, sniffing the air, blinked at her, cowering. Then indignantly it turned away as if angry at being startled.

Megan sagged against the wall, tears welling as the fear dissipated.

But she didn't have much time for recovery.

At the far end of the dim corridor a shadow materialized into the loping form of Peter Matthews, hunched over and moving slowly. He didn't see her and disappeared from view.

Megan paused for only a few seconds before she started after him.

The Shenandoahs and Blue Ridge keep the air in northwest Virginia clean as glass in the spring, and when the sun sets, it's a fierce disk, bright as an orange spotlight. Newscasters report on "sun delays" from the glare at various places on the highway.

This radiant light, behind Tate, lit every detail in the trees and buildings and oncoming cars as he sped down I-66 at eighty miles an hour.

He skidded north on the parkway, then east on Route 50, pulled into the county police station house and climbed out of the car. He practically ran into Dimitri Konstantinatis as he too happened to arrive, carrying two large Kentucky Fried Chicken bags.

"Oh-oh," the detective muttered.

"What oh-oh?"

"That look on your face."

"I don't have a look," Tate protested.

"You had it comin' into my office when you were prosecutor and you needed that little bit of extra evidence—which'd mean I'd lose a weekend. And you've got it now. *That* oh-oh."

They walked inside the building and into Konnie's small office.

"You didn't call me back," Tate said.

"Did so. Ten minutes ago. You musta left. What's that?"

Tate set the letter Megan had written him and the knucklebone he'd found in his house that morning, both in Baggies, on the cop's desk.

"Prints," Tate said.

"A prince among men—yes, I am. So, what's going on?"

"I want you to run the letter through Identification. Something's up. Bett's acting funny."

"You complained about that when you were married," Konnie pointed out. "Crystals, mumbo jumbo, long distance calls to people'd been dead a hundred years."

"That was cute funny. This's weird funny. Witnesses've been disappearing and not calling back and it's just too much of a coincidence. And I think I know who's behind it."

He also told Konnie about his run-in with Jack Sharpe.

"Ooo, that was bright, Counselor, and you were packing your gun to boot?"

Tate shrugged. "Was your idea for me to get one."

"But it *wasn't* my idea to threaten an upstanding member of the Prince William mafia with it. Grant me that at least."

"I've been on his bad side since I routed his lawyers at the injunction hearing last week."

"What's wrong with a nice theme park 'round here, Tate? You'd rather have what we got *now* in Manassas? A track fulla big wheels slugging it out in a mud pit. *I'd* vote for Disneyland, with them fun rides and cotton candy and knock-the-clown-in-the-water shit."

"I'm just telling you that Jack Sharpe would love for me to be out of commission come that argument at the Supreme Court in Richmond next week. And I think he's had somebody in a van following me. Sorry, no tag, no model."

Konnie nodded slowly. Then added, "But he's got boys he'd hire for that. And they could hire other boys. No way could you trace it back to him. And you think anybody'd snitch on Jack Sharpe?"

"I'm not a prosecutor anymore, Konnie. I don't want to make a case. I want to find Megan. Period. End of story."

"And kneecap the prick who did it."

Tate pushed the bags containing the letter and the bone toward Konnie again. "Please."

Another mournful glance at his cooling dinner. "Be right back."

"Wait." Tate handed him another Baggie. "Exemplars of Megan's prints on the keys and mine on that glass. And remember you handled the note too."

Konnie nodded. "The prosecutor in you ain't dead, I see." Carrying the bags, he walked down the hall toward the forensic lab. He returned a moment later.

"Won't be long. I *was* looking forward to supper."

Tate ignored the red-and-white KFC bag and continued. "Now, there was a gray Mercedes following her. Can you check that out?"

"Check what out?"

"Registered owners of gray Mercedeses."

"I was asking before: year, model, tag?"

"Still none."

Konnie laughed. He typed heavily on his computer keyboard. "This'll be worth it just to see your expression."

As he waited for the results Konnie peeked into the tallest Kentucky Fried bag, kneaded his ample stomach absently. "You know what the worst is? The worst is when the mashed potatoes get cold. You can eat the chicken when it's cold because everybody does that. On a picnic, say. Same with the beans. But when mashed potatoes get cold you have to throw them out. Which is bad enough but then you think about them all night—how good they would've been. *That's* what I mean by the worst."

The screen fluttered. Konnie leaned forward.

"Here's what we got. I did Fairfax, Arlington, Alexandria, Prince William and Loudoun. Mercedes, all types, all years, gray."

Tate leaned forward and read: *Your request has resulted in 2,603 responses.*

"Two thousand," Tate muttered. "Man."

"Two thousand *six* hundred."

Tate knew from his prosecuting days that too much evidence was as useless as too little.

"If you're just not buying the runaway stuff"— Konnie sighed—"we're gonna have to do more thinking. All right, you think Sharpe's a possibility and I don't think he's above snatching a girl. But there anybody else? Think hard now, Tate. Anybody hassling her?"

"Recently?"

"Like last year's weirdos don't count?" Konnie snorted. "When*ever!*"

"Not that I know of. I have to say there was a rumor . . . it was just a rumor . . . she might've been seeing . . . well, having sex with some older men. And maybe there was some money involved. I mean, they were paying her."

If Konnie felt anything about this he didn't show it. "You have any idea who? Where?"

"Some kids at this place called the Coffee—"

"—Shop. They been trying to close that piss hole down for a year. Well, I can poke around there. Ask some questions. Now, was she in any cults or anything?"

"No, don't think so."

"You or Bett in anything like that?"

"*Me?*"

"All right, your wife."

"Ex," Tate corrected.

"Whatever. She did that sort of stuff."

"It was strictly softball with her. No Heaven's Gate or Jonestown or anything like that. Bett wouldn't even put up these Indian posters because they had reverse swastikas on them. Nothing to do with Nazis; she just thought it was bad karma."

"Karma," Konnie scoffed. "Any relationships of yours go south in a big way recently?"

"I—"

"'Fore you answer, think back to every one of them twenty-one-year-olds you promised diamonds to and then ran for the hills."

"I never proposed to a single one," Tate said.

"Never proposed to *marry* 'em, maybe."

"You don't get *Fatal Attraction* after three dates. That's about the longest term I went."

"Sad, Tate, sad. How 'bout Bett?"

"I don't know. But I don't think so."

"Any relatives acting squirrelly? Might've wanted to take the girl and run?"

"Only relative nearby's Bett's sister, Susan. Outside of Baltimore. She'd never do anything to hurt her. Hell, she was always joking about adopting Megan."

This got Konnie's attention. "Adopting her? You sure she's not involved in this? Maybe she went over the edge, decided to get herself a daughter."

"Imagine Bett but fifteen pounds lighter. She couldn't kidnap a bird."

"But she could've *hired* somebody to. She could have a wacko boyfriend."

"I just can't see it, Konnie."

"Gimme her name anyway."

Tate wrote it down.

"Okay, how 'bout any business associates of either of y'all? Clients? Or the bad guys? Other than Sharpe."

"Bett's got this interior design business. I don't think her clients're the sort for this kind of thing. Me, all I've been doing are wills, trusts and house closings—except for the Liberty Park case."

Konnie grunted. The detective got a call. Grabbed the phone. Nodded. Slammed it down. "Interesting . . . That was the lab. Only her prints and yours on the bone. And mine, yours and hers on the letter. But . . . there were some smudges on the bone that might've been from latex gloves. Can't say for certain. But that starts me wondering. Think it's about time to do a Title Three."

"A wiretap?"

"Yours and your wife's phones both."

"Ex."

"You keep saying that. Broken record. That's in case you get a ransom call."

"I thought this wasn't a case."

"It's becoming one. Tell me again what happened this morning at your place. I mean exact."

Tate remembered this about Konnie: he was a working dog when it came to dredging for evidence and hammering on suspects and witnesses. Only exhaustion would slow him down—and even then it never stopped him.

Tate gave another recap of the events.

"So you never actually saw her at your house?"

"No," Tate said. "I got back home about ten A.M. from the office then got suited up and went to check on a busted pipe."

"The sharecroppers there?"

"No. Not on Saturday. I never saw anybody at all. Just the lights go out around ten-twenty."

"All of 'em?"

"Yeah."

"Didn't you think that was funny?"

"No. Megan doesn't like bright lights. She likes candlelight and dimmers."

This gave Tate a burst of pleasure—proving to Konnie that he knew *something* about the girl after all.

"It was dark as pitch this morning," the detective mused. "With all that rain. Most people'd want *some* light, you'd think. 'Less they didn't want to be seen from the outside."

"True."

"And shit, Tate, wait a minute. Why'd she go to your place at all?"

"To leave the letters and get the backpack."

"Well, doesn't she have any suitcases or book bags at your wife's? Sorry, your *ex's*. Your dee-vorced spouse's."

"Sure she does. You're right. *Most* of them are there, as a matter of fact. And she had her book bag with her at Amy's. And a lot more clothes and makeup at Bett's place than mine."

The cop continued, "You and Megan hardly ever saw each other."

"True again."

"So you wouldn't go into her room much, would you?"

"Once a month maybe."

"So why'd she leave the letters there? Why not at her mother's?"

That would've made more sense, true. The detective added, "And hell, why go to the house and leave some letters this morning around the time you were going to meet her? I tell you, if I was going to leave a note to diss my folks and run I'd leave it someplace they *weren't* going to be. Don'tcha think?"

"So he made her write 'em and planted them himself. Whoever he is."

"That's what I think, Counselor . . . Here's what I'm gonna do. Order some serious forensic work and then have a chat with the captain. Guess what? This's just become a case. And in a big way." Konnie pulled a drumstick from the bag and charged down the hall.

Tate returned home.

No messages and no one had called; the caller ID box was blank.

Twelve hours ago he had wanted Megan and Bett out of his life again. He'd gotten his wish and he didn't like it one bit.

So Brad had left Bett. He didn't know what to make of that. Why? And why now? He had a feeling that whoever was behind Megan's disappearance was behind this too.

Then his thoughts segued to Belize, the trip he and Bett had planned to take. A second honeymoon. Well, a *first* honeymoon technically—since they'd never taken one after their wedding.

He looked out over the dark sky, at the spattering of a million stars. Tate laughed to himself. What a kick if they'd run into each other. He wondered how Bett would have reacted to Karen. No, Cathy.

Probably not well.

Not a jealousy thing so much as a matter of approval. She'd never liked his taste in women.

Well, Tate didn't either, now that he looked back at his lovers over the past ten years.

Belize . . .

Was there actually a possibility that he and Bett might take that trip together still—after they found Megan?

Whatever happened with Brad, the presence of a fiancé didn't seem as insurmountable as simply the concept of Tate and Bett taking a trip together. At one time their joined names had been a common phrase among their friends. But that was a long, long time ago.

Yet—this was *feelings* again, not Cartesian logic— yet somehow he believed that they'd get along just fine. The fight today had been as bad as any they'd had fifteen years ago. And yet there'd been a reconciliation. This astonished him. That never would have happened in the past.

He sighed, sipped his wine, looked out at the Dalmatian nosing about in the tall grass. Thinking now of Megan.

But even if husband and wife were to get together again, what would the girl come home to? And more important . . . *who* was the person coming home?

Was the girl's drinking and the water tower incident more than just a onetime fluke? Was *that* the real Megan McCall, a bitter young woman who slept with men for money? Or was there another person within her? One Tate didn't know well—or maybe one he hadn't even yet met?

Tate Collier felt a sudden desperation to know the girl. To know *who* she was. What excited her, what she hated, what she feared. What foods she liked. What clothes she'd pick and which she'd shun. What bad TV shows she'd want to watch.

What made her laugh. And what weep.

And he was suddenly stung by a terrible thought: that if Megan had *died* this morning, the victim of a deranged killer or an accident, he'd have been distraught, yes, terribly sad. But now, if that happened or—the most horrifying—if she simply vanished forever, never to be found at all, he'd be destroyed. It would be one of those tragedies that breaks you forever. He remembered something he'd told Bett when they'd been married, a case he was working on—prosecuting an arson murder. The victim had run into a burning building to save her child, who'd survived, though the mother had perished. He'd read the facts, looked up to Bett and said, "You'll kill for your spouse but you'll die for your child . . ."

In rhetoric, lawyers use the trick of personification—picking words to make their own clients seem human and sympathetic and their opponents less so. "Mary Jones" instead of "the witness" or "the victim." Juries find it far easier to be harsh to abstractions. "The defendant." "The man sitting at that table there."

It's a very effective trick and a very dangerous one.

And it's just how I've treated Megan over the years, Tate now thought. He rose, walked into the den and spent a long time looking for another picture of her. He was terribly disappointed he couldn't find one.

He'd given his only snapshot to Konnie and Beauridge that afternoon.

He sat down in his chair, closed his eyes and tried to create some images now. Images of the girl. Smiling, looking perplexed, exasperated . . . A few came to mind. He tried harder.

And harder still.

Which was why he hadn't heard the man come up behind him.

The cold finger of a pistol touched his temple. "Don't move, Mr. Collier. No, no. I really mean that. For your sake. Don't move."

Chapter Twenty-one

Jimmy, Tate recalled.

His name was Jimmy. And he was the man who'd been far more willing than Tate to engage in some gunplay in Jack Sharpe's immaculate foyer.

Tate glanced at the phone.

Jimmy shook his head. "No."

"What do you want?"

"Mr. Sharpe sent me."

Figured that.

The gun was really very large. The man's finger wasn't on the trigger; it was outside of the guard. This didn't reassure Tate at all.

"I have something for you to look at."

"Look at?"

"I'm going to give it to you to look at. Then I'm going to take it back. And neither me or Mr. Sharpe'll ever admit we know what you're talking about if you ever mention it. You understand?"

Tate didn't understand a thing. But he said, "Sure. Say, is that loaded?"

Jimmy didn't respond. From the pocket of his leather jacket he took a videocassette. Set it on the table. Backed up. Nodded toward it. Tate walked over, picked it up. "I should play it?"

Jimmy's face scrunched up impatiently.

Tate put the cassette in the player and fiddled with the controls until the tape started to play. The scene on the TV showed a building, some bushes. The date and time stamp revealed that it had been made that morning, at nine forty-two. He didn't recognize where. The tape jumped ahead four minutes; now whoever was making the tape was driving, following another car down a suburban street. Tate recognized the car being followed. It was Megan's Tempo. Because of the rain he couldn't make out who was driving.

"Where did you get this?" Tate demanded.

"Watch, don't talk," Jimmy muttered. The gun was pointed directly at Tate's back.

Another jump on the tape. To nine-fifty that morning. Tate recognized the Vienna Metro station. The man taping—of course, one of the private eyes hired by Sharpe, despite his protests to the contrary—must have been afraid of getting too close to his subject. He was about fifty yards away and shooting through the mist and rain. Megan's car stopped at a row filled with other cars. There was a pause and then motion. After a moment he caught a glimpse of someone. A white man, it seemed, wearing a dark jacket, though he couldn't be sure. Tate could see no distinguishing features. Then there was more motion. Finally a gray Mercedes pulled out of a space and a moment later Megan's car eased into where the Merce had been. At 10:01 the Mercedes sped out of the lot.

The tape went fuzzy. Then black.

Tate stared, his heart pounding. Thinking of the vague motion he'd seen—pixels of light on the screen, distorted to start with, more distorted in the rain and fog. But he believed it might have been the man lifting a heavy object from the trunk of Megan's car and putting it into the Mercedes. An object about the size of a human body.

"That's all," Jimmy said. "Could you eject it?"

Tate did. "Did he see anything else?" he asked.

"Who?" Jimmy asked.

"You know who. The private eye. Can I talk to him? Please?"

Jimmy nodded at the table. "If you could just set the tape there and back up."

Tate did. He knew he wouldn't get an answer. This was as far as Sharpe was willing to go. But he asked one more question. "Why did he show this to me? He didn't have to."

Jimmy pocketed the cassette, gun still held steadily at Tate. He backed to the door. "Mr. Sharpe asked me just to mention the old adage that one good deed deserves another. He hopes you'll remember that next Thursday at the argument down in Richmond."

"Look—"

"He said he didn't think you'd agree. He just asked me to mention it."

Jimmy walked to the sliding door, through which he'd apparently entered. He paused. "The answer to your question? I myself would guess it's because he's got two daughters of his own. Good night."

After he'd gone Tate drained his wineglass with a shaking hand and picked up the phone and dialed a number.

When Konnie answered Tate said, "Got a lead."

"Asking or telling?"

"Telling."

"Go on."

"Long story. That case with Sharpe?"

"Right."

Tate said, "It wasn't just me he had a PI tailing. It was Megan too."

"Why? Dig up dirt?"

"That's my guess. Lawyer's daughter scores drugs. Sleeps around. Something like that. Anyway, a friend of his just showed me a tape." Tate described it.

"Hot damn. Get it over here—"

"Forget it. It's been atomized. But I think it was Megan the perp was moving from one trunk to another. She was probably drugged." Tate prayed the girl had merely been unconscious.

"Tags?"

"Nope. Sorry."

"Damn, Tate. Why'd you think they put those cute little signs on cars?" After a pause Konnie continued. "Okay. So—you don't think it's Sharpe?"

"He didn't have to show me diddly. He didn't even bargain—well, not too hard. You know, throw the case and I'll tell you what the PI saw. He could've done that."

"Would you've agreed?"

Tate didn't hesitate for an instant. "Yes, I would have."

"Okay, so it's not Sharpe. Then let's think. She's got a stalker after her. He's checking out her routine. Following her. When she goes to school, when she goes to pom-pom practice."

Tate tried to picture Megan as a cheerleader. "As if."

"He knows where she's going to be this morning. He gets her, drugs her, drives her to Vienna, where he's left his own car. He's got to switch wheels. The Mercedes."

"Right."

"Leaves her car with the timetable. So it looks like she's headed off on Amtrak . . . He took off to wherever he was going to stash her. Which means what, Counselor?" Tate couldn't think.

When he said nothing Konnie gave a harsh laugh. "Damn, I'd forgot how I had to hold your hand when we were putting all those bad guys away. What's sitting right *under* her car at the moment?"

"Tread marks! The Mercedes's tread marks."

"There's hope for you after all, boy—if you apply yourself and work real hard. Okay, Counselor, this's gonna take some time. Listen, you sit tight and have some nice hot mashed potatoes. And think of me when you eat 'em."

Konnie Konstantinatis's first lesson in police work was to watch his father fool the tax men like 'coons tricking hounds.

The old Greek immigrant was petty, weak, dangerous, a cross between a squirrel and a ferret. He was a born liar and had an instinct for knowing human nature cold. He put stills next to smokehouses, stills next to factories, stills in boats, disguised them like henhouses. Hid his income in a hundred small businesses. Once he smooth-talked a revenuer into arresting Konnie's father's own innocent brother-in-law instead of him and swore an oath at the trial that cost the bewildered man two years of his life.

So from the age of five or six Konnie had observed his father and had learned the art of evasion and deception. And therefore he'd learned the art of seeing through deceit.

This was a skill to be practiced slowly and tediously. And this was how he was going to find the man who'd kidnapped Tate Collier's daughter.

Konnie arranged for a small crane to lift Megan's car out of its spot, rather than drive it out and risk obliterating the Merce's tread marks.

He then spent the next two hours taking electro-static prints of the twelve tire treads that he could isolate and differentiate—ones he determined weren't from Megan's car. He then identified the matching left and right tires and measured wheelbases and lengths of the cars they'd come from. He jotted all this, in lyrical handwriting, into a battered leather notebook.

He then went over the entire parking space with a Dustbuster and—hunched in the front seat of his car—looked over all the trace evidence picked up in the paper filter. Most of it was nothing more than dust and meaningless without laboratory analysis. But Konnie found one obvious clue: a single fiber that came from cheap rope. He recognized it because in one of the three kidnapping cases he'd worked over the past ten years the victim's hands had been bound with rope that shed fibers just like this.

Speeding back to the office, the detective sat down at his computer and ran the wheel dimensions through the motor vehicle specification database. One set of numbers perfectly fit the dimensions for a Mercedes sedan.

He examined the electrostatic prints carefully. Flipping through *Burne's Tire Identifier,* he concluded that they were a rare model of Michelin and because they showed virtually no wear he guessed the tires were no more than three or four months old. Encouraging, on the one hand, because they were unusual tires and it would be easier to track down the purchaser. But troubling too. Because they were expensive, as was the model of the car the man was driving. It was therefore likely that the perp was intelligent, which suggested he was an organized offender—the hardest to find.

And the sort of criminal that presented the most danger.

Konnie then started canvassing. It was Saturday evening and although most of the tire outlets were still open—General Tire, Sears, Merchants, Mercedes dealerships—the managers had gone home. But nothing as trivial as this stopped Konnie. He blustered and bullied until he had the names and home phone numbers of night staff managers of the stores' record-keeping and data-processing departments.

He made thirty-eight phone calls and by the time he hung up from speaking with the last parts department manager on his list, faxes of bills of sale were starting to roll into police headquarters.

But the information wasn't as helpful as he'd hoped. Most of the sales receipts included the manufacturer of the customer's car and the tag number. Some had the model number but virtually none had the color. The list kept growing. After an hour he had copies of 142 records of the sales of that model of Michelin in the past twelve months to people who owned Mercedeses.

He looked over the discouragingly lengthy list of names.

Standard procedure was to run the names through the outstanding warrants/prior arrests database. But a net like that didn't seem to be the sort that would catch this perp—he wasn't a chronic 'jacker or a shooter with a long history of crime. Still, Konnie was a cop who dotted his *i*'s and he handed the stack to Genie. "You know what to do, darling."

"It's seven forty-two on a Saturday night, boss," the assistant pointed out.

"*You* had dinner at least."

"Lemme tell you something, Konnie," the huge woman said, nodding at the KFC bags. "Throw those out. They're starting to stink."

Dutifully, he did. As he returned to his desk he grabbed his ringing phone.

"'Lo?"

"Detective Konstantinatis, please?"

"Yeah."

"This is Special Agent McComb with the FBI. Child Exploitation and Kidnapping Unit."

"Sure, how you doin'?" Konnie'd worked with the unit occasionally. They were tireless and dedicated and top-notch.

"I'm doing a favor for my boss in Quantico. He asked me to take a look at the Megan McCall case. You're involved in that, right?"

"Yup."

"It's not an active case for us but you know Tate Collier's the girl's father, right?"

"Know that."

"Well, he did some pretty good work for us when he was a commonwealth's attorney so I said I'd look into her disappearance. As a favor."

"Just what I'm doing, more or less. But I'm gonna present it as an active case to my captain tonight."

"Are you really?"

"Found some interesting forensics." Konnie was thinking, Man, if I could turn the tire data over to the feds . . . the FBI has a whole *staff* of people who specialize in tires.

"That's good to know. We ought to coordinate our approaches. Do some proactive thinking."

"Sure." Konnie's thinking was: They might be the best cops in the world but feebies talk like assholes.

The agent said, "I'm up at Ernie's, near the parkway. You know it?"

"Sure. It's a half mile from me."

"I was about to order dinner and was reading the file when I saw your name. Maybe I could come by in an hour or so. Or maybe—this might appeal to you, Officer—you might want to join me? Let Uncle Sam pick up the dinner tab."

He paused for a moment. "Why not? Be there in ten minutes."

"Good. Bring whatever you've got."

"Will do."

They hung up. Konnie stuck his head in Genie's office, where she was looking over the warrants and arrests request results. "Everything's negative, Konnie."

"Don't worry. We got the feds on the case now."

"My."

He took the stack of faxed receipts from her desk, shoved them into his briefcase and headed out the door.

Konnie was feeling pretty good. Ernie's served some great mashed potatoes.

Chapter Twenty-two

Aaron Matthews sat at a booth in a dark corner of the restaurant, looking out the window at a tableau of heavy equipment, bright yellow in the dusk, squatting on a dirt hillside nearby.

This was an area that five years ago had been fields and was now rampantly overgrown with town houses and apartments and strip malls. Starbucks, Chesapeake Bagels, Linens 'n' Things. Ernie's restaurant fit in perfectly, an upscale franchise. Looked nice on the surface but beneath the veneer it was all formula. Matthews stirred as the waddling form of Detective Konstantinatis entered the restaurant and maneuvered through the tables.

Watching the man's eyes, seeing where they slid—furtively, guiltily.

Always the eyes. Matthews waved and Konstantinatis nodded and steered toward him. Matthews had no idea what official FBI identification looked like and wouldn't have known how to fake some if he had but he'd dressed in a suit and white shirt—what he always wore when seeing patients—and had brought several dog-eared file folders, on which he'd printed FBI PRIVILEGED AND CONFIDENTIAL with stencils he'd made from office materials bought at Staples. These sat prominently in front of him.

He hoped for the best.

But after glancing at the files the detective merely scooted into the seat across from Matthews and shook his hand.

They made small talk for a few moments— Matthews using his best government-speak. Stiff, awkward. If the fake files hadn't fooled the cop the stilted language surely would have.

The waitress came and they ordered. Matthews wasn't surprised when the detective ordered milk with dinner. Matthews himself ordered a beer.

He said, "I'm afraid we don't have many leads. But from what you were telling me you think there's a chance she was kidnapped?"

"First I just thought she ran off. But there's apparently a tape that shows somebody switching her car with this gray Mercedes around the time she vanished. And maybe hustling the girl into the trunk, unconscious."

"I see," said Aaron Matthews, who felt fire burn right through him. His battleship gray 560 sat in the parking lot, fifty feet from them. Resplendent with its stolen license plates.

A tape? Who'd taken it? He was furious for a moment but anger was a luxury he had no time for.

"You've got this tape?"

"Vanished into thin air. Long story."

"Oh."

"Don't envy you that job," the detective said. "Looking for missing kids all day long. Must be hard."

Revealing a sentimental side Matthews wouldn't have guessed he had.

Matthews said in a soft voice, "It's where I feel I can make the most difference." Their drinks came. They clinked glasses. Matthews spilled some beer on the table. Wiped it up sloppily with a cocktail napkin.

"Detective—"

"Call me 'Konnie.' Everybody else does."

"Okay, Konnie. I hate to ask but I don't know this Collier and the question's come up. Do you think there was anything between him and the girl?"

"Naw. Not Tate. If anything, just the opposite."

"How's that?"

"Hell, I didn't even know he *had* a daughter until we'd been working together awhile. It's not that. I do think somebody 'napped her. No motive yet, though might be a case Tate's working on. He's decided this local real estate guy didn't do it. But I'm not so sure. I also have some thoughts about the girl's aunt— apparently she's pretty jealous of her sister having a child."

Bett's sister . . . How did Konnie know about *her?*

"I 'statted some tire treads and got a list of a hundred and a half people bought that brand of tire in the past year. Could I give you the receipts"—he patted the briefcase—"have your people check 'em out?"

"Be happy to. Have you done anything with them yet?"

"Just run 'em through the outstanding warrants and arrests. Nothing showed up."

Planning for the kidnapping, Matthews had bought new tires for the car two months ago; he couldn't afford to be slowed up by a flat. At least when he'd taken the car into General Tire he'd given a fake name and paid cash.

"But then I got to thinking," Konnie continued, "on the way over here, what I shoulda done—I shoulda looked at the receipts and found out who paid cash. Anybody who did, I figure it'd be a fake name. I mean, those tires cost big money. Nobody pays cash for something like that. So what your folks could do is check the tags and see if the name matches—on all the cash receipts. If they don't then that's our prime suspect."

Jesus in heaven. Matthews hadn't swapped plates when he'd taken the car in to have the new tires mounted. The tag would reveal his real name and the address of his rental house in Prince William County. Which didn't match the fake information he'd given the clerk at the tire store.

"That's a good idea," Matthews said. "A proactive idea." He sounded casual but he wanted to scream. A dark mood hovered over him.

The food came and Konnie ate hungrily, hunched over his meal.

Matthews picked at his. He'd have to act soon. He flagged the waitress down and ordered another beer.

"You want to give me those receipts?" Matthews nodded at the briefcase.

"Sure, but let's go back to headquarters after. It's right up the street here. You can fax 'em to your office."

"Okay."

The second beer came. Konnie glanced at it for a second, returned to his food.

"This Tate Collier," Matthews said slowly, savoring his microbrew. "Sounds like a good man."

"None better. Best fucking lawyer in the commonwealth. I get sick of these shits getting off on technicalities. When Collier was arguing the case they went to jail and stayed there."

Matthews held up the beer. "To your theory of tires."

The detective hesitated then they tapped glasses. Matthews drank half the beer, exhaled with satisfaction and set it down. "Hot for April, don't you think?"

"Is," the detective grunted.

Matthews asked, "You on duty now?"

"Naw, I been off for three hours."

"Then hell, chug down that milk and let me buy you a real drink." He tapped the beer.

"No thanks."

"Come on, nothing like a nice beer on a hot day."

"Fact is, I gave up drinking a few years back."

Matthews looked mortified. "Oh, I'm sorry."

"Not at all."

"I wasn't thinking. A man drinking milk. Shouldn't have ordered this. I *am* sorry."

The cop held up a calm hand. "'S no problem at all. I don't hold with making other folk change their way of life 'cause of me."

Matthews lifted the glass of beer. "You want me to get rid of it or anything?"

As the cop glanced at the beer his eyes flashed— the same as they had when he'd walked through the bar, looking longingly at the row of bottles lined up like prostitutes on a street corner.

"Nope," the detective said. "You can't go hiding from it." He ate some more mashed potatoes then said, "Where you find most of the runaways go?"

Matthews enjoyed each small sip of the beer. The detective eyed him every third or fourth. The aroma from the liquid he'd spilled—on purpose—filled the booth with a sour malty scent. "Always the big city. What a lure New York is. They think about getting jobs, becoming Madonna or whoever the girls want to become nowadays. The boys think they'll get laid every night." Matthews sipped the beer again and looked outside. "*Damn* hot. Imagine that battle."

"Bull Run?"

"Yep, well, I call it first Manassas but that's because I'm from Pennsylvania." Matthews enjoyed another sip. "You married?"

Or did the wife leave the drunk?

"Was. Divorced now."

"Kids?"

Or did they cut Daddy off cold when they got tired of him passing out during *Jeopardy!* on weeknights and puking to die every Sunday morning?

"Two. Wife's got 'em. See 'em some holidays."

Matthews poured down another mouthful. "Must be tough."

"Can be." The fat cop took refuge in his potatoes.

After a minute Matthews asked, "So, you a graduate?"

"How's that?"

"Twelve steps."

"AA? Sure." The cop glanced down at his beefy hands. "Been four years, four months."

"Eight years for me."

Another flicker in the eyes. The cop glanced at the beer.

Matthews laughed. "You're where you are, Konnie. And I'm where I am. I was drinking a fifth of fucking bad whiskey every day. Hell, at least that. Sometimes I'd crack the revenue of a second bottle just after dinner." Konnie didn't notice how FBI-speak had turned into buddy talk, with syntax and vocabulary very similar to his.

"'Crack the revenue.'" Konnie laughed. "My daddy used to say that."

So had some of Matthews's patients.

"Bottle and a half? That's a hell of a lot of drinking."

"Oh, yes, it was. Yes sir. Knew I was going to die. So I gave it up. How bad was it for you?"

The cop shrugged and shoveled peas and potatoes into his mouth.

"Hurt my marriage bad," he offered. Reluctantly the cop added, "I guess it *killed* my marriage."

"Sorry to hear that," Matthews said, thrilling at the sorrow in the man's eyes.

"And it was probably gonna kill me someday."

"What was your drink?" Matthews asked.

"Scotch and beer."

"Ha! Mine too. Dewar's and Bud."

Konnie's eyes grew troubled. "So you . . . what?" The cop nodded at the tall-neck bottle. "What happened? You fell off, huh?"

Matthews's face turned reverential. "I'll tell you the God's truth, Konnie." He took a delicious sip of beer. "I believe in meeting your weaknesses head-on. I won't run from them."

The cop grunted affirmatively.

"See, it seemed too easy to give up drinking completely. You understand me?"

"Not exactly."

"It was the coward's way. A lot of people just stop drinking altogether. But that's as much a failure to me . . . sorry, don't take this personal."

"Not at all, keep going. I'm interested."

"That's as much a failure to me as somebody who drinks all the time."

"Guess that makes some sense," the cop said slowly.

Matthews swirled the beer seductively in his glass.

"Take a man addicted to sex. You know that can be a problem?"

"I've heard. They got a twelve-step for that too, you know?"

"Right. But he can hardly give up sex altogether, right? That'd be unnatural."

Konnie nodded.

Oh, he's with me, Matthews thought. Hell, *this* is like sex talking your way into a man's soul. He felt so high. "So," he continued, "I just got back to the point where I could control it."

"And that worked?" Konnie asked. The toady little man seemed awestruck.

"You betcha. I stopped cold for two years. Just like I told myself I'd do. This was all planned out. Sometimes it was tough as hell. I'm not gonna sugarcoat it. But God helped me. As soon as I had it under control, two years to the day I stopped, I took my first drink. One shot of Dewar's. Drank it down like medicine."

"What happened?"

"Nothing. Felt good. Enjoyed it. Didn't have another. Didn't have anything for a week. Then I had another shot and a Bud. I let a month go by."

"A month?" Konnie whispered.

"Right. Then I poured a glass of scotch. Let it sit in front of me. Looked at it, smelled it, poured it down the drain. Let another month go by."

The cop shook his head in wonder. "Sounds like you're one of them masochists or whatever you call 'em." But there was a desperation in his laugh.

"Sometimes we have to find the one thing that's hardest for us and turn around and stare right at it. Go deep. As deep as we can go. That's what courage is. That's what makes men out of us."

"I can respect what you're saying."

"I've been drinking off and on for the past six years. Never been drunk once." He leaned forward and rested his hand on the cop's hammy forearm. "Remember that feeling when you were first drinking?"

"I think—"

"It made you relaxed, peaceful, happy? Brought out your good side? That's the way it is now." Matthews leaned back. "I'm proud of myself."

"To you." The cop swallowed and tipped his milk against the beer glass. His eyes slid over the golden surface of the brew.

Oh, you poor fool, thought Aaron Matthews. You don't have a soul in the world to talk to, do you? "Sometimes," he continued pensively, "when I have a real problem, something eating at me, something making me feel so guilty it's like a fire inside . . . Well, I'll have a shot. That numbs it. It helps me get through."

"No foolin'." The fork probed the diminished pile of potatoes.

Let's go deep.

Touch the most painful part . . .

"If I found myself in a situation where there was somebody I loved and she was drifting away because of the way I'd become—well, I'd want to be able to face whatever had driven her away. I could show her I was in control again and—who knows?—maybe I could just get her back."

The cop's face was flushed and it seemed that his throat had swollen closed.

Matthews sipped more beer, looked out the window, at the dusk sky. "Yes sir, I hated living alone. Waking up on those Sunday mornings. Those March Sunday mornings, the sky all gray . . . The holidays by myself . . . God, I *hated* that. My wife gone . . . The one person in the world I needed. The one person I was willing to do anything for . . ."

The detective was paralyzed.

Now, Matthews thought. Now!

"Let me show you something." Matthews leaned forward, winking. "Watch this." He waved to the waitress. "Shot of Dewar's."

"One?" she called.

"Just one, yeah."

Numb, the cop watched the glass arrive.

Matthews made a show of reaching down and picking up the brimming glass. He leaned forward, smelled the glass, then took the tiniest sip. He set the glass down on the table and lifted his hands, palms up.

"That's it. The only hard liquor I'll have for two, three weeks."

"You can do that?" The cop was dumbfounded.

"Easiest thing in the world. Without a single problem." He returned to his beer and called the waitress over. "I'm sorry, honey. I'll pay you for it but I changed my mind. I think I better keep a clear head tonight. You can take it."

"Sure thing, sir."

The cop's hand made it to the glass before hers. She blinked in surprise at the vehemence of the big man's gesture.

"Oh, you want me to leave that after all?"

The cop looked at Matthews but then turned his dog eyes to the waitress. "Yeah. And bring my friend here another beer."

A fraction of a pause. Their eyes met. Matthews said, "Make it two."

"Sure thing, gentlemen. Put it on your tab?"

"Oh, no," Matthews insisted. "This's on me."

Matthews, wearing his surgical gloves, drove Konnie's car out of the parking lot of the strip mall and toward the interstate. The cop was in the passenger seat, clutching a bottle of scotch between his legs like it was the joystick in a biplane. His head rocked against the Taurus's window. Spit and liquor ran down his chin.

Matthews parked on a side road, not far from Ernie's, lifted the bottle away from Konnie and splashed some on the dashboard and seat of the car, handed it back. Konnie didn't notice. "How you doing?" Matthews asked him.

The big man gazed morosely at the open mouth of the bottle and said nothing.

At the strip mall where they'd bought the scotch Matthews had pitched out a trash bag containing the tire receipts and all the rest of the notes on the Megan McCall investigation. The doctor now climbed out of the car, pulled Konnie into the driver's seat.

Konnie gulped down two large slugs of liquor. He wiped his sweating, pasty face. "Where'm I going?"

"You're going home, Konnie."

"Okay."

"You go on home now."

"Okay. I'm going home. Is Carol there?"

"Your wife? Yeah, she's there, Konnie. She's waiting for you to come home. You better hurry."

"I really miss her."

"You know where to go, don't you?" Matthews asked.

"I think . . ." His bleary eyes looked around. "I don't know."

"That road right there. See it?"

"Sure. There?"

"Right there," Matthews said. "Just drive down there. That'll get you home. That'll get you home to Carol."

"Okay."

"Good-bye, Konnie."

"Good-bye. That road there?"

"That's right. Hey, Konnie?"

Matthews looked at the rheumy eyes, wet lips.

"You say hi to Carol for me, won't you?"

The cop nodded.

Matthews flicked the gearshift into drive and stepped back as Konnie accelerated. He was driving more or less down the middle of the road.

Matthews was walking back to Ernie's to pick up the Mercedes when he heard the sudden squealing of brakes and the blares of a dozen horns, signaling to Konnie that he'd turned his dark blue Taurus onto the exit, not entrance, ramp of I-66 and was driving the wrong way down the interstate. It was no more than thirty seconds later that he heard the pounding crash of what was probably a head-on collision and—though perhaps only in his imagination—a faint scream.

Chapter Twenty-three

Night now.

The corridors of the asylum were murky, illuminated only by the light from two outdoor security lamps bleeding in through the greasy windows.

Megan McCall, gripping her glass sword, moved silently through the main wing. She couldn't get the comic books out of her mind, the tentacles gripping screaming women, the monsters raping them.

Moving toward the boy's room. Closer, closer.

She stepped into the large lobby. In the dim light, shadows filled the space. She *believed* he was back in his room but he could have been anywhere.

Megan felt a breath on her neck and spun around, practically feeling the metal rod he carried swinging toward her head. Gasping.

Nothing but a faint breeze.

Was he asleep in there? Reading? Jerking off?

Fantasizing about her?

About what he was going to *do* to her?

The hospital corridors were like a maze. She lost her way and was no longer sure where his rooms were. Made several false turns and found herself back where she'd started. Feeling desperate now. Megan was afraid that he'd find the trap—her only advantage against the boy. She walked more quickly, listening carefully. But she heard no obscene breathing, no lewd whispering of her name. In a way the silence was *more* frightening than his mutterings, not having the least indication where he was.

Then she turned a corner and found his room. She saw light spilling into the corridor from the open door. It flickered and darkened for a moment.

He was inside.

Megan, sweating. Megan, scared.

Scared of dying, scared of the monster who lives up the hall, scared of the whispering bears.

Well, you wanted him, Crazy Megan whispers. *What're you waiting for? Go get him.*

Megan started to tell C.M. to be quiet. But suddenly she stopped—because a thought hit her with the strength of the cinder blocks piled up in her trap. It was this: that Crazy Megan not only isn't crazy, she's completely sane. And more than that: C.M. is the only one of them who's real.

Crazy Megan is the genuine Megan—the Megan who danced on the scaffolding of the water tower on a dare, just to get Bett or Tate or *somebody* to notice her. The Megan who secretly dreamed of going to San Francisco for a year after high school and then to college in Paris. The Megan who made fierce love with a sexy black boyfriend who—fuck you, Dr. Hanson—I *do* love after all! The Megan who wanted to poke her finger into her father's face and scream at him, "The inconvenient child's back and you've got her whether you like it or not!"

Oh, yeah, Crazy Megan's the sane one. And the other one's just a loser.

"Okay," she said out loud. "Okay, prick, come and get me." The shadow of Peter Matthews froze on the wall.

The light clicked out and the corridor filled with darkness.

"Come on, you fucker!" she shouted.

There was a ring of metal—he must have picked up the rod.

She couldn't see clearly but she could just make out his form lumbering slowly from the doorway. He looked up and down the hall and then turned toward her. "Megan . . ."

God, he's big.

"Megan!" he rasped.

He started toward her. Moving much faster than she'd expected from the shuffling lope she'd heard earlier.

Her courage dissolved. What a fucking stupid idea this is! Hell, it's not going to work. Of course it isn't. He'll get her.

"No!" she screamed in panic.

Get going! Crazy Megan shouts. *Run.*

She backed up fast, knowing that she should be watching where she was going but afraid to take her eyes off him for an instant.

Feeling the wall behind her. Nearly tripped on a table. She spun around, pushed it aside.

And when she looked back he was gone.

We're fucked, Crazy Megan whispers hopelessly.

He could be anywhere now! Coming up around her from the left or the right.

And, of course, she remembered, he'd have keys to the place; he could hide in one of the locked rooms and wait for her to pass by. And then . . . move from room to room and come up behind her.

There was nothing she could do now except return to the dead end corridor where she'd set up the trap. Get there as fast as she could and wait.

But in her panic she was turned around. Was it back *that* way? Or down *this* corridor? She gazed down two hallways. Which? He could be down either of them. She could hardly see a thing in the darkness.

There, she thought. It's got to be that one. I'm sure.

Almost sure.

She sprinted. She slammed into a fiberglass chair, sending it flying. She stayed upright but the noise of the furniture hitting the wall was very loud.

Megan froze. Had he heard? Had—

Suddenly a huge form stepped from the corridor about two feet away, lunging toward her. "Megan . . ."

Megan screamed, couldn't get the knife up in time. She closed her eyes, swinging her left fist toward where his face was. She connected hard and must have broken his nose because he wailed in pain and dropped back, around the corner.

She ran.

Turned one corner and paused at the entrance to the hallway that led to the trap.

He followed, moving toward her.

She made sure he got a good look at her, to see which way she was going, then started toward the trap.

But she stopped. Wait! Was it *this* corridor? No,

the next. Wait. Was it? She glanced into the murky shadows and couldn't see.

Peter was getting closer. *Which fucking corridor?* Crazy Megan shouts.

I don't know, I don't know, they all look alike . . .

He was twenty feet away.

Come on, snaps C.M. *Get it together.*

No choice. It better be this one.

Megan ran to the end of the corridor.

Yes! She'd been right. There was the trap. She crouched down and picked up the end of the rope. At the far end of the corridor Peter paused and glanced toward her.

More muttering. Like an animal. She remembered the newspaper picture: his odd mouth, probing tongue, the crazy eyes. The grin at his mother's funeral.

I'm so fucking scared . . .

You're gonna nail him, Crazy Megan says.

In the darkness he didn't even seem to be walking. He just floated closer to her, growing larger and larger, filling the corridor. He stopped right before the trap. She couldn't see his eyes or face in the shadow but she knew he was leering at her.

More muttering.

He stepped closer.

Now!

She pulled the rope.

The denim snapped neatly in half. The cinder blocks shifted slightly but stayed where they were.

Oh, no. Oh, Christ, no! *That's it,* Crazy Megan cries. *It's over with.*

He moved forward another two steps.

She swept the knife from her pocket, looked at his shadowy form.

I'm going to die. This is it. I'm dead. He'll break my arm, take the knife away from me and fuck me till I die . . . Megan's by herself now—Crazy Megan has gone away, Crazy Megan is dead already.

He stepped forward one more foot. The dim light from outside fell on his face.

No . . .

She was hallucinating.

Megan gasped. "Josh!"

"Megan," he mumbled again. Joshua LeFevre's face and neck were bloody messes, his hands, arms and legs too. Large patches of skin were missing from his arms and legs. He dropped to his knees.

Just as the cinder blocks started to tumble toward him. He glanced hopelessly at the hundreds of pounds of concrete and didn't even try to get out of the way.

"No!" Megan cried.

She leapt forward and pushed him aside. The blocks just missed them both and crashed into the floor, firing splinters of stone through the air.

"Megan," he said, the name stuttering out from his torn throat. Blood sprayed her face as he spoke. Then he passed out.

Tate Collier's Lexus skidded up to the pay phone on Route 29.

He leapt out, looking around desperately.

He saw no one.

"Hello?" he called in a harsh whisper. "Hello!"

He glanced at the old diner—or what was left of it

after an arson fire some years ago—and piles of trash. Deserted.

Then he heard a moan, followed by some violent retching.

Tate ran into the bushes. There Konnie sat, bloody and drenched in sweat, vomit on his chin, eyes unfocused. He'd been crying.

"Jesus. What happened?" Tate bent down, put his arm around the man. When Konnie'd called him twenty minutes ago he'd said only to meet him here as soon as possible. Tate knew he was drunk, only half conscious, but had no other clue as to what was going on.

"I'm going down, Tate. I fucked up bad. Oh, Christ . . ."

Bett . . . now Konnie . . . What a day, Tate thought. What a day.

"You're hurt."

"I'm okay. But I may've killed people, Tate. There was an accident. I left the scene." He gasped and retched for a minute. "They're looking for me, my own people're looking for me." He coughed violently.

"I'll call an ambulance."

"No, I'm turning myself in. But—"

He rolled over on his side and retched for a few minutes. Then caught his breath and sat up.

A squad car with flashing lights cruised past slowly. The searchlight came on but it missed the bushes where Tate crouched beside the detective.

"Listen to me," Konnie said. "You have to get to the office. You need to look at the receipts."

"Receipts."

"For the tires. Go to the office, Tate. Genie

should've made a copy of them. I'm praying she did. Ask her for them. But move fast 'cause they're going to impound my desk."

"Genie? That's your assistant?"

"You remember her. The list of receipts, okay?"

"All right."

"Then look for whoever paid cash for the tires."

"Cash for the tires. All right."

"She ran warrants but that's not . . . that's not what I shoulda been looking for. Tate, you listening?"

"I'm listening."

"Good. Look for the receipts where the customers paid cash. Then run the tag numbers of their cars. If the registered owner doesn't match the name on the receipt that's our boy. The one took your daughter. I got a look at . . ." He caught his breath. "I got a look at him."

"You saw him?"

"Oh, yeah. The prick suckered me good. He's white, forties, dark hair. Six feet. About one seventy. Said he . . . *Claimed* he was Bureau. He suckered me just like my daddy suckered people. Shit. God, I'm sick."

"Okay, Konnie. I'll do it. But now I'm getting you to the hospital."

"No, you're not. You're not wasting another fucking minute. You're going do what the hell I told you. And be there for my arraignment. I can't believe what I did. I can't believe it." His voice disappeared in a cascade of retching.

Tate found his old commonwealth's attorney ID badge at home and ran back to his car, hanging the beaded chain around his neck.

The date was four years old but was in small type; he doubted anyone would notice.

In twenty minutes he was walking into the police station. No one paid him any attention. He signed the log-in book and walked into Konnie's office.

A heavyset woman, red eyed and crying, looked up.

"Oh, Mr. Collier. Did you hear?"

"He's going to be all right, Genie."

"This's so terrible," she said, wiping her face. "So terrible. I can't imagine he'd take to drinking again. I don't know why. I don't know what's going on."

"I'm going to help him. But I've got to do something first. It's very important."

"He said I should help you when he called. Oh, he sounded so drunk on the phone. I remember he used to call me up and say he wouldn't be coming in today because he had the flu. But it wasn't the flu. He sounded the way he was tonight. Just plain drunk."

Tate rested his hand on the woman's broad shoulder. "He's going to be all right. We'll all help him. Did you make a copy of the receipts?"

"I did, yes. He always tells me, 'Make a copy of everything I give you. Always, always, always make a copy.'"

"That's Konnie."

"Here they are."

He took the stack of receipts, owners of Mercedeses who'd bought new Michelins. On four receipts the cash/check box was marked. He didn't recognize any of the names.

"Could you run these tag numbers through DMV

and get me the names and addresses of the registered owners?"

"Sure." She sniffed and waddled to her chair, sat heavily. Then she typed furiously.

A moment later she motioned him over.

The first three names matched those on the receipts.

The fourth didn't.

"Oh my God," Tate muttered.

"What is it, Mr. Collier?"

He didn't answer. He stood, numb, staring at the name Aaron Matthews, Sully Fields Drive, Manassas, the letters glowing in jaundice yellow type on the black screen.

Chapter Twenty-four

The Court: *The prosecution may now present its summation. Mr. Collier?*

Mr. Collier: *My friends . . . The task of the jury is a difficult and thankless one. You're called on to sift through a haystack of evidence, looking for that single needle of truth. In many cases, that needle is elusive. Practically impossible to find. But in the case before you,* the Commonwealth versus Peter Matthews, *the needle is lying out in the open, evident for everyone to see.*

There is no question that the defendant killed Joan Keller. He was seen walking with the victim, a sixteen-year-old girl, by Bull Run Marina. He was seen leading her into the woods. He was later seen running from the park five minutes before Joan's body was found, strangled to death. The mud in which her cold corpse lay matched the mud found on the knees of the defendant's jeans. When he was arrested, as you heard from the testimony, he blurted out to the officers, "She had to die."

And in the trailer where he lived, the police found hundreds of comic books and horror novels, depicting big, hulking men doing unspeakable things to helpless women victims—victims just like Joan Keller.

The defense can see that shiny needle of truth as clearly as you and I can. There's no doubt in their minds, either, that the defendant killed that poor girl. And so what do they do? They try to distract us. They raise doubts about Joan's character. They suggest that she had loose morals. That she'd had sex with local boys . . . sometimes for money. Or for liquor or cigarettes. A sixteen-year-old girl! These are nothing more than vile attempts to distract you from finding the needle.

Oh, they talk about accidental death. "Just playing around," they say. The killer was a troubled young man, they say, but harmless.

Well, I'd say the facts of the case prove that he wasn't harmless at all, don't you think?

Harmless men don't strangle innocent young women seventy pounds lighter than they are.

Harmless men don't act out their sick and twisted fantasies on helpless youngsters like Joanie Sue Keller.

Ladies and gentlemen, don't let the defense hide that needle of truth from you. Don't let them cover it up. This case is simple, extremely simple. The defendant, through his premeditation, his calculation, his knowing, purposeful intent, has taken a life. The life of a young girl. Someone's friend . . . someone's sister . . . someone's daughter. There is no worse crime than that. And he must be held fully responsible for it.

The great poet Dante said that the most righteous requests are answered in the silence of the deed. I'm not asking for hollow words, ladies and gentlemen. No, I'm asking for your courageous deed—finding this dangerous killer sane, finding him guilty and recommending to the court that he pay for young Joan Keller's life with his own. Thank you.

Orator Tate Collier had done everything right in the closing statement. It was short, colloquial, filled with concrete imagery. He'd referred to Peter Matthews as "the defendant" and to the girl as "Joan"— depersonalizing the criminal, humanizing the victim. The reference to the "needle"—getting the jury used to the thought of the needle used in lethal injections— was a particularly good touch, he'd thought.

He'd even added the request for the death penalty because that was something they could bargain with in their minds—trading the boy's life for a finding of sanity and a long prison sentence.

And that was exactly what happened.

He won, the boy was found sane and guilty. And was sentenced to life without parole. Which had been Tate's goal all along.

And a week later the young man who'd beaten capital punishment was executed by a far more informal means than lethal injection—a dozen prison inmates, identities unknown, had used broomsticks and sharpened spoons to carry out the sentence. And it took them three hours to do so.

Justice?

After he'd heard of Peter's death, Tate had sat at his desk for a long moment, wondering why he felt so troubled at the news. Then he walked into the commonwealth's attorney's file room and read through evidence in the case once again.

They were the same files and documents he'd read before the trial, of course. But he examined them now untainted by the passionate drive to convict the young man. He looked more carefully at the picture they painted of the boy—not "the defendant." But Peter Thomas Matthews, a seventeen-year-old boy, a resident of Fairfax, Virginia.

Yes, Peter had a collection of eerie comics and Japanimation tapes. But many of them, Tate had learned in preparing for trial, were best-sellers in Japan—where they'd taken on an artsy cult status and were reviewed seriously and collected by young people and adults alike. What was more, the boy also had a collection of serious science fiction and fantasy writers like Ray Bradbury, Isaac Asimov, William Gibson, C. S. Lewis, J. R. R. Tolkien, Jules Verne, Edgar Rice Burroughs. Peter had spent hours copying long, poetic passages from these books and had tried his hand at illustrating scenes from them. He'd also written sci-fi and fantasy short stories of his own, which weren't bad for someone his age.

Yes, some psychiatric evaluations called the boy dangerous. But others said he merely had a paranoid personality and was given to panic in stressful situations. He had no history of violence.

In getting ready for the case, Tate had also learned about Joan Keller—the victim. The girl had been sexually active since age twelve. She'd experimented with "weird things," possibly erotic asphyxia. She'd seduced older men on several other occasions and would have been the complaining witness in at least one statutory rape case, except that she'd refused to cooperate. She'd been treated for being a borderline personality and had been suspended twice for assaults—against both girls and boys at her school, including one involving a knife.

Peter had abrasions on his face and neck when he was brought to the lockup. He claimed that Joan had struck him with a rock when she got tired of his awkward groping—after *she'd* taken *his* hand and slipped it into her panties.

And the statement the boy had made—about how Joan "had to die"—was disputed by a local fisherman near the scene of the arrest. He claimed the boy might have said, "She never had to die . . . She shouldn't have hit me."

But silver-tongued Tate Collier had managed to keep all of this damning evidence out of the trial or had shattered the credibility of the witnesses presenting it.

Your Honor we will not try the victim in this case Your Honor a well-written short story has no probative value in this case whatsoever Your Honor that fact is immaterial and has to be stricken please instruct the witness . . .

The defense lawyers had come to him with a plea bargain request: criminally negligent homicide, suspended sentence, three years' probation and two years' mandatory counseling.

But, no. Peter Matthews had laid his hands upon the neck of a sixteen-year-old girl and had pressed, pressed, pressed until she was lifeless. And so a plea bargain wouldn't do.

The Court: *The defendant will rise. You have heard the verdict of the jury and have been adjudged guilty of murder in the first degree. The jury has not recommended the death penalty and accordingly I hereby sentence you to life in prison . . .*

He went to prison and the last thing anyone remembered about Peter was his telling a guard he was going to play with his new friends. "Won't that be way cool?" Peter asked. "We're going to play ball, a bunch of us. They want me to play ball. Awesome." Then he disappeared into the laundry room and was found, in several pieces, five hours later.

Why, Tate had wondered back then as he sat alone in the musty file room, had he been so vehement about prosecuting the boy? *Why?*

The question he'd asked himself often in the past few years.

The question he asked himself now. What would have been so bad if the defendant . . . if *Peter* had been put on probation and gone into a hospital for treatment?

Wasn't that reasonable? Of course it was. But it hadn't been then, not to the Tate Collier of five years ago. Not to Tate Collier the whiz-kid commonwealth's attorney, the man who spoke in tongues, the Judge's grandson.

Why?

Because the thought of a killer depriving parents of their child was unbearable to him. *That* was the answer. *That* was all he thought. Someone stole away a girl just like Megan. And he had to die. To hell with justice.

Tate had never seen Peter's father, Aaron Matthews, at the trial or hadn't paid any attention to him if he'd been there. The man was a therapist, Tate remembered from reading the boy's history and evaluations. Lived alone. His wife—a therapist as well, and reportedly more successful than her husband—had committed suicide some years before.

Aaron Matthews . . .

Well, he could give the police a name and address now. They'd find him. He only prayed Megan was still alive.

Now, in Konnie's office, he dialed Bett's home phone. Her voice mail gave her cell phone number and he dialed that. She didn't answer. He left a message about what he'd learned and told her that he was at the county police station.

He started down the hall, striding the way he'd walked when he'd been a commonwealth's attorney and cut up these offices as if he owned them, playing inquisitor to the young officers as he grilled them about their cases and the evidence they'd collected.

He pushed through the door to the Homicide Division and was surprised to see three startled detectives stop in the tracks of their conversations. He smiled ruefully, remembering only then that he was a trespasser.

One detective looked at another, an astonished gaze on his face.

"I'm sorry to barge in," Tate began. "I'm Tate Collier. It's about my daughter. I don't know if you heard but she's disappeared and—"

In less than twenty seconds he was facedown on a convenient desk, the handcuffs ratcheting onto his wrists with metallic efficiency, his Miranda rights floating down upon him from a gruff voice several feet above his head.

"What the hell's going on?" he barked.

"You're under arrest, Mr. Collier. Do you understand these rights as I've read them to you?"

"For what? What're you arresting me for?"

"Do you understand your rights?"

"Yes, I understand my fucking rights. What for?"

"For murder, Mr. Collier. The murder of Amy Walker. If you'll come this way, please."

Chapter Twenty-five

She cradled him, sobbing.

Megan had eased Joshua LeFevre into the pale light from the outside lamp. He was even more badly injured than she'd thought at first—terribly battered—riddled with slashes and bite marks, the wounds crusted with dirt and dried blood. One eye was swollen completely closed. Most of his dreads had been torn off his scalp, which was covered with mud and scabs.

He could speak only in a ghostly, snapping wail. No, it hadn't been Peter Matthews's leering voice she'd heard; it was Josh's. His throat was split open and his vocal cords had apparently been cut. When he breathed, air hissed in through both his mouth and the slash. The bleeding seemed to have stopped but she bound the denim rope around his throat anyway. She could think of nothing else to do.

"*Thought* it was you," he gasped. "I couldn't see. My eyes, my eyes. I thought it was you. But you didn't answer."

Megan lowered her head to his chest. "I thought you were his son. I thought you were going to kill me. Oh, Josh, what happened? Was it the dogs? Outside?"

He nodded, shivered—from the pain, she guessed, as much as the cold.

"That . . . man?" he struggled to ask. "He kidn—"

She nodded. "Did you call the police?"

"No," he gasped. "I didn't know what was going on. I stopped him but he tricked me . . ." He coughed for a moment. "Thought you . . . thought you were going with him."

"What happened?" she asked tearfully.

The stuttering explanation: he'd followed her and Matthews here then the doctor had attacked him and left him for the dogs. But before they could finish him off a young deer had trotted past and they left Josh to pull her down.

His beautiful voice, Megan thought, crying. It's gone. She had to look away from his face.

He'd found a metal rod to use as a cane, he continued, and made his way into the hospital to find a phone. But there weren't any. Then he learned that the doors didn't open outward, that the place was a prison.

She gently touched a terrible wound on his face. Even if they managed to get him to a doctor soon would he survive? He'd lost so much blood.

"Were you . . . you weren't his lover, were you?"

"What?" she blurted.

"He said you were. He said . . . He said you wanted to get rid of me."

"Oh, Josh, no. It was . . . whatever he said, it was a lie."

"Who is he?" LeFevre rasped.

"We don't have time now. Can you walk?"

"No." He breathed heavily and winced. "Can't do anything. I've about had it."

She pulled him farther into the alcove, hid him from view. "Wait here."

"Where . . . you going?"

"Lie still, Josh. Be quiet. I'll get something to use for bandages," she said, rising.

"But he might be there."

She showed him the glass knife. "I hope he is."

"I'll tell you whatever you want to know. But for God's sake send somebody after my daughter."

"Once more from the top, please, sir."

Tate was still stunned from the news that Amy had been found naked and stabbed to death on Tate's farm.

"There's a man named Aaron Matthews. He drives a gray Mercedes. He lives on Sully Field, off Route twenty-nine near Manassas. He's been following my daughter for the past couple weeks. Or months. I don't know. And—"

"We've got our own agenda here, Collier," the young homicide detective—a dead ringer for the security guard at Megan's high school—said gruffly, his patience gone. "You don't mind, we got a lotta ground to cover."

"Is Ted Beauridge around?"

"No. One more time, sir. From the top."

He was in an interrogation cubicle and he was perched on an uncomfortable metal chair. At least the cuffs were off.

"Matthews killed Amy. Megan had told her about being followed. He thought she might have some information—maybe he just killed her to get me out of the picture."

And *I* gave him her name, Tate thought. He was sure the man who called from the FBI—Special Agent McComb—was Aaron Matthews, probing to get information to stop their search for the girl. He forced or tricked Megan into writing those notes and when they kept looking for her anyway, he turned on them.

"How'd you find out about the body?" Tate asked. "An anonymous call, right?"

The detectives looked at each other. They were slim and in perfect shape. Shoes polished, guns tucked neatly away. Law enforcement machines.

"It was *Matthews* who called. Don't you get it?"

"Her mother said you'd been stalking Amy. That Child Protective Services has been investigating you."

"What? That's bullshit. Call them."

"On Saturday night, sir? We'll call on Monday."

"We don't have until Monday."

The cop continued lethargically, "Mrs. Walker also said you tried to break into her house today."

"Amy was going to give us Megan's book bag. I knocked on the door and tried to open it when no one answered."

"Uh-huh."

"There *is* no Child Protective Services investigation. It's him! It's Matthews. He's trying to stop me from finding Megan. Can't you see?"

"Not exactly, sir. No."

"Okay. When did this anonymous call come in? Within the last half hour? Believe me, Matthews killed Amy and dumped the body on my land. I saw somebody watching the house this morning."

"Did you report it?"

"Well, no, I didn't."

"Why not?"

Tate remembered thinking, as he stood in the rain-swept field that morning, Hey, looks like the Dead Reb. But it wasn't. It was Aaron Matthews, waiting until I left the house then tossing the dog a bone, planting Megan's letters, leaving fast.

"I just didn't. Look, he knows I'm after him—Konnie was running a check on the Mercedes. It turned out to be his. That's not a coincidence."

"How do you account for the fact that this girl was murdered with a kitchen knife that had your fingerprints on it?"

"Because it was probably from *my* kitchen. Talk to Konnie about this morning. He—"

"Detective Konstantinatis is in custody and he's also in no shape to talk to anybody. As I'm sure you know."

"Beauridge, then. They were out to my house. Matthews broke in, planted some fake letters that Megan supposedly wrote and he must've stolen the knife at the same time. Or stolen it tonight. It's an easy house to break into."

"The cause of death was shock due to blood loss after her throat was slashed and her chest and abdomen punctured thirty-two times. There was some mutilation too."

"Fuck of a way to kill someone," the other detective added.

Tate's face grew hot. Megan's terrified eyes were the most prominent image in his thoughts.

"We've checked out your house and found you'd

packed most of your girl's stuff away. Her bedroom looked about as personal as a storeroom."

"She lives with her mother."

"No pictures of her, no clothes, nothing personal. The impression we got was you'd been planning to say adios to Megan for some time. That's making us wonder about this whole kidnapping story."

"There were some witnesses. There's a teacher . . . Robert Eckhard. He saw—" But he stopped talking when he saw the expression on their faces.

"You a friend of Eckhard?"

"I don't know him," Tate said cautiously. "I just heard that he'd seen the car that was following Megan."

"Have you ever talked to him?"

"No. I just told you—why?"

"Robert Eckhard was arrested today on numerous counts of child pornography and endangering the welfare of minors."

"*What?*"

"Could you describe your relationship with him?"

"With Eckhard? There *is* no relationship . . . Jesus Christ. I don't know him! Please! Just send somebody out to check out this Matthews!"

A rhetorician never pleads. Tate's talents were deserting him in droves. Think smarter, he raged at himself. He could talk his way out of this. He *knew* he could. There must be some way. What would his grandfather, the Judge, have done?

All cats see in the dark . . .

Midnight is a cat . . .

"Officer," Tate said calmly, offering a casual smile, "you've got nothing to lose. Absolutely nothing. I'm not going anywhere. If you check him out, if you send a couple officers out to his house then I'll tell you whatever you want to know. Anything. No hassle. We have a deal?"

One of the detectives sighed. He shrugged and stepped out the door.

Therefore Midnight sees in the dark.

Tate pictured Megan, bound and gagged, lying somewhere in a basement. Matthews standing over her. Undressing. It was a terrible image and, once thought, wouldn't go away.

"Have you ever had sexual relations with Amy Walker?"

He tamped down his anger. "I've never met her," he answered.

"Did you send your daughter off somewhere because she knew you were stalking Amy Walker? And did you fabricate a kidnapping charge?"

"No, I didn't do that." Struggling now to stay calm, to stay *helpful.* Really struggling. He looked at the doorway through which the other cop had disappeared. Were they sending a hostage rescue team to Matthews's house? Or just patrol officers? Matthews could trick them. He could lull them into complacency—oh, yes, *he* had the gift too. Tate now understood.

You can't negotiate with someone like Matthews. You need to act—immediately.

The silence of the deed.

"Did you kill Amy Walker?"

"No, I did not."

"When was the last time you drove your daughter's car?"

"A month or so ago, I think."

"Is that how your fingerprints got on the door handle of her car?"

"It would have to be."

"Could we run through the events just prior to her disappearance once more?"

"Prior?"

"Say, for the week before."

Tate glanced out the door, squinted. Looked again. The second detective came back into the cubicle. Tate asked, "Did you send a team to his house? I should have told you to send hostage rescue. Not regular officers. And don't listen to him. Whatever he says, Megan's there, in the house. Tell whoever's on their way not to listen to him."

"He wasn't home."

"What?" Tate asked. He didn't understand. The officers couldn't have gotten there so quickly.

"I called him. He wasn't home."

"You *called* him?" Tate's heart stuttered.

"Relax, sir, I didn't tell him anything. Just asked him to give us a call about some parking tickets." The slick young cop seemed proud of his cleverness.

"Jesus Christ, you don't *have* to tell him anything. Are you crazy?"

"Sir, we don't have to pay any attention to your story at all, you know. We're doing you a favor."

Tate sat back, glanced into the hall again.

After a moment he looked back at the officers again. Closed his eyes and sighed. "You win. Okay, you win."

"How's that, sir?"

"I'll waive my rights and tell you everything I can think of. No confession but a full statement about my daughter and Amy Walker. But I want some coffee and I've got to use the john."

They looked at each other and nodded.

"I'm coming with you," the first detective muttered.

Tate laughed. "I was a commonwealth's attorney for ten years. I'm not going to escape."

"I'm coming with you."

Tate gave a disgusted sigh and walked into the scuffed halls, which resembled a suburban grade school. He ambled to the men's room and pushed inside. The detective was directly behind him.

He stood at the urinal for an inordinately long time. When he'd finished and washed his hands he stepped to the door and pushed it open, bumping into the woman who was juggling three large law books and several pads of foolscap, which tumbled to the floor.

"Sorry," Tate said, bending down to pick up the books.

Bett McCall glanced at him, said, "No problem." And slipped the pistol out of her purse and into his hand.

Tate didn't even pause to think—he simply spun around, shoved the Smith & Wesson into the belly of the shocked detective and pushed him back into the men's room as Bett calmly retrieved the books.

In one minute Tate had gagged and cuffed the furious cop and relieved him of his gun. He tossed it in the wastebasket.

"The cuffs too tight?" he asked.

The detective stared angrily.

"Are they too tight?"

A nod.

Tate snapped, "Good."

And stepped out into the corridor as a faint rumble arose in the john, like a low-Richter earthquake. The detective was trying to pull down the stall.

When he'd looked into the hallway from the interrogation room he couldn't believe that he'd seen her standing there, motioning with her head down the hall. "How did you get in here?" he asked as they walked briskly toward the exit.

"Told them I was a lawyer."

"You cite a case or two?"

"I could have." She smiled. "I memorized the names of a couple on your desk. I was going to tell the desk sergeant I had to see my client because these new cases had just been put down."

"It's 'handed down,'" Tate corrected.

"Oh. Glad he didn't ask."

"I don't know if we can get out that way. I came in under my own steam but the desk officer might know I've been arrested." He looked back down the corridor. "Five minutes, tops, till they come looking."

She rearranged the books she was carrying so the cover showed. A school hornbook, *Williston on Contracts.*

He laughed. "That'll fool 'em." Then asked, "You got my message?"

She nodded. "I called Konnie and his assistant told me you'd been arrested. I couldn't decide whether to get a lawyer or the gun. I figured we didn't have time to wait for public defenders. My car's outside."

The old Bett McCall might have meditated for days, hoping for guidance. The new one went right for the Smith & Wesson.

They paused just before they turned the corner beside the guard station. He took a breath. "Ready?"

"I guess."

"Let's go."

Tate started forward, Bett at his side. The guard glanced at them but out they strolled without a hitch, signing the "time departed" line in the logbook scrupulously—one a phony prosecutor and one a phony defense lawyer and both of them now felons.

Aaron Matthews was driving, seventy, then eighty miles an hour.

Anger had given way to sorrow. To the same piercing hollowness he'd felt in the months after Peter had died in prison. Sorrow at plans gone wrong, terribly wrong.

Matthews had been at his rental house, off Route 29, waiting to see if he'd finally stopped Tate Collier. He believed he had. He'd given up on the subtlety, given up on the words, given up on the delicious art of persuasion. Stiff with anger, he'd dragged the Walker girl, screaming, from the trunk of his car. Said nothing, convinced her of nothing—he'd just slashed and slashed and slashed . . . All of his anger flowing from him as hot and sudden as the blood from her body. He'd called from a pay phone to report seeing a body then had sped home.

There the phone had rung. He hadn't answered but listened to the message as the officer left it. Some bullshit about traffic tickets. "Give us a call when you get home. Thank you."

It meant, of course, that they knew about him. Or suspected, at least.

How had it happened? Why hadn't they just tossed Collier into the lockup and ignored him? Maybe he had actually convinced them that he was innocent and that Matthews had kidnapped the girl. The fucking silver-tongued devil! An angry, sorrowful mood exploded within Matthews like napalm.

It was only a matter of time now before they found Blue Ridge Facility. They knew his name, they'd find out his connection there, and they'd find Megan.

He stared out the window for a moment. Then closed his eyes.

In a perfect world, moods don't burn you like torches, juries work pure justice and revenge befalls sinners in exact proportion to their crimes. In a perfect world Matthews would have kept Megan McCall as his child forever, a replacement for Peter. And Tate Collier would have lived in despair all his life, never knowing where she was—knowing only that she'd fled from him, propelled by undiluted hate.

But there was no chance for such symmetry now. All his hopes had unraveled. And there was only one answer left. To kill the girl and leave. Flee to the West Coast, New England, maybe overseas.

He'd lost his son, Tate Collier would lose his daughter.

A kind of cure, a kind of justice, a kind of revenge . . .

He spent a few minutes preparing some things in his house then hurried to his car. He sped out onto the highway, toward the distant humps of mountains, a sensuous dark line above which no stars became stars and the moon showed as a faint, white crescent of frown.

• • •

Cleaning the deep wounds was the hardest part.

She'd found a cheap sewing kit in the bedroom and a bottle of rubbing alcohol in the medicine cabinet.

He took the stitches bravely (even though *she* cringed every time the needle pierced his skin). But when Megan poured a capful of alcohol on the wounds he shivered frantically at the pain.

"Oh, I'm sorry."

"No, no," came his garbled voice. "Keep at it, Ms. Beautiful . . ."

Her eyes teared when she heard the nickname he'd used the night he picked her up.

"Even if you get out, you'll never get past 'em. The dogs. He's got four or five of the big fuckers."

"You're sure you can't walk?"

"I don't think so," he gurgled. "No."

"Okay, you stay here. I saw a door going to the basement. I think I can break it open. I'm going to see if there's a door or window down there. Maybe it'll lead outside."

He nodded, breathed, "I love . . ." and passed out.

She stacked the cinder blocks around him so that if Matthews glanced this way he wouldn't see the young man.

She listened for a moment to his low, uneven breathing. Then, knife in one hand, she started down the corridor.

Megan was almost to the intersection of the corridors when she heard the creak of a door opening. Then it slammed.

Aaron Matthews had returned.

Chapter Twenty-six

They drove in silence through destitute parts of Prince William County. They passed tilled fields, where the taproots of corn were reaching silently down into the dark, red-tinted earth. Barns long ago abandoned. Decaying tract bungalows, where postwar dreams had withered fast—tiny cubes of vinyl—and aluminum-sided homes. Shacks and cars on blocks.

Through Manassas, where the fearsome Rebel yell was first heard, then through the outlying farms and past the Confederate Cemetery.

"It was him, Tate," Bett said, breaking a long silence.

"Who?"

"A man came to see me. He said he was her therapist but he wasn't."

"It was Matthews?"

"He called himself Peters."

"His son's name was Peter," Tate mused. "That must be why he picked it." Glanced at her. "What happened?"

She shook her head. "He seduced me. Nothing really happened but it was enough . . . Oh, Tate, he looked right into my soul. He knew what I wanted to hear. He said exactly the right things."

You can talk your way into somebody's heart and get them to do whatever you want. Judge or jury, you've got that skill. Words, Tate. Words. You can't see them but they're the most dangerous weapons on earth. Remember that. Be careful, son.

She continued, "He'd called Brad. I think he pretended he was a cop and told him to get to my house. We were together on the couch . . . I was drunk . . . Oh, Tate."

Tate put his hand on her knee, squeezed lightly. "There was nothing you could've done, Bett. He's too good. Somehow, he's done all of this. Dr. Hanson, Konnie . . . probably Eckhard too, the teacher. Just to get even with me." They drove on in silence. Then Tate realized something. "You got here too quickly."

"What?"

"You couldn't have been in Baltimore when you got my message."

"No, I got as far as Takoma Park and turned back."

"Why?"

A long pause.

"Because I decided it had to stop." Instinctively she flipped the mirror down and examined her face. Poked at a wrinkle or two. "I was running after Brad and I should have been going after Megan." She continued, "I realized something, Tate. How mad I've been at her."

"At Megan? Because of what we heard at the Coffee Shop?"

"Oh, Lord, no. That's *my* fault, not hers." She took a deep breath, flipped the mirror back up. "No, Tate. I've been mad at her for years. And I shouldn't've been. It wasn't her fault. She was born at the wrong time and the wrong place."

"Yes, she sure was."

"I neglected her and didn't do the things I should have . . . I dated, I left her alone. I did the basics, sure. But kids know. They know where your heart is. Here I was, running after Joe or Dave or Brad and leaving my daughter. Time for that to stop. I'm just praying it's not too late."

"We'll find her."

The roads were deserted here and the air aromatic with smoke from wood cooking fires, common in this poor part of the county. The Volvo streaked through a stop sign. Tate skidded into a turn and then headed down a bad road.

"We're in trouble, aren't we?" she asked.

"We sure are. They don't put out all-points bulletins anymore. But if they did we'd be the main attraction in one."

"They don't know my car," Bett pointed out.

He laughed. "Oh, that took all of thirty seconds for 'em to track down. Look, there. That's his place."

Matthews's small bungalow was visible through a stand of trees some distance away. A rusting heating-oil tank sat in the side yard and the stands of uncut grass were outnumbered by patches of red mud. The house was only two miles away from Tate's farm. A convenient staging point for a break-in and kidnapping, he noted.

"What are we going to do?" Bett asked.

Tate didn't answer her. Instead he took the gun out of his pocket. "We're going to get our daughter," he said.

Thirty yards, twenty, fifteen. Tate paused and listened. Silence from inside Matthews's house.

He smelled the scent of wood smoke and pictured the kidnapper sitting beside the fireplace with Megan bound and gagged at his feet.

The shabby house chilled his heart. He'd seen places like it often. Too often. When he was a commonwealth's attorney he'd always—unlike most big-city prosecutors—visited the crime scenes himself. This was what detectives dubbed a section-sixty cottage, referring to the Virginia Penal Code provision for murder. Shotgun killings, domestics, love gone cruel then violent . . . There were common elements among such houses: they were small, filthy, silent, brimming with unspoken hate.

The Mercedes wasn't in the drive so it was possible that Matthews hadn't heard the message from the police. Maybe Megan was here now, lying in the bedroom or the basement. Maybe this would be the end of it. But he moved as silently as he could, taking no chances.

He glanced through the window.

The living room was empty, lit only by the glow of embers in the fireplace. He listened for a long moment. Nothing.

The windows were locked but he tested the handle on the door and found it was open. He pushed inside, thinking only as he did so: Why a fire on a warm night?

Oh, no! He lunged for the doorknob but it was too late; the door knocked over the large pail of gasoline.

"God!"

Instinctively Tate grabbed for the bucket as the pink wave of gas flowed onto the floor and into the fireplace.

"What?" Bett cried.

The gas ignited and with a whoosh a huge ball of flame exploded through the living room.

"Megan!" Tate cried, turning away from the flames and falling onto the porch. His sleeve was on fire. He slapped out the flames.

"She's in there? *She's in there?*" Bett shouted in panic and ran to the window. Scrabbling away from the flowing gasoline, Tate grabbed Bett and pulled her back. He covered his face with his hand, felt the searing heat take the hairs off the back of his fingers.

"Megan!" Bett cried. She broke the window in with her elbow. She peered inside for a moment but then leapt back as a plume of flame burst through the window at her. If she hadn't leapt aside the fire would have consumed her face and hair.

Tate ran around the back of the cottage, broke in the window in one of the bedrooms, which was already filling with dense smoke.

No sign of the girl.

He ran to the other bedroom—the cottage had only two—and saw that she wasn't there either. The flames were already burning through the bedroom door, which, with a sudden burst, exploded inward. In the light from the fire Tate could see that this wasn't a bedroom but an office. There were stacks of newspaper clippings, magazines, books and folders. Maps, charts and diagrams.

Sirens sounded in the distance.

Bett came up behind him. There was a burn on her arm but she was otherwise okay. "Tate, I can't find her!" she screamed.

"I don't think she's here. She's not in either of these rooms and there's no basement."

"Where *is* she?"

"The answer's in there," he shouted. "He only set the trap so nobody could find any clues to where he's got her."

He picked up several bricks and shattered the glass-and-wooden grid in the window. "Oh, brother," he muttered. And climbed inside, feeling the unnerving pain as a shard of glass sliced through his palm.

The heat inside was astonishing, smoke and embers and flecks of burning paper swirling around him, and he realized that the flames weren't the worst problem—the heated air and lack of oxygen were going to knock him out in minutes.

He raced to the desk and grabbed all the papers and notebooks he could, ran to the window and flung them outside, crying to Bett, "Get it all away from the house." He went back for more. He got two more armfuls before the heat grew too much. He dove out the window and rolled to the ground heavily as the ceiling collapsed and a swell of flame puffed out the window.

He lay, exhausted, gasping, on the ground. Dizzy

and hurt. Wondering why on earth Bett was doing a funny little dance around his arm. Then he understood. The file folder he held had been burning and she was stamping out the flames.

The sirens were getting closer.

"Great," he muttered. "Now they're gonna add arson to our rap sheets."

Bett helped him up and they gathered all the notebooks and files he'd flung into the backyard. They ran to the car. Tate started it and skidded out of the drive, passing the first of the fluorescent green fire trucks that were speeding toward the house.

They turned north and drove for ten minutes until Tate figured there was no chance of being spotted. He parked near a quarry in Manassas. A grim, eerie place that looked like it should have been a serial killer's stalking ground though to Tate's knowledge there'd never been any crime committed here worse than pot smoking and drinking beer and sloe gin from open containers.

Tate and Bett pored over the singed files and papers, looking for some clue as to where Matthews might have taken Megan.

The files were mostly articles, psychiatric diagnostic reports, medical evaluations. He also found surveillance photos of Megan. Dozens of them. And of Tate's house and Bett's. Matthews had been planning this for months; some of the pictures had been taken during the winter. In one notebook Megan's daily routine was described in obsessive detail.

More patient notes.

More articles.

More diaries. With shaking hands Tate and Bett read through them all but there was no clue as to any other buildings, apartments or houses where he might have taken the girl.

"There's nothing," Bett barked in frustration. "We've looked at everything." Tears on her face.

Tate gazed at the mess of scorched papers and files on their laps. His eye fell on a patient diagnostic report. Then another. He flipped through them quickly. Then read the name and address of the hospital where the patients had been evaluated.

He snatched up his cell phone and, eyes on one of the reports, made a call to directory assistance for Calvert, Virginia. He asked for the number for the Blue Ridge Mental Health Facility.

"Please be out of order," he whispered.

"Why on earth?" Bett asked.

"Please . . ."

"We're sorry," the electronic voice reported, "there is no listing for that name. Do you have another request?"

He clicked the phone off. "That's where she is. An old mental hospital in the Shenandoahs." He tapped the reports. "Matthews was a shrink. I'd guess he was on the staff there a few years ago. It's probably closed and that's where he's taken her."

"You sure?"

"No. But it's all we've got."

"Go, Tate."

He pulled onto the highway and steered toward the interstate. Thinking with frustration that they'd have to drive the entire way right on the speed limit. They could hardly afford to be stopped now.

Glass knife in front of her, Megan walked through the hallways.

There was silence, then the shuffling of footsteps. More silence.

I hate the quiet worse than his footsteps.

I'm with you there, Crazy Megan shares.

Then the steps again but from a different place, as if the intruder were a ghost materializing at will.

Five minutes passed. Another noise nearby, behind her. A sharp inhalation of breath. Megan gasped and turned quickly. Aaron Matthews was twenty feet away. His eyes widened in surprise. She stumbled backward and fell over a table, went down hard. Grunted in pain as the edge of the table dug into her kidney.

Despite the pain, though, she leapt to her feet, lifting the knife threateningly. She assumed he'd charge at her. But he didn't. He merely frowned and said, "Oh, my God, Megan, are you all right?"

Crouching, eyes fiery, breath hard, gripping the cloth handle of her wicked knife. Staring at his dark eyes, his large shoulders and long arms. Why wasn't he coming at her?

She glanced behind her.

"Wait," he said with a heart-tugging plea in his voice. "Please, don't run. *Please.*"

She hesitated.

He sighed. "Oh, I know you're upset, Megan, honey. I know you're scared . . . You hate me and you have every right to. But please. Just listen to me."

He held his hands up. "I don't have a knife or gun or anything. Please, will you listen?"

His eyes were so sincere, radiating sympathy, and his voice so imploring . . .

"Please."

Megan kept her tight grip on the knife. But she straightened up. "Go ahead," she whispered. "I'm listening."

"Good," he said. And offered her a smile.

Chapter Twenty-seven

"I didn't know you'd gotten out of your room," Aaron Matthews said.

"Cell," she corrected bluntly.

"Cell," he conceded, watching her eyes carefully. "But I should've guessed." He laughed. "You're the independent sort. Nobody was going to lock you away. It's one of the things I love about you."

Matthews noted how she fixed her gaze on his eyes. How her pale lashes stuttered when he'd said the word "love."

How had she done it? he wondered. He'd been over the cell so carefully—and the lock was still on the door. Had she gotten through the ceiling? The wall? And she was wearing some of his clothes. So she'd found his living area. What else did she know?

However it had happened, Matthews was surprised. It showed more mettle than he'd expected from the spoiled little whiner.

"Are you all right? Just tell me that." He looked her up and down.

No answer.

He continued, "I'm sorry about your clothes. When you passed out from the medicine I gave you . . . well, you had an accident. I'm sorry. I didn't think it would happen. I'm washing your clothes in the laundry room here. They're drying now. They should be ready soon. I didn't touch you. I swear."

He glanced at the knife in her hand. A long shard. He thought at first that there was something about the glass itself that was particularly unnerving, the sharp, green edge of the triangle. But then he decided that, no, it was her *face* that scared him. She was prepared—no, eager—to use the weapon. And so much in control . . . she'd be a hard one to crack. Harder than in Hanson's office, where her defenses were down and her self-esteem bubbling near empty.

He eased forward. "Oh, Megan, I'm so sorry."

The point of the knife tilted toward him and Matthews froze. He said in his best therapist's tone, "I didn't want it to happen this way."

He fell silent. And to fill the intolerable gap of silence she asked, "What way?"

"This . . ." He lifted his arms to the hallways. "If there'd been anything else I could have done, I would have. I promise you."

"What do you mean?"

He leaned against the wall, closed his eyes. "You don't really know me. But I know you. I've known you for a long time."

She shook her head, frowning, confused. The tip of the knife was pointed lower.

"My name's Aaron Matthews . . ."

She'd've learned his real name, of course—from looking through the desk in his rooms here. But tell someone the truth—no matter how much you've lied to them in the past—and you nudge them closer toward you, if ever so slightly. He continued right away—Matthews had a spell to weave and spells work best when cast quickly. "I worked with your father on a case last year. He hired me as an expert witness. To evaluate a suspect. We were talking before the trial. Just making conversation. And I asked about children, if he had any, and he said . . ." Matthews paused and his face grew somber. He continued, "I'm sorry, honey, but he said no, he didn't."

Megan's beautiful light eyes widened. Shocked for a moment. Then they grew deeply sad, as they had in Hanson's office. A child betrayed, a child alone.

What are the bears whispering to you?

"But I'd heard somebody mention his daughter and I asked him about you. He looked embarrassed and said that, well, yes, he *did* have a daughter. But she lived with her mother. He said you were technically his child but that was all. I told him about my son, Peter. See, he had some problems at birth. Serious mental problems."

Another flicker of lash. So she knew about him too. He said, looking down, "But I've always felt that, despite all that, I loved my boy and wanted him to be with me. I mentioned that to your father. But he didn't say anything. I asked him how often he saw you . . . He said virtually never. I asked him about you and he didn't seem to know much at all. And then—" Matthews stopped abruptly, like a man finding himself in a minefield.

"What?"

"Nothing."

"No, tell me," she said with faint desperation in her voice.

"He said some things about you."

"Please." The knife was pointed straight down. Her face was no longer fierce. "I want to know."

"He said being more involved with you would be . . . awkward."

"No, he didn't," she whispered. "He didn't say that at all, did he?"

"I'm not sure . . ." Matthews stammered, putting a vulnerable look on his face.

She muttered, "He said being involved with a child would be *inconvenient*. Right?"

"Yes," Matthews conceded, sighing. "I'm so sorry, Megan. But that's what he said. And when I heard it, all I could think of was how I hoped you had a good relationship with your mother. I hoped *someone* cared. I felt so bad for you."

A faint laugh then her face went still. "My mother. Yeah, right."

He cocked his head, offering her another sympathetic glance. And continued, "Well, I went to see her. When you were in school one day."

"You did?"

Matthews eased a few inches closer. He decided that anger wouldn't work with Megan, unlike with her boyfriend, Josh. The madder she got, the more dangerous she'd be. No, the way to get inside her defenses was to tap into her sorrow and loneliness.

"I lied, Megan. I'll admit it. I told Bett I was a counselor with your school and I wanted to know how you were doing. I was shocked to find that she didn't

have much time for you either. She told me she was
engaged, trying to make that relationship work, was
totally absorbed with Brad, didn't have much time
for . . . well, she said, for baby-sitting."

"She said *that?*" Megan gasped.

"In fairness she said you were very mature and
didn't need a lot of hand-holding."

"How would she know?" Megan muttered.

Matthews swayed toward her but the coldness
returned to her eyes and she asked, "But why the fuck
did you kidnap me?"

"Because I wanted to give you a second chance,
Megan."

"Kidnapping me? What kind of chance is that?"

He looked down and rocked back and forth on
his feet, moving a good six inches closer to her. "Oh,
Megan, yes, I kidnapped you. But I'd never hurt you.
That was the last thing on my mind." If she'd seen the
room, she'd probably also seen the kitchen. He said, "I
can prove it. I'll show you the kitchen. It's filled with
food that you like. I found out what you liked and I
bought a lot of it."

She nodded. Her defenses slipped a bit more. "You
were the one following me for the past couple weeks."

"That's right. I followed you. And I talked to people
about you too. Teachers, students. And the more I
learned about you, the more I couldn't understand
your parents. You're creative, you're funny, you're
pretty, you have a sense of humor, you were artistic . . .
You were everything a teenage girl ought to be. Why
didn't they want you? Your parents, I mean?"

Her lip began to tremble. She wiped tears.

"It was so unfair," he whispered. "I wanted to give you the love that they never did. Parental love, I'm speaking of. I hope you know that . . . I think you're beautiful but I don't desire you physically." He nodded toward her padded cell. "I could have done that when you were unconscious if I'd wanted to."

Her eyes told him that she understood it. That she'd checked her body for tenderness, for moisture.

But the eyes hardened again. She asked, "But there's more, isn't there? There's another side to it."

He smiled. "Oh, you're smart, Megan. You're very smart. Yes, there's another side. *I* wanted another chance too. I told you about my son. The problems I mentioned? They were pretty serious. My wife . . . she drank and had a Valium habit when she was pregnant. I tried to get her to stop but she wouldn't. My son had permanent brain damage . . . Oh, I wanted a normal child. Someone I could spend time with. Have fun with. Someone I could spoil." He remembered something Bett had told him earlier that evening. "I wanted someone to play games with, to spend Christmas and Easter with, Thanksgiving. To make oatmeal and pancakes for. To hang out with on Sunday in sweats and sneakers and read the paper and rake leaves."

From somewhere, he summoned a tear.

"You wanted me to be your daughter," Megan said softly.

"Yes! But there was no way you would've agreed on your own. Or even listened to me. You would've thought I was some kind of crank and called the police. So I did what I had to. I waited until I had a chance—

Dr. Hanson's mother getting sick—and I arranged with him to see you."

"That part was true?"

"Oh, yes. Of course it's true. We're friends, Hanson and me." He smiled indulgently. "Though I think I'm a better therapist than he is. I get right to the core of the problem."

"Yeah, you sure as hell do." She offered a faint smile in return.

"You didn't like those letters, I know. But I had to make you see how angry you were with your parents. I had to make you see the truth."

"That's why you made me write them?"

"Yes."

"What did you do with them? Did you send them?"

He frowned. "The letters? No, I threw them out. Writing them was for *you*, Megan. I thought maybe, here, we could get to know each other for a while. I'd hoped you'd stay for a few weeks, a month. If it worked out, fine. We could move to San Francisco, you could start college there in the fall."

He'd moved another few feet closer to her. He was slumped, diminished, looking mournfully at the floor. Matthews had decided how she'd die: He'd strangle her. Her eyes would grow wide and he'd stare at them, drink them in as she died. Pull the glass knife from her hand and get a grip on her neck. Squeeze and squeeze and squeeze until the tip of her protruding tongue stopped quivering. And squeeze some more after that.

It was the way Peter had killed the slut who'd tried to seduce him. Maybe it was the way Peter himself had died. The body was so mutilated the prison doctor hadn't been able to be certain of the cause of death.

Tears flooded the eyes of the inconvenient child.

"Oh, Megan, I'm sorry. I'm so sorry. I just thought that you deserved so much more than you had."

She was shivering with the sobs.

"A father who wanted to be rid of you. What a terrible thing . . . He wanted to get you out of his life and get back to those ridiculous young women he chased after. And your mother . . . a dear woman but a child herself, really. I thought about all sorts of things—how I could adopt you, get you into a foster home . . ."

"You really thought that?" she asked, wiping her face. Her attention was wavering from the glass blade. Her hand was in the shadows at her side. The hallway was dim and he couldn't tell whether the knife was pointed downward or at him.

"Yes, I sure did. I talked to a lawyer about adoption. He said I wouldn't have a chance, not with your natural parents around, however neglectful they were." His voice was soft, lulling.

Megan wiped her face again. "I just wanted to be loved."

"And they didn't love you, did they? They didn't give you any love at all."

"No."

"Oh, I would've done things so differently . . . and that's why I took this chance. I'm risking life in prison just to see if something might work out between us. I just wanted you to have a home." He too was crying now. "I just wanted a family! That's all *I've* ever wanted too."

She was sobbing uncontrollably now, hand over her face. "Yes! That's it. A home. I never had a home. I wanted a father so badly."

Matthews stepped closer, reached out a tentative hand and touched her cheek, wiped away a tear. He could almost feel her under his hands, peeing and thrashing as she died. He'd leave her body out for the dogs. So that Collier would have to live with the terrible memory of what the crime scene photos revealed.

"I wish I could have done it differently," he said. "I mean, this place is so disgusting, Megan. But I didn't have any choice. For both our sakes."

"I just—"

He reached out his other hand and put his arm around her shoulder. Rubbed her back.

"I just wanted a home . . . only a home." She struggled to breathe.

"I know you did." His right hand moved down her face to her neck. His left slipped down her arm until he gripped the glass knife she held.

He gently pulled it out of her hand.

Got you! he thought.

But then he glanced down, frowning. It wasn't a knife at all. In his hand was a plastic Bic pen. But he'd seen the blade . . . He looked into her face.

Saw the leering smile.

"Nice try," Megan whispered.

And with her left hand she jammed the glass blade deep into his side. Once, then again. And again.

A flash of terrible pain shot through him and

Matthews howled. He twisted hard away from her and the blade snapped on a rib, leaving a long glass splinter inside him.

Now Megan screamed—an insane wail—and as the doctor groped for his wound she slammed her open palm into his face. A huge pop as his nose broke and blood spurted. He went down on his knees. She kicked him near the knife wound and his vision went black from the astonishing pain.

She came forward but he swam back to consciousness quickly and now it was his fist that connected hard—slamming into her jaw, sending her backward into the wall. By the time he was on his feet she was disappearing down the dark corridor.

He touched the wound. The pain was bad. But it was nothing compared with the feeling of shock that raged through him. *She's* the one who fooled me! Suckered me in nice and close, got *my* defenses down. My God, the whole time I thought I was playing her but she led me right into the trap . . .

Her father's daughter, Matthews thought in fury and disgust.

He dropped to his knees and began working the fragments of glass out of his wound, actually savoring the pain; he wanted to remember it. He wanted to feel what Megan was about to experience.

Chapter Twenty-eight

The basement . . .

She plunged into the dim corridors of the hospital, looking for the basement door she'd seen earlier.

Her jaw ached and the back of her head too—from where she'd slammed it into the wall after he hit her. For just a moment she'd thought about leaping on him again—seeing him lying there, blood filling his shirt, blood dripping from his nose. He'd looked half dead. But she wasn't sure that he was hurt as badly as he seemed. He might have been faking. If he lied with words, he'd lie with actions.

So she ran—to find the basement door.

She heard Matthews's unearthly scream—it seemed to shake the walls—and then footsteps.

Making slow circles through the corridors, she finally found the door, the one leading to the basement. She grabbed a cinder block and smashed it down on the hasp and lock, which snapped off easily.

Megan flung the door open, looked down into the musty place. For a moment she was paralyzed.

No choice, girl, Crazy Megan the tour guide shouts. *Move, move, move.*

But Josh, she protested silently, I can't leave him.

Hey, if you die, he dies. Go!

She clomped down the stairs and found herself in a dimly lit warren of corridors. Trotting slowly from room to room, she took care to avoid the standing water so she wouldn't leave footprints he could follow.

Please, a door, a window . . . Oh, please.

She heard the creak of footsteps from the ceiling above her as Matthews made his way to the door she'd just broken open. She found a door leading outside. It was locked. And the windows too were sealed. Another door. Nailed shut.

Goddamn him! C.M. blurts. *Why'd he padlock the fucking door upstairs if we can't get out this way?*

Megan didn't bother to answer. She couldn't figure it out either. She returned to a room near the base of the stairs and glanced again at one of the windows. The bars on these were wider than the ones on the main floor but she doubted that she could get through.

Fucking hips.

Don't start! Megan muttered silently and started to turn away. Then she paused, looked back. Thinking: Okay, maybe I can't get through the bars. But I can make him *think* I did.

She smashed the glass and pushed an overturned plastic bucket beneath it so that it looked like she'd climbed out.

Then she ran back into the warren of dark storerooms to find someplace to hide.

Most of the cardboard boxes piled in the rooms were too small to conceal her. And she didn't have the strength to pull herself up into the pipes that ran along the ceiling.

His steps were approaching the door upstairs. Then he started down.

Megan ran into a cluttered storeroom, the farthest one from the stairs. It was filled with cartons, small ones like the others. But over to the side of the room, in the shadows, was a long metal box. It was almost too obvious a choice to hide in but this room was nowhere near the window where she'd faked her escape. And it was pitch-dark in here. Matthews might not even see the box if he bothered to look.

Could she get it open? And was it empty?

But Megan stopped asking questions. Matthews was now in the basement. A shuffle of footsteps, a moaning wheeze from the pain of the wounds, words muttered to himself.

Now! Crazy Megan prods her. *Go, girl!*

Megan unlatched the trunk. It took all her strength to lift the thick lid.

And it took all her willpower not to scream as she looked inside and saw the blue-white flesh, the limp hair, the closed eyes, a dark, shriveled penis, the long yellow fingernails . . . Cuts and gouges covered the young man's entire torso, which was further mutilated by the large *Y* incision from the autopsy. An ear and an arm had been crudely stitched back onto his body.

It was Matthews's son, Peter. She recognized the eerie face from the newspaper clipping.

Oh, God . . . My God . . . Tate, Bett . . . Somebody!

The footsteps were closer now. They sounded only thirty or forty feet away.

Go on, Crazy Megan urges. *Do it.*

I *can't* do it, Megan thought. No way in hell.

Get inside, C.M. chokes. *You have to.*

Either you fight him with your fists, she told herself, or you hide in here. Those're your choices. A moment's pause. The doctor was now right outside the doorway, it seemed. Then Megan closed her eyes—as if that would lessen the horror—and climbed into the box, lying down on the corpse, on her back, shivering fiercely. She let the lid down. The air reeked of sweet formaldehyde, pickled flesh—she recalled the scent from biology class, hating to be in school at the time but now praying that she could somehow be transported back to that time and place.

And beneath her, terrible cold.

Nothing's colder than cold flesh.

Then she heard, faintly, a moan very near. Aaron Matthews was in the room.

Crossing a gap in the Shenandoahs, Tate glanced out the window of Bett's car at the darkened bungalows and ramshackle farmhouses, abandoned barns, the black pits that opened into the network of caverns that laced the earth beneath the Shenandoahs and the Blue Ridge.

They sped past walls of ominous forest—the stark pines, the scrub oak, the sedge, the young kudzu and Virginia creeper. Tate imagined dozens of eyes peering at them and he thought of the Dead Reb once again.

Ten minutes later, well into the Blue Ridge, Tate pulled Bett's Volvo into an all-night gas station. The elderly attendant glanced at them cautiously when he asked about the mental hospital.

"That old place? Phew." The man cast a dark look westward.

"Where is it?"

"You get back on the interstate and go one more exit . . ."

"We'd rather stick to back roads, if we can." The state troopers would be looking for him on the highway, a fact Tate didn't share.

The man cocked his head, shrugged. "Well, that road there. Route one seventeen? Take it west ten, twelve miles till you see a Buy-Rite gas station. Then go left on Palmer and just keep going."

"We'll see the hospital?"

"Oh, you'll see it. Can't miss it. But I'd wait till sunup. You don't wanna go there this time of night, no sir. But you asked for directions, not opinions."

Tate handed him a twenty and they sped off down the road.

They'd driven several miles when a no-nonsense siren burst to life a quarter mile behind them. It was a county trooper. The light bar flashed explosively in Tate's rearview mirror. He accelerated hard.

"You think he knows it's us?" Bett asked.

"If he doesn't he will when he calls in your tags." Tate's foot wavered. "What do I do?"

"Drive like hell," Bett muttered. "Try to lose him."

He did.

For about two miles it looked as if they'd get away. The Swedes make a good car but it was no match for the souped-up engine of the pursuing Plymouth. "Can't make it," he told her.

He eased up on the gas. "I'll talk to him. Maybe he'll at least send a car to the hospital."

"No," Bett said. "Pull over."

"What?" Tate asked, jockeying the skidding car onto the gravel shoulder and braking.

Bett ripped her purse open and dug inside. She paused, took a deep breath, then sat upright, staring in the rearview mirror at herself, stroking her cheek as Tate had seen her do so often.

What's she up to? he wondered.

"Bett!" he cried as she lifted the nail file to her face and dragged it hard across her skin.

Blood poured from a gash deep in her cheek.

"Oh," Bett wheezed. "It hurts."

Tate stared at the blood, running more black than red down her neck and falling onto her chest in delicate paisleys.

"Get out of the car!" reverberated the metallic voice through the rectangular mouth of the PA speaker atop the car.

The young trooper stood beside the open door of his squad car. His blue-black pistol, dwarfed by the lawman's huge hand, was aimed at Tate's head.

"Get out of that vehicle! Keep your hands up."

For a moment neither of them moved.

Then Bett's door opened so fast Tate thought that another deputy had snuck up behind them unseen and pulled her out. But, no, she was moving on her own. She screamed shrilly as she rolled onto the grassy shoulder of the road. The leather strap of her purse was wound around her wrists as if she were tied up. Without the use of her hands she fell hard and dust mixed with the blood covering her face.

"Help me!" she cried. "He kidnapped me!"

"Don't move. Nobody move!" the trooper called, swinging the muzzle toward Bett. Tate sat perfectly still, hands on the wheel.

Bett scrabbled toward the cop.

"He's got a knife!" she cried. "Help me, please. He cut me. I'm bleeding. Help me!" She put the harrowing wail of a frightened child into her voice as she stumbled forward. "He was going to rape me! Get me away from him! Oh, please . . . Oh . . ."

The trooper gave in to his instincts. "Over here, miss. You'll be all right. He's that fella from Prince William, isn't he? The one killed that girl? Where's the knife?"

"In his belt. He picked me up at a rest stop," she cried. "He kidnapped me!"

"Put your hands up!" the trooper called over the microphone. "And I mean now!"

Tate did.

"What happened?" the cop asked Bett, who was stumbling closer.

"Cut me . . . I need a doctor . . ." The words were lost in the sobbing.

"You in the car. Leave your right hand up and with your left reach out the window and open the door. Don't lower that right hand."

Tate didn't move.

"I'm not telling you again! I have a—"

"Put it down!" came Bett's raw scream from inches behind his head. Tate's pistol was resting at the cop's throat.

"Oh, shit."

"Do it!"

"I've got him covered, lady. You do anything to me and he's gone. I'll shoot him. I swear . . ." But he said this out of shame, not resolve, and when Bett screamed, "We're after my daughter and I'll kill you right now if I have to," the cop's disgusted grunt was followed by the sound of his large pistol hitting the dirt.

Bett stepped away from the man, who towered over her. He went limp as he saw the ferocity in her face, maybe wondering just how close to death he'd come. He sagged against the car.

"All right," Bett muttered. "Lie down on the ground. There. On your stomach."

Tate was out of the car and jogging toward them.

"There're other troopers coming, lady. They'll be here in minutes."

"All the more reason to *move!*"

He eased down. Bett handed the cop's pistol to Tate.

"Cuff him and let's go," she said.

But Tate put his hand on her shoulder. "No. You're staying."

"No, Tate," Bett said, holding a wad of Kleenexes up to her bloody chin. "I want to come."

What could he say to her? That there wasn't anything she could do and Tate needed to focus on saving Megan—if she could be saved? That it was important for her to stay here and tell the police exactly what had happened, send them out to the hospital? They were both surefire arguments. But Tate answered instead from his heart and told her the truth. Simply: "I don't want to risk losing you."

She looked at the dark blood on the Kleenex and up at Tate once more. She nodded.

"Now, listen to me," he said gravely. "When they get here, just set the gun down and put your hands up. They'll be nervous and looking to shoot. Do exactly what they say. You hear me?"

She nodded. He touched her cheek, wiping away some blood.

"A sexy woman with a scar—won't be a man in the county'll keep his hands off you."

"You'll get her, won't you, Tate?"

"I'll get her."

He kissed her forehead and ran to the car.

He floored the accelerator, splattering the squad car with gravel and dirt. As he drove over a crest in the road, the tach nosing into the red crescent of the warning zone, he caught a glimpse of Bett in the rearview mirror, crouching beside the prone trooper, undoubtedly apologizing earnestly. Still, the pistol that was gripped in both her hands was pointed steadily at his face.

She couldn't take it anymore.

Crazy Megan was gone, dead and sleeping with the fishes.

The depleted air suffocated her. The smells— the rot and the sweet scent from embalmed skin— wrapped themselves around her throat and squeezed.

Which was bad enough. But then the panic started to sizzle through her body like electricity. The claustrophobia.

"No, no, no," she said, or maybe she just thought it. "No, no . . . Let me out, let me out, let me out . . ."

334 / Jeffery Deaver

Suddenly she wasn't even worried that Matthews was outside the casket, waiting for her. It didn't matter; she couldn't stay inside a moment longer.

Megan pushed against the lid of the coffin.

It didn't move.

She tried again, with all her strength. Nothing.

"Ah," she gasped. "Oh please, God, no . . ."

He'd locked her in! She pounded on the lid then heard a wild laugh outside. Words she couldn't distinguish. More laughter.

More words, louder: ". . . two having fun together . . . likes you . . . Peter likes you . . ."

"Let me out, let me out!"

Her voice rose to a wild keening, her whole body shivered in violent spasms.

"You fucker you fuck let me outoutoutout!" With both her fists Megan pounded on the lid until they bled, banged it with her head, feeling with horror Peter's cold face against her neck, his cold penis against her thigh.

From outside Aaron Matthews beat on the lid too, responding to her pounding. Then more laughter. And finally more tapping, like a drummer, keeping perfect time with the rhythm of her raw screams.

No subtlety, no nuance . . .

Tate Collier came to the end of Palmer Road and saw the mental hospital in front of him. He aimed Bett's car directly toward the gate, got his speed up to about forty and bounded over logs and potholes in the neglected surface. He saw the infamous gray

Mercedes parked in the staff-only carport. He saw a faint light in one of the windows.

He had no plan other than the obvious and as he skidded around a fallen pine and straightened for the final assault on the gate he pressed the accelerator down harder, sealing his resolve.

He pressed his hands into the steering wheel, pinning himself into the seat. The car plowed through the chain link. The air bag popped with an astonishingly loud bang. He'd forgotten about it and hadn't closed his eyes. He was momentarily blinded and lost control of the car. When he could see again he found the vehicle skidding sideways, narrowly missing the Mercedes. The Volvo crashed obliquely into the cinder blocks, stunning him.

Tate leapt out of the car and ran to the first door he could find. Gripping his pistol hard, he flung all his weight against the double panels.

He was expecting them to be locked. But the doors swung open with virtually no resistance and he stumbled headfirst into a large, dim lobby.

He saw shadows, shapes of furniture, angles of walls, unlit lamps, dust motes circling in the air.

He saw faint shafts of predawn blue light bleeding in through the windows.

But he never saw the bat or tire iron or whatever it was that hummed through the air behind him and caught him with a glancing blow just above the ear.

IV

THE SILENCE OF THE DEED

Chapter Twenty-nine

A hand stroked his hair.

Lying on his side, on a cold floor, Tate slowly opened his eyes, which stung fiercely from his own sweat. He tried to focus on the face before him. He believed momentarily that the soft fingers were Bett's; she'd been the first person in his thoughts as he came to consciousness.

But he found that the blue eyes he gazed into were Megan's.

"Hey, honey," he wheezed.

"Dad." Her face was pale, her hair pasted to her head with sweat, her hands bloody.

They were in the lobby of the decrepit hospital. His hands were bound behind him with scratchy rope. His vision was blurry. He got up and nearly fainted from the pain that roared in his temple.

Aaron Matthews was sitting on a chair nearby watching them both like the helpless prisoners that they were.

What astonishing black eyes he has, Tate thought. Like dark lasers. They turned to you as if you were the only person in the universe. Why, patients would tell him anything. He understood why Bett had been powerless to resist him earlier that night when he'd come to her house. Konnie too. And Megan.

Then he saw that Matthews was hurt. A large patch of blood covered the side of his shirt and he was sweating. His nose too was bloody. Tate glanced at Megan. She gave a weak smile and nodded, answering his tacit question if she was responsible for the wound. He lowered his head to the girl's shoulder. A moment later Tate looked up. "You've lost those five pounds you wanted to," he said to her. "You're lean and mean."

"It was ten," she joked.

Matthews finally said, "Well, Tate Collier. Well . . ."

Such a smooth, baritone voice, Tate reflected. But not phony or slick. So natural, so comforting. Patients would cling to every word he uttered.

"I was just doing my job," Tate finally said to him. "Peter's trial, I mean. The evidence was there. The jury believed it."

Megan frowned and Tate explained about the trial and the boy's murder in prison.

The girl scowled, said to Matthews, "I knew you'd never worked with him on cases. Those were just more lies."

Matthews didn't even notice her. He crossed his arms. "You probably don't know it, Collier, but I used to watch you in court. After Pete died I'd go to your trials. I'd sit in the back of the gallery for hours and hours. You know what struck me? You reminded me of myself in therapy sessions. Talking to the patients. Leading them where they didn't want to go. You did exactly the same with the witnesses and the juries."

Tate said nothing.

Matthews smiled briefly. "And I learned some things about the law. *Mens rea.* The state of a killer's mind—he has to *intend* the death in order to be guilty of murder. Well, that was you, all right, at Pete's trial. You *murdered* Pete. You intended him to die."

"My job was to prosecute cases as best I could."

"*If,*" Matthews pounced, "that was true then why did you quit prosecuting? Why did you turn tail and run?"

"Because I regretted what happened to your son," Tate answered.

Matthews lowered his sweaty, stubbly face. "You looked at my boy and said, 'You're dead.' You stood up in court and felt the power flowing through you. And you *liked* it."

Tate looked around the room. "You did all this? And you went after all the others—Konnie and Hanson and Eckhard? Bett, too."

"Mom?" Megan whispered.

"No, she's okay," Tate reassured her.

"I had to stop you," Matthews said. "You kept coming. You wouldn't listen to reason. You wouldn't do what you were supposed to."

"This is where you were committed, right?"

"Him?" Megan asked. "I thought he'd worked here."

"I thought so too," Tate said, "but then I remembered testimony at Peter's trial. No. He *was* a therapist but *he* was the one committed here." Nodding at Matthews. "Not Peter." Tate recalled the trial:

Mr. Bogan: *Now, Dr. Rothstein, could you give an opinion of the source and nature of Peter's difficulties?*

Dr. Rothstein: *Yes sir. Peter displays socialization*

problems. He is more comfortable with inanimate creations—stories and books and cartoons and the like—than with people. He also suffers from what I call affect deficit. The reason, from reviewing his medical records, appears to be that his father would lock him in his room for long periods of time—weeks, even months—and the only contact the boy would have with anyone was with his father, Aaron. He wouldn't even let the boy's mother see him. Peter withdrew into his books and television. Apparently the only time the boy spent with his mother and others was when his father was committed in mental hospitals for bipolar depression and delusional behavior.

Matthews said, "I was here, let's see, on six intakes. Must have been four years altogether. I was like a jailhouse lawyer, Collier. As soon as the patients heard I was a therapist they started coming to me."

"So *you* were 'Patient Matthews,'" Megan said, eyes widening. "In the reports about the deaths here."

"That's my Megan," Matthews said.

She said to Tate, "They closed this place because of a bunch of suicides. I thought it was *Peter* who'd killed them."

"But it was you?" Tate asked Matthews.

"The DSM-III diagnosis was that I was sociopathic—well, it's called an antisocial/criminal personality now. How delicate. I knew the hospital examiners in Richmond were looking for an excuse to close down places like this. So I simply helped them out. The place was too understaffed and too incompetent to keep patients from killing themselves. So they shut it down."

"But it was really just a game to you, right?" Megan

asked in disgust. "Seeing how many patients you could talk into suicide."

Matthews shrugged. He continued. "I got transferred to a halfway house and one bright, sunny May morning, I walked out the front door. Moved to Prince William County, right behind your farm. And started planning how to destroy you." Matthews winced and pressed his side. The wound didn't seem that severe.

Tate recalled something else from the trial and asked, "What about your wife?"

Matthews said nothing but his eyes responded.

Tate understood. "She was your first victim, wasn't she? Did you talk her into killing herself? Or maybe just slip some drugs into her wine during dinner?"

"She was vulnerable," Matthews responded. "Insecure. Most therapists are."

Tate asked, "What was she trying to do? Take Peter away from you?"

"Yes, she was. She wanted to place him in a hospital full-time. She shouldn't have meddled. *I* understood Peter. No one else did."

"But you made Peter the way he was," Megan blurted. "You cut him off from the world."

She was right. Tate recalled the defense's expert witness, Dr. Rothstein, testifying that if you arrest development by isolating a child before the age of eight, social—and communications—skills will never develop. You've basically destroyed the child forever.

Tate remembered too how he'd handled the expert witness's testimony at Peter Matthews's murder trial.

The Court: *The Commonwealth may cross-examine.*

Mr. Collier: *Dr. Rothstein, thank you for that trip*

down memory lane about the defendant's sad history.
But let me ask you: psychologically, is the defendant
capable of premeditated murder?

Dr. Rothstein: *Peter Matthews is a troubled—*

Mr. Collier: *Your Honor?*

The Court: *Please answer the question, sir.*

Dr. Rothstein: *I—*

Mr. Collier: *Is the defendant capable of pre-*
meditated murder?

Dr. Rothstein: *Yes, but—*

Mr. Collier: *No further questions.*

"All he needed was *me!*" Matthews now raged. "He
didn't need anyone else in his life. We'd spend *hours*
together—when my wife wasn't trying to sneak him
out the door."

"Did you love him that much?" Tate asked.

"You don't have a clue, do you? Why, you
know what we did? Peter and I? We *talked.* About
everything. About snakes, about stars, about floods,
about explorers, about airplanes, about the mind . . ."

Delusional ramblings, Tate imagined. Poor Peter,
baffled and lonely, undoubtedly could do nothing but
listen.

Yet . . . with a sorrowful twist deep within him Tate
realized that this was something Megan and he *didn't*
do. They didn't talk at all. They never had.

And now we won't ever, he realized. We've lost that
chance forever.

Their captor fell silent, looking into a corner of the
hospital lobby, lost in a memory or thought or some
confused delusion.

Finally Tate said, "So, Aaron. Tell me what you

want. Tell me exactly." He closed his eyes, fighting the incredible pain in his head.

After a moment Matthews said, "I want justice. Pure and simple. I'm going to kill your daughter and you're going to watch. You'll live with that sight for the rest of your life."

So it's come to this . . .

Tate sighed and thought, as he had so often on the way to the jury box or the podium in a debate, *All right, time to get to work.*

"I don't know how you can have justice, Aaron," Tate said to him. "I just don't know. In all my years practicing law—"

Matthews's face writhed in disgust. "Oh, stop right there."

"What?" Tate asked innocently.

"I hear it," the psychiatrist said. "The glib tongue, the smooth words. You have the orator's gift . . . sure. We know that. But so do I. I'm immune to you."

"I won't try to talk you into a single thing, Aaron. You don't seem to be the sort—"

"It won't work! Not with me. The advocate's tricks. The therapist's tricks. 'Personalize the discourse.' 'Aaron' this and 'Aaron' that. Try to get me to think of you as a specific human being, *Tate.* But that won't work, *Tate.* See, it's Tate Collier the human being I despise."

Undeterred, Tate continued, "Was he your only child? Peter?"

"Why even try?" Matthews rolled his eyes.

"All I want is to get out of this and save our lives. Is that a surprise?"

"A perfect example of a rhetorical question. Well, no, it's not a surprise. But there's nothing you can say that's going to make any difference."

"I'm trying to save your life too, Aaron. They know about you. The police. You heard the message from the detective, I assume? On your answering machine?"

"They may figure it out eventually but since you're here by yourself, an escapee, I think I have a bit of time."

"What does he mean?" Megan asked. "Escapee?"

He saw no reason to tell her now that her friend Amy was dead. He shook his head and continued, "Let's talk, Aaron. I'm a wealthy man. You're going to have to leave the country. I'll give you some money if you let us go."

"Leading with your weakest argument. Doesn't that mean you've just lost the debate? That's what you say on your American Forensics Association tape."

The faint smile never wavered from Tate's face. "You saw my house, the land," he continued. "You know I've got resources."

A splinter of disdain in Matthews's eyes.

"How much do you want?"

"You're using a rhetorical fallacy. Appealing to a false need—for diversion." Matthews smiled. "I do it all the time. Soften up the patient, get the defenses down. Then, bang, a kick in the head. Come on, I didn't do this for ransom. That's obvious."

"Whatever your motive *was*, Aaron, the circumstances've changed. They know about you now. But you've got a chance to get out of the country. I can get you a half million in cash. Just like that. More by hocking the house."

Matthews said nothing but paced slowly, staring at Megan, who gazed back defiantly.

Tate knew, of course, that money wasn't the issue at all; neither was helping Matthews escape. His immediate purpose was simply to make the man indecisive, wear down his resistance. Matthews was right—this was a diversion. And even though the man knew it Tate believed the technique was working.

"I can't make you a rich man but I can make you comfortable."

"Pointless," Matthews said, shaking his head as if he were disappointed.

"Aaron, you can't change things," Tate continued. "You can't make it the way it was. You can't bring Peter back. So will you just let us go?"

"Specific request within the opponent's power to grant," Matthews recited, "requiring only an affirmative or negative response. Your skills are still in top form, Collier. My answer, however, is neg-a-tive."

"You tell me you're after justice." Tate shrugged. "But I wonder if it's not really something else."

A flicker in the doctor's eyes.

"Have you really thought about why you're doing this?" Tate asked.

"Of course."

"Why?"

"I—"

Tate said quickly, "It's to take the pain away, isn't it?"

Matthews's lips moved as he carried on a conversation with himself, or his dead wife, or his dead son. Or perhaps no one at all.

What a man hears, he may doubt.

What a man sees . . .

Tate leaned toward him, ignoring the agony in his head. He whispered urgently, "Think about it, Aaron. *Think*. This is very important. What if you get it wrong? What if killing Megan makes the pain *worse?*"

"Nice try," Matthews cried. "Setting up straw men."

"Or what if it has no effect at all? What if this is your one chance to make the pain go away and it doesn't work? Did you ever *consider* that?"

"You're trying to distract me!"

"You lost someone you loved. You lie on your back for hours, paralyzed with the pain. You wake up at two A.M. and think you're going mad. Right?"

Matthews fell silent. Tate saw he'd touched a nerve.

"I know all about that. It happened to me." Tate leaned forward and, without feigning, matched the agony he saw in Matthews's face with pain of his own. "I've been there. *I* lost someone I loved more than life itself. I lost my wife. I can see it in your face. These aren't tricks, Aaron. I *do* know what I'm talking about. That's all you want—the pain to go away. You're not a lust killer, Aaron. You're not an expediency killer. You're not a hired killer. You only kill when there's a *reason*. And that reason is to make the pain go away!"

And to Tate's astonishment he heard a woman's voice beside him. A smooth contralto. Megan, gazing into Matthews's eyes, was saying, "Even those patients you killed here, Aaron . . . You didn't *want* to kill them. I was wrong. It wasn't a game at all. You just wanted to help them stop hurting."

Excellent, Tate thought, proud of her.

"The pain," the lawyer took over. "That's what this is all about. You just want it to go away."

Matthews's eyes were uncertain, even wild. How we hate the confusing and the unknown, and how we flock to those who offer us answers simple as a child's drawing.

"I'll tell you, Aaron, that I've lived with your son's death every day since the Department of Corrections called and told me what happened. I feel that pain too. I know what you're going through. I—"

Suddenly Matthews leapt forward and grabbed Tate's shirt, began slugging him madly, knocking him to the floor. Megan cried out and stepped toward them but the madman shoved her to the floor again. He screamed at Tate, "You *know?* You know, do you? You have no fucking idea! All the days, the weeks and weeks that I haven't been able to do anything but lie on my back and stare at the ceiling, thinking about the trial. You know what I see? I don't see Peter's face. I see your *back.* You, standing in the courtroom with your back to my son. You sent him to die but you didn't even *look* at him! The jury were the only people in that room, weren't they?"

No, Tate reflected, they were the only people in the universe. He said to Matthews, "I'm sorry for you."

"I don't want your fucking pity." Another wave of fury crossed his face and he lifted Tate in his powerful hands and shoved him to the floor again, rolled him on his back. He took a knife from his pocket, opened it with a click and bent down over Tate.

"No!" Megan cried.

Matthews slipped the blade past Tate's lips into his mouth. Tate tasted metal and felt the chill of the sharp point against his tongue. He didn't move a muscle.

Then Matthews's eyes crinkled with what seemed to be humor. His lips moved and he seemed to be speaking to himself. He withdrew the blade.

"No, Collier, no. Not you. I don't want you."

"But why not?" Tate whispered quickly. "Why not? Tell me!"

"Because you're going to live your life without your daughter. Just like I'm going to live mine without my son."

"And that'll take the pain away?"

"Yes!"

The lawyer nodded. "Then you have to let her go." He struggled to keep the triumph from his voice—as he always did in court or at the debate podium. "Then you have to let her go and kill me. It's the only answer for you."

"Daddy," Megan whimpered. Tate believed it was the first time he'd heard her say the word in ten years.

"Only answer?" Matthews asked uncertainly.

Tate had known that eventually it would come to this. But what a time, what a place for it to happen.

All cats see in the dark.

Therefore Midnight can see in the dark.

He leaned his head against the girl's cheek. "Oh, honey . . ."

Megan asked. "What is it? *What?*"

Unless Midnight is blind.

Tate began to speak. His voice cracked. He started again. "Aaron, what you want makes perfect sense. Except that . . ." It was Megan's eyes he gazed into, not their captor's, as he said, "Except that I'm not her father."

Chapter Thirty

Matthews seemed to gaze down at his captives but he was backlit by dawn light in the picture window and Tate couldn't see where his eyes were turned.

Megan, pale in the same oblique light, clasped her injured face. A pink sheen of blood was on her cheeks and hands. She was frowning.

Matthews laughed but Tate could see that his quick mind was considering facts and drawing tentative conclusions.

"I'm disappointed, Collier. That's obvious and simpleminded. You're lying."

"When you were stalking Megan and me how often did you see us together?" Tate asked.

"That doesn't mean anything."

"You followed us for how long?"

A splinter of doubt, like a faint cloud obscuring the sun momentarily. Tate had seen this in the eyes of a thousand witnesses.

Matthews answered, "Six months."

"How many weekends was she with me?"

"That doesn't—"

"How many?"

"Two, I think."

"You broke into my house to plant those letters. How many pictures of her did you see?"

"Dad . . ."

"How many?" Tate asked firmly, ignoring the girl.

Matthews finally said, "None."

"What did her bedroom look like?"

Another hesitation. Then: "A storeroom."

"How much affection did you ever see between us? Did I *seem* like a father? I've got dark, curly hair and eyes. Bett's auburn. And Megan's *blond,* for God's sake. Does she even look like me? Look at the eyes. Look!"

He did. He said uncertainly, "I still don't believe you."

"No, Daddy! No!"

"You went to see my wife," Tate continued to Matthews, squeezing Megan's leg to silence her.

The doctor nodded.

"Well, you're a therapist. What did you see in Bett's face when you were talking to her? What was there when she was telling you about us and about Megan?"

Matthews reflected. "I saw . . . guilt."

"That's right," Tate said. "Guilt."

Matthews looked from one of his captives to the other.

"Seventeen years ago," Tate began slowly, speaking to Megan, finally revealing the truth they'd kept from her for all these years, "I was prosecuting cases, making a name for myself. The *Washington Post* called me the hottest young prosecutor in the commonwealth. I'd take on every assignment that came into the office. I was working eighty hours a week. I got home to your mother on weekends at best. I'd go for three or four days in a row and hardly even call. I was trying to be my grandfather. The lawyer-farmer-patriarch. I'd be a local celebrity. We'd have a huge family, an old manse. Sunday dinners, reunions, holidays . . . the whole nine yards."

He took a deep breath. "That was when your aunt Susan had her first bad heart attack. She was in the hospital for a month and mostly bedridden after that."

"What are you saying?" Megan whispered.

"Susan was married. Her husband, you remember him."

"Uncle Harris."

"You were right in your letter, Megan. Your mother *did* spend a lot of time caring for her sister. Harris and your mother both did."

"No," Megan said abruptly. "I don't believe it."

"They'd go to the hospital together, Harris and Bett. They'd have lunch, dinner. Go shopping. Sometimes Bett cooked him meals in his studio. Helped him clean. Your aunt felt better knowing he was being looked after. And it was okay with me. I was free to handle my cases."

"She told you all this?" Megan asked. "Mom?"

His face was a blank mask as he said slowly, "No. Harris did. The day of his funeral."

Tate had been upstairs on that eerily warm November night years ago. The funeral reception, at the Collier farm, was over.

Standing at a bedroom window, Tate had looked out over the yard. Felt the hot air, filled with leaf dust. Smelled cedar from the closet.

He'd just checked on three-year-old Megan, asleep

in her room, and he'd come here to open windows to air out the upstairs bedrooms; several relatives would be spending the night.

He'd looked down at the backyard, gazing at Bett in her long black dress. She hiked up the hem and climbed onto the new picnic table to unhook the Japanese lanterns.

Tate had tried to open the window but it was stuck. He took off his jacket to get a better grip and heard the crinkle of paper in the pocket. At the funeral service one of Harris's attorneys had given him an envelope, hand-addressed to him from Harris, marked *Personal,* apparently written just before the man had shot himself. He'd forgotten about it. He opened the envelope and read the brief letter inside.

Tate had nodded to himself, folded the note slowly and walked downstairs, then outside.

He remembered hearing a Loretta Lynn song playing on the stereo.

He remembered hearing the rustling of the hot wind over the brown grass and sedge, stirring pumpkin vines and the refuse of the corn harvest.

He remembered watching the arc of Bett's narrow arm as she reached for an orange lantern. She glanced down at him.

"I have something to tell you," he'd said.

"What?" she'd whispered. Then, seeing the look in his eyes, Bett had asked desperately: "What, what?"

She'd climbed down from the bench. Tate came up close, and instead of putting his arm around his wife's shoulders, as a husband might do late at night in a house of death, he handed her the letter.

She read it.

"Oh my. Oh."

Bett didn't deny anything that was contained in the note: Harris's declaration of intense love for her, the affair, his fathering Megan, Bett's refusal to marry him and her threat to take the girl away from him forever if Harris told Bett's sister of the infidelity. At the end the words had degenerated into mad rambling and his chillingly lucid acknowledgment that the pain was simply too much.

Neither of them cried that night as Tate had packed a suitcase and left. They never spent another night under the same roof.

Despite the presence of a madman now, holding a knife, hovering a few feet from them, Tate's concentration was wholly on the girl. To his surprise her face blossomed not with horror or shock or anger but with sympathy. She touched his leg. "And you're the one that got hurt so bad. I'm sorry, Daddy. I'm sorry."

Tate looked at Matthews. He said, "So that's why your argument doesn't work, Aaron. Taking her away from me won't do what you want."

Matthews didn't speak. His eyes were turned out the window, gazing into the blue dawn.

Tate said, "You know the classic reasons given for punishing crimes, Aaron? To condition away bad behavior—doesn't work. A deterrent—useless. To rehabilitate—that's a joke. To protect society—well, only if we execute the bad guys or keep them locked up forever. No, you know the real reason why we punish? We're ashamed to admit it. But, oh, how we love it. Good old biblical retribution. Bloody revenge is the only honest motive for punishment. Why? Because its purpose is to take away the victim's pain.

"That's what you want, Aaron, but there's only one way you'll have that. By killing me. It's not perfect but it'll have to do."

Megan was sobbing.

Matthews leaned his head against the window. The sun was up now and flashed on and off as strips of liver-colored clouds moved quickly east. He seemed diminished and changed. As if he were beyond disappointment or sorrow.

"Let her go," Tate whispered. "It doesn't even make sense to kill her because she's a witness. They know about you anyway."

Matthews crouched beside Megan. Put the back of his hand against her cheek, lifted it away and looked at the glistening streak left by her tears on his skin. He kissed her hair.

"All right. I agree."

Megan started to protest.

But Tate knew that he'd won. Nothing she could say or do at this point would change his decision.

"I'll call the dogs to the run. I'll be back in five minutes."

Chapter Thirty-one

"Is it true?" she asked, tears glistening on her cheeks.

"Oh, yes, honey, it's true."

"You never said anything."

"Your mother and I decided not to. Until after Susan died. You know how close Bett is to your aunt. She wanted her never to find out about the affair—it would've been too hard for her. The doctors only gave her a year or two to live. We were going to wait to tell you until she'd passed away."

"But . . ." Megan whispered.

He smiled wanly. "That's right. She's still alive."

"Why didn't you tell me last year, or two years ago? I was old enough not to say anything to Aunt Susan."

Tate examined the wounds on her palms. Pressed his hands against them. He couldn't speak at first. Finally he said, "The moment passed."

"All these years," she whispered, "I thought *I* must've done something." She lowered her head to his shoulder. "What a terrible thing I must have been for you. What a reminder."

"Honey, I wish I could tell you different. But I can't. You were half the person I loved most in the world and half the person I most hated."

"One time I said something to Mom," she said, weeping softly. "I'd been with you for the weekend and Mom asked how it went. I said I'd had an okay time but what could you expect? You were just an adequate father. I thought she was going to whip me. She freaked out totally. She said you were the best man she'd ever met and I was never, ever supposed to say that again."

Tate smiled. "An adequate father for an inconvenient daughter."

"Why didn't you ever try it again, the two of you?"

He echoed, "The moment passed."

"How much you must love her."

Tate laughed sourly to himself at the irony. The child who drove husband and wife apart had now brought them back together—if only for one day.

How scarce love is, he thought. How rarely does it all come together: the pledge, the assurance, the need, the circumstance, the hungry desire to share minutes with someone else. And the dear desperation too. It's miraculous when love actually works.

He looked her over and decided that the two of them, his ex-wife and her daughter, would be fine— now that the truth had been dumped between them. A long time coming but better than never. Oh, yes, they'd do fine.

Gritty footsteps approached.

"Now, listen to me," he said urgently. "When he lets you out find a phone and call Ted Beauridge at Fairfax County Police. Tell him your mother's probably in jail in Luray or Front Royal—"

"*What?*"

"No time to explain. But she's there. Tell him to get cops out here. She told them you were here but they might not've believed her."

The girl looked at him with eyes that reminded him of her mother's. Not the violet shade, of course—those were Bett's and Bett's alone—but the unique mix of the ethereal and the earthy.

Matthews appeared in the doorway.

They turned to look at the gaunt man standing before them, his muscular hand pressed to his bloody belly.

"Okay, get going," Tate said to her. "Run like hell."

"Go on," Matthews said, and reached forward to take her arm.

She spun away from him and hugged Tate hard. He felt her arms around his back. Felt her face against his ear, heard her speaking to him, a torrent of fervid words flowing out, coming from a source other than the heart and mind of a seventeen-year-old high school junior.

"Megan . . ." he began.

But she took his face in both her hands and said, "Shhh, Daddy. Remember, bears can't talk."

Matthews grabbed her again and pulled her away. Took her to the door.

He unlocked it and shoved her outside. The door closed with a snap behind her. Through a dirty, barred window Tate saw her sprint down the driveway and disappear through the gate.

"So," Collier said, glancing up at Matthews.

"So," he echoed.

"Outside?" the lawyer asked, looking around at the gloomy place. "Would that be all right? I'd rather."

Matthews hesitated for a moment. But then decided, why not? "Yes. That's all right."

He unlocked the door again and they stepped into the parking area and walked around into the grounds behind the asylum, past the wild rottweilers in their runs.

Matthews was thinking back to the times he'd been committed here. He recalled how beautiful these lawns and gardens had been then. Well, why wouldn't they be? Give five hundred crazy people grounds to tend and, brother, you've got a showplace. He'd sat for hours and hours and hours talking to other patients and—in his imagination—to his dead Peter. Sometimes the boy responded, sometimes not.

The dawn sun was still below the horizon but the sky was bright as they walked side by side through the tall grass and goldenrod and milkweed while dragonflies zipped from their path. Grasshoppers bounced against their legs, leaving dots of brown spit on their clothing. The dogs were in a frenzy behind them, sniffing the ground and bounding at the wire fence of their run, trying to escape and go after the intruder who walked beside their master.

"Look at this place," Matthews said conversationally. He waved his arm. "I remember it like it was yesterday. I remember the strange things people would say. The delusional ones, the paranoid ones, the depressed ones. The ones who were simply nuts—you know, Collier, the mind isn't an exact science, whatever the *Diagnostic and Statistical Manual* says. Some people are just plain crazy and that's all you can ever say about them. But I always listened to them. Why, people give themselves away like free samples at a grocery store. Hand themselves to you on platters. And what do they use? Words. Aren't words the most astonishing thing?"

Collier said, "You bet they are."

There wasn't much time, Matthews reflected. He supposed he had an hour or two until the police arrived. At best it would take Megan two hours to get to the nearest phone. Enough time to finish here, bury Peter, and get to Dulles for a flight to Los Angeles. Or maybe he should just drive west. Hide in the hills of West Virginia. He took a deep breath. "Stop here."

They were beside a shallow ditch. It would make a fine grave for Collier. And he'd decided that he'd kill the lawyer with a single shot to his head. No pain, no torment. And he wouldn't let the dogs have the body. Out of respect for a worthy adversary.

Then the lawyer stunned him by closing his eyes and whispering, "Our Father, who art in heaven . . ." He slowly completed the Lord's Prayer.

Matthews laughed then asked, "You believe in God?"

Collier nodded. "Why does that surprise you?"

"When I'd see you in court it seemed that only the judge and jury were your gods."

"No, no, I believe He exists. That He's merciful and He's just."

"Just?" Matthews asked skeptically.

"Well, He's the reason I don't send people to death row anymore . . . Do *you*? Believe in God?"

"I'm not sure," Matthews said.

"You know, I always wanted the chance to prove the existence of God in a debate."

"How would you do that?" Matthews asked, truly curious. "Resolved: God exists. Isn't that how debates start?"

Collier looked up at the purple sky. "You know Voltaire?"

"Not really. No."

"I'd make his argument. He said there had to be a God because he couldn't imagine a watch without a watchmaker."

Matthews nodded. "Yes, I can see that. That's good. That's compelling."

"But, of course, then you run into all of the counterarguments. The con side."

"Such as?"

"Incompatible religious sects, interpretations of holy scriptures proven wrong later, no empirical proof of miracles, the Crusades, ethical and secular self-interest, terrorism . . . That's an uphill battle, all right."

"No answer for that?"

"Oh, sure. I've got an answer."

Matthews was suddenly fascinated. After Peter's death he'd prayed every night for six months. He believed that the boy had answered some of those communiqués. It gave him clues, but not proof, that Peter's soul floated nearby. "What is it, what's the answer?" he asked hungrily.

"That a watch," Collier answered slowly, "no matter how well made, can never *comprehend* its watchmaker. When we claim to understand God, everything breaks down. If God exists then by definition He's unknowable and souls—yours, mine, Megan's, Peter's—are beyond our understanding. When we create human institutions to represent God they're inherently wrong so He has to exist apart from our flawed visions of Him."

"Yes, it makes sense. How simple, how perfect."

"You've thought about questions like this, haven't you? Because of Peter?"

"Yes."

Eyes on Matthews's, Collier said, "You miss him so much, don't you?"

"Yes, I do." Matthews stared down at the ground. For all he knew he'd stood on this very spot two or three years ago, studying slugs or dung beetles or ants, hour upon hour, wondering how, in their wordless world, they communicated their passions and fears.

"You can get help, Aaron. It's not too late. You'll be in jail but you can still be content. You can find a doctor to help you, somebody who's as good as you were."

"Oh, I don't think so. It's too late for that. One thing I learned—you can't talk somebody out of his nature."

"Your character is your fate," Collier said.

Matthews laughed. "Heraclitus."

He'd learned the aphorism from one of Collier's closing statements. He lifted the gun toward the lawyer.

Then Collier's eyes flickered slightly. "You won't turn yourself in?" Collier asked.

"No."

"I'm sorry," the lawyer said.

Matthews frowned. "What do you mean?"

"I'm so sorry."

A snap of brush behind him.

Matthews spun around. There stood Megan, holding the gun Collier had brought with him. Matthews had left it in the lobby of the hospital and had forgotten about it. The girl was ten feet away and was pointing the black muzzle at Matthews's chest.

Matthews laughed to himself. Oh, yes . . . He understood. Remembered her whispering to Tate before she'd walked out of the asylum. They'd planned this together. Collier would stall him—with his talk of theology—and Megan would pretend to run but would return for the gun. He remembered Collier protesting as they'd hugged. But she'd had her way.

Maybe she wasn't his blood kin but at the moment she was her father's daughter.

He glanced at her eyes.

"Drop the gun," she ordered.

But he didn't. He wondered, would she go through with it? She was only seventeen and, yes, she had anger in her heart—enough to attack him with a knife—but not enough to kill, he believed.

Character is fate . . .

He saw compassion, fear and weakness in her eyes. He could stop her, he decided. He could get her to lower the gun long enough to shoot her.

"Megan, listen to me," he began in a soft voice, gazing into her blue eyes, which *were* so unlike Collier's. "I know what you're thinking. I know what you've been through. But—"

The first bullet tugged at his side, near the knife wound, and he felt a rib snap. He was swinging his gun toward her when another shot struck his shoulder and arm.

Collier dropped to his knees, clear of the line of fire.

Megan stepped closer.

"Peter . . ." Matthews whispered, struggling to hold on to his pistol.

She pushed through the grass until she was only a few feet away.

Matthews squeezed the grip of the pistol. Then he looked up into her eyes.

Always the eyes . . .

Her gun fired again. And for an instant his vision was filled with a thousand suns. And in his ears was a chorus of noise—voices, perhaps.

Peter's among them, perhaps.

And then there was blackness and silence.

Chapter Thirty-two

The beach at San Cristo del Sol in Belize is one of the finest in Latin America.

Even now, in May, the air is torrid but the steady breezes soothe the hordes of tourists during their endless trips from the air-conditioned bars and seafood joints to the pools to the beach and back again. Windsurfing, paragliding, waterskiing and racing Jet Skis keep the surface of the turquoise water perpetually turbulent, and within the bay itself hundreds of snorklers and resort-course scuba divers engage in their elegantly awkward amphibious ballets.

The town is also a well-known staging area for those who wish to see Mayan ruins; there are two beautifully preserved cities within five kilometers of the main drag in San Cristo.

The Caribe Inn is the most luxurious of all the hotels in town, a Spanish colonial hacienda that has four stars from Mobil, and accolades from a number of other sources, proudly displayed behind the registration desk at which Tate Collier now stood, hoping fervently that the clerk spoke English.

The man did, it turned out, and Tate explained

that he had reservations, proffering passports and his American Express card.

"That's a party of . . . ?" the clerk queried.

"Party of two."

"Ah," the desk clerk responded. Tate filled out the registration card with ungainly strokes.

"So, you are from Virginia," the clerk said. "Near Washington?"

"*Sí,*" Tate responded self-consciously, ready for his pronunciation to throw the conversation off kilter if not insult the clerk personally.

"I have been there several times. I like the Smithsonian especially."

"*Sí,*" Tate tried again, forgetting even the words that conveyed some meaningless pleasantry—words he'd practiced on the flight. For a man who'd made his way in the world by speaking, Tate's command of foreign languages was abysmal.

He watched the clerk glance down at the reservation form with a momentarily perplexed frown on his dark, handsome face. Tate knew why. The clerk had taken a good look at the attractive woman who'd entered the hotel on Tate's arm a moment before, and though surely, in this line of work, the clerk had seen just about everything, he couldn't for the life of him figure out why these two would want separate rooms.

A man is, after all, a man . . . And an age difference of twenty years . . . well, that's nothing.

Megan came out of the lobby phone booth and walked to the desk just as the clerk was showing Tate a diagram of the available rooms. Tate pointed to two, first a smaller inside room, then a corner unit with a view of the beach. "I'll take this one. My daughter'll have the corner room."

"No, Dad, you take the nice one."

"Ah, this is your daughter?" the clerk said, his curiosity satisfied. "Of course, I should have known."

"I'm sorry?" Tate asked him.

"I mean, the resemblance. The young lady takes after you."

The man's suspicions crept back when he saw the two guests exchange fast glances and struggle to suppress laughter. Tate thought about pulling out driver's licenses and proving the relationship but then decided: it's none of this guy's business.

Besides, mystery has an appeal that documented fact will always lack.

They settled on the rooms and after Tate's card was imprinted they followed the bellhop through a veranda.

"Josh said his new physical therapist is great," Megan told him.

"Glad to hear it."

"But the way he put it was he said 'she's' great. Think she's old and fat?"

"We'll be back in six days. You can find out for yourself. When do you say *de nada* again?"

"After somebody thanks you. It means, 'It's nothing.'"

"They say *gracias* and then I say *de nada*." Tate repeated the words several times as if he were a walking Berlitz tape.

"Then I called Bett," Megan continued. "She's glad we got in okay. She said to take lots of pictures."

"I'll call her later."

"She, um, was going over to Brad's tonight. But she said it in a funny way. Like there was something going on. Is anything going on?"

"I don't have a clue."

Megan shrugged. "She said she talked to Konnie and he's coming to your office on Tuesday at nine to talk about the case."

The previous week Tate had made his first appearance in a criminal court in nearly five years—Konnie's arraignment. He'd answered the judge's simple query with simpler words. "My client pleads not guilty, Your Honor."

He had a novel defense planned. It was called "induced intoxication," and although he'd promised Megan that they would be spending the week doing nothing but seeing the sights and partying he'd hidden three law books in his suitcase and suspected the last day of the trip would find him with at least a rough draft of his opening statement to the jury—if not a set of deposition questions or two. He knew that as soon as Megan met a handsome young windsurfer—probably at the cocktail party that night—he would have at least a few hours free on most of the evenings.

He and Megan arrived at their rooms.

"Gracias de nada," Tate said, and slipped the confused bellhop an outrageously generous tip. A half hour later they'd showered and were in khaki shorts, T-shirts and wicker hats. Every inch *los turistas.* They walked down to the lobby and asked about how they might bicycle to the nearest Mayan ruin. The clerk arranged for the bike rental and gave them directions.

It was just past the afternoon siesta and most of the guests were headed for the white sand beach. But Tate and Megan snagged two battered bicycles from the rack in front of the inn and started away from town.

"Which way?" she called.

He pointed and they mounted up.

Despite the opposing foot traffic and the astonishing heat, they cycled fast along the cracked asphalt path straight into the dense, fragrant jungle, standing on the pedals, hollering and laughing, racing each other, as if every moment counted, as if they had many, many hours of missed exploration to make up for.

XO

Jeffery Deaver

Available in hardcover from Simon & Schuster

Turn the page for a preview of *XO*. . . .

Subject: Re: You're the Best!!!
From: noreply@kayleightownemusic.com
To: EdwinSharp18474@anon.com
2 January 10:32 a.m.

Hey there,
Edwin—

Thanks for your email! I'm so glad you liked my latest album! Your support means the world to me. Be sure you go to my website and sign up to get my newsletter and learn about new releases and upcoming concerts, and don't forget to follow me on Facebook and Twitter.

And keep an eye out for the mail. I sent you that autographed photo you requested!

XO,

Kayleigh

* * *

Subject: Unbelievable!!!!!
From: EdwinSharp26535@anon.com
To: ktowne7788@compserve.com
3 September 5:10 a.m.

Hi, Kayleigh:

I am totally blown away. I'm rendered speechless. And, you know me pretty good by now—for me to be speechless, that's something!! Anyway, here's the story: I downloaded your new album last night and listened to "Your Shadow." Whoahhh! It's without doubt the best song I have ever heard. I mean of anything ever written. I even like it better than "It's Going to Be Different This Time." I've told you nobody's ever expressed how I feel about loneliness and life and well everything better than you. And that song does that totally. But more important I can see what you're saying, your plea for help. It's all clear now. Don't worry. You're not alone, Kayleigh!!

I'll be *your* shadow. Forever.

XO, Edwin

* * *

Subject: Fwd: Unbelievable!!!!!
From: <u>Samuel.King@CrowellSmithWendall.com</u>
To: <u>EdwinSharp26535@anon.com</u>
3 September 10:34 a.m.

Mr. Sharp:

Ms. Alicia Sessions, personal assistant to our clients Kayleigh Towne and her father, Bishop Towne, forwarded us your email of this morning. You have sent more than 50 emails and letters since we contacted you two months ago, urging you not to have any contact with Ms. Towne or any of her friends and family. We are extremely troubled that you have found her private email address (which has been changed, I should tell you), and are looking into possible violations of state and federal laws regarding how you obtained such address.

Once again, we must tell you that we feel your behavior is completely inappropriate and possibly actionable. We urge you in the strongest terms possible to heed this warning. As we've said repeatedly, Ms. Towne's security staff and local law enforcement officials have been notified of your repeated, intrusive attempts to contact her and we are fully prepared to take whatever steps are necessary to put an end to this alarming behavior.

Samuel King, Esq.

Crowell, Smith & Wendall, Attorneys-at-Law

* * *

Subject: See you soon!!!
From: EdwinSharp26535@anon.com
To: KST33486@westerninternet.com
5 September 11:43 p.m.

Hi, Kayleigh—

Got your new email address. I know what they're up to but DON'T worry, it'll be all right.

I'm lying in bed, listening to you right now. I feel like I'm literally *your shadow* . . . And you're mine. You are so wonderful!

I don't know if you had a chance to think about it—you're sooooo busy, I know!—but I'll ask again—if you wanted to send me some of your hair that'd be so cool. I know you haven't cut it for ten years and four months (it's one of those things that makes you so beautiful!!!) but maybe there's one from your brush. Or better yet your pillow. I'll treasure it forever.

Can't WAIT for the concert next Friday. C U soon.

Yours forever,

XO, Edwin

Sunday

Chapter 1

THE HEART OF a concert hall is people.

And when the vast space is dim and empty, as this one was at the moment, a venue can bristle with impatience, indifference.

Even hostility.

Okay, rein in that imagination, Kayleigh Towne told herself. Stop acting like a kid. Standing on the wide, scuffed stage of the Fresno Conference Center's main hall, she surveyed the place once more, bringing her typically hypercritical eye to the task of preparing for Friday's concert, considering and reconsidering lighting and stage movements and where the members of the band should stand and sit. Where best to walk out near, though not into, the crowd and touch hands and blow kisses. Where best acoustically to place the foldback speakers—the monitors that were pointed toward the band so they could hear themselves without echoes or distortion. Many performers now used earbuds for this; Kayleigh liked the immediacy of traditional foldbacks.

There were a hundred other details to think about. She believed that every performance should be perfect, *more* than perfect. Every audience deserved the best. One hundred ten percent.

She had, after all, grown up in Bishop Towne's shadow.

An unfortunate choice of word, Kayleigh now reflected.

I'll be your *shadow. Forever. . . .*

Back to the planning. This show had to be different from the previous one here, about eight months ago. A retooled program was especially important since many of the fans would have regularly attended her hometown concerts and she wanted to make sure they got something unexpected. That was one thing about Kayleigh Towne's music; her audiences weren't as big as some but were loyal as golden retrievers. They knew her lyrics cold, knew her guitar licks, knew her moves onstage and laughed at her shtick before she finished the lines. They lived and breathed her performances, hung on her words, knew her bio and likes and dislikes.

And some wanted to know much more . . .

With that thought, her heart and gut clenched as if she'd stepped into Hensley Lake in January.

Thinking about *him,* of course.

Then she froze, gasping. Yes, someone was watching her from the far end of the hall! Where none of the crew would be.

Shadows were moving.

Or was it her imagination? Or maybe her eyesight? Kayleigh had been given perfect pitch and an angelic voice but God had decided enough was enough and skimped big-time on the vision. She squinted, adjusted her glasses. She was sure that someone was hiding, rocking back and forth in the doorway that led to the storage area for the concession stands.

Then the movement stopped.

She decided it wasn't movement at all and never had been. Just a hint of light, a suggestion of shading.

Though still, she heard a series of troubling clicks and snaps and groans—from where, she couldn't tell—and felt a chill of panic bubble up her spine.

Him . . .

The man who had written her hundreds of emails and letters, intimate, delusional, speaking of the life they could share together, asking for a strand of hair, a fingernail clipping. The man who had somehow gotten near enough at a dozen shows to take close-up pictures of Kayleigh, without anyone ever seeing him. The man who had possibly—though it had never been proven—slipped into the band buses or motor homes on the road and stolen articles of her clothing, underwear included.

The man who had sent her dozen of pictures of himself: shaggy hair, fat, in clothing that looked unwashed. Never obscene but, curiously, the images were all the more disturbing for their familiarity. They were the shots a boyfriend would text her from a trip.

Him . . .

Her father had recently hired a personal bodyguard, a huge man with a round, bullet-shaped head and an occasional curly wire sprouting from his ear to make clear what his job was. But Darthur Morgan was outside at the moment, making the rounds and checking cars. His security plan also included a nice touch: simply being visible so that potential stalkers would turn around and leave rather than risk a confrontation with a 250-pound man who looked like a rapper with an attitude (which, sure enough, he'd been in his teen years).

She scanned the recesses of the hall again—the best place *he* might stand and watch her. Then gritting her teeth in anger at her fear and mostly at her failure to tame the uneasiness and distraction, she thought, Get. Back. To. Work.

And what're you worried about? You're not alone. The band wasn't in town yet—they were finishing some studio work in Nashville—but Bobby was at the huge Midas XL8 mixing console dominating the control deck in the back of the hall, two hundred feet away. Alicia was getting the rehearsal rooms in order. A couple of the beefy guys in Bobby's road crew were unpacking the truck in the back, assembling and organizing the hundreds of cases and tools and props and plywood sheets and stands and wires and amps and instruments and computers and tuners—the tons of gear that even modest touring bands like Kayleigh's needed.

She supposed one of them could get to her in a hurry if the source of the shadow had been *him*.

Dammit, quit making *him* more than *he* is! *Him, him, him,* like you're even afraid to say his name. As if to utter it would conjure up his presence.

She'd had other obsessed fans, plenty of them—what gorgeous singer-songwriter with a voice from heaven wouldn't collect a few inappropriate admirers? She'd had twelve marriage proposals from men she'd never met, three from women. A dozen couples wanted to adopt her, thirty or so teen girls wanted to be her best friend, a thousand men wanted to buy her a drink or dinner at Bob Evans or the Mandarin Oriental . . . and there'd been plenty of invitations to enjoy a wedding night without the inconvenience of a wedding. *Hey Kayleigh think on it cause Ill show you a good time better than you ever had and by the by heres a picture of what you can expect yah its really me not bad huh???*

(Very stupid idea to send a picture like that to a seventeen-year-old, Kayleigh's age at the time. By the by.)

Usually she was cautiously amused by the attention. But not always and definitely not now. Kayleigh found herself snagging her denim jacket from a nearby chair and pulling it on to cover her T-shirt, providing another barrier to any prying eyes. This, despite the characteristic September heat in Fresno, which filled the murky venue like thin stew.

And more of those clicks and taps from nowhere.

"Kayleigh?"

She turned quickly, trying to hide her slight jump, even though she recognized the voice.

A solidly built woman of around thirty paused halfway across the stage. She had cropped red hair and some subdued inking on arms, shoulders and spine, partly visible thanks to her trim tank top and tight, hip-hugging black jeans. Fancy cowboy boots. "Didn't mean to scare you. You okay?"

"You didn't. What's up?" she asked Alicia Sessions.

A nod toward the iPad she carried. "These just came in. Proofs for the new posters? If we get them to the printer today we'll definitely have them by the show. They look okay to you?"

Kayleigh bent over the screen and examined them. Music nowadays is only partly about music, of course. Probably always has been, she supposed, but it seemed that as her popularity had grown, the business side of her career took up a lot more time than it used to. She didn't have much interest in these matters but she generally didn't need to. Her father was her manager, Alicia handled the day-to-day paperwork and scheduling, the lawyers read the contracts, the record company made arrangements with the recording studios and the CD production companies and the retail and download outlets; her longtime producer and friend at BHRC Records, Barry Zeigler, handled the technical side of arranging and production, and Bobby and the crew set up and ran the shows.

All so that Kayleigh Towne could do what she did best: write songs and sing them.

Still, one business matter of interest to her was making sure fans—many of them young or without much money—could buy cheap but decent memorabilia to make the night of the concert that much more special. Posters like this one, T-shirts, key chains, bracelets, charms, guitar chord books, headbands, backpacks . . . and mugs, for the moms and dads driving the youngsters to and from the shows and, of course, often buying the tickets as well.

She studied the proofs. The image was of Kayleigh and her favorite Martin guitar—not a big dreadnought-size but a smaller, 000-18, ancient, with a crisp yellowing spruce top and a voice of its own. The photo was the inside picture from her latest album, *Your Shadow*.

Him . . .

No, don't.

Eyes scanning the doors again.

"You sure you're okay?" Alicia asked, voice buzzing with a faint Texas twang.

"Yeah." Kayleigh returned to the poster proofs, which all featured the same photo though with different type, messages and background. Her picture was a straight-on shot, depicting her much as she saw herself: at five-two, shorter than she would have liked, her face a bit long, but with stunning blue eyes, lashes that wouldn't quit and lips that had some reporters talking collagen. As *if* . . . Her trademark golden hair, four feet long—and no, not cut, only trimmed, in ten years and four months—flowed in the fake gentle breeze from the photographer's electric fan. Designer jeans and high-collared dark-red blouse. A small diamond crucifix.

"You gotta give the fans the package," Bishop Towne always said. "That's *visual* too, I'm talking. And the standards're different 'tween men and women. You get into trouble, you deny it." He meant that in the country music world a man could get away with a look like Bishop's own: jutting belly, cigarette, a lined, craggy face riddled with stubble, wrinkled shirt, scuffed boots and faded jeans. A woman singer, he lectured—though he really intended to say "girl"—had to be put together for date night. And in Kayleigh's case that meant a church social, of course: the good girl next door was the image on which she'd built her career. Sure, the jeans could be a little tight, the blouses and sweaters could closely hug her round chest, but the necklines were high. The makeup was subtle and leaned toward pinks.

"Go with them."

"Great." Alicia shut off the device. A slight pause. "I haven't gotten your father's okay yet."

"They're good," the singer reassured her, nodding at the iPad.

"Sure. I'll just run it by him. You know."

Now Kayleigh paused. Then: "Okay."

"Acoustics good here?" asked Alicia, who had been a performer herself; she had quite a voice and a love of music, which was undoubtedly why she'd taken a job for someone like Kayleigh Towne, when the efficient, no-nonsense woman could have earned twice as much as a personal assistant for a corporate executive. She'd signed on last spring and had never heard the band perform here.

"Oh, the sound is great," Kayleigh said enthusiastically, glancing at the ugly concrete walls. "You wouldn't think it." She explained how the designers of the venue, back in the 1960s, had done their homework; too many concert halls—even sophisticated ones intended for classical music—had been built by people without confidence in the natural ability of musical instruments and voices to reach the farthest seats with "direct volume," that is, the sound emanating from the stage. Architects would add angular surfaces and free-standing shapes to boost the volume of the music, which did that but also sent the vibrations in a hundred different directions. This resulted in every performer's acoustic nightmare, reverberation: in effect, echoes upon echoes that yielded muddy, sometimes even off-key, sounds.

Here, in modest Fresno, Kayleigh explained to Alicia, as her father had to her, the designers had trusted in the power and purity of the voice and drum skin and sounding board and reed and string. She was about to ask the assistant to join her in a chorus of one of her songs to prove her point—Alicia did great harmonies—when she noticed her looking toward the back of the hall. She assumed the woman was bored with the scientific discussion. But the frowning gaze suggested something else was on her mind.

"What?" Kayleigh asked.

"Isn't it just us and Bobby?"

"What do you mean?"

"I thought I saw somebody." She lifted a finger tipped in a black-painted nail. "That doorway. There."

Just where Kayleigh herself had thought she'd seen the shadow ten minutes before.

Palms sweating, absently touching her phone, Kayleigh stared at the changing shapes in the back of the hall.

Yes . . . no. She just couldn't tell.

Then shrugging her broad shoulders, one of them sporting a tattoo of a snake in red and green, Alicia said, "Hm. Guess not. Whatever it was it's gone now. . . . Okay, see you later. The restaurant at one?"

"Yeah, sure."

Kayleigh listened absently to the thumping of boots as she left and continued to stare at the black doorways.

Angrily, she suddenly whispered, "Edwin Sharp."

There I've said *his* name.

"Edwin, Edwin, Edwin."

Now that I've conjured you up, listen here: Get the hell out of my concert hall! I've got work to do.

And she turned away from the shadowy, gaping doorway from which, of course, no one was leering at her at all. She stepped to center stage, looking over the masking tape on the dusty wood, blocking out where she would stand at different points during the concert. It was then that she heard a man's voice crying from the back of the hall, "Kayleigh!" It was Bobby, now rising from behind the mixing console, knocking his chair over and ripping off his hard-shell earphones. He waved to her with one hand and pointed to a spot over her head with another. "Look out! . . . No, Kayleigh!"

She glanced up fast and saw one of the strip lights—a seven-foot Colortran unit—falling free of its mounting and swinging toward the stage by its thick electric cable.

Stepping back instinctively, she tripped over a guitar stand she hadn't remembered was behind her.

Tumbling, arms flailing, gasping . . .

The young woman hit the stage hard, on her tailbone. The massive light plummeted toward her, a deadly pendulum, growing bigger and bigger. She tried desperately to rise but fell back, blinded as the searing beams from the thousand-watt bulbs turned her way.

Then everything went black.